Abandoned

MIA in Vietnam

Bill Yancey

Front and Back Covers
by
Picture Perfect Cover Art
St. Augustine, FL

Abandoned: MIA in Vietnam
Bill Yancey
© Copyright 2016 by Bill Yancey
ISBN-13: 978-1533304056
ISBN-10: 153330405X

Yancey, Bill, 1947—
Abandoned / Bill Yancey
ISBN-13: 978-1533304056
ISBN-10: 153330405X

1. Mystery Medical – Fiction 2. Murder Mystery—Fiction 3. Military—Fiction

DEDICATION

In memory of

G. Barry Lockhart
February 17, 1947 – December 21, 1972
Francis C. Hammond High School, Class of 1965
United States Air Force Academy, Class of 1969
Captain, USAF B-52 co-pilot, KIA, Hanoi, Vietnam

&

Richard E. Bolstad
July 7, 1929 – February 21, 2014
Corporal, USMC, Korean War
Colonel, USAF A-1 pilot, Vietnam War
POW 1965-1973, Hanoi, Vietnam

Also by Bill Yancey

Elvis Saves
No One Lives Forever
The Last Day
What Your Doctor Won't Tell You About Your Lower Back
Invictus
Multidimensional Man
Reluctant Intern
Deadly Practice
Quantum Timeline

Acknowledgements

Special thanks to Pat Aller, for editing assistance. Any remaining mistakes are mine.

Special thanks to Tina Biron for help with Vietnamese language and customs.

Many friends and some of my family read the rough draft of this novel and offered insightful criticism. I would like to thank Lee Hyatt, David Biron, Jerry Anne Yancey, Mitos McKay, Bruce Berger, and Tom Yancey, for their suggestions and for taking the time out of their busy lives to improve the manuscript. Any remaining typographical errors, punctuation mistakes, or other blunders, however, are mine.

Praise for the author

(*Elvis Saves*)... is a fun read. A really evil guy named Lomax is trying to make a lot of money for his employer, Turner-Disney Entertainment, by coercing the American public into a frenzy over sightings of Elvis Presley. Despite his unlimited resources and utter ruthlessness, Lomax is thwarted by an entertaining group of characters. The author's obvious familiarity with details about the real Elvis Presley helps him to create B.J. Nottingham, a plausible and engaging Elvis impersonator...
A.K. Williams, *Roanoke Times*

In a fun, fast and furious thriller (*Quantum Timeline*) that mixes fact with fiction, Detective Engle chases suspects, uncovers conspiracies, rights wrongs and even finds love while bouncing around through the continuum.

Dr. Addison Wolfe is back. He's old, broke and more-than-a-tad bitter, but ready to start afresh with his new young wife and child.... Throughout (*Deadly Practice*) the retired M.D. explores the many frustrations of doctors in our modern world.... But the novelist Yancey doesn't let these mundane problems get in the way of a good mystery. Loaded with strong characters and a page-turning plot, *Deadly Practice* will keep you entertained until the wee hours of the morn.
C.F. Foster, *Florida Times Union*

Dr. Addison "Addy" Wolfe who appeared in Dr. Bill Yancey's previous novel, *Reluctant Intern,* has left behind the struggles of his internship years.... *Deadly Practice* offers a strikingly realistic picture of the drastic changes that have taken place in medicine.
Marie Vernon, *St. Augustine Record*

Amazon Books Reviews

Addison Wolfe is a charming, endearing character and his passion for truth and justice make him a very likeable protagonist. All of the characters in this clever tale, some with more warts than others....This is a fun read. I look forward to more adventures from Addison Wolfe.

...author did a great job at bringing the characters' emotions out of the book. And at each turn of page you have a surprise. If you want to spend some quality time with a good book this is a good choice.

Good guys and bad guys were surprising and the finely woven mystery was well crafted and believable. Characters were well developed and likeable. All in all a really good read.

For those of you who enjoyed Yancey's last novel, **Reluctant Intern**, you are in for another treat with **Deadly Practice**! This gem takes place about 20 years later with Addy relocating to an Urgent Care clinic in Florida, and brings with it lots of intense, fast, page-turning!

This book was so well written, I didn't want to put it down. I really hope he writes a sequel.

Dynamic characters, plot twists, and riveting medical scenarios kept me thoroughly invested in the lives of these soon-to-be doctors.

I enjoyed this absorbing tale of an internship year. There were the usual rotation anecdotes, and stories of hospital politics. But who would've expected romance, practical jokes, and attempted murder. I couldn't put it down.

This is a fascinating look at the world of medicine, and what it takes to make it in the medical world.

The book was very readable, the characters likeable, and the flow of the book very natural, making me want to read on until I was done. (I finished the book within 24 hours.) I would recommend this book to anyone.

All of the "horrors" of internship were included, but they made the characters more interesting, and kept the plot moving along and holding your attention, while the suspenseful part snuck up grabbed you from behind. A thoroughly enjoyable read, I look forward to recommending to anyone that will listen.

TABLE of CONTENTS

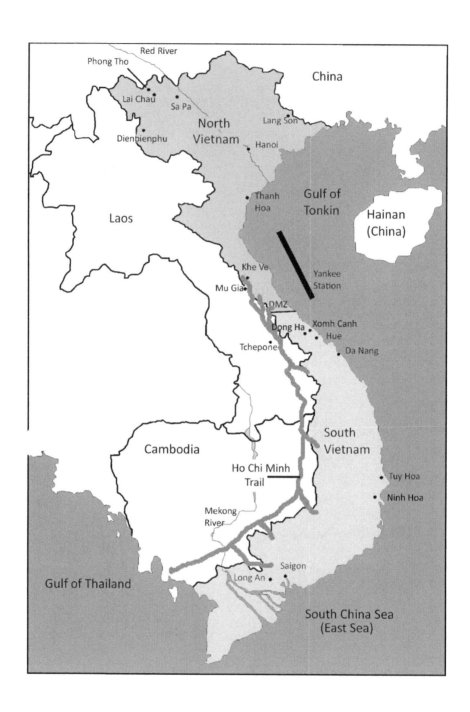

CHAPTER 1

Regaining his senses, Jimmy Byrnes swung a high kick at Deke Jameson's head, but the huge sailor had anticipated the move. He caught Byrnes's foot and threw him over the safety cable. Byrnes caught the side of the ship with one hand. Gripping the edge of the deck, he dangled briefly and tried to pull himself back onto the sponson. Jameson stepped on his fingers and Byrnes dropped into the Gulf of Tonkin.

One of the other sailors immediately yelled, "Man overboard!"

Jameson spun and grabbed the man's face with one hand, his other on the man's shirt at his collar. Pinching the man's cheeks between thumb and forefinger, Jameson growled, "Unless you want to join him, I suggest you shut up. Got it?"

Color drained from the sailor's face as he mulled the ultimatum. "Sure, Deke. Sure," he said. Jameson released his grip on the man's face.

"And if anyone asks, this never happened." Jameson glared at each of the men on the sponson. They nodded silently. "Okay. Let's go. Act natural." Leaving the fire hose and life jackets where they had fallen on the deck, the men exited the sponson and returned to their berths. The busy hangar deck crews and mechanics paid no attention to them as they closed the hatch behind them.

**

That's how the fight ended. It started with alarms sounding over the PA system, and then an announcement, "Fire! Fire on the hangar deck! This is no drill! All hands to General Quarters!"

The USS *Oriskany*, an Essex-class aircraft carrier, had more than 100 fires and fire drills during its deployment to Vietnam, from June, 1967, until this very early morning in January, 1968. This most recent minor fire had originated on one of the yellow tractors that moved aircraft around the hangar deck. Apparently the ignition switch had shorted out. Smoke from the burning insulation in the dash filled the forward hangar bay. General Quarters sounded. The entire crew manned their fire fighting stations, at 0113 hours.

No one onboard *Oriskany* took fires lightly. About fifteen months before, on October 26, 1966, a magnesium flare ignited accidentally in the forward hangar deck bay. The sailor handling the burning flare threw it into the flare locker. He closed the locker's heavy steel door and dogged it shut, using the metal handles that surround watertight doors. He assumed the flare would suffocate in the closed compartment.

Instead, that single flare ignited all the magnesium flares in the locker. The resultant explosion blew off the hatch door, set a helicopter on fire, and led to a major fire. As a result forty-four crewmen died, including many pilots unfamiliar with the layout of the ship and escape routes. One hundred fifty-six other sailors suffered injuries, from smoke inhalation to serious burns.

The aircraft carrier returned to the United States for repairs. The fire severely damaged the electrical system in the forward one third of the ship. In need of aircraft carriers to prosecute the air war in North and South Vietnam, the navy rushed *Oriskany* through a repair and sent her back to Vietnam in June of 1967. Among the miles of damaged electrical cable in the ship, there were circuits that frequently shorted out and started electrical fires. Every three days, or so, another fire began somewhere in the ship's forward third. Having experienced one major fire, the crew never underestimated the possibility of another. Not on a ship that carried tons of bombs, rockets, flares, and fuel for seventy aircraft, itself, and its destroyer escort.

In addition, *Oriskany's* crew had witnessed the near sinking of the

USS *Forrestal*, which caught fire in the Gulf of Tonkin on July 29, 1967. 134 sailors and airmen perished. Another 161 suffered serious injury. Leaving herself under-protected, *Oriskany* had flown every spare fire hose, breathing apparatus, and other fire fighting equipment to the *Forrestal* by helicopter. The same choppers retrieved injured sailors and brought them to *Oriskany*'s sickbay for triage and treatment.

No one on *Oriskany* took fire at sea lightly. No one.

After the ship's crew extinguished the fire and secured the vessel, some old animosities flared.

"Hey, Chink!" the big sailor yelled.

Byrnes looked up, involuntarily. Usually he didn't respond to insults about his heritage. He attempted to ignore the lowlife who would disparage his ancestors. The voice had been so loud and so close that it startled him. He had reacted to the noise, not the words. When he saw who had yelled, he frowned. "Get lost, asshole," he said, almost loud enough to have been heard over the din of the noisy hangar deck. He returned to his task, rolling up the four-inch fire hose on the sponson.

An extension adjacent to the hangar deck, the smaller sponson deck had been originally designed to be an anti-aircraft gun position forward of the port elevator. He had hung one heavy, brass, connecting end of the hose over the edge of the sponson. As he rolled up the hose he squeezed water from it, which fell fifty feet into the Gulf of Tonkin from the aircraft carrier.

"I'm talking to you!" the huge man bellowed. Six-foot four-inches, with a heavy build, his beginning beer gut hung over his worn dungarees, barely covered by his white T-shirt. The irate sailor blocked Byrnes's passage to the hangar deck from the sponson.

Byrnes tried to ignore the man. He shouldered the heavy canvas rolled hose and tried to push his way through the hatch. Behind the man, Byrnes saw several more sailors staring at him. Behind them, the hangar deck crew he led had returned to work. They were repositioning aircraft moved away from the fire. Squadron mechanics needed to finish preparing for the final day on the line for *Oriskany* and her air wing. The ship's company thought the Vietnam War would likely end for the ship at noon the next day. From Yankee Station she was scheduled to steam to Subic Bay in the Philippines. From there, the next stop was Alameda, California and a complete overhaul. No one expected the war to continue until *Oriskany* could rejoin the fleet. They were wrong, of course.

A large open hand hit Byrnes in the chest, pushing him backward on the small sponson. He lost his balance and dropped the fire hose. Catching himself with his back to the lifeline, he spread his arms out along the top cable, waited, and watched. Three cables on metal posts surrounded the sponson deck keeping ship's crew from falling overboard.

Byrnes knew the large sailor, Deke Jameson. He had testified against him for stealing laundry and had helped to send the man to the brig at the beginning of the cruise. As he watched, two other men joined the angry sailor on the sponson. Two more took positions on the far side of the hatch, facing away from the sponson. Jameson, the largest sailor, turned and closed the hatch door. Byrnes braced himself, taking deep, slow breaths, eying his opponent.

"You're quiet now, Gook," Jameson growled. "What did you say earlier? Did you call me an asshole? The guys in supply division aren't happy that you cost me my rating and sent me to the brig. Are you, guys?" He stepped closer to Byrnes. Nodding in agreement, the other two moved silently to Byrnes's left and right.

Byrnes waited until Jameson raised a fist and reared back to throw a roundhouse punch. With a swift kick to Jameson's groin, he crippled him temporarily. Screaming, Jameson dropped to his knees and then rolled to the deck. "Kill him," he yelled.

One of the other sailors, chambray shirt unbuttoned and hanging loose at his beltline, tried to grab Byrnes around the waist. Byrnes pulled the man's shirt over his head and face, and then brought a knee up and into his face. That man also crumpled to the deck. Jameson had managed to raise himself onto knees and hands. Byrnes kicked him in the ribs, rolling him onto his back.

Through the elevator opening to the hangar deck, Byrnes saw his crew working. He called to them. With the racket from the ship making headway through the ocean and the din generated by equipment used by the mechanics and his crew, no one heard him. He dodged a poorly thrown punch from the third sailor, and hit him with a combination of punches to stomach, chest, and face. Blood squirted from the man's nose as the bones crunched under Byrnes's knuckles. The third man joined the other two on the deck.

Byrnes stepped around and over the three combatants. He picked up the rolled fire hose, slinging it upward onto his shoulder. Silently, he pushed open the hatch to the hangar deck. Swung by another sailor, a metal, fire extinguisher canister bounced off the fire hose and hit him in the head, preventing him from leaving the sponson. One of the men from the hangar deck rushed him, while the other pulled the hatch closed. Dazed and wobbly as he fell backward, Byrnes reached out and grabbed the locker door that held floatation devices that stood next to the hatch. The locker door opened and twenty life jackets spilled onto the deck.

The man from the hangar deck grabbed Byrnes, knocking him down and pinning him to the deck. Jameson regained his footing, pulled Byrnes to his feet, and began swinging his fists at him faster than the stunned Byrnes could block the blows. Retreating, Byrnes stumbled over the life vests and fell face forward onto the cable lifeline.

At the same time, *Oriskany* had reached the southeastern end of its assigned position on Yankee Station in the Gulf of Tonkin. During their struggle the sailors had missed the announcement about preparing for a high-speed turn to starboard. The aircraft carrier turned sharply to begin its return run to the northwestern end of Yankee Station. She had an appointment with an early morning launch of aircraft, her last strike against North Vietnam before heading home. All the men on the sponson leaned onto the cable fence as the ship listed mildly to port. A dozen life preservers rolled into the sea.

Then came the blocked kick and the fall overboard. Byrnes plunged into the Gulf of Tonkin.

CHAPTER 2

Blam! Blam! In Addison Wolfe's dream, the car on which he was changing a flat tire fell off the jack. Startled, Wolfe flailed, jumping backward from the falling automobile. At the same time, he realized he had been dreaming and awoke. Fully awake in an instant, he sat up. Not since medical school had he been able to wake slowly. Either he was wide-awake or he was asleep. There was no sleepy gray area between.

Blam! Something hit the window next to his bed. He jumped again. It sounded like someone had slapped the glass. Unable to see through the blackout curtain his wife required to sleep, he yelled, "What do you want?"

"Dad. It's me Kayla, Kayla Anne. Are you alright?"

Wolfe pushed up the curtain, cursing the statisticians who had decided curtain ropes risked increased infant mortality. His daughter leaned on the window pane, face distorted, nose pushed to one side, hands cupped around her cheeks and forehead. "Of course, I'm alright," he growled. "Come to the screen porch." He pointed to his left.

Kayla turned to her right and marched to the porch. Her father pulled on trousers over his undershorts and strode to the sliding glass door. After fiddling with the dual locking mechanism for a minute, he walked across the porch pavers and unlocked the back screen door. "Lose your key?" he asked.

"It's in the dorm at Flagler. I spent the night at a friend's. Got a ride here." Kayla scanned the small, two-bedroom home, taking in the chaos. "Maid hasn't been by, yet, this morning?" she asked.

"Very funny, honey," Wolfe said, wrapping his arm around his daughter's shoulders. "How's summer school going? Must not be too tough if you can party in the middle of the week."

"First summer session is over, Dad. We had exams the day before yesterday. Second session starts Monday."

"Short break. What brings you to the *cemetery*, as you call it?"

"Mom made me promise to look in on you this week. She said you would be alone for a while. Where did she go?"

"She took your brother to Costa Rica to bird watch," Wolfe said, padding his way to the small kitchen to make some coffee.

"How long have she and Junior been gone? This place is a disaster," Kayla said, eyes roaming over the mess in the great room: several day's worth of newspapers on the couch and floor. Dirty dishes sat on the end table, dining table, and floor. Sweat clothes occupied one of the recliners. "Those jogging clothes are pretty rank, Pops. Are they headed for the washing machine?"

"No, I can get one more walk out of them. Don't sweat as much as when I used to jog. So now I'm walking three miles, three times a week. Swimming in the clubhouse pool twice a week. Working out with weights twice a week, too." Wolfe listed his ideal retirement workout schedule, one he didn't follow too closely.

"Really, Dad?" She eyed his dirty, holey, old T-shirt, bare feet, and week's growth of beard. "When was the last time you left the house?"

Wolfe rolled his eyes, thinking. He said, "Let's see, the kids are out of school, so they don't need tutoring – "

"Did you really like tutoring reading?" Kayla asked.

"A frickin' elephant, I did."

"What?"

Wolfe smiled, recalling a first grader's first attempt at reading a caption in an alphabet zoo book. He said, "That's *Hooked on Phonics* for *African Elephant*."

"And the last time you left the house?" Kayla asked.

"I needed some bananas last week." He pointed to the black bananas hanging from the holder on the counter. They oozed liquid essence of banana onto the granite countertop.

"Yech," Kayla said. "You go take a shower and shave. I'll fix you some breakfast."

"I only shave on Sunday and Wednesday now," Wolfe protested. "It's only Thursday...."

"Friday. Get your ass in the shower or I'll call Mom." She held her cell phone in front of her. "By the way, why didn't you answer your phone when I called this morning?"

"Same reason you can't call your mother. The reception stinks," Wolfe said. He picked up his telephone from the table and tossed it to her. "See for yourself. No bars."

Catching his phone, she looked at it then at her phone. She flashed the front of hers at him. "Four bars," she lied. "Shower, Dad."

Shoulders slumped and head bowed, Wolfe shuffled slowly toward the master bedroom and bathroom. She heard both doors close and lock. When the shower water ran, she went to work.

In thirty minutes Wolfe reappeared, clean-shaven and smelling fresh. She had loaded the dishwasher and the washing machine. A bowl of oatmeal, toast, and two scrambled eggs, along with orange juice, waited for Wolfe at the dining table.

"Smells good," he said. Inspecting the room, he added, "You didn't throw out any of the newspapers, did you? There are some articles in them –"

"They're all in the recycle bin, if you really want to search for them," she said.

Wolfe sat heavily in front of the food. One elbow on the table, he poked at the eggs with his fork for a while, and then stirred the oatmeal with his spoon. He didn't eat much.

Kayla waited in silence for ten minutes, watching her father's facial expressions, frown on her face. When he finally put the silverware down and looked up at her, she said, "Get your jogging shoes. We're going for a walk."

"I just took a shower," Wolfe said. "I'll need another if we walk. It's already eighty degrees out there."

"It's Florida, Dad. Deal with it." Wolfe trundled into his room and retrieved his worn ex-jogging shoes.

Using her father's keys, Kayla locked the front door. "Wait, my phone." Wolfe said.

"Is dead. That was the real reason you couldn't answer. I plugged it into the charger," Kayla said.

They walked on Copperhead Circle toward the Cascades clubhouse. Wolfe said nothing.

After reaching Legacy Trail, about a quarter mile from his house,

Kayla had to speak. "You're depressed, Dad."

"Yeah, I suppose I am. A little. Maybe."

"What did you do to drive Mom away?" she asked.

"Nothing."

"Really? I don't think she has spent six months here in this so-called *active adult community* since you moved in, what, two years ago?"

"About that. Well, it's better than those *inactive adult communities* you compare it to," Wolfe said.

"It *is* like a cemetery, in ways. Maybe three steps prior: this, then assisted living, then nursing home, then inactive adult community," she said. "But that's not why Mom isn't around, is it?"

"Well, she's much younger than I am," Wolfe said.

"She knew that when she married you. Something else?"

Wolfe fell silent. Kayla waited. She had learned some things in her two semester-psychology course. Prime directive: wait the patient out. Silence asked better questions than most therapists did.

"I did retire, you know," Wolfe said.

"Yes...."

"I spend a lot more time at home than she was used to."

"And...."

"She was much more efficient as an office nurse. You know, multitasking," he said.

Kayla waited, steering him away from the clubhouse and toward Inverness Drive, lengthening their walk around the block.

"But she wasn't interested in the best way to load the dishwasher, or the most efficient way to do laundry, or how food should be stored in the refrigerator or pantry. They are both small here and if you don't pack them so the most used stuff is up front, then you spend all day re-arranging things to get what you need."

"When did you become an efficiency expert?" she asked and immediately regretted the inference.

"I'll have you know that as an intern and physician I learned one hell of a lot about being efficient."

"Sorry, Dad. I didn't mean that," Kayla said quickly, blushing. "I meant that's what Mom must have thought, after years of running the household without your help. Why don't we get you a hobby? Something you can do and stay out of her hair."

"I've tried. Thought of a lot of things," Wolfe said. "But some are too expensive, like building or converting another internal combustion vehicle to electricity. She was really upset with that. I spent twenty grand on it over four years, but then never drove it. I guess the driving wasn't the challenge that building it was."

"Was that EVie, the electric vehicle you gave to the college so the students could disassemble it and reassemble it?"

Wolfe shrugged. He said, "Yeah. Great tax deduction. But who needs tax deductions when you're living on social security?"

"Don't play poor with me, Dad. You may live on social security, but your house and automobiles are paid for. And you have some investments."

"Not good enough for your mother," Wolfe said. "Remember, she's the daughter of a very, very successful, rich radiologist. And she remembers her old life style. She thought she married another rich doctor, not a struggling one."

Kayla put her arm around her father. He felt thin, less substantial than the last time she had hugged him. *Old age, and two families, had worn him down. Maybe he had reason to be depressed.* "You're not sick are you?" she asked.

"Aside from the usual osteoarthritis in my knees, spinal stenosis in my back, the pernicious anemia, and Barrett's esophagitis, I'm as healthy as a horse. Except my BUN and creatinine are climbing slowly. Too many anti-inflammatories, likely. But you aren't interested in that, or you would be applying to medical school, right?" he asked.

"Right," she agreed. "But still, a hobby."

"I thought about electronics, too expensive. Even bought a guitar. Can't sit still long enough to practice with my back pain. I'll find something eventually, or it will find me."

"What do you mean it will find you?"

Wolfe said, "I have a bad habit of becoming obsessed by something. Like EVie. Like the RV. Once I decided to buy it, I spent innumerable hours researching it. I had thought about buying one to live in as a medical student, almost did. Fought off the compulsion. But when I was working as a doc, the fixation hit me again. Couldn't resist."

"So it found you?"

"Yep," Wolfe nodded.

"Going to sell it?"

"Never," Wolfe said. "My neighbors here in the Cascades tried to get me to do that. It fits within their rules, much to their chagrin. They tried to fine me $100 a day, until they read their own rules. That was a fun fight." Wolfe smiled for the first time since she had come home.

"Anyone else driving you crazy?" she asked, going with what seemed to make him happy.

"Yeah," he said. "One of my neighbors knocked on the door the other day. As you know I help keep the borrowing library in the clubhouse alphabetically arranged. When I get out of the house." She nodded. "When I first started, I carried a clipboard back and forth when I walked to the clubhouse. To remind myself to do things, like print the dividers."

"And?"

"Well, a month ago, a little old lady with a heavy cane knocks on my door. She shakes the brass head of the cane at me and says, 'Are you the guy who walks around the neighborhood with a clipboard?' 'Maybe,' I said. 'Why?' 'Well my husband saw you in our backyard taking pictures the other day and I want to know what you were doing, sonny?' She also claimed to be a retired BAM drill sergeant."

"A retired what?"

"B-A-M, broad-assed marine. That's swabbie talk. Don't repeat it, especially around her. I believe her. She was muscular and mean. although she was 50-plus pounds overweight. Probably from all the medication she might be taking for PTSD."

"Geez. What did you do?" Kayla asked.

"Well I explained that I thought I was on common property, taking a picture of a huge red-shouldered hawk that had landed on her roof. I took it for your mom. She's gone overboard with this birding stuff. Kind of reminds me of dogs and squirrels. She can't complete a sentence, or drive safely if a bird flies by. I started yelling, 'Squirrel!' whenever she gets distracted by a bird."

"And I wondered if you did something to drive her away," Kayla said.

"It's a joke," Wolfe said.

"Which part?" Kayla asked. "Do you really yell squirrel, and that's the joke? Or, are you joking about yelling squirrel?"

Wolfe smiled. "Both are jokes," he said. "I don't do it much."

"Because she's not here much," Kayla said.

"True," Wolfe said. He started to laugh. "Anyway, I showed this old biddy the pictures of the bird on her roof that I have on my cell phone. That appeased her. She went away happy. As she left, I asked her why she cared about me walking to the clubhouse with the clipboard. 'Listen, sonny, we old folks here have nothing to do but keep track of our neighbors,' she said. 'Get used to it.' That explains the neighbor who didn't like the fact that I covered the garage door windows. 'Ugly,' she said. I gave her the choice of leaving the windows covered or watching my jock straps dry after I jogged. I put them on the clothesline I hung in front of the windows. She agreed the covered windows weren't as ugly as my jockstraps. She's since become a friend."

The walk on Inverness led back to Copperhead and then to his house. The morning paper lay in the driveway behind the van conversion. Four more morning papers lay on the bricked front porch where a neighbor had thrown them. Having not seen Wolfe for several days, the neighbor assumed Wolfe was out of town and had worried about rain ruining the papers. Wolfe gathered the newspapers, two already yellowing, as Kayla unlocked the front door.

"More articles to clip," she said. "Don't become a hoarder, Dad. This place is only 1600 square feet."

"Might find my next hobby in one of these," Wolfe said. He pulled the clear plastic cover off the oldest paper and spread it before him. Kayla removed wet clothing from the washing machine and tossed it into the dryer. Once the dryer started up she returned to the great room and found her father engrossed in the paper.

"Dad," she said quietly, then again louder when he didn't respond.

"Oh, sorry, dear," Wolfe said. "Aircraft carrier did in my ears, as you well know."

"Find something interesting in the paper?" she asked. "I've got to get back to the dorm. I have things to do and a date tonight. Can't waste my short time off."

Wolfe stood and put his arm around his daughter. "Well, it was good to see you, Kayla. I love you. Drive carefully," he said.

"Dad. You have to drive me back to Flagler. A friend dropped me off. Remember?"

"Oh, yeah," Wolfe said. "I was distracted by the paper."

"What about the paper?"

"On the front page of today's paper, there's a story about an attempted murder at Flagler Hospital. Someone pushed a bolus of potassium into a dead man, and then left a note: *This is for Jimmy Byrnes*. I knew a Jimmy Byrnes in the navy. He was a yellowshirt on the *Oriskany* hangar deck crew when I got to Vietnam. Probably a coincidence. Why would someone push potassium into a dead man? Makes no sense."

Bill Yancey

CHAPTER 3

Wolfe drove the large van conversion into the parking lot between the Anastasia Bookstore and the Villa Zorayda Museum, setting the brake. He reached to his right and grabbed Kayla's hand before she jumped out. "Study hard, KayLan," he said, using his pet name for her, an abbreviated form of Kayla Anne. He left the engine running and the air conditioner blowing cold air. Seconds after shutting either one down the van's interior temperature would shoot to a hundred degrees or more.

"As always, Pops," she said. Remembering what else was nearby, besides Flagler College, she asked, "Don't you go to Price's for haircuts?" She eyed his shaggy mop of hair. "How long has it been?"

Running his hand through his graying mane, Wolfe thought for a second. "Two months, I guess. Don't need haircuts as often, since it's thinning."

"That's a matter of opinion," she said. "It looks pretty bad, especially that hairy neck. And you can wander through the bookstore when you're done. Might find something to do in the hobby section. We've got to work on your depression."

"I told you. Something will grab me. I'm easily infatuated," Wolfe said, staring at three barely dressed co-eds walking through the parking lot.

"I don't expect Mom wants you to take up girl watching, Dad. Did you ever have a crush on a girl?" Kayla leaned back in the captain's chair and explored her father's countenance. His expression went from

15

gloomy to bright. A smile crossed his lips.

"Only with every girl I ever met," he said. "Your mother knew that about me. She kept me out of circulation after the twins' mother died, until I had convinced myself she was my next wife."

"Explain that, the crush on everyone," Kayla said. "I've had similar feelings about boys. Men, I guess."

Wolfe stared at the ceiling for a long minute, then tried to frame an answer. "Well, it seems I have a hard time differentiating between casual flirting, or a woman being nice to me, or commiserating with me, and telling the difference between that and being interested in me. Should one of those women who walked through the parking lot just now wave to me, my heart would have done flip-flops."

"That ever get you in trouble?" Kayla asked.

"All the time. I believe I've had more first dates with no second dates than all my male high school and college classmates put together." Wolfe said and laughed. "I dated a college student after Lisa died, not really a date. She volunteered in my clinic for several weeks. I took her to dinner, as a reward, her last night in the clinic. After dinner we walked back to my car. I grabbed her hand. She pulled her hand from mine and turned to face me with tears in her eyes. 'You're like a father figure to me,' she said. 'Why would you do that?' I said I would like to get to know her better. She said, 'You're so *old*.' Mind you, I was forty-two. She was twenty-two. Only six years younger than your mom. Anyway, I immediately came to my senses and apologized for misinterpreting her kindness and interest. But she never spoke to me again."

"Ew," Kayla said. "Twenty years. And now you're almost seventy and Mom is fifty-five."

"Sixty-nine."

"Whatever. I don't think I could date someone twice as old as I am."

"Better start looking now. Gets harder as you get older," Wolfe agreed, smile on his face. "By the time you are fifty, eligible bachelors who are one hundred years-old are rare." He started to laugh, quietly at first, then louder as his daughter joined in.

Wolfe turned the ignition key off and opened his door. "Where are you going, Dad?" Kayla asked jumping down from the passenger seat. They met behind the van.

He put his arm around her shoulder. "I suppose I'll get a trim while I'm here. Can you lend me twenty bucks? Price's doesn't take credit cards."

Kayla opened her purse. "I think –"

"Just kidding, honey. I've got money." Wolfe scanned the parking lot. "Maybe I will hit the bookstore afterwards and check out the hobby section. Worse thing that could happen is I might find a good book."

Kayla squeezed her father around his waist. He seemed a lot more vigorous than he had earlier in the morning. "And I didn't even have to threaten to call Mom! Are you still going to let me bring the Prius to school in the fall, so I don't have to beg for rides?"

"As long as you can find a safe, cheap place to park it," Wolfe said.

"I was thinking about leaving the dorm and sharing an apartment with some girls senior year."

Wolfe's face clouded briefly. "We'll talk about it," he said, using a tone Kayla knew usually meant *no way in hell.*

Not wanting to dwell on his negative thoughts, she gave him a peck on his cheek. "Okay, Pops. Call me if you want me to come home and cook you a real meal for supper. Love you." And she was gone, across King Street and into the Flagler campus.

Wolfe brushed away a tear and turned to walk around the building to the entrance of Price's barbershop. Mike gave him a quick trim and told him several jokes, but still couldn't fix the bald spot in the back.

***

Wolfe ran his hand through his short haircut, *just long enough to comb a part.* He mulled over the fact that his wife would be upset. *If she were home.* She liked longer hair on him, although with his thinning gray hair, he thought every possible longer hairstyle looked like a comb-over. Sweating in a hot Florida summer made the look worse. He detested comb-overs and would rather have his tanned scalp show through the gray locks. *Nice contrast.*

None of the books in the hobby section of the bookstore excited his interest. Those on remote-controlled aircraft and drones attracted him momentarily until he read how the FAA had gotten involved in the sport.

Someone left that day's *St. Augustine Record* in one of the cushioned chairs scattered around the bookstore. Picking up the paper, he scanned the headline he had seen at home, *Attempted Murder at Flagler.* Settling into the comfortable chair, Wolfe read the entire article.

The night before, a retired navy chief had succumbed from his maladies on the medical ward. No attempt had been made to resuscitate him. Apparently he and his family had decided against extreme life saving measures, although the article didn't mention why. *Probably HIPAA,* Wolfe thought. *In the old days, there would have been a paragraph or two on the man's congestive heart failure, liver disease, or failed kidney transplant.*

The nurse noted his passing in her log, but left the body in the bed for the morgue crew to process for the funeral home. When she returned to the room with the orderly from the morgue, they found a needle on a syringe, later noted to contain a concentrated solution of potassium, sticking into one of the patient's intravenous ports. Attached to the pole holding the bag of intravenous solution was the note: *This is for Jimmy Byrnes.* A review of the security video showed a man slipping into and out of the dead man's room, after his death. Police were searching for a *person of interest*. No name given. No picture of the person in the paper.

Wolfe turned to the obituaries in the back of the first section. The family hadn't put a death notice in, yet. The article mentioned the dead man had been in his late seventies, so his career in the navy could have overlapped Wolfe's brief sojourn on the high seas. That would also have made it contemporary with the Jimmy Byrnes that Wolfe had known on the *Oriskany.*

No one would be able to tell he had sat in the chair and read the paper. Wolfe folded it neatly and laid it in the chair. When he read the funnies as a boy, his father had been insistent that he return newspapers to their original folded, neat order. That way the next reader, usually his father, could find the sections he wanted. The habit had followed Wolfe for a lifetime. His insistence that Jennifer, Kayla's mother, follow the same routine was but one more irritant in their marriage.

Empty-handed, Wolfe left the bookstore. When he returned to the van a light bulb went off in his head: *The Chief would know about Jimmy Byrnes.*

Chief Noble had been an ABH-2 – aviation boatswains mate petty officer second-class – in the V-3 Hangar Deck Division on *Oriskany* when Wolfe had been an airman. During Wolfe's internship in Jacksonville, he had had to drive his roommate and fellow intern, Iggy Harrison, to the VW dealership to pick up his car one Saturday morning. And who should present Iggy with his bill but retired USN Chief Noble.

It had taken Wolfe a minute to recognize the black ex-sailor, dressed in blue trousers and white shirt with the VW logo on it. Noble wasn't convinced of who Wolfe was until they had gotten together briefly for a beer later that week. Although they didn't see much of each other during Wolfe's internship, they kept in touch more often after Wolfe returned to St. Augustine to work at the *After Hours* urgent care centers.

"I'm coming. I'm coming," Noble's voice boomed through the glass storm door, over the sound of barking dogs. "Oh, my God, look who has come calling," Noble said. He pushed the glass door open. The three pit bull mixes wagged their tails and barked, then climbed on Wolfe and tried to lick his face. He entered Noble's home on Lincoln Street, in the Lincolnville historic section of old St. Augustine.

"Hey, Chief," Wolfe said, shaking the older man's right hand with both of his. "I was up the street getting a haircut. Thought I'd drop in for a visit. I would have called first, but my cell phone is at home charging."

"I hate those things," Noble said, referring to cell phones. "No one ever drops in unannounced any more. They always call first. When you get to be my age, you'll like surprises. I do."

"Surprise!" Wolfe shouted, spreading his hands out wide. The outburst started the dogs barking again. They quickly quieted down.

"Come in. Come in. Have a seat here in the living room. You look good, Doc. Retirement must be going well for you," Noble said. He ushered Wolfe into the living room, filled by two recliners and a large flat screen television. "Sit in my wife's chair. She's over at Bethel Baptist. Women's meeting, you know. Want a drink? Iced tea? Lemonade?"

Wolfe smiled, remembering a younger Noble as a hard-charging, heavy-drinking man. He teased the retired chief, saying, "That's it? No liquor. Not even a beer?"

Noble shook his head. "Lord, no," he said and laughed, shaking his head. "The doctor mentioned once that alcohol wasn't good for my gout or my liver. Daloris cleaned out the liquor locker that day. I can't get a drink from any of my neighbors, either. I think she told everyone in Lincolnville. They won't even let me in any of the bars downtown."

"She must love you a lot," Wolfe said. "I'll take a half lemonade/half iced tea, if the iced tea is sweet. But only if it's no trouble."

"No trouble at all," the older man said, turning to go to the kitchen. He returned with a glass of pale iced tea and handed it to Wolfe. "So what really brings you to Lincolnville?"

"Did you read the paper this morning?" Wolfe asked.

"Well, I read some of the online version. My grandson set it up on the computer for me."

"See the article about the attempted murder at Flagler Hospital?"

"Don't believe I did," Noble said, scratching his unshaved chin.

Wolfe told Noble about the article. He ended his dissertation with, "Could the note be referring to *our* Jimmy Byrnes?"

Noble leaned back in his chair. "You don't know about Jimmy?"

"Know what?" Wolfe said.

"He's long dead. Navy said it was suicide."

"When?"

"Our cruise, yours and mine on *Oriskany*. Last day on the line. He didn't show up for work. Why don't you remember this? We mustered the entire crew, many of them on the hangar deck. Counted noses. The marine detail and the chiefs checked every compartment. No trace of him. The last time anyone had seen him was during the fire the night before."

"Big fire? I wasn't on the ship then," Wolfe reminded Noble. "Got a ride in a helo to the *Ranger*. You guys went home. I stayed for another cruise. Remember?"

Noble cocked his head, examining Wolfe carefully. "Maybe. Small electrical fire in a tractor. Anyway, we turned the ship around and went back to where it had been the night before when the tractor caught fire. It's a huge ocean, Doc. No trace of him there, either. The destroyers stayed for two more days searching. Someone said we even radioed the Russian trawler that tailed us to see if they had found him. Nothing."

"So the navy gave up and decided he committed suicide by jumping overboard?" Wolfe asked. "No investigation into foul play? You know he didn't have many friends, especially in the supply divisions. I remember he caught that asshole, Deke Jameson, red-handed stealing dungarees from our laundry. Went to Captain's Mast and testified against him, too, even though they threatened him. Several other witnesses refused to show up. Got the jerk a month in the brig and the captain busted him from second-class to seaman."

"Yeah," Noble said, pausing to search his memory, "And if I remember, S1-S7 had it in for Byrnes from then on. His pay was always screwed up. His laundry slashed. They messed with his chow. One of the barbers even purposely screwed up his haircut. Chief Powell and I went down to the barbershop and stood there while the supply chief trimmed Byrnes's hair to fix the damage. As best as it could be fixed. Took a month to grow out."

Wolfe smiled. "I remember Rocky used to complain about how long

Byrnes's hair was."

"There was one crazy son of a bitch. Our beloved V-3 Hangar Deck Division Officer, Rocky the Flying Squirrel. He had wings, but the navy wouldn't let him near an aircraft, except as a passenger," Noble laughed. "Every time he'd tell Byrnes to get a haircut, we had to remind him that Byrnes had to see a civilian barber at the next port of call to keep him away from the ship's barbers."

After an hour of reminiscing, the two old salts had brought each other up to date since their last pow-wow. Wolfe stood, holding his hand out to Noble, signaling his intention to leave. "Stay for lunch?" Noble asked.

"No thanks, Chief. Got some things I need to do," Wolfe said.

"You sure? The wife will be home soon. If you're here, she'll be less of a bother. If not, I'll have to leave for a while," Noble pleaded.

"Why, Chief, don't you get along with your wife?" Wolfe teased.

"Oh, I love my wife," Noble said. "Unfortunately, she missed me a lot while I was at sea and working for Volkswagen. Since I retired, she has made *me* her hobby. She wants me to go everywhere with her. She accompanies me to doctor appointments. I can't take a walk to the library without her wanting to come with me. She's smothering me!"

"Yoo-hoo, I'm home," Daloris called. The dogs had known better than to bark at her. She entered the room, wide grin on her face. She wore a red dress and hat, and she peeled off a pair of long white gloves as she walked. "Oh, you have company. Doctor Wolfe. So glad to see you again."

"Hello, Daloris," Wolfe said, putting his arm around her shoulders and leaning forward so she could give him a light kiss on the cheek. "You look all dolled up. Fashion show at the church?"

Daloris smiled coyly. "Why, thank you, Addy. Will you stay for lunch?"

"I asked him the same thing," Noble said, following Wolfe to the front door. The dogs sat, tails wagging, waiting for a chance to bark. One harsh look from Daloris and all three lay their heads down quietly.

"I'm sorry, Daloris. I've been gone from home all morning," Wolfe said. "I've got some things to do that I can't put off."

"Well, you say hello to Jennifer, Kayla Anne, and Junior for me, Okay?"

"Will do," Wolfe said.

CHAPTER 4

Vehicles filled the parking lot in front of the Flagler Hospital emergency room and all other lots surrounding the hospital also. Wolfe thought about parking in the physician's parking lot, but decided having to prove he was a retired doctor to the security guard would take more time than finding a spot in the last row. Besides, he wasn't there on hospital business and he no longer had an active pass card.

Entering the high-ceilinged foyer that led to the patient tower and the ER, Wolfe strode to the desk manned by an elderly woman wearing a pinkish jacket. She owned a wide smile and white false teeth too large for her mouth. "May I help you?" she asked.

"Does Luther Gundersen still work here?" Wolfe asked. Gundersen had been an ER doc who started *After Hours* urgent care with his partner, Francis Cordiano. There had been some irregularities in the billing by the *After Hours* corporation, ending with Cordiano going to jail for tax evasion, the breakup of the business, and the eventual divorce of Gundersen and his fourth wife. She got one of the clinics, the one Wolfe had worked in. Gundersen eventually lost his license. Flagler hired him as a marketing agent. He knew how to do that, in spades.

The volunteer flipped through the hospital directory on the computer screen. "Oh, here he is," she said. "He's in the Anderson Gibbs building in the administration suite. Should I call him? Whom shall I say is looking for him?"

"I'm Dr. Wolfe. I haven't seen Luther in a long time. I'd like to surprise him. How do I get to his office?"

"Go to your right, walk past the elevators, through those glass doors," she said. "Then go through the central building. Cross the patient drop off in front of the cafeteria and Anderson Gibbs is on the left.

"Thanks."

The door to Anderson Gibbs opened to mild chaos. Workmen moved ladders and sheetrock. A power saw cut steel 2 x 4s. Someone hammered in the background, while a power drill screamed off to Wolfe's left. Dust floated through the air. Wolfe smelled wood burning and gypsum. Gundersen stood inside the door with his hand out to Wolfe. "Addison," he said, "good of you to stop by." He beckoned Wolfe to follow and strode out the door. "Much too noisy in there to talk."

The door closed slowly, pinching off the racket completely. "Did you know I was coming?" Wolfe asked.

"The volunteers are required to phone us when someone asks about any of the executive staff by name," Gundersen said. "We haven't had any violent incidents yet, but you never know when an angry family member or jealous husband might show up. We've had security stop several people over the past two years. One psyche patient thought he was a terrorist."

"I'll keep that in mind next time I visit," Wolfe said smiling. He followed Gundersen to the cafeteria. "Next time I won't stop at the desk and ask directions."

Gundersen shrugged. He said, "Won't matter. Without the proper pass, you won't be able to get into the executive suite. And if you tailgate someone through the door, you will still have to pass through the metal detector and the scrutiny of the security team. That's what they are building."

"Why?"

"Homeland Security suspects all hospitals are potential targets. In general, we are undefended. Vulnerable. Besides they gave us a lot of money to do it. I got a new office out of it," Gundersen said, wicked grin on his face. "Of course, it went with a promotion."

"You must be doing well," Wolfe said.

Gundersen opened a door in the rear of the cafeteria. The two men stepped into the executive dining room, used by the physicians and administrators. "We'll talk over lunch. I assume that's why you came at this time of day?"

"I need to get out of the house more often," Wolfe said. "This is the second invitation to lunch I've had today. Thanks. I am hungry. I'll join you, if I can pay my own way."

"Sorry to disappoint you, Addison, but the meals are free for us, the docs, and the guests we bring."

Wolfe shrugged, "Guess I can't fight city hall."

After working their way through the cafeteria line, and finding a seat at a far table in front of an enormous window, the two men sat. They enjoyed the view of the Matanzas River, Old St. Augustine, and the Flagler Campus. For about thirty minutes they rehashed the demise of *After Hours*, the rise of *Healing Arts* in one of its proposed locations, and the unsolved disappearance of Sarafea Seville from *After Hours*. For fifteen of those minutes Gundersen outlined his non-medical career and rise to glory as marketing director, and his most recent promotion.

Wolfe listened with one ear, watching as patrons finished eating and departed, thinning the number of possible eavesdroppers. When at last the two were alone, Gundersen finished eating while Wolfe filled him in on how boring retirement was. Gundersen checked his watch and started to stand as Wolfe finished his monologue with how the older twins and his two younger kids were doing. Gundersen never had a feel for kids, just wives.

"Got to go, Addison. Even a star like me has to earn his living," Gundersen said as he started to rise.

"Before you go," Wolfe said. "Tell me about the attempted murder."

Gundersen sat down again quickly. He looked over his shoulder, and answered curtly, "Can't discuss it," he said.

"Do you know who can?"

"Nobody. CEO said it's a dismissal offense for anyone caught talking to the media."

"I'm not media," Wolfe said.

"Do you have a personal interest in the case?" Gundersen asked.

Wolfe explained the possible connection. "I want to find out if this is related to the Jimmy Byrnes I knew."

"Why? That's what, forty some years ago?"

"About that long, 1967. He was a good friend. I recently found out he is dead. For me, it's as if his death recently happened. I'd like to know if he's the guy in the note. If not, I know all I need to know," Wolfe said.

"Well, what if he is your buddy from the navy? What then?" Gundersen asked.

"Don't know. Maybe when the police find their person of interest, they'll let me talk with him to see what he knows. There's a chance

Jimmy was murdered. I don't remember him as having a fatalistic or suicidal personality."

Gundersen again scanned the room for eavesdroppers. He scooted his chair nearer to Wolfe. Both hands clasped together on the table, he leaned closer to the retired physician and whispered. "A resident from Shands Hospital in Jacksonville was on the ward that night. He's doing a community medicine rotation here in Flagler this month. The dead man was one of his long-term patients. I'd assume he knows more about the dead man than anyone else in this hospital. And the CEO can't fire him."

"Got a name?"

"If anyone asks, we never had this conversation," Gundersen said.

"Just like the old days," Wolfe said. "Where can I find this resident?"

"Medical ward, third floor. Name is Gadhavi, Amit Gadhavi."

"Indian?" Wolfe asked.

"Yep."

CHAPTER 5

Byrnes landed in the water face first, arms flailing. The force of hitting the water after a fifty-foot drop knocked the air from his lungs. The ocean forced its way into his nose, mouth, and sinuses. He surfaced coughing and spitting. Panic raged in his mind.

A ship making headway through the ocean creates a bow wave that travels down both sides of the ship and becomes its wake. 30,000 plus tons of aircraft carrier, air wing, supplies, and crew makes a huge bow wave and wake, even at slow speeds. Byrnes fairly surfed away from the ship and into the path of one of the trailing destroyer escorts. Though not as large as the carrier's, the bow wave from the destroyer pushed him farther away from the carrier.

He didn't wait to see if the ship would stop for him. Training at Annapolis took over, pushing aside the panic. Taking a deep breath and holding it, Byrnes doubled over and untied his shoelaces. Cursing the fact that he double knotted them, Byrnes kicked off one shoe, took a second breath, and untied the second. The steel-toed boondockers sank.

Slipping out of his dungarees the third-class petty officer treaded water in his skivvies and T-shirt, while he tied a knot at the end of each pant leg. He held the dungarees behind his neck. Kicking as hard as he could to gain altitude, he flung the open waist of the dungarees over his head and into the air, holding the waist with both hands. As when he had practiced the maneuver in the Olympic-sized pool at the Naval Academy, the dungarees inflated with air. Now he had a temporary life preserver, and time to search for rescue.

By then a mile distant and lit up by red deck lights, the carrier and two destroyer escorts steamed quickly farther away. Knowing it was useless to yell he did so anyway, "Man overboard! Man overboard!" Spinning in place, he searched for other ships. Large swells lifted him and he could see long distances in the moonlight, over the waves. No other ships appeared.

Close by he could see several objects floating on the water. As the air leaked out of his dungarees, Byrnes retrieved three life jackets that had fallen into the ocean during the fight. Using their straps he tied the three together, and slipped his arms through the center one. He secured it around his waist. Carefully, he tried to unknot his dungarees and pull them on, but they slipped away and sank. *Great*, he thought, *they'll find my body in my underwear. If they find it.*

Unable to sleep in the rough water and still hopeful of rescue, Byrnes watched as the sun rose several hours later. He had to pull his T-shirt over his head to keep from being sunburned as the day wore on. Toward evening, dark clouds gathered on the western horizon. As the sun sank in the west, lightning flared all along the horizon in towering black clouds. Thunder boomed; lightning drew near. The wind rose, and with it the amplitude of the waves. Byrnes sank into deep troughs and then found himself flung to the tops of huge waves. He clung to the flotation devices, arms wrapped tightly in front of his chest.

By early the next morning, he was exhausted, hungry, and thirsty. Allowing his arms to float at his sides, he leaned back into the center life jacket, white T-shirt covering his face. Depression set in. He was 60-120 miles from shore, depending upon where *Oriskany* was at the time he fell overboard. His only hope was that a ship would cruise by before he died of thirst, went crazy, or a shark found him. He wrapped his fist around the jade pendant that hung from his neck and said aloud a Buddhist prayer his mother had taught him, "Hail to the jewel in the lotus. Help me to overcome all obstacles and hindrances." How long he slept, he could only guess. The sun shone high in the sky when he woke to the sound of voices.

Three Asian men in a sampan floated nearby on the flat, glass-like, calm sea. Byrnes pulled the shirt from his face. His movement startled the men in the boat and they started yammering at each other in an unfamiliar language. Raising a hand, Byrnes waved. "Help. Help." His yelling excited the men even more. Two of the men paddled the small boat in his direction. The third man put his hand out to grab the life preserver closest to the boat. He pulled Byrnes to the side of the sampan.

Once Byrnes had both hands on the edge of the wooden boat, the three men struggled to pull him into it. He was of almost no help, too weak. Rolling over the gunwale and onto his back on the wooden deck inside the boat, the powerful scent of fish wafted into his nostrils. Byrnes tried to express his gratitude. He gasped for breath. Once his heart stopped pounding, he continually nodded his head and said, "Thank you, thank you," through parched lips and sunburned face. The men sat him in the shade of the curtain that covered the hatch to the mid-deck wooden shelter. Fishing poles of various lengths and two bamboo poles attached to small fishnets lay on the deck between the shelter and the side of the boat. Along the far side of the boat a large fishing net filled the deck from the bow to the stern.

The men spoke quietly among themselves. Eventually, one offered the American a metal cup of water. Sitting unsteadily at the stern of the boat, Byrnes gulped the warm fresh water. He handed the cup back, pantomiming for them to fill it again.

The oldest of the three men – two looked young enough to be his sons – shook his head. He pointed to the forward section of the ship. Past the small covered shelter amidships, Byrnes saw the stump of a mast and some hemp line lying on the deck. The sail and most of the mast were gone. His rescuers needed rescuing, too. They rationed their water.

For an hour, Byrnes and the older man tried to communicate through sign language and pictures scraped into the wood of the old boat with a metal belt buckle from a life preserver. He finally understood that the men had survived the same storm he had endured. For three days, it had driven them farther out to sea than they had intended to go. The wind had snapped the mast, and blown the sail and mast over the side.

Pointing to the small outboard motor hanging on the stern of the boat, Byrnes made puttering noises like a motorbike. The old man shook his head. He led Byrnes to the engine. Flipping the choke over, he ordered one of the younger men to pull the starter rope. On the third pull, the engine puttered briefly, and then died. It did the same on the fourth pull. The second young man pulled four more times. The engine refused to run.

Byrnes tapped on the gas tank. The old man pointed to the ocean. Seawater had gotten into the fuel during the storm. Byrnes searched for a gas can. There were two 20-liter cans of gas inside the shelter. One was half full, the other almost completely empty. He pointed to those. The old man again pointed at the ocean. Both somehow had been contaminated during the storm, possibly as they tried to fill the gas tank on the outboard.

Reaching behind him, Byrnes fingered the covering to the hatch. It rippled slightly in the gentle breeze. The curtain felt like leather, or at least a waterproofed material of some type, almost the same consistency of suede or the chamois his father had him use to dry the family automobile. Motioning slowly, the American pointed to the knife that hung on one of the younger men's belt. It had a wooden handle and a razor thin, long, sharp blade. With his other hand, he pointed to the curtain at the opening of the shelter. He held his hand out for the knife. After the older man nodded, the younger one handed the knife to Byrnes, handle first.

While the men watched, Byrnes first poured the entire contents of the nearly empty gas can into the half-full can. Using the knife, Byrnes carved a large square of the leather from the bottom of the curtain. He grabbed one of the fishnets on a short bamboo pole. Fashioning a pouch from the leather-like material, he pushed the piece of curtain into the fishnet. Leaning over the side of the sampan, Byrnes dipped the pouch into the ocean. As he suspected, the covering was waterproof. A puddle of seawater remained in the pouch.

After dumping the seawater back into the ocean, Byrnes wrung the pouch as dry as possible. Changing his mind about using the original square and net, he laid them on the deck and cut another large square from the curtain. He fashioned another pouch in a second fishnet and pantomimed pouring a small amount of gasoline from the half-full can into the pouch. The old man nodded, and one of the young men poured several ounces of gasoline onto the leather. Byrnes squeezed the piece of curtain, forcing gasoline through it. The fuel dripped from the outside of the pouch. He wrung the pouch again between his sunburned hands. When he was convinced the gasoline had soaked through the material and not dissolved it, he nodded. The young man filled the pouch again, while Byrnes held the pole so the pouch hung over the large opening in the empty gas can. From the underside of the material, gasoline dripped into the can.

Byrnes held the can between his legs. When the leather cup was full, he yelled, "Stop!" The startled man stopped pouring. The contaminated liquid in the leather pouch drained slowly into the gasoline can, all except a small amount of water. Byrnes tossed the water over the side and, after repositioning the pouch over the can, he nodded, imploring the man to pour more contaminated gasoline into the pouch. Pouch full again, he yelled, "Stop!"

"Dung lai," the old man said then and each time the pouch filled. Once they finished filtering the contaminated fuel, Byrnes pointed to the fuel tank on the outboard. The two young men lifted the engine from its mount and poured the gasoline from the tank into Byrnes's jerry-rigged filter. Then they tightened the engine back onto the stern of the small boat using the two clamp bracket screws that held it in place.

Byrnes pointed to the spark plug. He made a motion of unscrewing it and pulling it out, thinking it might have been fouled with oil when the men turned the engine over. The old man went into the shelter and returned with a spark plug wrench. Carefully, he unscrewed the sparkplug and handed it to Byrnes. The American inspected the plug. He dried it with his now dry T-shirt, noting there was no oil on it. Using the younger man's knife, he scraped gently at the ground and center electrodes until they appeared silver instead of black. He handed the spark plug back to the old man, who reinserted it into the engine and tightened it in place.

Under the direction of the old man, one of the younger men set the choke and yanked on the starter cord. Nothing happened, except a brief clap from the engine that Byrnes thought promising. The man pulled the rope again. The engine sputtered, ran for thirty seconds longer than it had before and quit. Impatient the old man stepped forward. He repositioned the choke to half open and pulled the rope himself. Byrnes saw the sinews in the old man's arms, legs, and neck strain when he pulled the rope with both hands. The engine roared to life, making a pleasant buzzing sound.

The old man steered the sampan toward the west and the setting sun. Both younger men clapped Byrnes on the back. One went to the container of fresh water and filled the metal cup with water. He offered the cup to the old man, who refused it. Pointing to Byrnes, the old man said, "Con co," and smiled. The American drank his second cup of water in two days.

CHAPTER 6

Wolfe thought he had found Amit Gadhavi, MD, on the third floor of the patient tower, in the Medical Intensive Care Unit. An older man, obviously the resident's mentor and cardiologist, dictated to the doctor-in-training as the young man took notes on his cell phone, swiping on the face of his phone as quickly as the older man spoke.

The two wore long white coats and stood at the counter in front of the nurses' station. Wolfe observed that the resident's pockets held only a stethoscope, not the bundle of books, papers, and 3x5 cards that Wolfe remembered from his residency. Everything he had carried in his pockets during internship and residency in the 1970s, this resident had on his phone. Plus, access to almost all knowledge, medical and otherwise, accumulated by the human race over the last 10,000 years. Wolfe waited quietly for the two to finish their discussion.

One of the nurses looked up from her paperwork and spoke to Wolfe, "May I help you, sir?"

Wolfe nodded and spoke in a whisper. "I'm Dr. Wolfe. Is that young man Dr. Gadhavi?" He nodded at the dark skinned man talking with the white haired physician.

"No, that's Dr. Guerrero," she said. "Dr. Gadhavi just left for a medical conference at Shands. Not two minutes ago. If you hurry, you can probably catch him in the physicians' parking lot. It's to the right as you exit...Oh, you'd already know that."

By the time she finished speaking, Wolfe was opening the door to the emergency stairway. "Thanks," he said before the door closed behind him, muting the sound of Wolfe scampering down the stairwell.

A handsome, well-tanned young man with a long white coat slung over one shoulder stopped at the volunteer's desk before leaving the building. Wolfe strode up behind him, hoping this time he had the correct physician. He heard the man say, "Dr. Roberts will be fielding all calls for me until I come back tomorrow, but if you can't get a response from him, please text me."

"Yes, Doctor," a petite black woman said. She wore the standard pink volunteer's jacket.

"Doctor Gadhavi?" Wolfe asked quietly from behind the man.

The physician turned and examined Wolfe closely. Seeing nothing to denote Wolfe was a hospital employee or physician, the young man assumed Wolfe to be a patient and responded curtly, "Sorry. I can't talk right now. I'm late for a conference. Make an appointment in clinic. These ladies can help you." He spun around and headed toward the revolving door.

"Sorry," Wolfe said, grasping the young physician's arm. Gadhavi turned his head and stared at Wolfe while continuing to move in the direction of the parking lot. "I didn't introduce myself. I'm Dr. Wolfe."

Not knowing Wolfe's role at Flagler Hospital, Gadhavi stopped walking. He turned to face Wolfe. It would not behoove him to irritate someone who might have input about his rotation. "I'm sorry, Dr. Wolfe," he said. "I will be late for medical rounds if I don't leave right now. Can this wait? I'll be back tomorrow."

Wolfe beamed. "No problem," he said. "We can talk while you drive. I did an internship at Shands about thirty years ago. They called it University Hospital then. I'd like to see how your instructors do medical rounds these days."

Gadhavi continued to walk toward his car. "I'm not coming back until tomorrow. How will you get back here?"

"Well, let me worry about that. Okay? Sweet ride," Wolfe said. He pulled open the passenger door to the doctor's red Audi A5.

"So, Dr. Wolfe, where do you practice? I haven't seen you around Flagler," Gadhavi said. The little Audi accelerated through a yellow light at 312 and US 1, switching lanes at the same time.

Wolfe knew the ride to Shands Jacksonville wouldn't take long if the resident continued to drive like Danica Patrick. He needed to ask his questions about the attempted murder. First, however, he had to make Gadhavi receptive to an interrogation. "I'm retired," he said. "Did family practice and urgent care stuff until two years ago. What year are you?"

"Third year. I start a pulmonary fellowship in July, in Miami."

"Looking forward to that, I bet," Wolfe said.

"Most of my family lives in Ft. Lauderdale. Mother is a lawyer. Father practices Oncology."

"When did they leave India?" Wolfe asked.

"In the '70s. They weren't fans of Indira Ghandi's politics," Gadhavi said. He steered the Audi onto I-95 north, merging between two semis and accelerating into the middle lane. Seconds later he had transitioned to the left lane. To Wolfe it looked like they were going about five miles an hour faster than the other traffic, which he knew generally traveled between 75 and 80 mph. I-95 had the highest accident rate of all roads in St. Johns County. Another vehicle, a purple Porsche 911 whipped past them on their right as if they were at the Burger King drive through. Wolfe noted the wet pavement, a rain shower having apparently ended minutes before. A few thunderstorms hovered over the beach several miles to their right.

Startled, Wolfe said, "I'd like to ask you some questions before someone kills us on this racetrack. That okay with you?"

Gadhavi turned his head toward Wolfe. He grinned. Even, white teeth filled his mouth. "The answers will do you no good if you are dead," he said.

"Peace of mind is what I'm after," Wolfe said.

"Okay," Gadhavi said. "Shoot."

"The man who died yesterday and then was found to have received a bolus of potassium —"

"I can't discuss that," Gadhavi said, taking a quick glance at Wolfe. The Audi continued to purr along, weaving into the middle lane to pass slower vehicles in the left lane as needed. "The police and the hospital administrator were pretty specific about not talking to anyone but them."

"I understand that," Wolfe said nodding. "I don't want information about the attempted murder investigation, or anything that HIPAA might find inappropriate."

Confused Gadhavi asked, "What else is there that you could want to know?"

"The man mentioned in the note, Jimmy Byrnes," Wolfe said. "He might —"

"Beats me," Gadhavi said, interrupting.

"Alright, try this," Wolfe said. "I don't need to know your patient's name, his diagnosis, his medical condition, or his chart number, phone number, or any of the other dozen identifiers that get administrators' knickers in a twist. I do need to know if your patient ever mentioned being on an aircraft carrier in Vietnam."

Silently, the resident stared through the windshield. Wolfe noted the backup of traffic headed in the opposite direction and wished traffic were slow in his direction also. Gadhavi slowed, temporarily stymied by tractor-trailers in every lane. 65 mph seemed slow after the rush to the Duval County line. The smell of diesel exhaust from the three trucks filtered into the Audi.

"I don't believe that question would upset the Sheriff, or HIPAA," Wolfe said, prodding the resident.

"Oh, Sorry," Gadhavi said. "I agree. I was replaying my initial history and physical with the patient in my head. He was a retired chief in the navy. Supply services, if I remember. He did spend time on an aircraft carrier in Vietnam. Enlisted in 1953, right after the Korean War, I believe. From southern Georgia. Stationed several times out of Mayport. After retiring from the navy, he took a job with a boat building company, Luhrs, in St. Augustine. Retired from that months before the great recession."

Amazed, Wolfe said, "Do you know all your patients' background histories that well?"

Gadhavi shrugged. "I guess," he said.

"I don't suppose you remember the name of the aircraft carrier?" Wolfe asked. "I can give you a list of names to choose from."

"I remember he said it came back to the States for a complete overhaul after a serious fire." Gadhavi slowed and cut across three lanes of traffic to exit from I-95 at 8th Street in Jacksonville.

"That narrows it down. Only three aircraft carriers had major fires during Vietnam: *Oriskany*, *Forrestal*, and *Enterprise*," Wolfe explained. "*Forrestal* came back to the Newport News shipyard in Virginia. *Oriskany* went to Alameda, California. And I would guess *Enterprise* went to Pearl Harbor, since her fire happened off Hawaii. Do you know if he went to the East Coast?"

"Definitely not," Gadhavi said. "He told me all about taking part in the sexual revolution in San Francisco during the overhaul. *Humping the hippies*, he called it."

Stunned, Wolfe sat back in his seat, silent. *The Jimmy Byrnes I knew may have known this man. But how were they related? And what did the note mean?* Gadhavi pulled his Audi into the Shands parking deck and into an empty space. "We're here," he said. "Sorry, Dr. Wolfe, but I have to rush along."

Wolfe climbed out of the vehicle, reached across the convertible top and shook the young man's hand. He said, "Call me Addy, short for Addison. I'll be in touch later after the police release his name. I'll want you to contact the family for me to see if they'll talk to me."

"Sure thing," Gadhavi said. He turned and walked briskly to the nearest hospital entrance.

Wolfe trundled slowly behind him, hands in pockets, mind in 1967.

CHAPTER 7

"Hey Wolfe, wake up." Wolfe opened his eyes. A chunky sailor in dungarees and chambray shirt stood at the foot of his hospital bed. Next to him stood a mop-haired civilian, Robert Martin, a grin on his face. With his hair in his eyes, Martin reminded Wolfe of John Lennon.

"Oh, Crespi," Wolfe said, peering through swollen eyelids. The words were difficult for Martin and Crespi to understand. Wolfe's face was so edematous he found it hard to breathe at times. He looked at his hands. They were still bright red and about twice-normal size. "What's up, Mike? Hey, Bobby," Wolfe acknowledged the civilian. The steady drumbeat of rain on the window drew Wolfe's gaze from his friends.

"Yeah," Crespi said, "monsoon again. They say there will be four more months of this stuff. I've never seen rain like this. You guys?"

"Yeah. It was like this last year, too," Martin said. "Every year from May until October it pours. I think the navy base averages a hundred inches of rain per year." Days before Martin had finished his freshman year in college at Washington State University. His father, a civilian, ran the Subic Naval Station engineering division. During World War II, the elder Martin had served as an enlisted driver with Patton's 3rd Army in Europe. He and two other men had driven the general's jeep all over France and Germany in the last year of the war. After the war ended, Martin found a pretty French woman to be his war bride and brought her home with him. Once home, he returned to college and earned an electrical engineering degree. He wanted Bobby to study engineering, but the younger Martin wanted to teach, like his mother.

Crespi scanned Wolfe's face, then his hands. "We got orders, Addy. And we got an east coast carrier, buddy. One cruise and we return to Norfolk. Maybe a Med cruise after that," he said, excitedly. Crespi grinned, white teeth in sharp contrast to his dark, Middle Eastern skin, made shades darker by working in the Philippine sun the previous two weeks. His orthodox Jewish ancestors had left Palestine in the 1920s and settled in Maryland.

Crespi had met Wolfe in the US Navy transit barracks on Bolling AFB, in Washington, DC. An unemployed reservist, married with a baby on the way, he had volunteered to go on active duty to keep his family fed. He had suspected the navy would send him to Vietnam, since he had no extra navy apprentice schooling. Although his wife cried torrents when he left, he promised to be home before the baby was born. He also explained to her that nothing bad ever happened to sailors. They didn't participate in combat, as far as he knew. In two years of reserve service, he had managed to finish basic training and earn a promotion to E-3, airman. He outranked Wolfe, who was still an airman apprentice, E-2. The only reason Crespi was an airman was the navy had a reserve squadron of aircraft stationed on Bolling AFB close to his home in suburban Maryland. Otherwise, he would have been a seaman.

Wolfe, on the other hand, had chosen to be an airman in boot camp. He had an uncle who flew fighters in the air force. With his eyesight, Wolfe would never fly as pilot-in-command, but he could be near the jets he loved to watch. Maybe, if the navy sent him to electronics school, he could work on aircraft one day or be a crewman. His uncle's death from cancer led to meeting Crespi. The navy allowed Wolfe to go home on bereavement leave at the end of boot camp. After the funeral, he found himself in the transit barracks, along with Crespi and two hundred other sailors, including Maryland Lt. Governor Raphael Pisenecki's son, Raymond.

"Hey, Pisenecki," Wolfe shouted one day while they toiled on a work detail. The navy wanted the transients to earn their keep. That morning they spit-polished the Chiefs' Club. Wolfe ran the buffer, while third-class petty officer Pisenecki sat in a chair supervising. "Are you really related to the lieutenant governor?"

"How many Piseneckis do *you* know?" the sailor shot back.

"Okay," Wolfe granted, "not many. So why are you here? Couldn't your father get you out of active duty?"

"Yeah. He probably could have," Pisenecki admitted, "but I wanted to be here. Actually, I want to serve in Vietnam, kill some commie gooks."

"Will you get to do that as a Seabee?"

"Probably," Pisenecki said. He went back to reading the paper he had pulled from the trash can, feet on the desk.

Crespi, Wolfe, and a hundred other sailors left the transit barracks in a bus. The bus took them to National Airport, where they boarded a passenger jet to San Francisco. The two-hour layover at SFO turned into an eighteen-hour delay while mechanics swapped out an engine on the jetliner. Crespi and Wolfe sat on either side of Martin on the long flight from San Francisco to Clark AFB. Unable to leave the terminal during the repair, and unable to sleep sitting upright on the jet, the three had had minimal sleep over the previous 36 hours by the time they arrived. The punch-drunk trio were best buddies.

Crespi and Wolfe rode in the navy bus from Clark to Subic Bay Naval Station. The 42 mile ride took three hours. On display all along the so-called highway, Wolfe saw some of the most abject poverty the world knew. Peasants lived in plywood and corrugated plastic-roofed houses covered with nylon sheeting, no windows. The smell of raw sewage wafted through the windows. The bus had no air conditioning.

Adult and child Filipinos climbed over the piles of trash discarded from the colossal American bases at Clark AFB and the US Naval Base at Subic Bay, searching for food and other treasures. Naked kids stood at the side of the road begging for anything the sailors might discard.

Having a civilian friend in Subic meant that Crespi and Wolfe had someone to visit when not participating in work details at the transit barracks. There were so many sailors awaiting ships their overseers had a hard time dreaming up busy work to keep the men occupied.

After a short workday, many men, especially the old salts, put on their whites and headed to Olongapo City, the whore-infested bar-crammed camp outside the gates of Subic. Drunk, bloody, injured sailors returned nightly to the barracks to wallow in their own vomit and piss. The Tijuana of the Philippines sounded more and more like a Wild West cesspool to Wolfe. Crespi refused to go to Olongapo on liberty, having promised his wife he wouldn't drink or chase women. Wolfe never felt an urge to explore the local environment, happy to pal around with Crespi, Bobby, and his family, even if Mr. Martin force-fed them on the need to get an education after their enlistments ended. The Martins kept the two sailors fed and entertained for two weeks while they awaited their assigned ship.

Then the navy sent Wolfe and Crespi on a gardening detail: mow the lawn and trim the hedges around the BOQ, Bachelor Officers Quarters. That would have been an easy six-hour workday. The two had made plans to walk to the Martins' place and escort Bobby to the station theater. *For A Few Dollars More*, the spaghetti western with Clint Eastwood, had arrived at Clark and Subic on the same plane as the sailors. Fifty cents got a sailor, a dependent, or a civilian contractor, a ticket, a small Coke, and a medium sized bag of popcorn.

The sudden burning in Wolfe's right hand stopped him from trimming the hedges. Within minutes he had a shooting pain that ran to his right shoulder. Before he could yell for help, he found it difficult to breathe. If Crespi hadn't been close by, he would have died from the anaphylactic reaction to an insect sting. The chunky airman called for help on the BOQ telephone. An ambulance from the dispensary arrived and a corpsman injected Wolfe with Benadryl and epinephrine.

Lifting his head from the pillow, Wolfe asked Crespi, "So, what ship did we get?"

"USS *Forrestal*. The first supercarrier," Crespi said.

Wolfe had never heard of the ship. "I thought the navy christened ships after famous battles, or famous ships. I never heard of a battle named *Forrestal*."

"Navy heroes, too. He was Secretary of the Navy and Secretary of Defense," Crespi said. "He fought for the funds for the navy to buy the supercarriers. Committed suicide at Bethesda Naval Hospital. Won the battle, lost the war."

"Oh," Wolfe said, properly chastised for not knowing his navy history. "When do we leave?"

"I sign on tonight. They said you will be better in the morning. Ship goes on line in three days."

Martin's smile never diminished. "We're going to miss you guys," he said. "But, the carriers return to port every month or so. Frequently they come back to Subic. Occasionally they go to Japan or Hong Kong. In fact, my parents and I are going to Hong Kong in August, before I go back to college. Maybe I'll see you guys there."

Wolfe never made it onboard *Forrestal*. The navy didn't clear him for duty for another two weeks. By then, *Forrestal* was on Yankee Station, in the middle of the Gulf of Tonkin. USN aircraft pounded the North Vietnamese so severely that the carriers had run out of the 1000-pound bombs favored for the A-4 Skyhawks. Someone thought it would be a good idea to use up the old 1000-pound bombs stored in the Philippines. These weapons were of an older design and at least ten years-old. They had been improperly stored in Okinawa and Subic Bay and exposed to salt spray. The formulation of explosive in these 1000-pound bombs could not withstand the heat of a fire as well as the newer explosives could. When the USS *Diamond Head* unloaded its cargo of older bombs onto the *Forrestal*, the stage was set for a tragedy.

CHAPTER 8

"I hated the guy," Sluggo Maxwell said over the telephone. Chief Noble had called Maxwell and given him Wolfe's cell phone number after Wolfe's visit. No less irritating than he had been as a sailor, Maxwell managed to annoy Wolfe by calling him at 10:00 p.m. He woke Wolfe from a sound sleep. In Maxwell's defense, he lived on the West Coast where it was only 7:00 p.m.

"Why was that?" Wolfe asked, sitting in bed with his cell phone and the pad of paper and pen he kept next to the bed. He frequently awoke in the middle of the night with a brainstorm, chore, or list of things to buy. Rather than allow the thoughts to keep him awake, he jotted them down and returned to sleep. His worst problem was trying to interpret his handwriting after he got up in the morning. Writing in the dark, to keep from waking his wife, did not improve his penmanship.

"I thought he was arrogant," Maxwell said. "For instance, he never went out for a beer with the crew. I never saw him blasted, except that one time you and he went over in Sasebo. He drank with you."

"Not exactly," Wolfe said.

"And he didn't pitch in with a donation when we ordered that sex book," Maxwell continued without listening to Wolfe. "We each contributed five bucks. Farrell ordered the book from some publisher in Australia."

"I heard about that," Wolfe said. "Was that the photographic Kamasutra book, supposed to have color photos of at least fifty different sex positions?"

"That's right."

"I think I remember Byrnes laughing at you guys. He said most of the V-3 Division had spent a lot of money and the publisher had ripped you off. Can't remember what the con was, though," Wolfe said, trying to retrieve the memory.

"The people in the photographs were dressed," Maxwell said, voice angry. "A hundred bucks worth of false advertising. We were bummed."

Wolfe chuckled. Byrnes and he had laughed belly laughs when Byrnes had related the yarn about the previous cruise. *Dumbass squids*, Byrnes had called his comrades at the time.

"Some of the guys thought he couldn't cross his legs because he had such big balls, but I thought he was egotistical," Maxwell said. "A real friend would have hung out with his crew and buddies. He was always doing stuff no one else did, like jogging on the flight deck. Who the hell runs three miles, half of it against a thirty knot wind, while at sea? He had to be some kind of health nut. Or just plain nuts."

"I remember him doing pull-ups on the ladder rungs welded to the sponson near the forward elevator while waiting for the flight deck to drop recovered birds," Wolfe admitted. "Never before knew a guy who could do twenty-five pull-ups. I remember he did a hundred push-ups one night, too."

"See what I mean," Maxwell said. "An arrogant, asshole show-off."

"So what did you do after getting out of the navy, Sluggo?"

"I don't answer to Sluggo any more," Maxwell said. "I went to law school. My clients call me Marlow Millard Maxwell, Esquire."

"That's a mouthful," Wolfe said. "What do your friends call you now?"

"I said I went to law school, Boot. I don't have friends," Maxwell said, laughing. "Actually, most of my friends call me Max."

"That is better than Sluggo," Wolfe said. "And you can call me Doctor Boot from now on. Do you ever get to the East Coast?"

"On occasion I have participated in class action suits and have had to spend time in Chicago or New York," Maxwell said. "But my primary practice is in personal injury law and it's busy. I don't leave California often."

"Still using your boxing skills?" Wolfe asked. Maxwell had earned his nickname. He had been the last man standing during a shipboard *Smoker*. Thirty sailors duked it out in a boxing ring on the hangar deck while on the way to port after an extensive line period. The rest of the ship's company watched, and made bets. Each participant had one hand tied behind his back and a blindfold over his eyes. If a sailor fell down, that eliminated him from winning the prize – two free nights in a hotel, all expenses paid, in Japan. Maxwell earned the title *Sluggo* and the prize when he accidentally hit the second-to-last man with an elbow while winding up to punch him. He had had no idea the other sailor stood directly behind him. Maxwell's elbow caught the man in the back and pushed him forward so fast he tripped and fell to the canvas.

"Don't do martial arts any more," Maxwell said. "I have an ex-cop on payroll for the heavy work. You did some boxing, too, if I remember."

Wolfe thought for a minute. "Yeah. I suspect it was right after I joined the ship. You guys were practicing and I went a round or two with Saulson."

"Gave him a black eye, too," Maxwell said.

"That was an accident," Wolfe said. "He didn't block an easy jab. My being left-handed gave him fits."

"Didn't you have a fight with Grender, too?"

Again, Wolfe had to pause and search his memory. He chuckled when he remembered the brief altercation. "Oh, yeah," he said. "Grender was mouthing off on the sponson while we were in port. He was supposed to be working. I told him to shut up. He swung at me and missed. I hit him in the jaw with a left and he went down to the deck. From there he kicked at me like a baby while he screamed in pain. Byrnes told him to get up and go sweep the hangar deck. But he never mouthed off at me again."

"I remember," Maxwell said.

"Can you tell me anything else about Jimmy that took place before I joined *Oriskany* in P.I., Max?" Wolfe almost called his ex-shipmate Sluggo.

"To be honest, Boot, er, Doc, I never think about the man. After he committed suicide, I spent a long time asking myself if the friction between us had contributed to his state of mind. Still can't say. The memories are painful, so I avoid them. Didn't like him, but he obviously had some deep psychological issues. No one should commit suicide, not even an asshole like him."

Bill Yancey

CHAPTER 9

"Doc! Doc!" Wolfe heard the high-pitched squeal of a little girl's voice behind him. Turning his head, he spotted a tiny towheaded kindergartener racing down the frozen food aisle toward him, arms open wide. When she reached him, she wrapped her arms around his leg. Barely as tall as the middle of his thigh she shrieked again, "Doc!"

"Lillian, Lillian!" an older woman spouted, as she chased after the child. "Sorry," she said when she reached Wolfe. "I don't know what got into my granddaughter. Say you're sorry to the man, Lillian. We have shopping to do."

Mournful eyes locked on Wolfe's, pleading. Lillian resisted the pull of her grandmother. "But, Doc," the child said.

Wolfe laughed and patted the girl on her head. He said, "It's okay. I'm one of the reading tutors at Ketterlinus Elementary." Unwrapping Lillian's arms from his leg, he knelt and placed his right arm all the way around the child. She smelled of a fresh bath and shampoo. "Are you practicing your reading this summer? You want to be ready for first grade in the fall, don't you?"

"Oh, yes," Lillian replied. "Grandma and I read the funnies in the paper every day after Mom drops me off at her house. And she takes me to the library every week."

"Oh," the older woman said, hand to her mouth, "You're *that* Doc. She talks about you all the time." A crooked smile spread across her face and her chest puffed out with pride. "Lillian is reading third grade books from the library now, aren't you Lillian? Why do the kids call you

Doc?"

"Well, I'm a retired physician," Wolfe explained. "I didn't want them to have to call me Dr. Wolfe. And the teachers didn't want them to call me Addison. It was a compromise, I guess." He stood. "High five," he said to the child.

She wound up as if she threw pitches for the Atlanta Braves and slapped Wolfe's hand with a loud smack. Then she giggled when he said, "Ow! You've been practicing that, too."

Her grandmother took her by the hand and dragged her down the aisle. "Say goodbye, dear. Nice to meet you, Doc." The child waved at Wolfe until she disappeared around the end of the aisle.

"Nice to meet you, too, ma'am," Wolfe said.

"Cute little girl," another customer said. "What's her last name?"

"I wish I could remember," Wolfe said, turning to his shopping cart. He pulled out his cell phone and scanned a list of the groceries he needed to buy. At the same time the telephone rang. Wolfe puzzled over how to answer the phone without erasing the list, and then finally remembered. "Wolfe," he said.

"Dr. Wolfe, this is Amit Gadhavi," the resident said. "How are you today?"

Wolfe smiled. "Except for being reminded about how bad my memory is, Dr. Gadhavi, it's been a pretty good day. How about you?"

"Oh, fine," the resident said. "You got back to Flagler Hospital without incident then?"

"Well, no. I went directly home from the medical conference. Took an Uber," Wolfe said. "Speaking of the conference, you guys sure rely on technology a lot. Do you ever talk to patients or touch them? One of my neighbors had groin pain. I told him it was probably a hernia. He saw four physicians and had normal x-rays, CT scan, blood work, and urine tests before anyone made him turn his head and cough. He did have a hernia when checked, but modern medicine turned the diagnosis into a $3000 odyssey. Surgery for the hernia is next week."

"You must have noticed that the older attendings said the same thing in the meeting summary," Gadhavi said.

Wolfe nodded to himself while holding the cell phone to his ear. "You're right. Sorry. I got off on a tangent. What's up?"

"Did you see the obituary in the *St. Augustine Record* this morning?" Gadhavi asked.

"I did. Was the retired chief petty officer in the obituaries the man who died the other day?"

"Yes. His family, wife and daughter actually, are coming in this afternoon to pick up his personal belongings. They have been released by the sheriff. Shall I ask them to stay and talk with you?"

Wolfe nodded, and then answered. "That would be terrific. I have to take some frozen food home from Publix, but I can be there in an hour an a half. Would that fit their schedule?"

"Yes. That works well. They said they would be here in about two hours," Gadhavi said. "I'll have his chart out for them to see, also. You may want to see that, if they'll give you permission."

"That's fine," Wolfe said. "I'll be there right after I put this stuff in the freezer." *And find the newspaper to remind myself of the man's name,* he thought.

"See you then," Gadhavi said.

"Good-bye," Wolfe said. His phone clicked. He went back to looking at his grocery list.

* * *

Parking on a Sunday at Flagler Hospital proved easier than on the previous Friday. Gadhavi led him to the MICU consultation room, a combination bereavement, informed consent, good news, bad news room. Comfortable seating and subdued lighting, along with the pastel colors and insulated quiet in the room, made family members more comfortable when discussing stressful situations.

Gadhavi introduced Wolfe to the dead man's wife, an elderly, short, nervous, thin woman, who obviously needed a cigarette, or a beer. Her daughter, about fifty-years-old, gray and slightly overweight, grasped her mother's hand as the two sat on a couch behind a walnut coffee table. A six-inch thick, paper, medical chart held their attention. It sat closed on the table in front of the women. Beside each woman was a clear plastic bag with a built in handle. Both bags held clothing and personal items, evidently the dead man's.

"Mrs. Clemons, Mrs. Wright," the resident physician said, nodding first to the older woman and then her daughter. "This is Dr. Wolfe, the man I talked to you about. If you would like me to stay, I will be happy to. Otherwise, I'll be in the MICU. The nurse will find me if you need me."

The older woman waved Gadhavi out of the room. "We'll be fine, Doctor," she said. "I doubt Dr. Wolfe bites and I'm sure you have other things you would prefer to do." Gadhavi backed through the door,

51

closing it tightly behind him.

"Please sit, Dr. Wolfe," the daughter said. She pointed to a chair across the table from them.

"Thank you for agreeing to chat with me," Wolfe said as he sat down. "I am sorry for your loss. You have my condolences."

"Thank you," the women murmured together.

The older one continued, "Dr. Gadhavi says you may have been in the navy with my Richard?"

"There's a possibility that's true," Wolfe admitted. "I don't know that I knew your husband, but I did know a man named Jimmy Byrnes."

"Who was he?" the daughter asked. "And what does he have to do with my father?" She pulled a tissue from her large purse and dabbed her eyes.

"Well," Wolfe said, "If he is the Jimmy Byrnes I remember, then he served on the USS *Oriskany* with me and maybe your father in 1967. He was a good friend. We worked on the hangar deck together. He made ABH-3, third-class petty officer, weeks before I transferred to a different ship." Turning his head toward the older woman, he added, "I guess the first question is this: Was your husband on *Oriskany* in 1967, Mrs. Clemons?"

Clemons nodded, silent tears fell in her lap. She made no effort to staunch the flow, or to catch them with a tissue. "We lived in Oakland, California. Missy," she pointed to her daughter, "was barely a year old. We were having financial difficulties. When he left for the cruise, I thought I'd never see him again. We were talking about a divorce. I went home to Chicago to live with my parents. After the overhaul and *Oriskany* came back from another WestPac cruise, Richard was promoted to second-class petty officer. We could then afford an apartment. When Missy was four, we moved back to Oakland to be with him. And he went on another cruise, on a different ship."

"I'm sure that being a navy wife and raising a family is complicated, when your husband spends so much time at sea," Wolfe said. "It was much easier for me, being a bachelor." Clemons nodded. Her daughter stroked her hand.

"He wasn't a bad man," Clemons said. "There were a lot of temptations on the cruises. Booze, women, even some drugs. Eventually, he became an alcoholic, got cirrhosis. The corpsmen treated him for multiple venereal diseases, too. We only stayed together for Missy's sake. I left for a while, but came back when he got so sick."

"Mom's been nursing him for twelve years," Wright said.

"That's a long time," Wolfe said. "Don't know that my wife would do that for me."

"She would if she loved you," Clemons said, "even if you are a son of a bitch. Sorry, Doctor. I miss him, but I'm happy he is no longer in pain. And, I guess, I will always be angry with him."

"Of course," Wolfe said, nodding.

"Can you find out who this Byrnes is and what he has to do with my father?" Wright asked.

"Now that I am pretty certain he was the man I knew onboard *Oriskany*, I would very much like to find out what he has to do with your father," Wolfe said. "Would you give me permission to read his medical chart and contact his friends from the Navy? And do you have a list of his friends from his time on active duty?"

Wright pulled a palm-sized black notebook from her purse. "This is Daddy's little black book," she said. "I was going to burn it to save Mom the heartache of going though it. If you would do us the favor of contacting everyone in it who is still alive and informing them of my father's death, I will give you this address book and sign a release so you may have a copy of his medical record."

CHAPTER 10

"Wolfe!" a yellow-shirted man Wolfe didn't recognize barked at him. Wolfe, wearing a blue jersey, had been sitting on the seat of the tractor, looking out the hangar bay opening to the elevator, watching the sea roll by. The elevator spent most of its time at the flight deck level, coming down to the hangar deck level only to drop off or pick up aircraft. He had been on *Oriskany* for a little over three weeks and had learned the names of most of his comrades. The man continued, "You and Higgins go with Byrnes. On the double."

Byrnes, Wolfe knew. He also wore a yellow jersey and was one of the aircraft directors in the crew in which Wolfe struggled to learn terminology and his new menial labor job. The blue-jerseyed sailors physically pushed aircraft around the hangar deck, when the tractor and spotting dolly could not fit in a space, or were not available. That was most of the time on the crowded hangar deck. Constructed during World War II and commissioned shortly after, *Oriskany* had been designed for smaller aircraft. Blueshirts also carried the chocks and chains used to immobilize and tie aircraft to the deck. It was their job to break down the tie-downs prior to moving a plane and then to re-attach them after it had reached its new position. The job was dirty, the heavy chains often coated with grease, fuel, and grime. It was also slightly dangerous. The underside of every aircraft bristled with antenna, rocket and bomb fins, and devices that secured fuel tanks, bombs, and other devices to the aircraft. To get firm leverage on the aircraft without pushing on control surfaces or other fragile parts, blueshirts crawled under the planes and pushed on the landing gear struts, bomb racks, fuel tanks, or bombs. Occasionally, after being distracted, a blueshirt would have a foot or hand run over, or have the skin on his back raked by a bomb fin. In the subtropical heat, on a ship with no air conditioning, the back breaking work had everyone in the crew smelling of sweat and salt.

The yellowshirts determined the direction the plane went by giving instructions to either the driver of the tractor or a man who pivoted the nose wheel of the aircraft with a long steel pole, the nose wheel steering bar also known as the tiller. A fully loaded A-4 Skyhawk, better known as the Scooter, could weigh almost 20,000 pounds, an F-8 Crusader almost twice that. During air operations the hangar deck crew routinely worked 15-18 hour days. They moved aircraft to the flight deck for launches. Later they moved aircraft dropped from the flight deck to the hangar deck during recoveries. Most recovered aircraft descended to the hangar on elevator #1 in the middle of the forward hangar bay. One plane after another arrived quickly from the flight deck. From there the three crews took turns pushing the planes toward the stern, filling all three hangar bays. That left room on the flight deck for the recovery of aircraft to continue. After air operations ended, they spotted and re-spotted aircraft for the squadron mechanics, so they could make certain each aircraft was in flying condition for its next sortie.

Depending upon how exhausted the aircraft handlers were, they either lounged for the two hours between launch and recovery, or worked at duty stations, cleaning up messes on the hangar deck made by the mechanics, polishing brass, or repairing or upgrading hangar deck equipment. The navy required all support and maintenance equipment, generators, tractors, aircraft jacks, rolling ladders, and more to be painted yellow. Sailors referred to the collection as *yellow gear*.

Coated in salt from evaporated sweat, his blue jersey ringed by many layers of white, Wolfe rolled out of the yellow tractor seat and stood quickly. He located Byrnes, who waved at him and Higgins from a hatch in the third hangar bay. "Run!" the yellowshirt yelled.

Higgins beat Wolfe to the hatch by a step. The three men climbed the ladder on the outside of the ship to a sponson several feet below the flight deck. Catching his breath, Higgins, another lowly blueshirt, asked Byrnes, "What's up? Why the rush?"

Silently, Byrnes pointed to the starboard horizon. A funnel of black smoke ascended from a large ship about five miles away. After they fixed the ship in their gaze, Byrnes said, "*Forrestal* may be dying." Pointing next to the rolls of fire hose on the sponson, he added, "When I give you the word I want each of you to carry a fire hose to the helo after it lands. Keep your heads down. The rotor blades dip occasionally. There will be injured men from *Forrestal* on the chopper. We'll take them off the helo. Four of us to each stretcher. We'll carry them down to sick bay. Got it?"

Wolfe nodded, staring in the distance. He had heard stories about *Oriskany's* fire. It seemed unreal that *Forrestal* would repeat the disaster less than a year later. More men joined their group, and another crowd of sailors watched them from the other side of the flight deck, the Landing Signal Officer's station. If they stood upright, their shoulders were even with the flight deck. "Down!" Byrnes shouted. They squatted and the blast of prop wash from the chopper's rotors and its jet exhaust blew over their heads.

"Go!" Byrnes ordered. Wolfe climbed the last ten steps on the ladder to the flight deck, arms around the coil of canvas hose. In a crouching run, he ran as fast as he could toward the helicopter and tripped, landing on the roll of hose. V-2 division had set up the arresting cables used to stop aircraft by their tail hooks. The cables stretched across the deck from port to starboard and about six inches in the air. Wolfe's foot had caught one of the cables. Scrambling to his feet, he completed his mission in time to grab the fourth handhold on a stretcher.

"Oh, and mind the arresting gear," Byrnes said to Wolfe, no trace of sarcasm in his voice.

The man on the stretcher howled in pain. Only shreds of his shirt remained, the rest burned away. From the waist up, his skin peeled in large sheets. A medic poured water over gauze on his face and chest as the four men struggled to carry him down to the hangar deck and then to sick bay.

Over the next two hours, Wolfe, Higgins, and Byrnes made four such journeys. The injuries looked worse with each trip. Finally, they ran out of firefighting equipment to load onto the helos. They made three more trips to sickbay. Exhausted the men climbed again to the flight deck. A large flight deck yellowshirt waited for them to gather around him on the sponson. "*Forrestal* feels she can continue air operations after the fire is out. She needs men to take the place of her injured flight deck crew. I'm looking for volunteers."

Wolfe never hesitated. He raised his hand. Ten other sailors did the same. "Never volunteer, Wolfe," Byrnes said.

"I have a friend over there," Wolfe said.

The flight deck chief took the men's names. "Okay. Back to your duty stations. We don't expect any more casualties to come here. *Bonny Dick* is taking them now," he referred to the USS *Bon Homme Richard,* another World War II era aircraft carrier nearby. "I'll contact you if you are needed."

The Air Boss or the admiral canceled flight operations for the day. Wolfe spent two hours under several aircraft moving them for the mechanics. Byrnes got into an argument with an aviation mechanic because the man refused to tie down his aircraft jacks securely. The yellowshirts and blueshirts constantly moved the jacks to avoid hitting them with an aircraft. Dinging an aircraft on a jack, another aircraft, or part of the ship earned a yellowshirt director or his safetyman the ire of the hangar deck chief. Too many dings and a yellowshirt might find himself reduced to blueshirt status, as a driver or nose wheel tiller man. If the chief was angry enough or the damage serious enough, he might even be demoted to tying down and pushing.

Chief Powell ran the hangar deck as his own personal fiefdom. Even the hangar deck officer knew better than to argue with him. Out of the corner of his eye, Wolfe saw the pot-bellied, gray-haired chief step out of hangar deck control and stare in his direction. Elevator #3 operator put down his sound-powered headphones and sauntered over to Wolfe. He and the third bay crew stared out the starboard elevator space at *Forrestal* less than a mile away. The two destroyers, USS *Rupertus* and USS *MacKenzie,* which had been spraying *Forrestal* with foam and water in an effort to control the multitude of fires had pulled away from the carrier. At one point they had been within feet of the huge ship. They joined a third destroyer, USS *Tucker,* searching the debris field for survivors and bodies of crew who were blown or jumped overboard. The dark black smoke had lightened to a haze gray funnel that climbed into the sky. "What did you do to piss off the chief?" the elevator operator asked Wolfe.

Blank look on his face, Wolfe shrugged. "I haven't done anything all day, except carry fire hoses and injured up and down ladders. Don't imagine that could have pissed him off."

"Well, he's pissed about something," the operator said. "Wanted me to tell you to double time to control. Wants *a word*, he said. By the way, that's never a good thing."

"Great," Wolfe said, turning and jogging between aircraft and yellow gear to the second hangar bay and hangar deck control.

Four men occupied the ten by twelve foot room, seated on a couch or two chairs or standing behind the status board: the Hangar Deck Officer, Lieutenant Rogers; Chief Powell; Airman Jake Snow; and first-class petty officer, Guy Munford. Chief Powell had returned to his usual position in hangar deck control, sitting next to Snow on tall stools behind the Plexiglas *Ouija board*, a desk-sized Plexiglas representation of the hangar deck. On the board, V-3 Division Chief Powell choreographed the movement of aircraft on the hangar deck. Flat, plastic, scale silhouettes of aircraft sat parked on it, as they were in the hangar deck. Lt. Rogers and Munford sat in plush lounge chairs near the huge coffee machine drinking coffee.

Airman Jake Snow wore a sound-powered headset. A microphone hung under his mouth. Pushing a button on the large round microphone, Jake the Snake spoke to the elevator operator in Hangar Bay 2, "Elevator #2, F-8, VF-162 #213, needs an engine swap. Coming down in two minutes."

Chief Powell took a flat silhouette of an F-8, marked it 162/213 and positioned it on the Ouija board in a space large enough to enable an engine swap. He then turned his attention to Wolfe. "Where did you think you were going, Wolfe?"

Wolfe looked at the chief, confused. "Pardon me, sir?"

"Don't sir, me, Wolfe. Save that for Lt. Rogers," Powell said pointing at the officer who smiled wanly when Wolfe glanced in his direction. Wolfe returned his attention to the chief. "I work for a living. Got it?"

"Yes, si- Chief," Wolfe said, glancing again at Rogers, who seemed to blush slightly. Munford grinned. The totally bald petty officer enjoyed Rogers's discomfort sitting in Chief Powell's domain.

"I said: Where did you think you were going when you volunteered to work the flight deck on *Forrestal*?" Powell repeated.

"To the *Forrestal*, Chief," Wolfe said, even more confused.

"Well," Powell continued, "if they need your assistance, Boot. Which I doubt by the way, since you barely know your way around this ship, and never stepped foot on the flight deck until today. And if you *do* go to the *Forrestal*, I will place you on report as AWOL. Got it?"

Totally bewildered, Wolfe shook his head. "You don't want me to help the *Forrestal's* crew?" he said.

"Correct. I want you working in Hangar Bay 3, on *Oriskany*. Now, get back to work."

"Yes, Chief."

Munford spoke as Wolfe left the control room. "If you can't find something to do at your duty station, you let me know, Wolfe." Then he howled like a wolf baying at the moon. The others in the compartment laughed.

Byrnes found Wolfe later, after chow. He slept soundly on the wing of an A-4. Mechanics had disassembled the aircraft into three large pieces: a large forward section including the wings, the back half of the fuselage and tail section, and an engine. Both the old engine and newer engine sat in rolling frames as the aviation mechanics worked on swapping them. The noise they made did not disturb the exhausted Wolfe. Byrnes had to shake Wolfe's leg repeatedly to wake him. "The crew's looking for you," Byrnes said.

Groggy, Wolfe replied. "I'll be there as soon as I get my boondockers on." He reached for his shoes.

Byrnes grabbed his arm. "Not for work. You are about to have an initiation, a pink belly."

"Are you serious?" Wolfe asked. "What is this, a sorority?"

Byrnes laughed. "I suggest you keep every derogatory remark to yourself and submit. The harder you fight, the worse it will be." He turned and walked away. Thirty minutes later Wolfe's crew dragged him bodily from the A-4, carried him to hangar deck control, held him to the deck, pulled up his shirt, and slapped his stomach until it glowed red.

"I heard you put up a battle," Byrnes said the next morning when Wolfe walked up to the tractor on which he sat. Wolfe nodded. It had taken all three crews to subdue him. The mechanics had laughed but offered no assistance. "Told you not to fight back, didn't I? Well, let's see the damage," Byrnes said. He had not participated in the ritual. Wolfe pulled up his shirt. His chest and stomach were bright red, with hints of blue and purple outlines of fingers in places. Byrnes gave Wolfe's stomach a quick backhand slap, eliciting a grimace but no sound from Wolfe. Involuntary tears filled Wolfe's eyes. He turned and walked away from the tractor and toward his duty station.

With flying operations suspended as *Oriskany* rendezvoused with the hospital ship USS *Repose* to offload injured and then follow *Forrestal* to Subic Bay, Byrnes pulled Wolfe from his duty station. He began instructing Wolfe on how to drive a tractor that afternoon. He and Wolfe hitched two tow bars to the tractor, one after the other, first on the rear of the tractor, then on the front. Wolfe practiced following

Byrnes's directions. The second tow bar took the place of an aircraft. After about an hour, they parked the tractor, Wolfe stayed in the driver's seat. Byrnes sat on the tractor's front deck next to a pile of tiedown chains.

"Not bad, Wolfe," Byrnes said. "You'll make a decent driver with a little more practice. I want everyone in the crew to know how to do every job. Makes us more efficient. We can divide into two smaller crews if necessary. Once you can drive and have more experience under the aircraft, I'll teach you about being a safety watch. Any questions?"

Still angry about the pink belly and Byrnes's late insult, Wolfe shook his head. Byrnes laughed. "Still pissed?"

Wolfe nodded. Byrnes continued, "You've worked hard. We still have some time. Let's BS a while." He waved off some of the hangar bay crew, when they began to cluster around the tractor. "Back to work, you slackers," Byrnes laughed. "I'm working with Wolfe today. You already know this stuff. The boot needs more training."

The crew wandered away laughing. "Suck ass," was the nicest comment Wolfe heard anyone direct at him.

"What do you want to know that you don't know already?" Byrnes asked.

"There's no such thing as a left-handed padeye wrench, is there?" Wolfe said.

Grinning, Byrnes shook his head. "Padeyes are welded to the deck. No right-handed wrenches or ignition keys for choppers either."

Turning personal, Wolfe asked the airman yellowshirt, "What nationality are your ancestors? You could pass for American Indian, Chinese, Japanese, or Filipino."

"My mother is Japanese," Byrnes said. "My father is from Ohio, European, mainly Irish. He flew Hellcats in World War II, was one of the first Americans to occupy Japan."

"Navy family, or draftee?" Wolfe asked.

"Long line of sailors, all the way back to John Paul Jones if you believe my grandfather. He was at Pearl Harbor on December 7, 1941. My father graduated from the Naval Academy in 1942, flew off carriers during the war."

"Is he still flying?" Wolfe asked, beginning to like the Japanese-American sailor.

"No," Byrnes said, changing the subject abruptly. "Time for chow. Tell you what, I'll buy." Byrnes grabbed the whistle that hung on the lanyard around his neck and blew it. The remainder of the crew gathered around the tractor parked near the starboard elevator opening. He spoke to the elevator operator. "Tell hangar deck control we're going to chow," he said. "You, too."

After communicating through the sound powered phones, the operator gave Byrnes a thumbs up. The crew headed for the chow line. Usually one or two men went to chow at a time, so as not to handicap the crew while working. Infrequently did the whole crew manage to eat together. With air operations cancelled, the crew would not be missed.

CHAPTER 11

Wolfe sat at his dining room table talking on his cell phone. It felt warm in his hand, the lithium ion battery having had a workout. The charging cord ran across the table and into the transformer next to the buffet. "You have my deepest sympathies," Wolfe said to the person on the other end of the call. "And I will relay your condolences to Mrs. Clemons."

He heard the front door to his house open and a quiet voice say, "Dad? Dad? Are you home?"

Quietly, he closed the spiral loose-leaf notebook, after scribbling himself a quick note. He laid Chief Clemons's black book on top of the notebook. "In here, KayLan," he said. He rose to his feet, stiff knees and back joints painful. He had been sitting far too long.

"Wow!" she said, entering the room. "What happened to the man-cave, bachelor pad? The curtains are open, sunlight is streaming in. No piles of dirty laundry. No dirty dishes in the sink. You've even showered and shaved. What's up?"

"Nothing," Wolfe said.

"Nothing?"

"Well, I found a project. Kind of," he said and shrugged. He placed one arm around her shoulder and planted a kiss on her forehead. "How's my baby girl?"

"No longer a baby, as you well know. First week of the second summer session was a bitch, though," Kayla Anne said. She slipped into the kitchen and rummaged through the pantry. Not finding anything appetizing in the pantry, she opened the freezer side of the refrigerator. Eyes widening, she pulled a Nutty Buddy ice cream cone from the fridge and began to unwrap it. "Mind if I eat this? You must have twelve in there. Mom know?"

"Your mom's not here. And she refused to make desserts while she was. Thought I would follow the same diet. Fat chance! Wanted to maintain her figure, she said."

"And yours."

"I don't have a figure. I'm a man," Wolfe said.

"Sure you do, Pops. It's a zero."

Wolfe shook his head. He worked at maintaining his weight by exercising, when not depressed. Unfortunately, gaining weight made him depressed. "You came home to pick on me?" he asked.

His daughter sat in the chair across from his, munching on the ice cream cone in one hand. He sat in front of his notebook. "No," she said. "I want to borrow the car for the weekend. A friend and I want to go to Cumberland Island and Savannah."

"Serious friend? And he doesn't have his own car?" Wolfe teased.

"*Her* family is local, too. They don't let her have a car at school, either. Like my parents. Too strict, you know?" She picked up Clemons's black notebook and thumbed through it with one hand before Wolfe could stop her. He reached for it, but she leaned backward out of his reach. "A lot of women's names in here, Dad. Is this your little black book?"

"That's private," he said, leaning farther forward and pulling it from her hand. "Belonged to a recently deceased navy chief. His wife lent it to me."

Intrigued, Kayla asked, "Why?"

"She wanted me to contact the people in it and tell them her ex-husband had died. She took care of him while he was sick, but she can't stomach the idea of calling his ex-girlfriends and navy buddies who helped break up their marriage."

"So, was this guy a friend of yours, or one of your patients?"

"We had mutual friends on one of the carriers I was on, eons ago," Wolfe said.

"Ancient history. Still using Roman numerals back then, I suppose," Kayla said.

"Too funny." Wolfe reached into one back pocket and retrieved the key to the Prius. Leaning farther forward, he pulled his wallet from his other back pocket, withdrew a twenty-dollar bill, and handed that and the key to Kayla Anne. "It needs gas. Drive carefully."

"That's it? No lecture about studying hard over the weekend. About summer school being so much harder than a regular semester? What's going on, Dad?"

Absently, Wolfe said, "Nothing." He opened the notebook and leafed through several pages. His daughter tried to read what he had written, but the notebook was upside down to her, and her father's handwriting, like most physicians, was indecipherable. "Have a good time."

Kayla's eyes widened. She pouted and said, "You're trying to get rid of me, aren't you? Maybe I should stay home today and tomorrow. I'll cook meals for you. Keep an eye on you, like Mom wants me to."

Wolfe stood. He walked around the table and gently pulled her out of her chair by the elbow. "Dad," she said, startled. Silently, he walked her through the laundry room and opened the door to the garage. Tenderly directing her into the garage, he pressed a button on the small black box on the wall. The garage door began to open. "You won't need the car?" she said.

"I'll drive the van if I have to go anywhere. Good-bye," he said. "Have fun. Drive carefully. Be back by 6 p.m. on Sunday." Without waiting for her to respond, he closed the door. He locked the deadbolt and walked to the great room. On his way to the dining table, he flipped the deadbolt on the front door, also. With his jet engine induced severe tinnitus, he didn't hear the car start or the garage door close, but he knew they had because Kayla did not reappear. Sitting at the table, he forgot about his daughter.

***

"Thanks for letting me interrupt your weekend, Chief," Wolfe told Noble. The two men sat on the metallic bench near the Bridge of Lions. To their right a boisterous crowd of middle school-aged kids played miniature golf. A sea breeze cooled them while palm trees shaded them from the tropical sun. At seventy-five degrees, the morning temperature seemed perfect. The smells of the ocean and sight of sea gulls nearby reminded Wolfe of being onboard the carrier.

"No problem," Noble said. "Always available for a friend, night or day, weekday or weekend. Anytime."

"Wife still smothering you?" Wolfe asked, smile on his face.

"Like a wet blanket in a car wash," Noble said. He laughed. "I really don't like you, Doc, but I'll do anything to get away from that woman, except divorce her. That would be expensive."

Wolfe laughed, "And here I thought you loved me, Chief."

"You can call me Maurice," Noble said, grinning at his own joke. "Haven't I told you that before?"

"Yeah, but I find it difficult to do. Old habits are hard to break. Besides, if I called you anything other than Chief, I expect *Smoke* might slip out. Did you resent that nickname? I apologize if it bothered you."

"Different time, different place, Doc," Noble said. He leaned his head back and scanned the sky, pointing. An E-2D from the Grumman factory flew low overhead, approaching the St. Augustine airport and the Grumman hangar where it had been assembled.

Wolfe nodded, seeing the new navy aircraft. The turboprop engines and their curved propeller blades whined as the aircraft glided overhead. The giant radome on top of the fuselage made its silhouette distinctive. He squinted through the sunlight at the modern version of the earlier E-2s he had moved around on aircraft carriers forty years before, "Always brings back memories," he said.

"There weren't many black sailors then," Noble said. "We put up with what we had to, in order to survive. Hell, when I joined at the end of the Korean War, the services had only been integrated for about five years. Truman ordered that in 1948. I thought I was going to be forced to be a cook, or worse, some admiral's orderly. It wasn't until the '70s, though, that Chief of Naval Operations Admiral Zumalt managed to force real desegregation." Noble paused, evidently mentally rehashing a poignant moment in that battle. Wolfe watched him swallow hard, grit his teeth, then relax. "So, what do you want to know?" he asked Wolfe.

Wolfe pulled Chief Clemons's black notebook from the side pocket of his cargo shorts. He handed it to Noble. "You were on *Oriskany* the same time as Clemons. Do you know anyone in this book?"

Noble opened the book. Slowly he thumbed through the pages, mumbling to himself. "Yeah, Akers. Geez, she was such a whore. Anderson, V-2, catapults. Andrews, what an ass. Carter," he laughed.

"What's so funny?" Wolfe asked.

"This guy Carter. Second-class, engine mechanic. Black dude. White wife. Always in trouble with the captain. He'd go out to sea. His wife would max out his credit cards. We'd come home after a cruise. The captain had to have disbursing hold his pay until the credit cards were paid off. The poor s.o.b. had to work a second job in order to eat. He'd get the cards paid off in five to six months and make up with his wife. Then we'd go on another cruise. And she'd do the same thing all over again." Noble laughed. "Wish I knew how that turned out."

"I'll ask if I get in touch with him. Know anyone else?"

Flipping pages slowly, Noble scanned the book some more. "Freeman. Black cook. Whenever anyone asked him if he was going to re-up, he'd say no. He told everyone he had an offer to work on the railroad in Thailand. Someone would always ask him, 'Doing what?' He'd say, 'Laying Thais.' He died from AIDS in Bangkok in 1990. So I guess he got the job."

Wolfe grimaced. As a physician, he knew more than he wanted to know about AIDS and HIV. He waited. Noble turned the pages slowly.

"Well, even you know this bastard," Noble said. He leaned toward Wolfe on the bench, tilting the book for Wolfe to see more clearly. "Deke Jameson. Thief. Liar. He had a posse. Haven't seen their names in here yet, though."

"Look on the last page," Wolfe said. "There's a list of names there. They aren't alphabetical. Couldn't figure that out. Five of them have asterisks by their names."

Nodding, Noble turned to the last page. After scanning the list, he said, "And there they are, the unholy posse: Jameson, Andrews, Gregg, Carr, Montgomery, Little. Yep. The names with the asterisks are guys who are dead. Montgomery died in Kuwait. A drunk driver killed Holden in a head-on collision in Puget. This is Jameson's posse, all right, if you include Clemons. They were tight. No one else ever joined their clan, or clique, I guess. We used to debate what they saw in one another, finally laughed it off. Someone suggested they had found a treasure map and each man kept part of it. After they retired they were going to piece it back together and dig up the gold."

CHAPTER 12

Byrnes woke to the sampan crew's yelling and screaming. He could see land on the horizon to the west. Sitting in the shade inside the shelter amidships, he couldn't see the sun. He assumed it was close to being directly overhead. Seagulls trailed the little boat looking for leftovers from the fishermen, unaware that they had only enough food for themselves. In the three days they spent being pushed westward through the calm seas by the little outboard engine, Byrnes had consumed a lot of sushi and rice. The fresh water had run out the night before and he could feel thirst beginning to gnaw at him. Between the shouts for joy, Byrnes recognized a quiet he hadn't heard for a while. The little motor was silent.

The old man pulled back the remains of the curtain Byrnes had sacrificed to filter gasoline from water. He beckoned to Byrnes to come to the stern and look at the engine. "Con co," he said, smiling. On his way, Byrnes picked up the gasoline cans and shook them, one after the other. As he suspected, they were absolutely empty.

Opening the top to the gas tank on the motor, Byrnes looked inside. The shiny interior of the empty tank reflected the overhead sun. Not only was the tank bare, it was dry. He pointed a finger inside the tank and shook his head. The old man nodded. Byrnes assumed the sampan crew had been aware of how low they had been on gas.

Over the next six hours the winds and currents pushed the little boat north and west, tantalizingly close to shore. They saw other sampans in the distance, but their crews did not acknowledge the waves and screams of his desperate boatmates. When the sun set, the wind died. The coastal current continued to push the small craft north. The crew took turns on watch.

Byrnes snuggled down in the bow, wearing his white T-shirt and the pair of cotton trousers lent to him by the crew. Although the waist fit him, the legs of the pants only reached to his mid-calf, since he was six inches taller than all of the other men. After Byrnes had donned the trousers for the first time, the old man had scraped a picture of a long legged bird on the wooden deck. He had pointed to it with his bony finger and then to Byrnes, "Con co," he said. Touching Byrnes in the chest and then the image. "Con co." The boat crew's nickname for Byrnes was *Stork*.

The rocking of the boat and his dry mouth woke Byrnes in the middle of the night. He looked out over the calm sea, surprised he had fallen asleep on watch. With the moon high in the cloudless sky, Byrnes thought he saw a flashing red light in the distance. He went inside the shelter and woke the older man.

Once on deck the old man pointed to the light and nodded. He went back in the cabin and returned with a stick wrapped with rags at one end. Pulling a plastic tube of matches from his pocket, he extracted a single match. Scraping it on a dry, rough piece of the cabin, he fired it up and used it to ignite the rags. Standing on the bow, he waved the burning torch back and forth until it burned out. Dipping it into the ocean, he quenched the smoldering piece of wood and laid it on the deck. Slapping Byrnes on the shoulder, he shrugged his shoulders and returned to his mat inside the cabin. Byrnes returned to his watch. When the sun turned the horizon pink, he allowed himself to fall asleep again.

A powerful, throbbing, diesel engine woke him and the crew of the sampan. A patrol boat coasted alongside. Byrnes headed for the cabin and met the older man and two younger men exiting. They had big grins on their faces. Byrnes stayed inside the shelter while the crew jabbered with the crew of the patrol boat. He didn't understand the language, but he appreciated the gasoline the patrol boat crew poured into the sampan's gas cans. A ten-liter rectangular can of fresh water also made its way from the patrol boat to the sampan. The old man poured some of the gasoline into the tank on the engine. It sprang to life and purred like a kitten on the first pull of the starter rope.

As the crew waved good-bye to the patrol boat, Byrnes stuck his head out of the shelter. He took a long look at the machine guns fore and aft on the powerful boat. His gaze rested for the longest time on the ensign flown from its stern: a red flag with a yellow star in the center, the North Vietnamese maritime flag.

Pulling itself within a half mile of shore, the sampan journeyed slowly south. Byrnes saw small fishing villages every ten to twenty miles. It took two more days before the sampan reached its home waters and the fishing village from which the three men had left weeks before.

With consummate skill and care the older man handled the tiller and engine. He brought the boat up a small river and then onto a sandy beach next to several more sampans. On the sand stood nearly forty people waving and shouting. Byrnes saw women with tears in their eyes. Two held infants. Older children clung to the skirts of some elderly women. Everyone smiled and spoke at the same time. He understood only a few words of Vietnamese: nuoc – water, con co was stork, dung lai meant stop, and di di meant go go.

The crew of the sampan leapt to the ground, where the crowd mobbed them. They disappeared into the sea of black heads. Byrnes stood in the boat enjoying the reception but unable to understand most of the words, except Xomh Canh, the name of the hamlet.

Eventually, the crew remembered the American. They returned and pulled him from the boat, introducing him to each individual in the throng as Con co. Each villager bowed slightly to him, which he returned. Many took his hands in theirs briefly; others slapped him on the back. All had huge smiles on their faces, obviously overjoyed by the return of a sampan thought sunk and fishermen thought drowned.

That evening, Byrnes found himself feted by the hamlet's inhabitants. Unable to understand the language he followed them from tiny house to tiny house. Some homes were brick; others constructed of coral, or wood. Some had tile roofs, most were thatched. There was no running water, except at a hand-pump-powered well in a central courtyard near the village banyan tree. Each home had an outbuilding, a latrine dug into the back yard. Electricity didn't exist. Candles lit tables with pictures of relatives and relics.

Everyone gave Byrnes something to eat or drink. He recognized the sweet potatoes, cabbage, bananas, and corn, which he gobbled down, still starving after the ordeal at sea. Some of the fish tasted good. The fermented sauce he declined not having developed a taste for it and annoyed by the smell. Egg noodles, dried squid, and seaweed he recognized, but left untouched after finding the cooked pork.

Byrnes knew better than to purposefully drink the smallest amount of alcohol. He had inherited the Asian gene that led to the red alcoholic facial flush and rapid intoxication. As a boot on his first cruise, he had presented to sick call vomiting his guts up after two beers. The navy corpsman called it the Asian alcoholic flush syndrome. He advised Byrnes to give up alcohol. However, it wasn't so easy deciding which drinks were weak wines and beer among the plain fruit juices and non-alcoholic drinks presented to him by the villagers.

The locals favored drinks with at least a small amount of alcohol for medical reasons. Alcohol killed bacteria in their liquids. There was no water sanitation plant in the province. Under the influence of the Vietnamese beverages, Byrnes soon staggered, woefully intoxicated. His face glowed red. Shortly thereafter he passed out in the home of the old man who owned the sampan.

Blinding sunlight streaming through a rudely opened door and a loud curse woke Byrnes the next morning. Briefly, he smelled his own vomit on the mat below his face. Then two men grabbed him by his arms and dragged him from the mat on which he had slept. Squinting into the bright sunlight, Byrnes saw more men in black pajama-like clothing standing in front of the old man's house. The old man and his wife argued with another man dressed in a khaki uniform, who carried a leather pouch slug over one shoulder, and wore a pith helmet on his head. The uniformed man gestured to several men in black. They stepped forward and pushed the elderly couple back until they stood with a crowd of villagers.

The man in khaki then strutted back and forth in front of the villagers, speaking in a loud voice, lecturing in the tonal language Byrnes did not understand. As his eyes adjusted to the glare, Byrnes managed to get a better view of the hat the speaker wore. A medallion about the size of a silver dollar — a gold star in a red background surrounded by a gold wreath —in the middle of a web band that circled the middle of the helmet. The man also had red patches on his collars. Byrnes's morale sank. The man had to be either a North Vietnamese Army officer or Viet Cong military cadre.

Finished with the lecture to the villagers, the man waved his arm. The crowd dispersed slowly, looking occasionally over their shoulders at Byrnes and the older man and his wife.

The man in the khaki uniform stood in front of Byrnes. Two men in black held the sailor in a tight grip. He barked in four or five languages before Byrnes understood, "Parlez vous francais, Con co?"

"Un peu," Byrnes said. It was quickly obvious that his two years of

French in high school didn't impress his interrogator. Aware of the Vietnamese hatred of the Japanese, following the occupation by the Imperial Japanese Army during World War II, Byrnes refused to respond to Japanese, which the man tried next.

Finally the man in khaki waved to one of the men in black, a thin, short man with half a left ear and a large horizontal scar across his left cheek. The uniformed man pointed at Byrnes. The second man spoke, "Do you speak English?"

Byrnes nodded, "Yes," he said.

"Are you American?"

"Yes."

Reaching out, the scarred man grasped the chain around Byrnes's neck. He lifted the jade pendant from under the sailor's T-shirt. Staring at the Buddhist icon, he said, "Mother of Quan. You are a Buddhist?"

"Yes."

The scarred man then spoke to the uniformed man in what Byrnes assumed was a dialect of Vietnamese, although it sounded different than that spoken by the villagers. The uniformed man spoke for several minutes to the man with half an ear, who then turned to Byrnes. "Are you a pilot?"

"No."

His interrogator paused. The officer spoke to him briefly. "A soldier?" he asked.

"No," Byrnes said.

"A spy?"

"No. A sailor. I fell off a ship," Byrnes said, pointing to the elderly man and his wife. "The old man and his crew found me in the ocean. They saved my life."

"They say you saved their lives."

Byrnes smiled. "We saved each other," he said.

"You are our prisoner, then," the man with the scar said. "Do not worry too much. The war will be over shortly. After our victory, we will exchange you for our comrades who the Americans and South Vietnamese traitors have captured."

"The war will be over soon?" Byrnes asked, stunned by the revelation.

"Since you are our prisoner, I can tell you that it will end on Tet, our New Year. In the year of the Monkey, the whole of South Vietnam will rise up against all the foreigners and throw your army into the sea." He nodded to the men behind Byrnes who tied his hands behind his back and pushed him down the road toward the edge of town and a small military camp. Geese owned by the villagers honked and scattered from the dirt road as the men marched through the hamlet.

Byrnes found himself in a tent, where he sat on the dirt floor, wrists bound behind him. Shortly thereafter, the men blindfolded him and led him on a long barefoot walk through the forest and into a cave. Inside the cave, he had his blindfold and restraints removed. Two men shoved him into a bamboo cage barely large enough to stand or lie in.

CHAPTER 13

Tied with its starboard side to the carrier pier in Subic Bay, many of *Forrestal's* most serious wounds were not visible from shore. She still listed slightly to port, a consequence of all the water poured onto the massive fire that raged on her flight deck and below. Nine 1000-pound bombs, all the older variety called Comp B for their chemical explosive ingredients, had exploded on the flight deck. All had come from the ordinance depot on the Philippines.

An electrical short on an F-4 Phantom accidentally fired a Zuni rocket. It flew into a drop tank full of JP-5 jet fuel on future senator and presidential candidate John McCain's A-4 Skyhawk. The resultant fire consumed a line of A-4s. McCain escaped by climbing out of the cockpit of his burning A-4 and dangling over the fire, while moving hand over hand, along the refueling boom. He dropped to the deck and scampered away before the first bomb exploded. Pilots in other aircraft were not so lucky.

The 1000-pound bombs that fell from burning A-4s dropped onto a burning flight deck and cooked off in the heat of the jet fuel fire. They exploded, blowing holes in the deck, shredding firefighting equipment, and killing wave after wave of sailors trying to extinguish the fires with fire hoses. Newer bombs would not have been set off by the flames. Holes punched into the flight deck by exploding bombs allowed JP-5 jet fuel from the A-4's tanks and an A-3 tanker aircraft to pour into compartments below the aft end of the flight deck. Burning fuel trapped men below decks, who died of burns or smoke inhalation.

The fires raged for two days, not completely extinguished until minutes before *Forrestal* docked in Subic Bay. From the pier, the acrid smell of burnt fuel, plastic, metal, and cordite was powerful enough to nauseate some observers on shore. *Forrestal's* crew had become accustomed to the stench.

Byrnes and Wolfe stood at the edge of the pier staring at the terrible burned hulk. Visitors were not welcome onboard the crematorium. Behind the ship's island – the carrier's control tower – soot coated the side of the ship. The black discoloration ran from the flight deck to the waterline. Wolfe doubted he wanted to board her, anyway. "They won't let us on board," he told Byrnes, "but I've got to find Mike Crespi to make sure he's okay."

Oriskany had followed *Forrestal* to Subic Bay from Vietnam, after trailing her to the hospital ship *Repose*. Doctors, corpsmen, and nurses on *Repose* took over the medical care of the injured. Both ships needed replenishment. The navy had decided to inspect *Forrestal* in Subic to see if she indeed could handle flight operations after a month's refit in Japan, as her captain suggested. There still existed the possibility that the navy might transfer some of *Oriskany's* crew to *Forrestal* to replace ship's company killed or injured. Many of *Forrestal's* aircraft had been incinerated or had been pushed overboard. Crews off-loaded by crane undamaged aircraft that had survived the fire. The navy planned to disperse these airplanes to squadrons on the remaining carriers in the Gulf of Tonkin on Yankee Station or Dixie Station in the South China Sea, if *Forrestal* went to Japan or to the States.

Glumly, Wolfe led Byrnes to the Martins's house on the naval base. "At least you can meet the Martins," Wolfe said. "Robert's a great guy. And you'll like his parents. His dad was in Europe with Patton in World War II. His mom is French, a war bride. Maybe they've heard from Mike."

Robert Martin answered the door, the usual wide grin on his face. "Addy! Come in. You'll never guess who's here."

Wolfe had already seen through the screen door. His tanned, heavy-set friend sat on the couch in the Martins's living room, telephone pressed to his ear. Unaware of Wolfe's presence, he talked quietly with his wife in Maryland. Another sailor sat next to Mike. Wolfe said, "Robert, this is Jimmy Byrnes, my work crew's boss on *Oriskany*."

The sailor sitting on the couch next to Mike stood and offered his hand to Wolfe and Byrnes. "I'm Arthur Anderson. Most folks call me Andy," he said. "I work with Mike on the hangar deck." Anderson stood more than six feet tall, his angular face had severe acne. Both men from the *Forrestal* were dressed in dungarees. Wolfe and Byrnes wore whites, a requirement for liberty. "I'm waiting to use the phone to call my folks in New York. Do you guys need to use the phone?"

Mr. and Mrs. Martin had allowed Mike and other sailors off *Forrestal* to use their telephone for free, absorbing the long distance charges. It was their way of contributing to the well-being of the crew. "Nah," Byrnes said. "We're from the *Mighty O.*"

Mike Crespi hung up the phone. He pulled a handkerchief from his pocket and silently wiped tears from his eyes. Wolfe noted the soot on the handkerchief. Anderson traded seats with Crespi who handed him the telephone. Anderson dialed the operator and soon conversed with his family.

Recognizing Wolfe for the first time, Crespi stood. His uniform did not fit well, chambray shirt bulging at the buttons, dungaree pants too long and rolled up at the ankles. He reached for Wolfe's hand, pulled him to his chest, and squeezed Wolfe in a bear hug. "Buddy," was all he said.

"God, I'm glad you're all right, Mike," Wolfe told his friend.

"Let's step into the front yard," Mike said. "I'm dying for a smoke, and I smell like burnt kerosene. Sorry we stunk up the house, Robert. Wish we had more than borrowed clothes to wear, too. Please thank your parents for letting me use the phone. There's a six-hour wait at the enlisted men's club to use a phone. The line wraps around the building twice. I'll be happy to pay for the –"

"Dad said, 'No'," Robert said. "And don't worry about the smell. It'll be gone soon." He followed Wolfe, Byrnes, and Crespi into the yard. The four young men sat in lawn chairs at a round table in the shade of an arboretum in the Martins's side yard. A Filipino yardman knelt in the garden, pulling weeds and thinning flowers.

"I thought you gave up smoking," Wolfe said, as Crespi tried to light a cigarette. The large sailor's hands shook so much that Byrnes took the lighter and lit the cigarette as it dangled, wavering, from Crespi's lips.

"I need one to calm down," Crespi said. "Besides, we've all been breathing smoke for two days. What harm is another fifteen minutes worth of carcinogens?"

"Did you fight the fire?" Wolfe asked.

Crespi shook his head. He sat in silence for nearly five minutes, inhaling large drags from the cigarette and letting the smoke slowly exit his mouth and nose. Anderson left the house, found a bench to sit on, and pulled it closer to the table. "Thanks," he said to Martin. The civilian nodded, eyes on Crespi.

"I almost died," Crespi said. "Almost half of my division is dead. Everyone who was in the compartment, except me."

"Flight deck crew?" Byrnes asked.

Crespi shook his head. "No. Hangar deck crew."

"I thought flight operations were going on," Wolfe said. "If we're flying, our whole hangar deck division is working."

"*Forrestal* is a supercarrier, Addy," Byrnes explained. "They have more men, probably work in shifts. It's enormous, much roomier. They can use the tractors and spotting dollies all the time, need fewer men to push aircraft."

Mike nodded exhaling more smoke. "We work 12 on/12 off, 0700 hours to 1900 hours. Or we did," he said. He looked into his lap and shook his head. "They're all dead," he said.

"Who?" Wolfe asked.

"V-3 on *Forrestal* sleeps in a compartment directly under the arresting gear. The guy on the top bunk can put his hand on the overhead above his bunk. That's a very thick piece of steel plate. On the other side of that piece of metal is the flight deck. Aircraft land there, catching the arresting cables, maybe six inches away. Six inches between you and death." Crespi ground his cigarette out on the sole of his shoe, and then tore the butt to shreds, scattering the remains in the yard under his chair. "It scared the hell out of me to sleep in that compartment with all the banging and thumping going on above me. Even though I was on the bottom of three bunks, it was noisy all the time. Everyone said I'd eventually get used to it. New guys get the bottom racks. And the 1900 hours to 0700 hours shift."

"So why are they dead?" Wolfe asked, not understanding how Crespi survived and no one else did.

"They had all heard those noises before. They weren't scared. I couldn't sleep. I heard something that sounded like an explosion, something I had never heard before in my month on the ship. I sat up, pulled on my pants, and ran to the hangar deck. The only two places I had learned to get to by then were the hangar deck and chow," he laughed, a hollow sound followed by a grimace and a shrug.

Anderson added to the tale for Crespi. "That first explosion was a 1000-pound bomb. The second went off right above our compartment making a large hole into it. A third bomb rolled into that hole, along with about a thousand gallons of burning JP-5. When it exploded, everyone still in the compartment died. That was everyone except Mike. The burning fuel ran through the compartments and corridors, down the ladders all the way to the engineering spaces below the hangar deck. The only reason I'm not dead is that I was working on the hangar deck along with the rest of the day crew."

Crespi finished his story, "We, me and the daytime hangar crew, fought some small fires on the hangar deck. Mainly burning JP-5. There were no explosions there. And no aircraft on fire. We had to move aircraft around to make room for a temporary sick bay and a morgue." He swallowed hard, looked at Wolfe. "The dead are stacked like firewood on the hangar deck, Addy. It's gruesome."

After an hour with Crespi and Anderson, Wolfe and Byrnes said good-bye to Mr. and Mrs. Martin, and Robert. They turned down the invitation for a meal, not wanting to add to the Martins's burdens. In silence they walked toward *Oriskany*, past *Forrestal*.

"What are you thinking, Addy?" Byrnes asked Wolfe.

"Was *Oriskany's* fire last year like that?"

"Yes and no," Byrnes said. "It was mainly a hangar deck fire. The forward bay filled rapidly with smoke. I took off running toward Bay 2, unable to see anything in the smoke. The bay fire doors slammed closed right behind me, caught the heel of my shoe and tore it off. If I had been a little slower, I would have been flat. Those doors are ten inches thick, weigh several tons." He laughed, an empty sound reminiscent of Crespi's laugh. "After we got the respirators on, hoses filled, and fought our way back into the bay, aircraft were on fire, along with all the flares. A lot of guys died."

"We didn't help much this time, did we?" Wolfe said.

"Sounds like all the hoses on their flight deck got shredded. They needed our equipment. We helped some. Maybe saved a life or two."

"The blood and guts and burns didn't bother me, although the screaming did. Maybe I should be a corpsman," Wolfe said, remembering the howls of the injured.

"Hell, Addy, aim higher than that. Be a doctor," Byrnes said, slapping him on the back.

"Okay," Wolfe said. "When I get out of the navy, I'll use the GI Bill to go to college. Then to medical school. Maybe then I'll be of some use in a disaster. Tell you one thing, though. If they ever give me a chance to work on a supercarrier, with day and night crews and no more pushing aircraft by hand, I'm taking it."

Byrnes grinned. "You and me both," he said.

The navy investigators decided *Forrestal* could not continue air operations. Within days she left Subic for the Newport News shipyard, another trip around the southern tip of South America. *Forrestal* would not fit through the Panama Canal. That left moot Wolfe's offer to join *Forrestal* as a flight deck crewman. The hangar deck chief did not have to report him AWOL. *Oriskany* returned to Yankee Station shortly thereafter.

CHAPTER 14

Byrnes thought he had been a POW for about two years, probably late in 1969, when the men guarding him dragged the severely injured air force pilot into camp. "Con co, you fix," An said, when they dropped the unconscious pilot at Byrnes's feet in the tunnel.

"I am not a doctor," Byrnes protested, although he knew there were no doctors or medics attached to the unit. The nearest hospital battalion was many miles away. Few seriously wounded Vietnamese soldiers lived long enough to receive medical care. The North Vietnamese were not going to waste manpower trying to transport an injured American pilot there.

"I kill then," An said. He reached for the pistol he kept in a worn, cracked, brown leather holster strapped to his belt. The pistol and a leather shoulder bag were the only evidence that An was the commanding officer of the company holding Byrnes captive. The Vietnamese wore no insignia, were lucky to have boots, shoes, or hats. In fact, that was how Byrnes distinguished newcomer replacements. They arrived with clothing. After months of jungle warfare, they either died, or wore out their clothing and boots. Re-supply, except for ammunition, rice, occasional canned food, and rare mail did not exist.

"Khong!" Byrnes said and stepped between the pilot and An. "I will try to help him."

An turned to leave the tunnel burrowed into the side of a cliff. "Lanh will bring medicine," he said as he left.

Byrnes removed the pilot's boots and flight suit. The lieutenant had soiled his underwear. The smell permeated the tunnel. One of the guards took the pilot's boots, trading his rubber sandals for them. Another searched the pockets of the flight suit, opening each zippered pocket. He removed pictures, a watch, and other trinkets before wadding the garment up and stuffing it into his pack. Comatose and lying on his back in a bloodied white T-shirt and soiled white boxer shorts, the pilot appeared dead, except for the shallow breathing. His right arm bent unnaturally above the wrist, as did his left lower leg between knee and ankle. Byrnes pulled up the man's shirt. His entire chest was one huge deep bruise. Both collarbones appeared broken. His face was so swollen, Byrnes could not pry open his eyes or see into his mouth. Air wheezed into and out of his badly flattened bloody nose.

Carefully, Byrnes straightened the fractures of arm and leg, splinting with sticks and strips of cloth torn from his own thin blanket. After washing the man's trunk as best he could with a rag and water from a wooden bucket, he laid the pilot on his back on the reed mat he used for a bed. Carefully he positioned the man's arms so that the collarbones looked straighter. He then bound a long piece of cloth around the pilot's armpits, chest, and back of his neck to hold them that way. One of Byrnes's high school football teammates had suffered a separated shoulder. He modeled the bandage after the splint his teammate had worn for that injury. It was the only bandage Byrnes thought might splint the fractures.

Soaking another piece of blanket in the bucket filled that morning in a stream where he bathed and washed his clothing, he placed it on the pilot's face. Gently, he washed the man's face and chest. Being careful not to cut the pilot, Byrnes stuck the blunt end of the handle to his cup in each of the man's nostrils and elevated the flattened nasal bones. The pilot never winced.

None of the fractured bones had torn through the skin, cutting down chances of a severe infection. Byrnes had watched a Vietnamese soldier die from tetanus only a month before. The North Vietnamese Army had no vaccines. Another soldier had died from a massive infection following a minor gunshot wound. They had no antibiotics, either.

Lanh, a corporal and unofficial medic, showed up with an herbal drink about an hour later. He had grown up in a remote village in North Vietnam, and had learned from the village healer which herbs and plants were useful as medications. After forcing the liquid down the unconscious pilot's throat, Lanh reached into his pouch and withdrew a leather bag of roots, mushrooms, and plant scrapings. He took a piece of Byrnes's blanket and soaked it in the wooden bucket of water. Dumping a ground-up portion of the concoction onto the rag, he wrung it over the pilot's chest. The solution dribbled onto the man's bruised ribs. Lahn then laid the rag onto his chest and pulled the bloody T-shirt down to hold it in place. He did the same for the man's face with a smaller rag. Byrnes's blanket existed no longer.

Byrnes dribbled water into the pilot's mouth hourly for three days. He cleaned the airman's new NVA, North Vietnamese Army, donated POW clothing and redressed him after sponge baths. Lanh replaced the bandages daily. On the fourth day, the pilot opened his eyes, but said nothing. The fifth morning, Byrnes said, "Good morning," to the pilot.

"You speak English," the pilot said. "I wish you had been around when the villagers beat the shit out of me. Oh, shit, that hurts."

"What hurts?" Byrnes asked.

"Everything. What does a guy have to do to get some pain medication around here? My wrist is killing me."

"The NVA don't have medics with their units. No medical supplies other than herbal stuff they find in the forest," Byrnes said. "Sorry. Lanh may have something you can chew on that has some pain-relieving properties. I'll see if he'll give it up for you. Don't get your hopes up. They don't like Americans much."

"They?" the pilot said, turning his head to get a better look at Byrnes. "Why didn't you say, 'We don't like Americans,'?" He examined Byrnes carefully, moving only his eyes to keep from increasing his pain. "Your English is excellent. Not even an accent. Go to school in the States?"

Piqued that the first American he had seen in two years didn't believe he was an American, Byrnes exploded. "Just because I have an Asian face doesn't mean I'm the enemy, asshole. My name is James T. Byrnes. Aviation boatswains mate third-class. I fell off a carrier, the USS *Oriskany*. I've been a prisoner here for about two years."

"Whatever," the pilot said, and became silent. He refused to talk to Byrnes any more that day.

An returned that night to see the pilot. Lanh had told his commander the American had been revived. "Does he talk?" An asked Byrnes.

"Not to Vietnamese," Byrnes said. "To him, I'm Vietnamese," he explained.

"Tell him an officer comes tomorrow. Will ask many questions," An said.

Byrnes had seen the pilot's flight suit. He knew the man's last name was Rhodes and he was a first lieutenant. "Lt. Rhodes, this is An, commanding officer for this company. He says an officer will ask you questions tomorrow. I assume he means an intelligence officer."

"Tell him to go fuck himself," Rhodes said. Byrnes laughed, for the first time in many months. "What's so funny?" Rhodes asked.

"I don't know how to say that. My Vietnamese is limited to food items, bathroom words, and some military stuff. I'm sure I know some cuss words, but not so sure what they mean. For instance Lanh frequently says, *di tieu*, when irritated, but I don't know what it means, yet. I'll say Khong and see how An reacts."

"What does Khong mean?"

"No."

"How do you say speak?"

"Noi."

"Let me say it." Rhodes turned his head toward An. "Noi khong," he said.

An's eyes widened. He looked at Byrnes. "Noi tieng viet?" he said. Byrnes shook his head.

Not one but two officers appeared in camp the next day. Both had reasonably new, clean uniforms and leather boots. They both spoke English better than Byrnes spoke Vietnamese. Almost too politely the first officer introduced himself as an intelligence officer and the second man as cadre.

"What's a cadre?" Rhodes asked.

"Those chosen to make certain we do not stray from the true path of enlightened communism," the first man said.

"We need to remain true to Marxist ideals," the second man said.

"Okay," Rhodes said. "Whatever. I'll save you some time. I'm only giving you my name, rank, and serial number."

"You might want to rethink that, Lieutenant," Byrnes said. "These guys can be brutal. I personally gave them my captain's name, Commander Donald D. Duck, and many other secrets. What good it does them I have no idea."

"All information goes to headquarters," the cadre officer said.

"Communications are unhurried –" Byrnes said. The first officer flicked his wrist in Byrnes's direction. One of the guards swung his rifle butt, hitting him in the chest and knocking the wind out of him. Another gesture led to Byrnes being marched from the tunnel at gunpoint.

By the time the interrogation ended the Vietnamese knew Rhodes flew an F-100D from the American airbase at Tuy Hoa, the name of his commanding officer, and that personnel from New York and New Mexico staffed the 355th TAC Fighter Squadron.

"I didn't hold up very well," Rhodes admitted when they returned Byrnes to the tunnel. "That guy kept pushing on the foot of my broken leg."

"They don't mess around," Byrnes said. "Don't worry about it. The best you can hope for is to pass on some false information, too."

Rhodes eventually accepted that Byrnes was an American. The bruises and two broken ribs from the rifle butt helped prove the point. That and his reaction on hearing that Joe Namath and the AFL Jets had beaten the NFL Baltimore Colts in the championship football game. "No fucking way!" Byrnes said. He tried to fill Rhodes in on his life over the previous two years.

The Vietnamese had moved Byrnes multiple times. At his first camp, in the cave near the fishing camp, they held him in the bamboo cage, allowed out only twice a day to use a nearby latrine. Meals were rice, pumpkin slices, and a liquid he dubbed grog. On rare occasions, usually when a water buffalo had been killed in an American bombing raid, his captors shared small pieces of meat with him. He guessed his weight to be about 130 pounds, down thirty from what he weighed on the carrier.

"Looks more like 120," Rhodes said. "With your Japanese heritage, you look similar to our NVA friends. Underfed. It would be faster to kill us than starve us, you know."

"I assume if they wanted us dead, we'd be dead already," Byrnes said. "Maybe they're worried about being on the losing side of a war and being labeled war criminals. They did mention something about using Europeans and Americans as hostages for trade."

"You seem to have survived well enough," Rhodes said.

"The beginning was scary. They tortured and killed several village province chiefs in front of me. 'A lesson for the South Vietnamese traitors who collaborate with you Americans,' they said. For about six months, they let anyone who felt like it hit me, poke me with a stick, or torture me with sharp objects. After an NVA officer told them I might be useful as a hostage, they stopped. Six months later they put me on work details with a guard. A month after that, they let me go without a guard. They believe I'm too weak to cause them serious trouble."

"Why didn't you take off?" Rhodes asked.

"Where would I go? I don't have a clue where I am."

Disgusted, certain he dealt with a coward, Rhodes said, "South. Or east to the South China Sea and then south. Steal a boat."

"When you're ready to travel, I'll let you lead the way," Byrnes said, knowing that would be a long while. By then Rhodes might understand the obstacles in his way.

The more weight Byrnes lost, the less of a threat he was to escape or make trouble. Eventually, they let him out of the tunnels during the day. They sent him to collect bamboo shoots in the forest to supplement their vegetables. Every night they again locked him in the cage.

The Vietnamese never saw Rhodes as a threat. The man could hardly walk until his fractures healed. And when they had, he still needed one of his crutches to hobble around the tunnel.

After such a long time in captivity and immersed in the Vietnamese language, Byrnes could communicate on a simple level with his guards. He had eventually learned what happened within days of his capture. The Viet Cong had staged a bloody offensive timed with a ceasefire on the Lunar New Year. The men who made up the fishing village of Xomh Canh joined the VC, many against their will to save family members from rape or torture.

Byrnes had recognized many of the village men as they gathered near the cave where the Vietnamese held him prisoner. One of the younger men who had been on the sampan with him toted an American M-16. No longer did he celebrate the American's help in saving his life. The sneer he showed Byrnes seemed real. Over three or four days, hundreds of soldiers streamed through the camp, armed with AK-47s, M-16s, rocket launchers, even M-1s and rifle types Byrnes didn't recognize. He thought they were probably Japanese or French weapons left over from World War II or the war for independence from the French.

He learned later that the men had marched some fifty miles south to the city of Hue, then the provincial capital, previously the Vietnamese national capital until 1945, and once the Imperial walled capital of the Nguyen Dynasty emperors.

"They surprised us," Rhodes said. "I was in the States then. I'll bet few of the enemy returned. The Tet Offensive started battles in over 100 towns and cities. The South Vietnamese Army and Americans rallied to destroy the Viet Cong, decimating their ranks. The defeat was total. Essentially the Viet Cong have ceased to exist as a fighting force."

"So, are we winning?" Byrnes asked. "It might end soon? One of my interrogators boasted the war would end on their terms within months of the offensive."

"Do these North Vietnamese act defeated?" Rhodes asked. "It's no longer a military question. Walter Cronkite pronounced the war lost. He's the most respected man in America, and had believed President Johnson when LBJ said the war was almost over. Then Tet happened. Now, no one believes Johnson. Everyone believes Cronkite. The will to win is dying. No one wants his kid to die in a losing cause. It's political now."

Byrnes never again saw the man with half an ear who had bragged of imminent victory. Nor did the sailor from the sampan return. Over several months North Vietnamese infiltrated the south, taking the place of the annihilated local VC militia. The presence of the northerners led to bombing by the South Vietnamese Air Force and the Americans. Initially, propeller driven aircraft, A-1s like the Spads off *Oriskany*, loitered overhead, strafing and bombing the northern troops. When the aircraft were on the prowl, Byrnes found himself joined in the caves or tunnels by up to thirty men.

The continued bombing made it necessary for his captors to change locations to avoid further destruction. Byrnes lost count of the number of moves. He scratched the pole the enemy allowed him to use as a walking stick to keep track of his days as a prisoner. His only possessions other than the same pair of pants the sailor on the sampan had lent him, his T-shirt, and a pair of sandals fashioned from tire tread, were a metal cup with a short flat handle and a bedroll, consisting of straw mat and worn wool blanket. He had sharpened the edge of the cup handle on a rock in an effort to make a defensive weapon, but ended up using it only to scratch a daily line on his walking stick.

Soon the propeller aircraft disappeared, replaced by slow-moving straight-winged jet aircraft Byrnes didn't recognize.

"Those were Tweety Birds, T-37s," Rhodes told him. "Repurposed USAF trainers. I flew them in Texas. The South Vietnamese fly them now."

When the American F-100s and B-52s appeared, they terrorized everyone, including Byrnes. The low flying F-100s fired cannon, and dropped bombs and napalm in support of ground troops and on targets of opportunity. They were not easy to avoid, but there was some measure of warning. Either a battle raged, or an obvious military target was nearby. The Vietnamese could minimize their effect by digging trenches and tunnels. Byrnes and the NVA spent days at a time underground, hidden from view, thankful for the safety provided by tunnels and caves.

"The Hun's not immune to ground fire," Rhodes said, "as I found out."

"The what?"

"Hun," Rhodes said, "as in F one *HUN*dred. Like Attila's people, the Huns."

B-52s were a completely different weapon system, a terror weapon. Only in North Vietnam did the enemy possess rockets capable of destroying a B-52. Too high in the sky to be seen, unless there was enough moisture in the air for them to leave long contrails, they frequently struck without warning. Each aircraft could carry up to a hundred 500-pound bombs. In flights of three or six, they laid a path of destruction unprecedented in war. The ground shook as if in an earthquake. A trail miles long and half a mile wide in which nothing survived – trees shattered and flattened, all wildlife shredded, and all military equipment obliterated – marked their passage. Entire brigades of North Vietnamese soldiers disappeared under such firepower.

One B-52 attack had taken place while Byrnes had been in a cave. Rubble closed the cave entrance, a fortunate thing as it kept shrapnel outside. All the men inside the cave, including Byrnes, lay on the ground praying to their respective gods or ancestors. The bombing was so terrifying that some men lost control of their bowels. Others went insane. After digging their way out of the cave, the soldiers found a corridor made up of bomb craters starting a kilometer from the camp, running through the center of the camp, and ending two kilometers away. They marched away that same night. Byrnes noted that most of the marches took them north and west.

"We're about ten miles south of the DMZ, now," Rhodes told him. He hobbled from the stream, naked. Using crutches fashioned from tree branches, he leaned over and picked up his cotton trousers, boxers, and T-shirt. No longer white, their dingy gray color reminded Byrnes of gray navy ships. Rhodes's fractures had taken four months to heal. The pilot also had endured a month of fever with malaria. He guessed his weight hovered near 140 pounds, forty less than his fighting weight.

"We're going to be moving again, soon," Byrnes said.

"Where to?" Rhodes asked while dressing.

"Always north. I heard Hanoi mentioned, but I don't know if that's our destination."

"Maybe we'll see Ho Chi Minh's grave," Rhodes said.

"Uncle Ho's dead?"

"Since September, this year. War's still on, though," Rhodes said, laughing.

CHAPTER 15

Lining the edge of the flight deck, the sailors stood at parade rest, dressed in their white uniforms. Wolfe and Byrnes stood on the edge of elevator #3 and looked out over the harbor in Sasebo, Japan, seventy-five feet below. Salt water, oil, and fuel smell, along with rainbows on oily patches of water, reminded them of every other waterfront they had seen. "Do you have a girlfriend?" Byrnes asked.

Wolfe shook his head. He said, "I thought I had one when I left home. No mail in three months. I may no longer have one. You?"

"The last girl I had an interest in, I danced with at the USO dance in San Diego. V-3 Division was there for fire-fighting school in April."

"How did that turn out?" Wolfe asked.

"We had a great time, I thought. She danced every dance with me. She was a good-looking blonde college student. She even laughed at my jokes. Most Californians don't look down on half-breeds like me."

"Is she writing to you?"

"Nope. When I asked her to go to the movies with me, she said her father wouldn't let her date sailors. He only allowed her to dance with them at the USO parties," Byrnes said. "Her father wasn't racist, unless sailors are a race."

Wolfe laughed. "Swabbies *are* a breed apart," he said.

"Do you drink?" Byrnes said while they watched the carrier slide into its final position in the crowded harbor. The ceremony was a decoration for the Japanese on shore. As far as Wolfe could tell, though, the only Japanese who paid attention to the display were the operators of the tugs that guided *Oriskany* to her mooring.

"Nah," Wolfe said. "I never developed a taste for that or smoking. I played football and ran track in high school. Thought it would give me an edge over the guys who did drink and smoke."

"Did it?" Byrnes asked.

"Don't know. Made the teams. Played first string some times. The guys I knew who drank and smoked still played, too." Wolfe said and shrugged.

"Well, I'm going on liberty with you," Byrnes announced when the formation broke up. "If I have something to do and someone to do it with, I won't be tempted to go to a bar."

"I hadn't planned on doing much," Wolfe said. "Thought I'd get some patches sewn on my work jacket. Maybe hit the theater. Also, I need some replacement contact lenses. Thought I'd look for those, too."

"Sounds good," Byrnes said. "Just keep me away from the bar district."

"Why?"

"I shouldn't drink," Byrnes said.

"Okay. Probably no one should drink. Why shouldn't you? Are you an alcoholic?"

Continuing their conversation, they climbed down the ladders from the flight deck to the hangar deck and walked forward to the boarding ladder. There they waited in line to ask permission to go on shore leave, show their liberty passes, salute the ensign, and climb down a long ladder to a flat barge tied to the side of the ship. Once on the barge, they crossed over a gangway to a huge flat-bottomed landing craft and joined two hundred of their closest friends on the twenty-minute boat trip to the Sasebo pier.

"No. I'd die before I became addicted to alcohol. I inherited a condition from my mother. A third of Orientals can't tolerate alcohol. I'm one. It tastes good, but we get quickly intoxicated and nauseated. Our faces blush and our hearts skip beats. I was born with my father's love of beer and this reaction from my mom. They don't go well together."

Wolfe found an optometrist by scanning billboards in downtown Sasebo. He spoke no English. Wolfe spoke no Japanese, but Byrnes knew quite a bit. "He wants you to sit in the chair facing the chart. He's going to try lenses on your eyes to see which fit best."

"He can't just measure the old scratched pair?" Wolfe asked. He reached into his pocket and pulled out a contact lenses case, handing it to Byrnes.

Byrnes translated, listened to the response, and said, "I think he says he wants to do a fitting. He's not sure how well your lenses fit after not being worn for a while."

"Okay," Wolfe said. He spent the next hour allowing the optometrist to put lenses in his eyes, check his vision on the chart, check the fit, and then try another set. By the time the man finished, Wolfe's eyes burned like fire and shone almost as red.

The optometrist bowed first to Wolfe and then to Byrnes. He spoke to Byrnes. Silently he stood and waited for Byrnes to translate. "He says he is sorry, but none of the lenses he has will fit an American's eyes."

Tears had run down Wolfe's cheeks as he suffered in silence for the previous hour. But he never refused to allow the optometrist to try another pair of lenses. "Really?"

"He says he has tried them all. He's afraid he will damage your eyes if he attempts any more. He suggests you go to an American eye doctor," Byrnes said and waited for Wolfe's response.

"Well, shit," Wolfe said. "Don't tell him that. Tell him thanks for trying. I'll see if I can get my dad to talk with my ophthalmologist. Maybe he would send me a pair, even though I can't make it to an appointment."

"Okay," Byrnes said. He relayed Wolfe's message and the two sailors left the office. Wolfe turned to look at the optometrist as they departed the building. The man bowed one more time and then waved cheerily.

"Did you suppose that was legitimate?" Wolfe asked Byrnes. "Or do you suppose he likes to torture Americans?"

"He was horrified, disgraced. Humiliated, even. I thought he was contemplating hari-kari." Byrnes said, laughing.

Wolfe laughed, too, despite the pain in his eyes.

Many shops displayed patches in their windows. Wolfe found three he liked. Dropping his work jacket in one of the shops, he arranged to pick it up later in the day. He chose a dancing Snoopy for his left shoulder. He asked the seamstress to modify the patch by embroidering *Happiness is May 16th* underneath Snoopy, his discharge date years in the future. He asked her to sew a large yellow patch on the back of the jacket, a copy of the South Vietnamese flag with a junk sailing in the foreground. The title read: Tonkin Gulf Yacht Club. For his right shoulder, he picked a round white patch with a baby red devil holding a trident, and wearing a white diaper. *Hot Stuff* had his own comic book in the States.

"Sure you don't want *Hot Stuff* as a tattoo?" Byrnes asked, pointing to the little devil in the shop window when they left. "I've seen guys in the showers with small versions of that on their asses or shoulders."

"I can always take the patch off the jacket if I like something better later," Wolfe said. "Tough to do with a tattoo."

They turned the corner, not having their next destination in mind and realized they had entered an area crowded with bars. Wolfe did an immediate about face followed by Byrnes.

Three sailors had followed them into the courtyard. Wolfe almost ran into them. "Sorry," he said, stepping around one of the men.

Two meaty hands grabbed Wolfe by the front of his uniform and spun him around until he faced a short, heavyset, drunk sailor. The man wore the stripes of a second-class petty officer. "Look what we got here," the man said to two first-class petty officers. He nodded toward the two green stripes on Wolfe's sleeve, "A boot." The other men, taller and thinner, supported the staggering drunk. They appeared to be inebriated, also.

"Excuse me," Wolfe said, trying to disengage from the drunk and avoid his booze-laden breath.

"Whoa, where you going, Boot?" the petty officer asked.

"Shopping," Wolfe said, placing his hands on the other man's in an attempt to disengage them from his uniform.

"You can't go shopping," the man said, laughing. "We're going to have a fight."

Wolfe shook his head, knowing the drunk could hardly stand much less fight. He laughed, trying to calm the drunk. "I can't fight you," he said, "You're a petty officer. I'd get in a lot of trouble."

"Oh, that's okay," the drunk said, "I'm going to hit you first."

Unable to pull free from the man, Wolfe shrugged. He turned his face toward Byrnes and handed him his sailor's cap. "Here, Jimmy, hold this for – " He never finished the sentence. The drunk hit him in his left jaw, leaving him with a three-inch gash inside his left lower lip and cheek, and dazed with a concussion. Not completely aware of his reaction, Wolfe balled up his right fist and swung at the drunk, rotating his body with his hips, legs, and shoulders. His fist connected solidly with the sailor's left jaw, breaking it. The drunk staggered backward and sat on the asphalt, semiconscious, his buddies unable to hold up his dead weight.

When Wolfe came to, he was holding one of the first-class petty officers around the neck and beating his head against a brick wall outside a bar. At the time he was thinking, *This is one hell of an interesting dream.* Byrnes had apparently dispatched the third drunk. That first-class petty officer lay in the courtyard face down near the seated man with the broken jaw. Two shore patrolmen pulled Wolfe from his opponent. "That's enough, sailor. That's enough," one said as they pinned his arms behind him. The inebriated sailor dropped to his knees, bloody hands clasped over his broken nose and lacerated scalp. Blood streamed down his face.

Dazed, Wolfe surveyed the crowd. Apparently the three bars that shared the courtyard had emptied to watch the fight. They formed a ring of white-suited sailors surrounding the combatants. Several witnesses consulted with more shore patrol. Wolfe searched the courtyard for Byrnes. He did not see his friend. As Wolfe became more and more aware of his surroundings, some of his memory returned. He pointed to the man sitting in front of him and the man face down. "He started it. And he helped him," he told the shore patrol.

"Got it," said the shore patrolman, sliding his nightstick into the loop on his belt. He motioned to other sailors. "Put them in the paddy wagon," he said. To Wolfe, he said, "You all right, sailor?"

"Sure," Wolfe said. "Can I go?"

"No. We have to investigate the fight. You'll have to ride with us to headquarters."

"Okay," Wolfe said placidly, wondering if he still dreamed. He went to climb into the cab of the truck. The shore patrolman walked him to the back of the van and helped him climb in, next to the three drunks.

When the paddy wagon arrived at the small navy building that held the brig for drunks, waiting sailors pulled them roughly from the van and placed them all in the same ten by ten-foot barred cage. Wolfe sat on a bench on one side of the cell. The three others sat opposite him. Wolfe's first thoughts were, *Where am I? Who are those guys? Why am I locked up?*

Over the next four hours, Wolfe's amnesia diminished. About the time the drunks started to sober, recover, and yell insults at him, he had remembered the pre-fight argument. The fact that he was off the *Oriskany* on liberty in Sasebo, Japan, creeped slowly into his consciousness. He remembered the shore patrol breaking up the fight. He never recalled hitting the heavyset drunk. The only part of the fight he remembered was bashing his opponent's head into the wall and being certain he was dreaming.

When one of the first-class petty officers stood and threatened to start the brawl all over, two hands reached through the bars of the cell, grabbed him from behind by the shoulders, and sat him down. "If you say one more word, or stand up again, I'll have your stripes," a shore patrolman said. He looked in Wolfe's direction. "You Wolfe?" he asked, as he unlocked the door to the cage.

Wolfe nodded.

"Come with me," the sailor said to Wolfe, ushering him into a large room that reminded Wolfe of a courtroom.

Sitting at a court-like bench in front of him, a first-class petty officer wearing a shore patrol armband looked down at Wolfe. "You been drinking?" he asked.

"I don't drink," Wolfe said.

"You hit a second-class petty officer and at least one first-class petty officer," the man said. "What do you have to say for yourself?"

Wolfe stared at the man for a minute. "I can't remember everything, but the second-class petty officer grabbed me. He said he wanted to have a fight and he was going to hit me first."

"That fits with the witnesses' accounts," the man at the desk said. "You can go back to your ship."

"Is my buddy here?" Wolfe looked around the room and did not see Byrnes. "I need to find him and take him back to the ship. And get my work jacket. Someone's putting patches on it."

"Better clean up your face first," the petty officer said. He turned to his left and spoke to another sailor. "Johnson, get this man into the head and get him cleaned up." Turning to Wolfe, he added, "Son, as soon as you get your work jacket, you go back to *Oriskany*. You are out of uniform without your hat."

Wolfe didn't recognize the sailor in the mirror. Blood covered his entire face, and most of his whites to his waist. Johnson brought him paper towels. After washing off all the blood he could remove, Wolfe started to leave the head. "What about those other guys?" he asked.

Johnson nodded. "Don't worry about them," he said. "They're in a heap of trouble. They had counterfeit liberty passes and are definitely intoxicated. More than one witness said they started the brawl. Their captain will likely take away some stripes. They're not off your ship, so you shouldn't see them again."

"Good," Wolfe said. "One more question, though. I'm still missing some memories. Which way is my ship?"

Johnson led him to the door of the building and stepped outside with him. He pointed. "At the end of this street, turn left. That road takes you to the pier. You can catch the landing craft at the pier. It'll take you to the *Oriskany*."

"Thanks," Wolfe said.

More memories seeped slowly into Wolfe's consciousness as he traversed the streets of Sasebo on this way to the pier. He recognized the shop where his jacket waited for him. The seamstress handed him a brown-paper package tied with string in exchange for his Japanese yen.

By the time he arrived at the pier, the sun had set. A rowdy crowd of drunk sailors, some already in the custody of the shore patrol, waited for the landing craft. After crossing over the gangway, Wolfe stumbled over a man lying on the deck of the landing craft. He recognized Byrnes. Stopping, he bent over and lifted Byrnes to his feet.

"Buddy, my buddy," Byrnes mumbled drunkenly. He threw his arms over Wolfe's shoulders. His eyes widened. "You look like shit. There's blood all over your uniform." He reached into his back pocket and pulled Wolfe's Dixie cup hat out. "I held your hat," he said, slurring his words. It took him several minutes to finish his thoughts, "Boy you dropped that...guy with one punch.... Sorry...I couldn't stay around...after I took out the second guy.... If shore patrol arrests me again...I'm in big trouble. You looked like...you were doing okay with...the third guy. They let you...out! Lost you...let you down...my fault. Drown...my...sorrows. Only two...maybe three...beers."

Over the twenty-minute boat ride to the *Mighty O*, Byrnes sneaked up behind groups of sailors and sucker punched them. He started at least ten fights. By the time the boat docked with the barge tied to the *Oriskany*, the entire landing craft raged in one huge mêlée. The drunks chased the shore patrol to the pilothouse of the craft. They locked the hatch to protect themselves and radioed the carrier. A dozen more shore patrol met the landing craft at the barge.

Wolfe pulled Byrnes to the stern of the craft, arm locked around his friend's neck. "You move, and we go to the brig," he said. Fortunately, Byrnes passed out. Wolfe and one of the shore patrol had to carry him over the gangplank and up the ladder to the ship. Once on the ship, other men from V-3 Hangar Deck Division helped Wolfe get Byrnes to his bunk.

The next morning Wolfe went to sick call. The corpsman who saw him looked inside his mouth. "We don't usually sew lacerations inside mouths," he said, "and it's been too long anyway." He handed Wolfe a bottle of mouthwash and a bottle of penicillin. "Rinse it three times a day. Take a pill four times a day on an empty stomach. Come back if it gets red and swollen more than it already is. And stay out of bars." From that point on Wolfe and Byrnes were close friends.

CHAPTER 16

Kayla piloted the Prius to Jacksonville International Airport. It rained for the entire trip from Flagler College, where Wolfe had picked up his daughter, to the airport. In those sixty miles, an hour and half of travel time, rain poured from the sky obscuring the road. The weather added thirty minutes to the drive. "Rain like this always reminds me of P.I." Wolfe said.

"Pi? 3.1416?" Kayla asked, teasing her father. She had heard her father say P.I. hundreds of times in the past and knew exactly what he meant.

"Not pi or apple pie," Wolfe corrected her at a subconscious level, an automatic response after many years. "P-I. As in Philippine Islands. Monsoon rains. That's the place I first saw rain like this."

"Tell me, again, Dad. Where are you going?" Kayla said, stopping the car in front of the Southwest Airlines baggage drop-off at the airport.

In a hurry, even though he knew there would be a long wait at the security check-in, and hoping not to miss his flight, Wolfe growled, "Washington. D.C., not the state."

"And why? Mom will ask."

"I'll be home before she will," Wolfe said, opening the hatchback door and pulling out his small carry-on.

"Dad!"

"Okay. Okay. I don't want her to give you a hard time." Wolfe closed the hatch and leaned through the passenger window. He said, "I'm going to see the family of a guy I knew in the navy. He's dead."

"Why are you going to see a dead guy?"

"I'm not going to see a dead guy. I'm going to see his mother. He's been dead for almost fifty years. I didn't know he was dead until last week."

"And why?" Kayla repeated her question, exasperated.

Stressed, in a rush, Wolfe said, "To pay my respects. He was a good friend. It's probably his fault I went to medical school. If he were alive, I'd choke him for that, though. Drive carefully. Love you." He turned and bolted through the glass doors.

Kayla saw him walk briskly to the escalator, and then disappear into the crowd. Taking her time, she navigated between the other vehicles, their drivers also scurrying to drop passengers quickly. Soon she was back on I-95 south, headed toward St. Augustine and Flagler College. She mumbled to herself. "If he was so important to you, why didn't you know he was dead until last week? You should have tried to keep in touch, don't you think?"

As the last person seated on the Boeing 737, Wolfe sat next to the obligatory crying baby, held by a teenaged mom. The father sat next to Wolfe in the middle seat. Mom and baby had a nice view of the aircraft wing. Dad wore his green USMC uniform, the two chevrons of a corporal on his sleeve.

"Marine Corps now issuing wives and children?" Wolfe asked between the child's howls after the aircraft leveled off at cruising altitude.

"No, sir," the corporal said. "I'm on terminal leave. Just left my folks' place in Palatka. On our way to Atlanta to visit my wife's family. Next week we go to Bethesda Naval Hospital for medical discharge."

Wolfe scanned the man carefully and noted no obvious scars or deformities, although he could not see the corporal's legs well. "TBI?" he asked, meaning traumatic brain injury.

The man nodded. "That and this," he said, folding his newspaper. He tapped with the tips of three fingers on his left thigh. The tapping resulted in the hollow sound of a long-leg prosthesis.

"Combat?" Wolfe asked.

"No, sir. Osprey crash in training."

"Sorry," Wolfe said. "Do you have a job lined up for when you are discharged?"

"He's going back to finish college. Then he's going to go to medical school," the man's wife said, leaning forward to make eye contact with Wolfe. The baby continued to shriek.

The corporal smiled. He winked at Wolfe. "Going to try, anyway, sir," he said.

"One of my medical school classmates lost a leg in Vietnam," Wolfe said. "He did well enough. Ended up as an ER doc in California, if I remember correctly. Mind if I hold the baby?" You two look like you could use a break."

The couple looked at each other and nodded. "He can't cry much louder," his mother said. She handed the baby to his father, who handed him to Wolfe.

"And I doubt he could kidnap him from the plane," the corporal added.

"A pediatrician taught me this trick during my pediatrics rotation as an intern," Wolfe said. He gently turned the infant over until it rested chest down on his left hand. Gently, he then folded each arm and each leg inward until they were all tucked under the infant, balanced on his left hand. The baby looked like a round ball. As each limb folded inward and under the child, his cries became softer and softer until he was silent. Then he went to sleep.

The young parents looked at Wolfe in disbelief. The corporal held his hands out for the child. "Want me to hold him now, sir?" he asked in a whisper.

Wolfe shook his head. "I've got him for the time being. You two relax for a while." Within ten minutes the man and woman had fallen asleep, her head on his shoulder. Wolfe held the infant for the hour flight to Atlanta. Both adults woke when the tires on the landing gear squealed as the aircraft touched down. The baby opened its eyes, took one look at Wolfe, and started to howl for his mother. Wolfe handed him back to the corporal who passed the infant to his wife. "Sorry," Wolfe said, "only one magic trick per flight. Thanks for your service, son."

"Were you ever in the military, sir?" the corporal asked.

"You *jarheads* called us *swabbies*," Wolfe said, laughing. "Do what your wife says. Finish college. Medical school can be rewarding, but it's not a crime if you don't get in. Sometimes I regret I did. I guess I would have been a better engineer. Listen to the college career counselors. You might make a great surgeon, or a better chemist." Wolfe stood in the aisle. The couple and baby joined him waiting to exit.

"I will, sir. Thank you for your service, too," the marine said, shaking Wolfe's hand.

"And for the trick for quieting the baby," his wife added.

Wolfe made faces at the infant as they exited the plane. The baby smiled.

On his second flight, Wolfe reviewed the obituaries he printed from the internet for Jimmy Byrnes, i.e. ABH-3 James T. Byrnes, III; his father, retired Admiral J. T. Byrnes, Jr.; and his Grandfather, Chief Petty Officer J. T. Byrnes, Sr.

Chief Petty Officer Byrnes had been at Pearl Harbor during the Japanese attack, one of only a handful of survivors from the USS *Arizona*. After the war, he had retired. He died of emphysema in 1958 and was buried in Arlington. His son, Admiral J.T., Junior, had flown from carriers in the Pacific during World War II. He saw service in the Battle of Midway and the Marianas Turkey Shoot, becoming an ace. He also flew jets in the Korean War in a ground support role. During Vietnam, he captained several ships, but never in the war zone, being in the Sixth Fleet, in the Mediterranean. He joined his father in Arlington in 1991. The navy had split his last duty station between the Pentagon and the Newport News Shipyard.

Wolfe's friend had the shortest obituary, essentially: "Lost at sea, body not recovered."

After his second flight landed at Reagan National Airport in Virginia, Wolfe rented a car and drove to the address he had found on the internet. An Emiko Byrnes lived in the house he found off Russell Road in Alexandria. According to his obituary, Admiral Byrnes had lived in Alexandria after retirement and had been survived by his wife, Emiko, and two daughters, Tamiko and Yasuko.

Wolfe parked the rental in front of the two-story colonial brick dwelling with a large, flat, front yard on a corner lot. He sat in the vehicle for about ten minutes, leafing through his notes and Clemons's black book. Nerves calmed somewhat, he walked to the front door. Taking a deep breath and releasing it slowly, he pushed the doorbell.

After several minutes, a neighbor walked by, struggling to control two large dogs on leashes. "You'll have to knock," the woman said. "The doorbell doesn't work." The animals dragged her down the street.

"Thanks," Wolfe said. He opened the screen door and knocked three times on the wooden door, then let the screen door close.

A gray haired woman opened the inner door. She appeared to be about Wolfe's age. Seeing her, he remembered sailors had had a difficult time guessing Japanese women's age when he was in Japan. They never seemed to age, or the women all lied well. "Mrs. Byrnes?" he said.

"Who's asking?" the woman said, arms folded across her chest. She made no effort to open the screen door.

"My name is Addison Wolfe. I was a friend of Jimmy's in the navy. On the *Oriskany*. Could we talk? I found out about his death not long ago."

"My mother doesn't do much talking," the woman said. "She has Alzheimer's." An older, smaller, Oriental woman appeared at the younger woman's side. She wore a kimono and wooden geta sandals over white socks that had a gap between first and second toes to fit around the sandal strap. "She's in Tokyo right now. Mentally, that is."

The older woman spoke in Japanese to the younger woman, and then bowed toward Wolfe. The younger woman bowed toward her mother. She then opened the screen door. "She heard you mention Jim's name. She wants me to be polite and let you in the house. I'm Tamiko Kimura. You said your name is Addison?" She opened the door farther, letting Wolfe into the house.

"My friends call me Addy," Wolfe said, following the younger woman into a large living room. The older woman disappeared to the left, where Wolfe saw a hallway and part of a formal dining room. "Is she going to talk with me?" he asked.

"Do you understand Japanese?" Kimura asked brusquely. She blushed. "Sorry, I have been busy. Responding to my mother's whims interrupts my day. I was never good with interruptions. Please, have a seat. May I get you something to drink? Never mind, my mother has decided we are drinking tea."

The older woman appeared with a woven bamboo tray, on which sat a small tea set, including three small cups. "I guess it would be impolite to refuse," Wolfe said, as she placed a napkin in front of him along with a saucer and cup.

Deftly, she poured his tea, and then a cup for her daughter and herself. She knelt in front of the coffee table, feet splayed to either side. Wolfe and Kimura sat on either end of the couch. "Arigato," Kimura said. The woman bowed her head silently.

"I'm Jim's sister, Tamiko. You can call me Tammy," the younger woman said to Wolfe. She held her small cup in her hands and swiveled toward him. She placed one knee on the couch. "What can my mother and I do for you?"

"First of all," Wolfe said, "I recently found out that your brother died shortly after I transferred from the *Oriskany* to another ship. He and I were really close for about six months. I have thought about him frequently over the last forty-odd years."

"But not close enough to track him down before now?" Kimura

frowned. She added, "Or to have found out about his death?"

Embarrassed, Wolfe blushed. He said, "We didn't have the internet then, of course. Keeping in touch was harder. And life always got in the way. College. Medical school. Family. You know."

Kimura nodded. "So why show up today? You said you just heard about his death?"

"I came to offer my very overdue condolences. Jimmy was a fine young man. It's probably his fault that I went to medical school." Wolfe told Kimura about the *Forrestal* fire, liberty in Sasebo, and other stories. During the telling, her face softened. Tears glistened slightly above her lower eyelashes, but never fell onto her cheeks.

"Thank you for relating that," she said when he finished. Wolfe saw Mrs. Byrnes nod in assent. Then the old woman stood, retrieved the tea cups, saucers, and napkins, and trundled slowly from the room. "She may, or may not, come back," Kimura said. "While she's away, I'll tell you a little about our family.

"My father graduated from Annapolis in 1942. From there he went to flight school in Pensacola and the war in the Pacific. He flew navy fighters from aircraft carriers in World War II and the Korean War. When Japan surrendered, the navy assigned my father to General Douglas MacArthur's occupation staff. It was his job to make sure Japanese military aircraft never flew again. He and his assistants spent seven months traveling around the country destroying Japanese navy and air force airplanes. His home base was in Tokyo, which is where he met my mother.

"I didn't learn this until after my father's death, but my mother was forced by her family to marry an American, any American. Arranged marriages were common before the war. Her parents thought it was their duty to sacrifice their daughter for the good of Japan and the emperor. Of course, my father never knew this or let on if he did. My mother surely fell in love with him over time. Although more than once I heard her refer to the arrangement as a *deranged* marriage after Dad died.

"Dad's family is an Irish mix. They drank a lot; could be violent at times, which may have been a plus for navy pilots but not civilians. Don't get me wrong, he was not Pat Conroy's Great Santini, even when drinking sake, but he did his share of boozing, fighting, and chasing women. He never beat the four of us. Berate, yes. Fists no. It was beneath him to strike a child or a female. His motto was, 'Never complain; never explain.' My parents weren't the most loving couple on the block. She hated him when he joked that farts were Kamikazes – Divine Winds. They stayed together for their children's sake, although my sister and I sometimes wonder if it was worth the drama.

"My brother was born almost nine months to the day after they married, in 1946. Shortly afterward my father got orders to San Diego. I was born there in 1948. During the two years in San Diego, my father's squadron transitioned from the Hellcat, his World War II fighter, to the new jets. He was flying Panthers when the Korean War broke out. He did two cruises on carriers off the coast of Korea. While he was there, my mother took my brother and me to Tokyo, where we lived with her family until after the war. Dad wrangled another assignment in Japan, at Naval Air Station Atsugi, only 30 miles from my mother's parents in Tokyo. So we spent a good five and one-half years in Japan."

"Jim was nine years-old and I was almost six when we arrived at Craig Field in Florida."

"I live in St. Augustine, Florida," Wolfe said, "a little south of Craig Field. It's a civilian industrial zone now."

"We hated America," Kimura said, frowning. Her face clouded, reliving grade school humiliations. "We never stayed anywhere long, thank goodness. My father had many short assignments. And he spent a lot of time at sea, flying off carriers or commanding ships. While he was gone, my mother instructed us in Japanese traditions, bowing to elders, knowing our station in life. She wanted Jim to be a Samurai warrior and follow the bushido code of conduct. You know, boy scout on steroids." Kimura laughed.

"In one school we were known as the *Lee* children. My younger sister, Yasuko, was Ug-Lee, and I was Home-Lee. Jim had less trouble with being accepted. He played sports in six different high schools. Although he was small compared to my dad, who was six-foot-two and weighed 190 pounds, he played defensive back at 140 pounds, wrestled, and ran track. In the summers, my mother forced him to take martial arts lessons. Ever the warrior. I suppose Mom was disappointed my sister and I didn't become geishas. When he graduated from Hammond High School here in Alexandria, he went to Annapolis – "

"Wait," Wolfe said, interrupting. "He went to Annapolis? We're talking about James T. Byrnes, III, ABH-3, from the USS *Oriskany*, correct? Am I in the wrong house?"

Kimura smiled. "It broke my father's heart when he quit the Naval Academy. Made him angry, too. He stopped talking to Jim for two years. They spoke briefly on the telephone right before Christmas 1967.

Oriskany was on R&R in Hong Kong then. I remember my father crying during that conversation, and again when the navy told us Jim had committed suicide. He was devastated by that news."

The sudden buzz of a smoke detector interrupted their conversation. "Uh-oh," Kimura said. She stood and walked quickly toward the dining room. Wolfe followed her through the dining room into the kitchen. Smoke poured off a pan sitting on the stove. "Mother!" Kimura said loudly.

After turning off the burner, Kimura opened the back door, allowing the smoke to escape into the yard. The smoke detector eventually shut off. After scanning the room to make certain there was no fire, she went down a hallway to the den. Wolfe followed. There they found Mrs. Byrnes asleep in a recliner in front of the television. It displayed a news broadcaster who spoke in Japanese. English translations scrolled across the bottom of the screen.

"That's her favorite show. Noon news from Japan," Kimura said. "The Alzheimer's affects her memory and her ability to stay awake. She occasionally forgets she has turned on the stove to warm the noodles. I'm afraid I can't tell you anything more about Jim today, Addison. I have an appointment this afternoon. Can you come back tomorrow?"

"Sure," Wolfe said. "What time would be good for you?"

"Mother goes to the senior day care center for six hours tomorrow. I take her, but I'll be back about 9:00 a.m. Anytime after that is good."

"Tomorrow about ten, then," Wolfe said. "I have a newspaper clipping and some information I'd like to share with you tomorrow."

CHAPTER 17

Wolfe returned about 10:15 a.m. the next morning. With him he carried his notebook and Chief Clemons's little black book. He waited for a good time to show them and the article from the *St. Augustine Record* about the attempted murder to Kimura. She showed Wolfe to her brother's room on the second floor, a virtual shrine to the dead sailor.

Jimmy Byrnes's family had framed and hung on the walls every sports letter he had earned, many academic awards, his letter of appointment to Annapolis, even grade school pictures he had drawn. Pictures of Mt. Etna, taken by Jimmy on a brief vacation to Italy between high school and the Naval Academy, hung next to pictures of Mt. Fuji photographed from his father's quarters at Atsugi. Yearbooks from *plebe* and *youngster* years at Annapolis lay open to his class picture on a teak desk. Tabs held the places of other entries with his picture, most notably to the 150 pound football team on which he played.

"They had to weigh in at less than 154 pounds the Wednesday before the games on Saturday," Kimura explained. "Jim never had trouble making weight, but he said some of the players had to sweat off as much as twenty pounds in order to play. He told me it sometimes took them three days to regain their strength."

Wolfe saw the list of teams Navy played against, all Ivy League schools and West Point. In the 1965-6 yearbook, the Navy 150 pound team had defeated Army 21-15. Wolfe pointed to the picture of Byrnes intercepting a pass. "They beat Army that year," he said.

"Jim paid too high a price for that victory," Kimura said. "When he was tackled at the end of the play, he twisted his knee. They never did figure out what he did to it, but it was never right after that. When he wanted to return to regular duty, they put him through a complete physical. Because of his knee, they told him he would never qualify to be a pilot. He was devastated. All he ever wanted to do was to fly off carriers like our father. In retrospect, I believe he quit the Naval Academy because he was so depressed. My father never forgave him for giving up. My mother could not accept it either."

In addition to the high school and college yearbooks, Kimura showed Wolfe a thick binder. It held at least a hundred letters and the envelopes in which they had arrived, each in an individual clear plastic three-ringed pouch. "All these are letters from friends after they heard the navy said he jumped overboard. Not a single person thought he was capable of killing himself."

The final pouch held twenty or thirty small cards, all addressed in the same tiny handwriting to Mrs. Byrnes and family. "That's how we know he didn't commit suicide," Kimura said. She pulled one of the letters from the pouch. "This is from Colonel Richard Rhodes. He was a POW with my brother in South Vietnam. He says Jim saved his life after the Viet Cong shot down his aircraft. Mother receives a card from him every Christmas reminding us of that and thanking her for having such a wonderful son." Tears again formed in Kimura's eyes. She sniffled slightly and they disappeared, almost too quickly for Wolfe to have seen them.

Stunned, Wolfe stood with his mouth open. "He didn't commit suicide?" He sat on the bed in the room. "I'm sorry, Tammy, I'm having a hard time adjusting to these rapid changes. Until a week ago, I thought your brother had lived through his tour and probably retired somewhere after a long career. A guy with whom we served on *Oriskany* told me he disappeared from the ship and the navy presumed him dead, a suicide. I thought you confirmed that yesterday. Now you tell me he was a POW. Did he come home after the war ended?"

"Colonel Rhodes is sure he died from friendly fire, a B-52 bombing raid," Kimura said. "I have Rhodes's telephone number. You can call him, if you like." She leafed through the binder and found a sheet of paper from which she copied Rhodes's address and telephone number. She handed the information to Wolfe.

Leaving Jimmy's shrine, Wolfe followed Kimura down to the main floor and sat in the small, wood paneled den. She sat in silence while Wolfe used his cell phone to call Rhodes. Enshrined on the walls of the den Wolfe found Admiral Byrnes's career. Pictures from Annapolis, of aircraft he flew, squadron mates, and ships he commanded decorated the walls. "He retired from the 6th Fleet in 1977," Kimura said. His last ship was the USS *Nimitz*. He supervised its construction and then retired."

Rhodes's telephone requested callers to leave a number and a message. "Colonel Rhodes, I am a friend of Jimmy Byrnes's. I'll call you again," Wolfe said, and left his telephone number.

Walking around the room, Wolfe examined each photograph carefully, noting the size difference between Jimmy and his father. The latter had played football at Annapolis, too, long before they had the 150 pound team. He was a fullback and linebacker, playing offense and defense at 190 pounds. Wolfe had no difficulty finding him in the team picture. "Navy won all three Army-Navy games my dad played in," Kimura said. "I believe he was more proud of that than of being an ace. He shot down seven enemy aircraft."

Finished examining the pictures, Wolfe sat again. He opened his notebook and took the newspaper clipping from it. Handing it to Kimura, he said, "This is why I am here. Initially all I wanted to know was if the Jimmy Byrnes mentioned in the note was your brother. Then Chief Noble told me about his disappearance. So I thought I'd pay my respects. Still don't know if the note refers to Jimmy, but the man who died in the hospital was on *Oriskany* with us."

He handed Clemons's black book and his notes to Kimura. "Could you go through these notebooks and see if you recognize any names. People Jimmy liked, or hated, too, I guess."

"I can't today or tomorrow," Kimura said. "My mother has two doctors' appointments. And my sister will be coming over from Maryland to visit. We will be extremely busy. We are trying to find a nursing home in which to transition my mother. It will be necessary fairly soon."

"I'm in no rush," Wolfe said. "I can come back in a week, or so. Do you suppose I could borrow Jimmy's Hammond High School yearbook and the two from the Naval Academy? I promise I won't lose or damage them."

Kimura surprised Wolfe by agreeing readily. "My sister and I will have to decide what to do with all Jimmy's stuff when my mother goes into a home. We will probably sell the house. Neither of us worships him the way my mother does. We may end up donating the yearbooks to his schools. Sometimes they let people who have lost their books scan the pictures and upload them to their computers. We are not as attached to them as you might expect, but please take care of them."

Rhodes returned his call seconds before Wolfe pulled into a parking place at his hotel in Crystal City, in Arlington. Not feeling guilty about leaving the expensive hotel, Wolfe asked for and received a late checkout time. In an hour he managed to find I-66 west and later I-81 south, toward Virginia Tech. Rhodes had retired from teaching, but still lived near the campus. The seventy-three year old ex-assistant commandant to the VT Corps of Cadets said he would be happy to talk with anyone, anytime, about Jimmy Byrnes.

Two hundred fifty miles southeast of Washington, Wolfe took the exit to Virginia 460 west from I-81 south, toward Christiansburg and Blacksburg. The drive was a homecoming of sorts. He had graduated from Virginia Tech before attending the Medical College of Virginia and had not been back since trying to convince his twin children by his first wife to apply to college there. Neither did.

CHAPTER 18

"We lost two more Spads," Byrnes told Wolfe, referring to the A-1 propeller driven attack aircraft, nicknamed after the Spads of WWI. They strolled back onto the hangar deck after chow. Byrnes had friends in most of the squadrons of Carrier Air Wing 16, plane captains he had known from the previous cruise. They shared the squadrons' gossip with him. "The pilots are going to be listed as MIA, although they think there's a chance they can be rescued. Choppers are looking for them now. Other pilots saw two parachutes. Both planes were hit by small arms fire."

"Damn," Wolfe said, "that's almost a plane a day and a pilot per week for the cruise. Five A-1 Skyraiders this week alone. The SAMs keep knocking down the A-4s, too."

"They're calling this month *Black October* in the ready rooms," Byrnes said.

As the two men walked past Hangar Deck Control, they heard a loud *BANG*! Spinning toward the sound, they saw an A-4 with its nose on a jack stand, nose wheel about a foot off the deck. Actually, only half the nose wheel remained on the strut. A shredded rubber tire hung from the remaining half of the metal nose wheel. Behind the aircraft, Wolfe saw a sailor lying on the deck, arms and legs outstretched, widening pool of blood surrounding his head.

Sprinting to the aircraft, Wolfe and Byrnes arrived at the same time as the man's squadron mates. An aircraft mechanic knelt next to the injured man. After a brief assessment, he pulled a small tarpaulin from one of the nearby tractors and laid it over the injured man's upper body and head. "He's dead," the AME said to other men dressed in green shirts. "Get a corpsman and a wire stretcher."

"Wheel blew up," Byrnes explained, walking with Wolfe to Hangar Bay 3. "They are supposed to either x-ray the wheel for fractures or place a chainmaille cover over it before pressurizing new tires. The tires wear out quickly hitting the deck at a hundred plus miles per hour. The wheels sometimes have hairline fractures."

"Well, I guess we don't have to worry about Gorecki not tying his jacks down in the future," Sluggo Maxwell said, and laughed loudly. The remainder of the hangar deck crew looked at him in disbelief. "What?" Maxwell asked. "You were all thinking it. I just said it."

"That's morbid, Sluggo," Wolfe said.

"Fuck you, Boot," the airman said. "Everything we do is dangerous. If you haven't noticed, this is an unsafe place to work even without the enemy shooting at us. Sure, the pilots have a dangerous job, but more people die from accidents in wartime than from enemy action. Remember the fire? Or fires, now that the USS *Forest Fire* has had one, too."

"I'm no longer a boot," Wolfe protested. "Made airman last month."

"I've been an airman for three years and you'll always be a boot to me, Wolfe," Maxwell said. The dark curly-haired man stalked away, followed by three crewmembers who agreed with him.

"Byrnes!" a deep voice from behind the men made Wolfe jump. He turned to see Chief Powell saunter into Bay 3. The spindly-legged, pot-bellied, balding, older man with an alcoholic red complexion rarely left Hangar Deck Control. In fact, Wolfe had never seen him in Bay 3, only on his way to chow or his quarters through Bay 2. The Chief laid his cup of coffee on the spotting dolly. He chewed on an unlit cigar. Stenciled on his yellow jersey above his stomach bulge were the words *Hangar Chief*.

"Yes, Chief," Byrnes said, turning to face the chief.

"Who's your best driver?" the chief asked, standing with legs spread and hands on hips, eyes boring into Byrnes.

Without hesitation, Byrnes said, "Wolfe."

"Wolfe?" Powell's eyes widened. "Hell, he's only been driving for three weeks."

Silently, Wolfe stood next to the tractor. He didn't realize Byrnes thought he was especially good, much less the best. And he certainly didn't know that Chief Powell knew exactly how long he had been driving.

"He's got the touch, Chief," Byrnes said evenly.

"Okay. If you say so, but if this don't work out and he goes in the drink, the fact that you recommended him is going in the report," Powell said. "Get your crew together. We have to spin an F-8. The port elevator is tied up with the accident. They're taking pictures and doing a brief forensic study before they'll let us move the A-4. And they still have to put a nose wheel on it. The starboard elevator is loaded with aircraft on the flight deck. The mechs in VF-111 want to swap engines on an F-8. It will be a lot easier to do if we spin it for them."

"I can do that," Byrnes said. "It'll be tight, though."

Powell chuckled, a hearty laugh that originated in his large beer belly and worked its way up to his gravelly throat. "I am certain I'm the only director who can do this, but I'm willing to let you watch and learn."

"Okay, Chief," Byrnes said. He knew better than to argue with Powell.

Powell gathered the entire Bay 3 crew together, in addition to the elevator operator, and the plane captain who would be manning the aircraft, his feet on the F-8's brake pedals.

"We're going to have thirty minutes to spin this bird and it will take every second to get it right and not drop the plane or the spotting dolly in the drink," Powell said. "Plane captain, you pay very close attention to me. If I close my fists and cross my arms, you lock those brakes up as tight as they get. Got it?" The plane captain nodded. He wore a brown jersey and soft brown cloth helmet with built in ear protection.

"Harris," the chief said to the elevator operator, "you are going to have to override the stanchion safety. The lifeline will have to be down in order to do this. We need more room. And you keep communications open with the bridge. If they turn this boat while Wolfe is out over the edge, we'll lose the dolly and the bird."

"Yes, Chief," Harris said.

"Wolfe," Powell said, studying Wolfe's eyes. "I can get someone else to do this if you want. No pressure."

Not entirely certain what the chief expected of him, but interested in the challenge, Wolfe said, "I'm your man, Chief."

The Bay 3 blueshirts gathered around the VF-111 squadron's F-8 Crusader and crawled underneath. Wolfe slid the spotting dolly under the red and white shark's teeth painted on the jet engine intake below the nose of the fighter plane. As soon as he locked the two hydraulic arms into the nose wheel, the chief gave the hand signals for the crew to remove the chocks and tiedowns. The chocks clanked and chains rattled as they hit the deck.

Powell put his right thumb in the air and Wolfe pushed a button. The two hydraulic arms on the spotting dolly raised the interceptor's nose wheel about a foot off the deck. "That's good," Powell said. "Now you do exactly as I say and you'll be fine."

Following Powell's directions Wolfe rotated the aircraft and moved the nose toward the stern side of the open space where the elevator sat when it was at the hangar deck level. As he watched, the metal stanchions dropped into the deck, as if the elevator awaited the aircraft and dolly. The metal cable lifeline sank into the deck with the stanchions. Instead of elevator, open ocean beckoned. Wolfe drove the dolly backward until it was three or four feet from the edge of the deck.

"Harris?" Powell yelled to the elevator operator, after motioning Wolfe to stop.

The elevator operator held his thumb up. "Captain says we're going twenty knots. Straight ahead. No turns anticipated."

Chief Powell looked into the cockpit. "Plane captain?"

"We're good. Have hydraulic pressure for brakes," the man yelled from the cockpit.

"Wolfe?"

Wolfe looked at the wide expanse of the ocean, and swallowed hard. "Ready, Chief," he said.

"Okay, eyes on me," Powell said. "Byrnes, get your crew out from under the aircraft. Are your safety men in place?"

"Yes, Chief." Byrnes said. He stood next to the chief, where Wolfe could see them both.

Following the chief's hand signals, Wolfe turned the motorcycle-like throttle of the dolly and swung the arm that controlled power to its two main wheels. He steered the yellow tractor by swinging the control arm. Whichever main wheel he pointed the arm toward got power, almost like steering a tank by changing power to the treads. If he twisted the throttle clockwise the dolly moved forward. Twisting the throttle counter-clockwise moved the dolly backwards. Wolfe sat over the third wheel of the strange, squat machine. Shaped like a block letter **Y**, the two main drive wheels were at the top of the **Y**. A castor wheel sat under the stem and Wolfe sat at the extreme bottom of the **Y**. Beneath and slightly in front of him the smaller, castor wheel spun freely and went wherever the two drive wheels pushed it.

The entire Bay 3 crew, and not a small number of aviation mechanics and other ship's company, watched in awe as the chief swung the F-8 in an arc, within inches of the other aircraft surrounding it. The usual sounds of machinery whining and tapping stopped as men held their breath.

Between watching the chief's signals, Wolfe glanced down at the castor wheel occasionally. As the wheel rolled past the stanchions and lifeline, Wolfe found himself hanging out, over the ocean, past the edge of the ship. Salt spray from the ship's bow wave landed on him, as the bow wave itself spread away from the ship becoming the ship's wake. He could see, hear, and feel the spray from the white foamy water as it slid sternward fifty feet beneath him. There were about three inches between the castor wheel and the lip of the hangar deck. Deftly, he controlled the drive wheels to maintain the castor wheel moving parallel to the edge of the deck. It rolled from the stern edge toward the bow of the ship. Wolfe felt his palms begin to sweat as he turned the throttle and added more power to rotate the aircraft, walking the castor wheel carefully along the edge of the deck.

As the nose of the plane neared the forward edge of the elevator opening, Powell motioned for Wolfe to take the nose of the plane toward the middle of the bay. The castor wheel rolled past the safety line and into the hangar. The stanchions came up behind the dolly. Wolfe exhaled for the first time in ten minutes. One of the safetymen blew a whistle. The chief crossed his arms with fists closed. The plane captain slammed on the aircraft brakes. The plane stopped moving suddenly, stalling the dolly.

"Six inches here," one of the yellowshirt safety men yelled. "You're going to crunch the tail on the bulkhead if you rotate any more. Take the nose forward if you can, Chief."

Powell motioned Wolfe to reposition the dolly after he restarted it. As Wolfe rotated the dolly by spinning the nose wheel on the F-8, the aircraft's tail moved sideways. Repositioning the dolly moved the aircraft slightly, even with its brakes on. Another whistle blew. Pulling his soggy chewed cigar from his mouth, Powell demanded, "What now?"

"Two inches away from the bulkhead now," the yellowshirt said.

"Okay, Wolfe," Powell said, holding his cigar in his hand. "You pull it forward as you rotate. Got it?"

Wolfe nodded. Powell motioned the plane captain to release the brakes. With a blend of rotation and forward motion, the dolly pulled the jet forward, nose into Bay 2, tail a fraction of an inch from the bulkhead. Chief Powell blew his whistle. All motion stopped. He spoke quietly with Byrnes, and then added loudly, "Okay, Byrnes, now you can spot this baby where the AMEs want it." After retrieving his coffee cup from the top of the spotting dolly, he turned and walked back toward Hangar Deck Control. Wolfe hadn't noticed that Powell had left his cup there. Pulling his cigar from his mouth, he stopped and spun, facing Wolfe, "Good thing you didn't spill my coffee," he said.

"You okay?" Byrnes asked Wolfe after the crew chocked and tied down the aircraft. The aviation mechanics had begun to swarm over the F-8 in preparation for dismantling it to replace the engine.

"Yeah," Wolfe said, "just couldn't get Maxwell's claim that more people die from accidents than enemy action out of my head."

"Your jersey looks a little wetter than before you started," Byrnes said.

"Hot and humid out there over the water," Wolfe said, grinning. "So you think I'm your best driver?"

"Used to be," Byrnes said.

"Used to be?"

Byrnes nodded. He said, "Yeah. Chief told me to promote you to yellowshirt. You start learning safety stuff today. Go to Hangar Deck Control and get your yellow jerseys and whistle."

CHAPTER 19

Retired USAF Colonel Richard Rhodes welcomed Wolfe to his home, a three story, wood-framed house on a narrow street a short block from the Virginia Tech campus. Wolfe shook hands with a well-built, gray-haired, seventy-three year-old. The colonel had a strong grip and a nose that looked like it had been broken more than once. From the second floor screened porch on the back of his house, Rhodes pointed out large gray stone buildings, the huge Lane Stadium, and Cassell Coliseum. "Except for a few months in winter, this is the nicest campus in Virginia," he said, offering Wolfe a seat in a round bamboo chair filled by a single, colorful, circular cushion.

"It's certainly beautiful today," Wolfe said. He had treated himself to a drive around the drill field of his alma mater and had seen unfamiliar Hokie Stone structures, new academic buildings and dorms. "My favorite season is the fall when the leaves change color."

Rhodes sat opposite Wolfe in an identical chair. "Football season is only two months away. It's our preferred time of year," Rhodes said. His smile changed to a frown briefly. "We're going to miss Coach Beamer, though. He was quite a guy. You said you went to school here?"

"After I got out of the navy," Wolfe said. "Used the GI Bill. I changed my major from engineering to pre-med. When I graduated, I went to medical school in Richmond. Practiced in Florida, mostly. Retired now."

"And from where did you know Jim Byrnes?"

"He and I were shipmates, enlisted sailors on the same ship for about six months. The aircraft carrier USS *Oriskany*," Wolfe said.

"So you knew about him being thrown overboard?" Rhodes said.

Wolfe's face drained color. His mouth and dry tongue stuck together. For a brief instant he thought he might vomit. The room tilted, and then returned to normal. Weak, he tried to answer Rhodes's question. "Sorry," he said. "Did you say he was thrown off the ship?"

"That's what he told me. Weren't you there?"

Wolfe told Rhodes what he had reminded Chief Noble. "I left *Oriskany* by helicopter when she returned to Yankee Station from Hong Kong. I had requested a transfer to another ship because *Oriskany* was going into a long dry-dock period. I wanted to stay in Southeast Asia. I was accumulating regular pay and combat pay, tax free, and I knew I needed the money for college when I was discharged." Wolfe caught his breath, and continued, "Last week I learned that the navy decided Jimmy had committed suicide. I didn't even know he was dead until I talked with a guy who was stationed on *Oriskany* with us. He's the one who told me the navy called it suicide."

Rhodes's face clouded. "Damn bureaucrats," he said. "I told them he was alive and a POW in South Vietnam, but they acted as if I had hallucinated. Of course they could have changed their reports and your friend never heard about it. At least his family is aware. I told them in person. Jim told me he got into a fight and someone pushed him overboard. I didn't tell his family that, though. It would have killed his mother, I think. Just told her he fell off the ship."

"How did you meet him?" Wolfe asked.

"I was flying a Hun, F-100 to you, out of Tuy Hoa, in support of South Vietnamese troops. ARVN, Army of the Republic of Vietnam," Rhodes said. "I can still feel and hear the throbbing of the engine, and the shudder and bang as it exploded. Flaming pieces of the engine went everywhere after being hit by machine gun fire from the ground. I had barely enough altitude to eject, but not enough to get out over the beach. Still can smell the burning fuel and the pine trees I fell through in the parachute, too. I got stuck hanging from a tree, feet only four feet off the ground. My wrist was broken and the parachute's quick release jammed. I couldn't free myself from the 'chute. The locals used me as a piñata until the NVA arrived and saved my ass."

Rhodes clasped his hands together around a cane, and looked at the floor between his knees. "Broke my ankle when they cut me down. Passed out, from pain I guess. Woke up in a cave with Jim. I thought he was a VC plant at first. That really ticked him off."

Rhodes explained to Wolfe how Byrnes's ministrations to him and the herbs from the VC medic had helped him heal as well as could be expected in the primitive conditions.

"You ended up in Hanoi with other pilots?" Wolfe asked. "Why didn't Jimmy go with you?"

"He did. Well, part way. He knew we would be moving north. He had been there at least two years before I was shot down in 1969 and had picked up some of the Vietnamese language." Rhodes stared out of the screened porch in the direction of the campus. "President Johnson stopped the bombing north of the 20th parallel in 1968 and the peace talks started. In my opinion the war had entered a political stage. What happened on the battlefield had little to do with the outcome. Americans had become war-weary. Our will failed. At times, we had them on the ropes, but never capitalized on it. You could tell when they were afraid they'd lose and have to repatriate us. For instance in the eleven days the B-52s bombed Hanoi in December, 1972, they basically gave up. They knew they were whipped. All our guards knew it. Conditions improved. Our rations went up. Speaking of rations, will you join me in a beer and some pretzels?"

"Don't drink, but I'll take the pretzels and a soft drink if you have one," Wolfe said.

Rhodes excused himself and hobbled without his cane into the main house, returning with a Coke for Wolfe, a beer for himself, and a huge bowl of pretzels. "Thanks," Wolfe said.

"Anytime," Rhodes said. "The NVA, North Vietnamese Army, camp commander, a guy named An, talked with Jim the night before we left. Jim had figured out Vietnamese names by then. Their surnames came first, ours come last. Almost no one uses his surname in Vietnam. The soldiers went by their first names with their rank, like Sgt. Bob, or Major Tom if they were English names. If there were two Sgt. Bobs, then they'd use their last name, too.

"Anyway, Major An told Jim that he had assigned six men to take us north to Hanoi. I guess the North Vietnamese were gathering all the POWs together to use as bargaining chips in the negotiations in Paris. Jim said the commander had ordered the men to make certain we arrived alive and healthy, but he couldn't vouch for the other North Vietnamese after we arrived. An had heard bad things about the treatment of POWs in South and North Vietnam.

"In the south, B-52s continued to fly missions against the NVA. The VC had practically ceased to exist after the Tet offensive. The ARVN and US troops had almost wiped them out. Mostly, they had been replaced by NVA soldiers. The Buffs, the B-52s, that's Big Ugly Fat Fucker, flew from Thailand, Guam, and Okinawa. I used to see their routes on the operations board in Tuy Hoa. Anyway, they were still flying and bombing suspected enemy strongholds south of the 20th parallel where we were. We were happy to be leaving the area they frequently hit, but anxious about what awaited us in Hanoi.

"Jim had a trick knee. It didn't bother him often, but when it did, he felt it. I had, and still have, a painful healed fracture above my left ankle. We had been starved in captivity, not maliciously though. The North Vietnamese had almost no rations. They sent troops out hunting for food; shot mountain goats, wild boar, even apes and tigers for protein to supplement their minimal rice diet. They assigned Jim and me to collect bamboo shoots, mushrooms, and tubers for the troops and ourselves. We had all lost a lot of weight.

"In any case, we started north both using canes. We moved slowly through difficult terrain and forest, two men ahead, two between Jim and me, and two behind. On our third day, we heard the unmistakable sound of a B-52 airstrike. The thunderous explosions marched directly toward us. As soon as the Vietnamese figured out we were in the crosshairs, they started running north pulling me with them. The two Vietnamese with Jim must have thought they had a better chance if they ran south. I saw them tugging at him. Then he was alone. They had abandoned him and had run.

"The train of 500 pound bombs went right between our two groups. Well, not exactly between us. We ran a short ways, the NVA yelling, 'Di, di,' Go, go. The four Vietnamese with me and I fell into a shallow ditch. We screamed our lungs out as the bombs marched past us, shrapnel flying inches from our bodies and directly overhead. The whole scenario took less than two minutes. It's the most scared I have ever been. Literally, nothing stood for a half mile south of us, where Jim and the two other Vietnamese had been. The bombs carved a half-mile wide, three-mile long path out of the forest. The men with me found a bent AK-47 barrel and some shredded clothing from the other group. They stopped looking after that."

"When was this?" Wolfe asked. He noted that Rhodes had perspired through his light sweatshirt, even though he sat in the shade on a cool screened porch.

"I got to the Hanoi Hilton on October 13, 1970, after a six week trek. So the bombing took place about the beginning of September, 1970. I used to joke that Friday the 13th came on Tuesday that month. Jim never showed up. More proof they didn't make it."

"How prophetic was the company commander about your treatment?" Wolfe asked.

"Really, it wasn't so bad by then. Most of the really horrific stuff was over, like the torture and isolation John McCain and others had suffered, like dislocated shoulders, hanging from ropes, and worse. By Christmas that year we were living in large group rooms, seven large rooms we called Camp Unity. There were about 350 POWs by then. The Vietnamese worried about an attempt to rescue us, so they concentrated us all in one place in the middle of the most heavily defended city in the world." Rhodes said.

"Jimmy knew McCain, too. Their families were friends." Wolfe said. "He was really depressed when McCain didn't return from his mission over Hanoi."

"Jim told me about the conversation they had before the flight. Were you there?" Rhodes said.

"Yeah," Wolfe said. "I had recently become a yellowshirt, one of the guys who direct aircraft around on the hangar and flight decks. Byrnes was mentoring me. The whole thing was strange. It was the only time I remember a pilot getting into an A-4 on the hangar deck. Usually we sent the aircraft to the flight deck with a plane captain in it. This time the pilot climbed up the ladder and the plane captain followed him. After he handed the pilot – I didn't know who he was then – his helmet, he came back down and started to disengage the ladder. Byrnes stopped him. He climbed the ladder and spoke with McCain for at least five minutes. When the elevator came down, Byrnes took away the ladder and acted as safety director. I had the crew back the plane onto the elevator and signaled the pilot to hold his brakes while the crew tied it down.

"After the elevator went topside, I asked Byrnes who the old guy was. He laughed. 'Just prematurely gray,' he said. 'That's Admiral McCain's son, John.' I asked him who Admiral McCain was, not recognizing the name. Jim laughed again. Admiral McCain was commander of US Naval forces in Europe at the time. I guess I should have known."

Rhodes smiled. He tilted his beer at Wolfe in a knowing toast. "I never knew anyone not in my direct chain of command either," he said.

Wolfe continued, "The really strange thing was the guy who held the tiller, the steel bar we used to steer an aircraft when the crew pushed them around the deck, came up to us an said, 'He ain't coming back.'

Jimmy hit Maxwell in the chest with an open hand. 'Shut up,' he said. Maxwell laughed and walked away. Jim called him an asshole. I reminded Jimmy that it was the anniversary of *Oriskany*'s hangar deck fire from the year before and that Maxwell was probably having a bad day. 'Nope, he's a psychotic asshole,' Jimmy said. 'I hope he's wrong.' He wasn't, and it's the reason I remember the conversation."

"John McCain told me that his discussion with Jim was the last big laugh he had before being shot down," Rhodes said. "Jim told him 'Welcome to the dumpiest carrier in the fleet.' McCain had transferred to *Oriskany* after healing from burns suffered on *Forrestal.* He asked McCain if he wanted him to load the candy dispenser so McCain could strafe the school kids. Then Jim told him not to blow up *Oriskany*, like he had *Forrestal*, or land in the water. Which he did in Pensacola. Pretty prophetic, himself, I'd say. McCain crashed in a lake in Hanoi."

"You're certain Jim died in that bombing?" Wolfe asked.

"Absolutely," Rhodes said. "There weren't even tiny pieces of those men left."

The two veterans sat in silence for a while, staring at their drinks.

"So, how long have you been here?" Wolfe asked.

"I'm a Tech grad, too," Rhodes said. "Charlie Company, class of '63. Back before the voluntary corps, the women on campus, and the women in the corps. I'm an antique, seventy-four years-old next month."

"Didn't you teach here, too?" Wolfe asked.

"Some aerospace engineering. Gave the senior cadets a talk on *Rules of Engagement* every year before graduation. After the air force said I could no longer fly and gave me a medical discharge," Rhodes tapped on his deformed left leg with his cane, "I used the GI Bill to get a master's degree in aerospace engineering, and then a PhD. Took six years. Came back here in 1980. Taught for a few years. Then the Corps of Cadets needed an assistant commandant. Got to wear the uniform again, which I liked. Was paraded around like a hero, which I didn't like. They said they wanted me to inspire the cadets. I retired in 2010."

"You don't think you were a hero, sir? You are to me," Wolfe said.

"I find it interesting that the Vietnam War POWs are considered heroes. The men who survived severe torture and those who attempted to escape were heroes, for sure. The rest of us weren't. We were guys who except for bad luck would not have been shot down. And except for good luck would not have survived. In some ways, we are the luckiest s.o.b.s to walk the face of the planet. But not necessarily heroes."

"You endured physical and mental torture and malnutrition. I've read about some of the abuse you guys lived through. I would not have survived, seemingly abandoned by my country in an unpopular war."

"That toughness was an act. We fought to maintain our dignity. It's all we had left. And it's what the North Vietnamese wanted most to deprive us of. None of us would break totally. We didn't want to fail our comrades. We made rules about how much a man had to take before giving in, and we supported those who eventually failed, which was all of us."

"I think you have answered all my questions, Colonel," Wolfe said standing. "May I take these into the kitchen for you?" He pointed to the beer and Coke cans.

"Naw, let'em sit," Rhodes said. "The wife will be home shortly. Where are you staying tonight? You could stay here if you want. But we'd have to talk about Tech football. I only allow myself an hour per day of reminiscing. Otherwise I have nightmares."

"No doubt, sir," Wolfe said. "Thanks for the offer. I already have a room at the Christiansburg Hampton Inn. I thank you for your time. You were very gracious to see me on short notice."

Rhodes stood, leaning on the cane. He held his right hand out to Wolfe and shook his hand. "Every friend of Jim Byrnes is a friend of mine, Doc. Come back any day. Have a safe drive back to D.C. Please give my regards to Mrs. Byrnes and her daughters."

Wolfe showed himself out of the house and drove the rental car to Christiansburg.

CHAPTER 20

Byrnes struggled. He descended a small rise within the forest. His right knee, swollen to twice its normal size, wasn't so much painful as inflexible and immobile. He had to swing it stiffly with each step. Left leg tiring from doing most of the work, he concentrated on not slipping on the slick muddy trail. The first explosion seemed miles away, and it may have been. He ignored it and walked on, although his escorts stopped and listened.

"Tam dung lai! Khoang lang!" one guard yelled. *Halt! Silence!*

Byrnes froze. The rhythmic pounding explosions of an air bombardment became obvious. The drumbeat moved in their direction from the east, their right. Byrnes looked up and saw Rhodes and four of the Vietnamese soldiers running for their lives. He started to move after them, but his two guards restrained him. They grabbed his wrists, spun him around, and pulled him after them, retracing their steps on the slippery trail.

After about thirty seconds, with the explosions marching closer and the ground shaking more fiercely, the two Vietnamese let go of Byrnes's arms and sprinted away, dropping rifles and backpacks. Byrnes struggled to run, hobbled by his bad leg. To his left he could see bombs explode, trees splinter, dirt thrown high in the air, flashes of red and white. The trail of bombs led directly toward him. Each explosion was louder than the previous. "Why?" he shouted. "Why bomb here? There's nothing here you assholes. It's a forest, for God's sake. An empty – "

A detonation to his left leveled trees. The concussion squeezed his chest, sucked air from his lungs. He stumbled, regained his balance. His foot caught a large tree root and he fell, sliding headfirst downhill on the muddy path. A bomb exploded directly behind him. Face down in a slight depression, the shrapnel from the blast blew by, inches over his head. Dirt rained on him like a muddy monsoon. Deafened by the sound, he curled in a ball and waited to die. More bombs exploded in front of him and to his right. He heard a scream. The bombs marched away to the west, and then stopped. The silence at the end of the attack went unheard. Byrnes was temporarily deaf, his ears ringing so loudly he couldn't hear himself cursing.

When he stopped shaking, Byrnes rolled over and lifted himself to his good knee, foot, and hands. The forest had ceased to exist around him. After hauling away the debris, the Vietnamese could have planted crops some day in the devastated clearing that remained. He had no doubt that Rhodes and the four NVA with him had died in the attack. And he was certain his guards had been killed also, until he heard the moans. Following the sounds, he found both guards pinned under the remains of a tree trunk. Both were injured. One man, Thien Vu, had obviously lost his left leg from slightly above the knee. A sharp, thin piece of hot metal shrapnel had sliced it off, cleaner than a surgeon's scalpel. The red hot sliver of bomb casing also cauterized most of the wound. Vong Binh, the second man, had managed to grasp a splintered piece of wood and use it as a shovel to claw his way out from under the huge tree. Blood covered Vong's face. Lacerations covered his arms. One of his fingers dangled uselessly, obviously dislocated.

Byrnes pulled off his rope belt and wrapped it around the amputee's left thigh. He found a tree branch and used that to wind the tourniquet tightly, staunching the minimal flow of blood. Thien screamed in pain and passed out. With the help of the second guard, Byrnes dug the man out from under the tree. Using his pouch of drinking water, he rinsed the stump of the leg and applied part of the man's torn shirt as a dressing.

After waiting an hour to see if Rhodes or one of the other men would return, Byrnes and Vong began the long, slow walk back the way they had come. Byrnes carried the only AK-47 they could find and the remains of a backpack. He used his cane to negotiate the trail. Vong carried Thien, wearing him like a rucksack, arms tied together over his shoulders and right leg tied around his waist. Byrnes marveled at Vong's stamina. He had been told the Vietnamese routinely carried their wounded and dead from the field after a battle, so the Americans would not know the true extent of their losses. Now he believed it.

The men had walked about three miles when they came to an intersection of trails they had seen earlier in the day. Vong indicated they would go to the left, rather than follow the trail south. He thought there might be an NVA camp to the east, possibly the target of the bombing.

An hour later they entered a camp, after a sentry challenged them. The NVA soldiers in the outpost relieved Vong of the wounded man, carried him into a wooden shed and laid him on a mat. This unit also had no medic, but the commander sent a runner to headquarters asking for a medic, or transportation for the wounded man.

"Where are you going?" the commander asked Byrnes, not realizing he addressed an American.

"Hanoi," Byrnes responded.

The commander smiled. "Why were you going to Hanoi?" he said.

"Binh should explain," Byrnes said. He handed the AK-47 to Vong and stood silently leaning on his cane while Vong enlightened the camp commander.

The longer Vong talked, the wider the commander's eyes became. When Vong finished the officer swung his foot at Byrnes, sweeping the cane out from under him. "Nguoi My!" *American!* he said as Byrnes fell to the ground. "Hinh su!" *Criminal!* He kicked Byrnes in the chest.

Vong stepped between Byrnes and the NVA officer. The officer spoke so rapidly, Byrnes could not follow what he said. The orders were clear to his soldiers, however. They pointed weapons at him and Vong. They relieved Vong of his AK-47. Then three men dragged Byrnes to the middle of the camp. They tied his hands behind him and put a rope around his neck. The other end of the rope went around a tree trunk. Standing Byrnes up, the men began to punch him in the face and body. Whenever he fell over they stood him up and continued to beat him. Eventually he fell unconscious and they left him in the dirt.

When Byrnes woke, he found himself in a bamboo cage, about four feet wide, long, and high. Even diagonally, he could not stretch out. The cage sat next to the tree where the NVA soldiers had beaten him. He lay semi-curled and listened. The camp slept. In time the sun rose.

Vong appeared in front of Byrnes's cage in the early morning. Apparently the NVA had beaten him as well. No longer dislocated his finger appeared straight, probably relocated accidentally during the beating. Welts and bruises covered his face.

"I am returning to my unit, Con co," Vong said. "I will tell Major An about the animal who runs this camp. I don't know if he can help you." The NVA soldier turned and walked away from the camp.

Byrnes did not look up. He spoke quietly to himself. "I should have shot you and Thien. I must have been out of my mind to try to help save Thien's life. And for what?"

CHAPTER 21

The Boxtops belted out *The Letter* as Wolfe stuffed uniform dungarees into his seabag. His fingers ran across the J-shaped flap in the green canvas bag that the parachute rigging shop had repaired for him. Someone had cut open the seabag while it lay in storage. As far as Wolfe could tell, nothing of value was missing. The civilian trousers and polo shirt he had bought in Subic to wear around the Martins's house were gone. Wolfe knew if he told anyone he had had civilian clothing in the bag, he would be on report. He let it go. Still, he felt violated. He wished he knew who had cut open the canvas bag. One of his compartment mates had to be the culprit because only the V-3 Division chief had the key to the storage space.

A hand reached out and rubbed the bristly short hair on Wolfe's head. "How's the head?" Byrnes asked, rubbing his hand back and forth, making the short hair stand on end. "Sutures are out."

Wolfe had ducked under the nose of an A-4 two weeks before to check clearance for the tractor and tow bar after backing the A-4 into a tight spot. Before he had given the plane captain the hand signal to release his brakes, the man had done just that. The expanded nose wheel oleo strut collapsed and the nose of the aircraft dropped suddenly. As sharp as a knife, the nose wheel door dropped six inches and sliced Wolfe's scalp to his skull.

Dazed, Wolfe backed away from the aircraft and put his hands to his head. While he stood there blood gushed from the wound and poured down his face. The scene in front of him took on a red-tinged hue. Two blueshirts wrestled him to the deck and threw a rag on his head. "Jesus Christ," Wolfe said when he came to his senses a few minutes later. "Lying down makes this bleed faster." He pressed the rag into the wound and climbed to his feet. "Maxwell, tell Byrnes I've gone to sick bay," he said. Thirty sutures later, Wolfe returned with a bottle of Tylenol and no hair. He worked the rest of the shift, but only as safetyman.

Wolfe pushed Byrnes's hand away, then rubbed his own scalp. His hair felt like the coarse stubble on his chin after not shaving for a week, even though he knew it had to be at least a quarter inch long. "Head's fine," he told Byrnes. "Guys on *Ranger* are going to suspect I recently got out of the brig, though."

The cheap record player in the three-chair lounge at the end of the compartment dropped another 45-rpm record. *Apple, Peaches, Pumpkin Pie* by Jay and the Techniques blasted through the space between the bunks. "You're going to miss that," Byrnes said, smiling. "I hear they've got a radio station and a television station onboard *Ranger*."

"Yeah," Wolfe said. "The next song is *Penny Lane*, followed by *Snoopy vs. The Red Baron*. I've got all twenty of them memorized. I bet you guys throw Smitty and his record player overboard before you get to Alameda."

"With luck he'll buy more records before we go to sea again," Byrnes said. "Can I carry something for you?"

"I've got it," Wolfe said. "My whole life fits in one seabag. Hard to believe, isn't it." He slung the wide strap to the bag over his left shoulder.

"Chief sent these up. I'll hang on to them until we get to the flight deck," Byrnes said. He waved ten copies of Wolfe's orders in front of him. They authorized his transfer to the USS *Ranger*, CVA-61,

Wolfe smiled. "She's newer than *Forrestal*, Jimmy. If I go to the hangar deck, they'll have two crews. No more 18-20 hour days or sweltering in this un-air-conditioned compartment."

"Keep on your toes, though. Remember what happened to *Forrestal*. And *Oriskany*."

Wolfe nodded. "Right."

He traipsed out of the compartment, shaking hands with his crew and the rest of the men in the division as he went. Everyone rubbed his scalp and wished him good luck, except Maxwell. "Bye, klutzy Boot," Maxwell said. He waved from the far end of the compartment. "Try not to participate in any more accidents. People *die* out here."

"Asshole," Byrnes said under his breath. "Bet you won't miss him."

Wolfe nodded. The two men wended their way through corridors and up ladders to the ship's island at the flight deck level. Opening the hatch to the starboard side of the island, away from flight operations, they stepped onto the flight deck, between twenty yellow hand trucks loaded with five hundred and one thousand pound bombs.

Toward the front of the island stood two other men, seabags next to them. A flight deck yellowshirt waved at Wolfe. "Got to go," he said to Byrnes. "See you in Alameda in seven to eight months."

Byrnes shoved the orders into Wolfe's left hand. Grabbing Wolfe's right hand with his, he shook it. He put his left hand on Wolfe's right shoulder and squeezed hard. Jet engines began to whine as aircraft warmed up in preparation for air operations. Byrnes shouted so Wolfe could hear him over the flight deck's wind and engine noise. "I won't be there, Addy. Navy has other plans for me."

Surprised, Wolfe shrugged. "Well, you know where I'll be. Keep in touch." He turned and walked toward the yellowshirt. Byrnes watched him climb into the SH-3 Sea King helicopter.

Wolfe sat on the port side of the chopper on a bench seat between the other two transferees. "Buckle up," the helicopter aircrewman told them. Wolfe never found the second seatbelt strap. Thinking how useless it would be if they went into the water, he hung on to the bench with one hand and half the seatbelt with the other, seabag lying between his legs. As the chopper lifted, it tilted forward. Wolfe had a brief glimpse of *Oriskany's* island, then nothing but white-capped sea and clear blue sky. Ten minutes later the chopper settled easily onto *Ranger's* forward flight deck. Wolfe never saw or heard from Byrnes again.

CHAPTER 22

Wolfe sat at the small table in his room at the Hampton Inn. He scribbled impressions of his interview with Colonel Rhodes in his loose-leaf notebook. When he finished, he pulled Byrnes's high school yearbook from his suitcase and flipped through it. Wolfe remembered the 1960s well. Only two years behind Byrnes in school, he remembered the ducktail hairstyle, DAs they had called them, for duck's ass. And the beehive hairstyle on the girls. And ring pins. *Jesus, was it really more than fifty years ago?* he thought.

Unwilling to spend a fortune on scanning the yearbooks, Wolfe compromised with himself. He wrote down the names of all Byrnes's friends who had written remarks in the book. There weren't that many. It appeared to Wolfe that Byrnes had had a small circle of close friends, mostly from the football, wrestling, and track teams pictured in the high school yearbook. In addition, there was a number of students in the same alphabet range as Byrnes's last name. These Wolfe assumed constituted homeroom acquaintances. In his barely legible handwriting, Wolfe made a list of the relevant high school students in his large notebook. He left space around each name, in case Byrnes's sister or mother knew a phone number or address. If Kimura knew where a few of these people lived, and if they lived near Washington, DC, he might be able to talk with them before he flew back to Florida.

He wasn't certain why he wanted to talk with friends of Byrnes, except he was also a friend. Maybe they could find some solace in talking about a man they all knew and liked. Maybe there had been some purpose in his short life that Wolfe had missed.

In the two Annapolis yearbooks, Wolfe found even fewer autographed pictures or comments. Byrnes again had friends on the 150 pound football team, but far fewer close friends. The only other signatures seemed to be from some midshipmen in his company.

As Wolfe slid the yearbooks back into his carry-on, someone knocked at the door to his room. Wolfe waited a minute, believing the person had made a mistake. He thought the visitor had probably meant to knock on the door to the adjacent room, given he didn't know anyone other than Colonel Rhodes in Blacksburg or Christiansburg.

The knocking repeated, along with a loud, masculine voice. It said, "Dr. Wolfe, I'd like to speak with you."

Surprised to hear his name, Wolfe went to the door and opened it. A man dressed in a dark suit stood outside Wolfe's room. "May I help you?" Wolfe asked.

The man reached into his inside coat pocket and produced a wallet, which he opened and flashed in Wolfe's face. Wolfe had a brief glimpse of a green identification card. The nearly transparent letters across the front of the ID read, CIA. The man spoke in a near whisper. "Agent Drugi Jaskolski, Doctor," he said. "May we talk in private?" He slipped his wallet back into his coat pocket.

Wolfe stuck his head out the door and looked both ways down the hallway, curious as to whether the man was alone. No one else stood in the corridor. "Sure, Agent Jaskolski. Come in. To what do I owe the pleasure of a visit by a CIA agent?"

"You may call me Drew, Dr. Wolfe," Jaskolski said, closing the door behind him. "All my friends do." The agent crossed the room quickly and pulled the curtains closed, darkening the room. Wolfe flipped on a light switch. Two desk lamps and an overhead light came on. "Mind if I borrow a bottle of water?" Jaskolski asked, opening the mini-fridge.

"Be my guest," Wolfe said, settling into one of the two chairs at a small table in the room.

Jaskolski sat next to Wolfe. Wolfe waited. He had no idea why a CIA agent would want to talk with him. Jaskolski opened the water, took a long swig with evident pleasure. "It's been a long, dry day," he said. "Mind if I ask you some questions?"

"Depends," Wolfe said. "About what?"

"James T. Byrnes, the third."

Surprised, Wolfe's eyes opened wide. "What would the CIA know, or why would they care about Jimmy Byrnes?" he asked.

Jaskolski placed both hands on the table, fingers intertwined. "Would you mind telling me why you visited Mrs. Emiko Byrnes yesterday and today?"

"Sure," Wolfe said. "I was a shipmate of Jimmy's on the USS *Oriskany*, during the Vietnam War. We were good friends."

"But, as far as we can tell, you've never visited before. It's been forty-eight years since you and he were on the hangar deck together," Jaskolski said. "Why go visit now?"

"Well," Wolfe started, "I recently found out that Jimmy died shortly after I left the *Oriskany*. Or, at least most people thought he had committed suicide by jumping overboard then. He apparently survived falling from the ship. Colonel Rhodes is sure he died some three plus years later, by friendly fire."

Jaskolski nodded. His face suggested to Wolfe that he already knew the answer to the question before he had asked it. And he also somehow knew Wolfe and Byrnes had been on the hangar deck together.

A troubling thought occurred to Wolfe. "And how would you, or anyone in the CIA, know if I had been to Mrs. Byrnes's house before now? Have you been surveilling her house? For forty-eight years?"

Ignoring the questions, the agent said, "When you joined the armed services, you were made aware that you might have to die for your country, were you not?"

Wolfe laughed. He said, "Part of the reason I joined the navy was so that wouldn't happen. If I wanted to die for my country, I might have joined the marines. But, yes. The navy made us all very conscious that servicemen, including sailors, sometimes gave their lives for their country. That fact was impressed upon me several times during my time in the service. Shipmates died in accidents. Men died in the *Forrestal* fire. Why do you ask?"

"There are over 1600 MIAs that served in Vietnam. We are sure a majority died in combat or air operations," Jaskolski said. "Some," he faltered, then continued, "Some have had to give their lives over a prolonged period of time as POWs. Long, slow deaths for their country, if you know what I mean?"

Suddenly angry, Wolfe shook his head. "No. I don't know what you mean," he said. Almost immediately he had an epiphany, "The POWs came home in 1973. Unless you mean there are still men in captivity, and the way they are giving their lives for their country is by continuing to be slaves, or worse to their captors. Is that what you mean? Are there still POWs in Southeast Asia who are alive and abandoned by our government?"

"You're a quick study, Doctor," Jaskolski said. "There are lots of ways to give your life for your country. A bullet to head or heart. Live without a limb or two for most of your life. Suffer a lifetime of PTSD or pain from wounds. Or get a life sentence in a gulag, if you get my drift. James T. may be dead. We don't know for certain. Probably, he is. What we do know is that we don't want you stirring up an international incident, because you recently found out that he died. It's the price some servicemen have to pay. Like it, or not. Do I make myself clear? The United States Government doesn't want you to remind the public of these sacrifices. Not with the possibility of MIAs in Iraq, Afghanistan, and Syria. Not to mention a dozen other countries, or the men who went missing during the Cold War. Understand?"

Stunned, Wolfe stared at the CIA agent. The man returned his gaze, unblinking. Wolfe said, "You mean there is a chance that some of these 1600 MIAs are still alive in Vietnam, Cambodia, wherever, and the government isn't trying to find them, or recover them? And it has no intention of trying? I'm not certain I can ignore that. What happens to me if I somehow cause an incident that brings this state of affairs to the rest of America's attention?"

The CIA agent chuckled. "Well," he said, "first of all, more than likely no one will believe you except possibly some conspiracy theorists. If, however, it appears that you are on track to embarrass your government, you might find out that you, too, can give your life for your country."

Shocked, Wolfe asked, "You'd have me killed?"

"Possibly," Jaskolski said, "More than likely you'd end up in prison for a long time, for tax evasion or some other crime. You might find the *After Hours* billing scam laid in your lap, for instance. You're sixty-nine years-old now. A fifteen-year sentence for Medicare fraud would be comparable to a life sentence. And who listens to prisoners when they maintain their innocence, or blame their predicament on a government conspiracy?" Jaskolski stood. He pushed the chair under the table. After taking a swig of water from the bottle, he tilted it in a toast to Wolfe. "Think about your family and your reputation, Doctor. Is the suffering you might cause worth finding out additional info about your friend?"

The CIA agent walked to the door of the hotel room and opened it. Wolfe remained silent as he followed the man to the door. "Good-bye, Dr. Wolfe," Jaskolski said and closed the door behind him.

"Good-bye, asshole," Wolfe said, after the door shut. "It may not have been worth the effort before, but it certainly is now." Looking toward the ceiling, imagining his friend looking down from his personal heaven, Wolfe thought, *We'll find you Jimmy, whether the government wants us to or not. Promise.*

CHAPTER 23

Tamiko Kimura sat in the waiting room of the Alexandria Hospital ICU. Wolfe sat next to her, his hand on hers. "When did she have the stroke?" he asked.

"Right after you left for Blacksburg. The ambulance brought her here. They say the blockage is on the right side of her brain," Kimura stared into her lap, tears dripping onto her clothing. "They say there is nothing they can do now except wait it out. They tried the clot dissolving medication. If her blood pressure goes up, they'll have to operate."

Wolfe nodded. If Mrs. Byrnes started to bleed inside her head, the blood would compress her brain, also requiring surgery. At her age, she had experienced some cerebral atrophy. That meant a little more space for blood inside her skull, a blessing and a curse. More space meant room for bleeding without damage to the brain itself. The smaller brain meant any damage would have a more serious effect. "Has she been awake?" he asked.

"She moans occasionally, but we haven't had a conversation yet," Kimura said. "The doctor believes she might wake up today." A taller, thinner, younger version of Kimura left the ICU and sat next to Kimura. "Dr. Wolfe, this is my younger sister, Yasuko Barnes. Yaz, Dr. Wolfe."

"Addison, or just Addy," Wolfe said, standing and offering his right hand to the woman.

She looked up at him momentarily and held his hand briefly, loosely, limply, and then dropped it. She spoke in a flat tone, not looking in his direction. "A pleasure," she said. "Mom's awake, Tammy. She wants to talk with you."

Kimura stood. "Excuse me Addy, I'm sure our time is limited, so I'll go right in."

"Of course," Wolfe said. After Kimura left, he sat next to Barnes. "Is she coherent?"

She ignored the question and examined Wolfe closely before asking, "You knew Jim?"

"In the navy."

Using a disdainful tone, Barnes said, "So, why did you visit my mother and sister? Did you not suppose that your visit might stress my mother? Might bring on a heart attack or a stroke?" Her frown and stare blamed Wolfe for her mother's condition.

"I'm sorry, Mrs. Barnes. I didn't know your mother was in fragile health, or I would have taken that into consideration," Wolfe said. "I apologize if my presence adversely affected your mother's well-being. The reason I came was to offer my condolences to your family over your brother's death. He was a good friend. I didn't know he had died until last week."

"Real close friend," Barnes said. The bitterness in her voice astonished Wolfe. "Kept in close touch all these years. I suppose – "

"Addy! Addy!" Kimura waved at him from the door to the ICU. "Come quickly. You stay there, Yaz. Only two visitors at a time, remember?" The younger sister sat down.

Wolfe walked over to Kimura who grabbed him by the elbow and pulled him into the ICU. The door closed quietly behind them. Wolfe found himself standing at the nurses' station, surrounded by ten ICU beds, each in its own glass cubical. Every cubical except one had a patient in it. All the patients had multiple electronic devices attached. Intravenous bags hung on poles in every room. Monitors beeped quietly, keeping electronic watch over their charges.

Kimura pulled him into the third glass room and closed the door behind him. "Your sister is certain I caused your mom to have a stroke," Wolfe said.

"My sister is not rational," Kimura said. "To her, if two things happen close together, then they are related. And the one that came first caused the second. No matter how bizarre the connection."

"Your mother's better?"

"You tell me," Kimura said. "Mother, Dr. Wolfe stopped in to say hello."

Emiko Byrnes's eyes opened and swept the room in front of her. A crooked smile appeared on her face, asymmetrical because the left side of her face barely moved. "Addison," she said. "So nice of you to come by. My Jimmy like you very much. You go see him. Okay?"

Startled by her words, but convinced she was confused after the stroke, Wolfe smiled and said, "Yes, ma'am." He looked at Kimura and wrinkled his brow.

"Yes," Kimura said, "I think she's a little befuddled, too. But did you notice? She spoke in English for the first time in six months."

"Oh, pshah," Mrs. Byrnes said. She waved her right hand at her daughter as if to dismiss her. Her left arm and hand remained motionless. Then she closed her eyes and appeared to drift off.

Wolfe and Kimura backed out of the room quietly. A nurse entered as they left. She brought a pan of water, washcloth, and towel. "Bath time," Kimura said. The nurse nodded.

Kimura and Wolfe spoke briefly with Barnes and decided to return to the Byrnes's residence. Barnes chose to remain in the waiting room in case her mother could see visitors again later. "Come get me in a couple hours," Kimura said, handing her car keys to her sister. "Dr. Wolfe and I will be at home." Barnes's head bobbed. She glared at Wolfe.

After reaching his rental car, Wolfe said, "Your sister seems to be furious with me."

"She's been irate for twenty some years. Since my father died," Kimura said. "He was a good man. She doesn't feel God should have taken him at such a young age."

"How old was he?"

"Seventy. He died of prostate cancer in 1991."

"Sorry. So your mom must be pushing ninety?"

"Ninety-four next week. God willing. Dad would have been ninety-five this year," Kimura said.

Inside the Byrnes's house, they sat at the dining room table, side by side. Wolfe placed the yearbooks on the table, next to the binder. It held the letters from Jimmy Byrnes's friends. He pulled out his notebook and opened it to where he had written down the names of Byrnes's assumed friends. "Do you know any of these people?" he asked. "There are some pictures missing from your brother's high school yearbook, too. Do you know about them?"

Kimura turned the notebook to get a better view of the names. She smiled. "My mother removed the pictures. They were of a girl Jim dated and liked a lot. Emily Rose. His first and only steady girlfriend. She liked him, too. They broke up when he left Annapolis. My mother didn't want Jim's future wife to worry about competing with an ex-high school sweetheart. While he was away in the navy, she cut out the pictures. Burned them, too. We only found out about it after the navy told us he was missing."

"Very considerate of your mother," Wolfe said, laughing. "Is that a Japanese thing?"

"No. A future mother-in-law thing," Kimura said. "She so badly wanted grandchildren with the last name Byrnes. My sister and I both thought about marrying almost any man named Byrnes to make her happy."

"Why did your brother and his girlfriend break up?" Wolfe asked.

"Her father was a marine colonel. A real hero. He was on a battleship at Pearl Harbor, and stormed the beaches in Okinawa as a lieutenant in World War Two. In Korea, he held a position against the onslaught of a Chinese battalion with only a company of men. Jim's girlfriend was pushing him to be a marine when he finished at Annapolis. He wanted to fly like my dad. When he quit, she apparently decided he was a loser. Found another midshipman, who did become a marine. And paid for it in Vietnam."

"A lot of that going around back then," Wolfe said. He pointed to the list of names, again. "Recognize some of these people?"

"How long will you be in northern Virginia?" Kimura asked.

"I have to go back to Florida this evening," Wolfe said. "In fact, I have to return the rental and get to TSA in the next hour or so. I can come back again in a couple weeks. Why?"

"It's probably not necessary for you to come back. Some of these people still live in the D.C. area," she said, and circled some names. "I'll get their phone numbers and email addresses together. If you give me your email address, I'll forward that information to you later this week. Okay?"

"That would be great," Wolfe said. He started to stand, pulling his cell phone from his pocket to check the time.

"You can't go yet," Kimura said. "I found something that might interest you." He sat again. She pulled the large binder closer to her and opened it. A piece of paper marked one of the slots. From that slot she pulled a long envelope. Inside the envelope was a yellow piece of paper from a legal pad. "Read this," she said, handing the paper to Wolfe.

Wolfe pulled his reading glasses from his shirt pocket. He unfolded the yellow lined page and read the marginally legible script. "The navy should do a more thorough investigation into your brother's death," it read. "He DID NOT commit suicide. And his disappearance was NO ACCIDENT!" Wolfe turned the page over. The backside was blank. There was no date. No signature. He scanned the envelope. There was no return address. "Who sent this, and when?"

Kimura pointed to the postmark cancellation over the stamp. "It was mailed on May 1, 1968, so I guess we got it soon after that," she said. "We never found out who sent it. The navy refused to re-open the investigation when we showed the legal affairs people the letter."

"Not much help then, is it?" Wolfe said.

"Except this," Kimura said. She pointed to the cancellation again. "The zip code is 32223. That's in Jacksonville, Florida, isn't it?"

Wolfe pulled his cell phone out and tapped on it quickly. He stared at the map that appeared on the phone. "32223. Mandarin. Southwest Duval County. Jacksonville, Florida. May I take a copy of that with me?"

Kimura handed him copies of the letter and the envelope that she had already made.

CHAPTER 24

"A little over six years," Byrnes said to the guard, Ngo Ty, who unlocked the bamboo cage. The guard had asked him how long he had been a prisoner after telling Byrnes the date, February 2, 1973. The smile on the North Vietnamese soldier's face made Byrnes apprehensive. In the past, anything that made an NVA soldier happy usually meant trouble for him. "Why do you ask?" Byrnes's spoke Vietnamese like a native, a native with a northerner's accent after six years as prisoner of the North Vietnamese Army in South Vietnam.

"The war is over for you Americans, Con co," the guard said. "Tet will be a grand celebration this year."

"What do you mean?" Byrnes asked. Only recently had the beatings stopped. NVA soldiers had poked him with sticks through the cage, thrown burning cigarettes at him, and punched him at every opportunity. Eventually, they had tired of abusing him when they realized he was no threat and could not strike back.

"In the Paris peace discussions, your country has agreed to leave Vietnam to its people," the guard said. He escorted Byrnes to the small pool in a stream where the NVA allowed him to bathe and wash his clothing once every two weeks. "We will still have to deal with the traitorous southerners, of course."

"No ceasefire?" Byrnes asked. He had heard similar claims in the past.

"Ceasefire, yes. But we do not have to leave the south. We will re-arm and restock, and finish the unification of Vietnam," Ngo said.

Byrnes looked at the guard, almost as emaciated as he was. "How long have you been in the south, Ty?"

"Corporal Ty, to you, American," the soldier responded.

"Sorry, Corporal Ty. How many years have you been a soldier?" Byrnes asked.

"Ten glorious years," Ngo said, standing taller and throwing out his chest as he walked. Byrnes saw the soldier's ribs behind the open, loose-fitting, unbuttoned, faded, light-green shirt.

"You have seen a lot of action then? Do you believe what the cadre tells you?" Byrnes said. He made conversation, more to pass the time and practice his Vietnamese language skills than to learn anything tactical or strategic.

Ngo sat behind the naked Byrnes on a rock. He put his AK-47 down beside him and constructed a cigarette from the tissue paper and tobacco he had in his shirt pocket. Byrnes washed with a rag. Having no soap, Byrnes used sand from the bottom of the stream to rub off dirt.

Ngo stared into the trees and blew smoke from his nostrils. Byrnes suspected his mind drifted to battles in which he had participated, bunkers in which he had hunkered down, and long marches which he had joined. As Byrnes knew, the strain had been almost more than humans could endure.

Ngo sounded wistful when he spoke. "We soldiers don't listen to the cadre," he told Byrnes. "They are old men, deluded men left over from the Viet Minh and the war with France. They no longer fight. We do not respect them. The communists were the only people who would help us escape from French colonial slavery. It was a convenient marriage. When this war is over, the cadre will disappear. Ho Chi Minh himself would disband them after the war ends, if he were still alive. United Vietnam will chart its own future. Not the Chinese or the Soviets."

"Are there many soldiers who feel this way?" Byrnes asked.

"All the younger men and most of the older ones," Ngo said. "Everyone except the older communists and their cadre. The generals will take care of the cadre after the war is over."

Byrnes began to wash his shirt, alternately rinsing in the dirty water and wringing it out after slapping it on a large rock. He pulled the rope belt from the loops of his cotton pants. He had braided the belt from parachute cord a soldier had given him. The parachute had dropped an American magnesium flare during a night battle. The NVA soldiers had found dozens of parachutes the next day.

Byrnes flung the belt onto shore near Ngo. Then he washed his light green faded trousers. Leaving the stream, he hung his clothing on some bushes to dry and squatted in the dry sand near Ngo and the belt. He dripped dry slowly in the sultry heat of the jungle, unable to tell sweat from pond water. The smell of rotting undergrowth filled his nostrils.

Ngo continued. "I left my village when I was eighteen, ten years ago. Five other boys from my village and I joined with a hundred others from the surrounding villages. We had all turned eighteen the year before. There was a great celebration. The whole village turned out to see us march away. The party had been going on for two days when we left. A few of the boys had drunk too much wine. They suffered in the march to the transportation rendezvous area.

"At a larger village we climbed onto four old French lorries. It took two days to get to our training site packed in those lorries, standing the whole time. At our basic training camp, they issued us our uniforms. Along with the hated political indoctrination, we trained for combat for three months, first with wooden weapons, then real weapons. Learning to kill with a shovel, bayonet, grenades, and this AK-47 took a long time. I spent more time digging trenches, foxholes, and tunnels, though. We also spent many days marching, learning to move undetected at night, and to hide from reconnaissance aircraft during the day. All of us who trained together formed a new battalion.

"Our battalion marched south, at night only, of course. It took us three weeks to cross the DMZ. We learned even more on the march. In our first battle, we overran an outpost, only losing a dozen men. We may not have the firepower of the traitors, or the air power of the Americans, but we have an unlimited supply of brave men. We march into battle unafraid. None of us would disappoint our ancestors or our comrades."

Byrnes saw his own reflection in the turbid pond water. His body had suffered. Over the years he had contracted malaria, had been malnourished to the point of starvation, and possibly suffered from mild cases of beri-beri and scurvy. Except that he was three to five inches taller than the NVA soldiers who guarded him, his build and appearance resembled his captors. He knew he had only a small chance to escape. He waited for the opportunity.

"Time to go, prisoner Con co," Ngo said. He continued to sit on the rock, blowing smoke at the trees, paying no attention to Byrnes. "Get your pants and shirt."

Byrnes bent down to pick up his belt. He stepped behind the Vietnamese as if to retrieve his clothing. Looping the belt over the NVA soldier's head, he wrapped it around the man's neck and tried to garrote the corporal.

Stunned, Ngo fought back. Byrnes held on to the rope as tightly as he could in his weakened state. Ngo pulled at him and tried to wriggle free, but soon passed out. Byrnes felt the corporal sag in his arms. At the same time something hit Byrnes in the back of his head. He fell to his knees releasing his grip on the belt and Ngo. Curled in a ball, Byrnes received multiple blows to his body from a rifle butt. He covered his face with his arms.

"See to Ngo," a voice said. Byrnes recognized the tone of the company commander, Major Ly. When the beating stopped, he looked up and saw three men, Ly and two sergeants. The two enlisted men splashed water on Ngo's face. Groggily, the corporal choked and spit, gradually regaining consciousness. When it became apparent that Ngo would survive, the commander drew his pistol and pointed it at Byrnes. "Dress," he said. "You men take Corporal Ty back to camp. I will deal with the prisoner."

After the men had dragged Ngo out of sight and Byrnes had finished dressing, he stood in front of the commander, arms held high. "Now what?" he asked.

"I should shoot you," Ly said.

Defiantly staring at Ly, Byrnes said, "You should."

Ly waved the pistol at Byrnes. He said, "Sit. Drop your arms. That would be ironic, since tonight I was going to let you participate in the Tet celebration. Your country is defeated. We expect all prisoners to be exchanged."

"Will that include me?"

"No longer. You have tried to murder one of my men. You must pay for that crime," Ly said. "I assume a year or two of hard labor in a work battalion would be appropriate. Don't you?"

Byrnes shook his head. He said, "My country's Military Code of Conduct requires that we try to escape. Article III says: 'If I am captured I will continue to resist by all means available. I will make every effort to escape and aid others to escape. I will accept neither parole nor special favors from the enemy.'"

"My country learned about modern warfare from the Japanese and the French," Ly said. "The French made us slaves. No one except the communists would help us throw off that yoke. The Japanese thought that to surrender was to disgrace oneself. To them, and to us, prisoners are non-persons – cowards, too afraid to die for their country. They have displeased their ancestors and failed their comrades. Therefore we can use them in any manner we see fit, or dispose of them if they are a burden. The Japanese enslaved us during the war. It took five years to rid ourselves of the Japanese, ten more to dispense with the French. Now we are trying to liberate your American puppets in the south. It has not been easy, almost twenty years, and there is more fighting to come. But we can finally see victory in our future. If you survive, you may see freedom again one day, too." Ly waved the pistol in the direction of the camp. Byrnes walked, hands by his side, to the camp and the bamboo cage. The beatings resumed.

CHAPTER 25

"Will you stay for dinner?" Wolfe asked Kayla Anne. She parked the Prius in the garage, having picked him up at the airport.

"Is that a subtle way of asking me if I'll cook your supper?" she asked.

"Yes and no," Wolfe said. "You are a much better chef than I'll ever be, but if you want me to rush you back to Flagler, I'll get fast food somewhere or go to a small restaurant. St. Augustine's full of restaurants, as you well know."

"I don't have a date tonight, and I've managed to stay on top of my Psychology assignments. If you promise to get me back to school before class at 8:00 a.m. tomorrow, I suppose I can stick around." She followed her father through the garage, past the washing machine and dryer in the laundry room and into the great room. "You can bring me up to date on your odyssey. Did you have any luck?"

Wolfe continued through the great room, and dropped his carry-on bag on his unmade bed. He returned to the dining room table and sat down. Pointing to another chair for his daughter to sit in, he absent-mindedly spread the pile of mail and newspapers she had collected for him while he had been away. "Yeah. Kind of," he said.

The doorbell rang. Wolfe stood. "Wonder who that could be," he said. Opening the door, he found a short, thin, gray-haired woman of

Indian descent about his age standing on the covered porch. "Dr. Wolfe," she said. "Welcome home. I brought you some cookies." The woman handed him a Tupperware box full of chocolate chip cookies. "My name and phone number are on a piece of paper inside. Call me when you finish and I'll come get the container." She winked seductively at Wolfe.

"Oh, Mrs. —"

"Brooker. Fran Brooker. You can call me Fran."

"Why, this is very sweet of you, Fran, but I can't accept —"

"Sure you can, Dad," Kayla Anne said from behind him. "Hello, Mrs. Brooker, I'm Kayla Anne Wolfe, his daughter. This is awfully kind of you. Would you like to come in for a minute?" Wolfe began shaking his head.

"Oh, I'm sorry, I can't now. Maybe later," the woman said. "I have other errands to run. Let me know when you finish the cookies."

"He will," Kayla Anne said.

"Thanks," Wolfe said. He nudged his daughter inside and closed the door behind them. Through the small side window he gave Brooker a quick wave and watched her make her way down the sidewalk.

"Quick. Go close the garage door," Wolfe said to his daughter.

"I thought you did that already," she said.

"If I had, I would not be holding a plastic container with cookies in it," Wolfe said. "Quickly, before anyone else sees that it's open."

Kayla Anne walked through the laundry room again, opened the door to the garage, and hit the button that controlled the big door. As it came down, she saw two other women make U-turns in the driveway and walk away from the house.

"What was that all about?" she asked her father when she rejoined him at the table. "It was kind of weird, like the *Night of the Living Dead*. They seemed to be attracted to your house while the garage door was open."

"I can explain," Wolfe said. "It started in The Villages, the town between Ocala and Leesburg. It's another retirement community. It's huge, though. More than 120,000 people live there, putting it in the top 20 of Florida communities by population count."

"I've heard of it. What started there? Giving cookies to neighbors who have been out of town?"

Wolfe laughed. "Not quite. It turns out that if you are single, widowed, widower, whatever, and you leave your garage door open in The Villages, you are inviting company. *Intimate company*. They have the highest rate of STDs per capita in the state."

"You're not single," Kayla Anne said.

"They haven't seen your mother in months," Wolfe said. "I'm sure there are rumors. Old folks love gossip."

Appalled, Kayla Anne scrunched up her face. "Old people have sex? And STDs? Ugh," she said.

"Yeah, I know," Wolfe said. "My tastes run to younger women." He made as big a leer as possible "Know what I mean? Like your mother, that is."

Kayla Anne pulled a throw pillow from the couch next to the table and swatted her father on the shoulder with it. "You old goat. I'm going to have to talk with Mom soon."

Wolfe smiled. "Wish you would. It gets lonely here at times," he said.

***

The next morning Wolfe woke late. He had not gotten much sleep. After dropping Kayla Anne at her dorm about 10:00 p.m., he had returned home. Not being too tired, he had started sorting his mail. He had not intended to read it, only to recycle the advertisements and junk mail. There were a few bills and two first-class letters. Nothing from his wife. Junior had sent him a postcard from Costa Rica with a picture of a huge iguana on the front. 'See you soon. Love, Ben,' his son had written on the back. *You'll have to practice that handwriting,* Wolfe told his son mentally. *It's much too legible for you to become a physician, Addison Benjamin Wolfe, Junior.*

After mulling over the thought of Ben becoming a physician, Wolfe found himself beset by thoughts of his own career. He didn't necessarily want his son to follow his example, and, if he did, he certainly hoped his son wouldn't make the same mistakes. Then the list of his mistakes ran through his mind. Unable to sleep, Wolfe decided to scan the newspapers that had accumulated. In one paper, a brief article reported that the police had apprehended the man who had injected potassium into the corpse at Flagler Hospital. Several people had recognized the man from security videos and had contacted the police after the images appeared on the evening news. Excited by that discovery, Wolfe slept fitfully the remainder of the night.

He re-read the article the next morning, which was how he ended up in Gainesville, Florida, looking for some coffee and lunch in the cafeteria of the Malcom Randall VA Medical Center.

After a brief meal and two cups of coffee, Wolfe made his way to the psychiatric unit of the hospital, a sprawling unit that occupied an entire floor. Exiting the elevator, Wolfe found himself in front of a desk manned by a hospital employee.

"Good morning," the young woman said. "How may I help you?"

Knowing doctors received more attention from staff than visitors, Wolfe said. "I'm Dr. Wolfe. I'm here to see Chief Fulton. Ralph Fulton, from Jacksonville."

The young woman looked at her computer screen and clicked the mouse a few times. "I'm sorry, Dr. Wolfe. Mr. Fulton isn't scheduled for any consults today. Are you a psychiatrist?"

Wolfe shook his head and smiled. "No. I'm here as a visitor. He and I served in the navy together in Vietnam. He is allowed to have visitors, isn't he? I called earlier."

Looking at her monitor again, the woman nodded. "Yes. You can see him in a little while. A St. Johns County sheriff's deputy is taking a deposition from him at the moment. Please have a seat. I'll let you know when you may speak with him."

Wolfe sat in a comfortable chair in the waiting room near a large window. Sunlight filtered into the room through sheer curtains, warming the chair. With a full belly and his lack of sleep, Wolfe's coffee failed to keep him awake. The next thing he knew, the lady at the desk called to him.

"Mr. Wolfe. Mr. Wolfe. You may see Mr. Fulton now."

"Sorry," Wolfe said, standing to stretch. "Didn't sleep well last night." He saw a green-uniformed deputy and a female court reporter, who towed a roll-around case the size of a carry-on bag, step onto the elevator. Wolfe approached the desk. The woman handed him a plastic clip-on pass.

The door behind her opened slowly. "Through the recreation area. Turn right into the hallway. Third room on the left," she said, as Wolfe entered the locked unit. The door swung silently closed. An audible click announced the relocking of the heavy steel door.

CHAPTER 26

Wolfe wove his way between the mental patients who sat, wandered, or stood in the open area. Some appeared normal, others far from it, talking to themselves and/or gesturing to unseen acquaintances. He turned right in the first hallway and stopped at the third door on the left. The door stood open. A tall, thin, vaguely familiar black man with reddish gray hair and a bushy, gray, handlebar mustache and beard lay in the single bed staring at the ceiling. He wore khaki pants, a sleeveless undershirt, and sandals. Tattoos covered both forearms and deltoids, but their pigments had faded and they were difficult to interpret on his dark skin. The room smelled of disinfectant.

From the hallway, Wolfe said, "Chief Fulton?"

The man sat up in the bed and looked at Wolfe. "Are you the physical therapist?" he asked, swinging his feet to the floor.

"No," Wolfe said. "I'm Addison Wolfe. You and I were on *Oriskany* together in 1967. In Vietnam." Wolfe had a vague memory of a younger version of this man, one of two sailors in dungarees and chambray shirts who sat at a table in front of a cash box. A chief, dressed in khakis with a thick wad of cash in his hands, stood behind him. "Weren't you in disbursements? S-4?"

A smile creased the retired chief's face. "Why, yes. Yes, I was. Where did you work? I don't remember you, but we have all changed in the last forty years. No?" He expressed himself with a mild southern accent. Atlanta, if Wolfe remembered correctly. He laughed a hearty laugh. "At least I have."

"Hangar deck," Wolfe said. "I was on *Oriskany* from June until December, 1967. Went to *Ranger* after *Oriskany* left Hong Kong."

Fulton's face clouded immediately. His voice dropped in pitch. He clipped his words. "So, you knew Byrnes," he said. "Is that why you are here? To kill me?"

"Whoa," Wolfe said, puzzled. "Hang on, Chief. I'm not going to kill anyone." He held his hands out to show Fulton they were empty. "I want to talk with you about Jimmy."

"He's killed my friends, you know?"

"Who killed your friends, Chief?" Wolfe asked, confusion worsening.

"Byrnes. Serves us right, of course; we deserve it," Fulton said. He leaned into the wall next to the bed and crossed his legs, Indian style in front of him on the bed. Lifting his head, he stared at the corner of the ceiling next to the window. Wolfe watched him cock his head, as if he listened to a noise, or voice. "I thought he'd come himself, not send an assassin."

"Mind if I sit?" Wolfe asked, pulling a chair from under the desk inside the room to his left. He sat without waiting for Fulton to reply. "I don't think Jimmy could have killed your friends. It looks like he's been dead for a while, killed by an airstrike in South Vietnam in 1970."

"Not true. I've seen him myself. He killed my friends."

"When did you see him?" Wolfe asked, hoping to dispense with the man's delusion and move on to other questions.

"About two weeks ago. He told me to put medication in Clemons's intravenous."

"And where did you see him?" Wolfe asked.

"He was in the emergency room. I saw him as I entered the hospital to visit Clemons. He pointed out the syringe lying on the red cart. Said I would die next if I didn't do what he said," Fulton said. He appeared to be more agitated the longer they talked about Byrnes.

"Okay," Wolfe said, "I'll concede you might have seen him. Why would he task you with pushing medicine into Clemons's intravenous?"

"Payback."

"Payback for what?" Wolfe asked.

Fulton dropped his head. No longer staring at the corner of the ceiling. He stared in his lap. Wolfe thought he saw a tear fall onto the bed sheet. He said, "We beat him up, threw him overboard."

"We?" Wolfe said.

"Deke Jameson's gang. The guys who embezzled from supply. We had leather flight jackets we sold, tool sets, ice cream, clothing. You name it; we trafficked in it at some point during Vietnam. At one point we had a hundred M-16s for sale. But we never got into drugs. No heroin. We were clean, man."

Suddenly, Wolfe understood. He said, "So when Byrnes caught Jameson red-handed stealing laundry, he interrupted a large smuggling operation. And put a dent in your profits?"

Anger swelled in Fulton's throat. He clenched his teeth briefly, jaw muscles bulging. Taking a deep breath, he relaxed and said, "Jameson couldn't keep from showing off. He told someone that no one would report him, no matter how blatant he was. He had too much power. What a laugh. Hell, we had to lay low until the cruise ended. He probably cost us a half million dollars over those six months," he said.

"I guess you had reason to be furious," Wolfe said. "If Jimmy survived the beating and being tossed off the ship, he also probably had grounds for revenge. *If* he survived. Why are you so sure he killed your friends?"

Fulton stood suddenly. He marched toward Wolfe, made a sharp turn to his left, and opened a closet, from which he pulled a scrapbook. He laid the six-inch thick, red-leather book on the desk in front of Wolfe. Orange, nylon, navy shot line bound the front and back covers of the book together. "It's all in here," Fulton said, handing the book to Wolfe. He returned to his bed and to staring at the ceiling.

Wolfe opened the loose-leaf book. The names of the men listed on the inside of the front cover were the same as those listed on the last page in Clemons's black book. Next to each name was a date and a page number. Clemons's date was the most recent. Wolfe turned to the page indicated. He found three newspaper articles about Clemons's death, including one Wolfe had found where the police had detained Fulton.

The clippings about Holden's death in Puget Sound mirrored Chief Noble's recollections. Holden, then a first-class petty officer in administration, left a bar late one night and had driven toward the ferry on his way to Seattle. Another vehicle had crossed the centerline of the highway and smashed into his car. He died at the scene. The owner of the other car had reported it stolen two days prior. Blood found in the second vehicle did not belong to the automobile's owner. The police never found the second driver. They assumed he was intoxicated, had survived, and walked home. Or, he had died in the woods trying to get home. They did not recover a body. They were unaware of any missing persons at that time. The hit and run case remained open and unsolved.

On October 12, 2000, Chief Petty Officer George Little died on the

USS *Cole* in Yemen when terrorists exploded a bomb near the ship. The guided missile destroyer had been refueling in Aden. Fulton had collected fourteen pages of newspaper and magazine clippings concerning the bombing. Little had been scheduled to retire at the end of the cruise, after nearly thirty five years on active duty.

Deke Jameson had the misfortune to be in a liquor store during a robbery that went sour. Held as a hostage, he died of a gunshot wound when one of the thieves used him as a shield and attempted to flee the scene. Ten pages were devoted to clippings about his death. Most of them mentioned the fact that the San Francisco Police Department did not recover the weapon that fired the bullet that killed him, even though they detained all the suspects in the robbery. An investigation cleared the police of any liability in Jameson's death.

Wolfe closed the scrapbook. "This is your proof that Byrnes is killing your friends?" he said. He realized that Fulton suffered from some form of mental disease, possibly Post Traumatic Stress Disorder, a psychosis, or both. Still, Fulton should have recognized that these men died from accidents. "These look like accidents."

"Byrnes designed them to look like accidents," Fulton said.

"Sailors who drink a lot of alcohol, frequent bars, and drive while intoxicated, die from accidents more often than sober civilians," Wolfe said. "Servicemen put themselves in harm's way. They die in combat, like Little in Yemen and Montgomery in Kuwait." He doubted the logic impressed Fulton. The man might never be rational again.

"No! No!" Fulton yelled. "Byrnes did this. Can't you see? Are you all blind?" He jumped from his bed and began to swing his fists at Wolfe.

Wolfe blocked the blows and backed out of the room without retaliating. Fulton followed him, ineffectual blows blocked by Wolfe's arms. "Nurse!" Wolfe yelled.

Two large muscular men in white pants and shirts came to his rescue. They restrained Fulton and walked him back into his room. "Sorry, sir," one of them said. "His medication seems to be wearing off. Maybe you should have a seat the waiting room." Wolfe agreed.

CHAPTER 27

"Is it okay if I put you on speaker phone, Mr. Young?" Wolfe asked the man on the other end of the telephone conversation. "That would make it easier to take notes." *And to keep the phone plugged in for recharging,* he thought.

"Sure, Dr. Wolfe," said the other man. "Can you speak a little louder?"

"I'll try," Wolfe said. "It may be the poor reception here where I live. If it's too bad, I'll drive to Starbucks, or somewhere else so we can talk more easily."

"Actually, you sound better on speaker," Young said. "Call me Steph, though. In your email, you said Tammy Byrnes gave you my name and email address?"

Wolfe nodded, circling Young's name on a nearly blank sheet of paper. The man was the first to agree to talk about Byrnes. "Okay, Steph, call me Addy. That's right. Her last name is Kimura, now, though. Tammy Kimura. She said you and Jim were friends? Is that true?"

Young laughed. The speaker option on Wolfe's cell phone made the laugh sound tinny. "Yeah. I suspect I was his only real friend at Hammond High School, with the exception of Emily."

"The girlfriend he broke up with after he left Annapolis?"

"They were pretty much broken up before he dropped out," Young said. "He came home one weekend sophomore year on crutches, leg in a cast. You could tell something was eating at him. Normally he had a huge smile on his face. *The inscrutable Oriental* we called him. Always smiling. You never knew what he was thinking, though. Don't get me wrong, I'm not being racist. My mother is also Japanese. My father was in the air force. Met her after the war."

"So you had a lot in common with Jimmy, Steph," Wolfe said.

"Yeah," Young said. "Except my father stayed put a lot more. He had four- and five-year tours in SAC and the Pentagon. I had been at Hammond all four years. Jimmy showed up at the beginning of senior year. He didn't expect to finish high school there, either. He thought his family would be moving between semesters. But his mom chose to stay in Alexandria when the navy transferred his father. I guess they had some marital problems."

"I knew him as an enlisted man in the navy, after he left Annapolis," Wolfe said. "What was he like in high school?"

"He had a lot of inner dragons, not demons like Caucasians," Young said, laughing again. "Your first impression of him was he had a chip on his shoulder, or he was arrogant. But he wasn't. He was very, very reserved, even for a Japanese. Except for Emily and me, I doubt anyone ever saw him open up, relax, and be himself."

"Was Emily Japanese, too?" Wolfe asked.

"No. She was short like an Asian. But she was a natural blonde, with a dynamite body. And she was smart. Editor of the school newspaper her senior year, the year after Jim and I graduated. Even she had a hard time getting him to open up at first. She traded her kisses for his information, I believe."

"Because he was new or because he was half-Japanese?" Wolfe asked. "He had no problems with speaking his mind in the navy. On the ship, some people may not have liked his honesty or candor, though. And when he drank he could really get wound up."

Young thought for a minute before continuing. Wolfe heard him talk to someone in the background. He continued, "He didn't drink in high school. His mother kept a tight rein on him. If you went to visit his home, and you were of Japanese descent like me, you saw him bow to his parents. His sisters bowed to him and their parents. All Japanese are made aware of their station in life. It's part of being Japanese, like eating pizza is part of being American. Captain Byrnes didn't go to church. Mrs. Byrnes took the kids to temple. She talked with the monks and Buddhist priests a lot.

"His dad instilled a lot of Annapolis in him, I'm sure, but his mother wanted him to be a Samurai. They even had two Samurai swords that hung over the mantel place. One was his father's. On graduation from the Academy, they were going to give him the other."

"Did you play football with him?"

"No. Thank goodness," Young said.

"Why *thank goodness*?"

"They said he was a demon on the field. He had played offensive and defensive lineman in some small high schools as his dad moved around the country. Playing against larger guys, he learned how to hit really hard and to take punishment and protect himself in collisions. I think he only weighed 135-145 pounds as a senior, too. On our team, they made him a cornerback. I rowed crew, but I used to hear the other players in the locker room complain about how hard he hit in practice. They went 6-4 that year. Hammond seldom had winning seasons."

"Did you two hear many racial slurs, Steph? He seemed to attract bigots in the navy," Wolfe said.

Young paused, then admitted, "There were some rednecks at school. I assume he converted all those on the football team." Young laughed. "It's hard to insult a guy who lays you out flat, especially if you outweigh him by fifty pounds. Some kid in homeroom called him a *gook* once. The football team held a rally at that student's locker later that day. They bent up the door to his locker so badly that the school had to replace it. The kid kept his mouth shut from then on."

"Was he comfortable in high school? His sister talks as if they both hated America."

"You have to understand there are great cultural differences between the United States and Japan," Young said. "Jimmy referred to us as mutts. He and his sister interpreted for their mother until her English improved. They grew up quickly. Their father was rarely home. They saw their role as protecting their mother and little sister. It was a burden, I'm sure.

"The Japanese are a monolithic culture. They revere the emperor, worship him as a god. My mother and his mother tried to impart Japanese cultures to us. My mother insisted that I was put on this Earth to make her miserable. I'm sure his mother felt the same way. We both rebelled at home. But neither of us felt comfortable enough to dissent at school. We were different. Different stands out. American high schools are intimidating, even for full-blooded American kids. And full-blooded Japanese are yin-yang anyway: loyal vs. treacherous; non-accessible vs. accessible; militaristic vs. aesthetic; submissive vs. resentful. You get the idea. We didn't fit in, in either culture. I still don't."

"I appreciate you taking the time to talk with me, Steph," Wolfe said. "I'm sure I'll think of more questions as I dig into this a little more."

"What, exactly, are you investigating?" Young asked.

"Initially, I was interested in finding out why someone would use Jimmy's name while trying to kill a dead man. I told you about that in the email. Then I wanted to make certain his family knew what a fine young man he was when I knew him. Then some asshole CIA agent told me I shouldn't have an interest in MIAs from the Vietnam War. That made me mad as hell. I may have to travel all the way to Vietnam to find out for myself what happened to him. I'm sorry I didn't know twenty years ago what I know now. By the way, have you kept in touch with Emily Rose?"

"She is Emily Thornton, or was until she divorced the jerk. Max Thornton was a star basketball player in her class at Hammond. They got married after college, had two or three kids and a divorce about ten years later. I expect she has remarried," Young said. He paused. "You know, I believe I know someone who has her email address. I have your email address; I'll send you all the information I can dig up. I'm curious myself as to what she's doing these days. Good talking to you, Doctor."

"Addy's fine," Wolfe reminded him. "Thanks, Steph. Keep in touch. Bye."

"Bye, Addy."

CHAPTER 28

"Your coffin will have to be bigger than that, Con co," Tran Hien said to Byrnes.

"Am I building mine this time, Corporal Hein?" Byrnes asked.

"Of course not," Tran said, smiling. "We need too many to let you rest."

Byrnes had been with the prisoner detail for over a year in 1974. He knew from listening to the guards that they were located in a forest near Thanh Hoa about 160 kilometers, or 100 miles, south of Hanoi. Not that he wanted to go to Hanoi. There were no more American prisoners in Hanoi. They had departed and been repatriated in the United States weeks before Byrnes had been marched into this camp. He had arrived along with a hundred other prisoners, mostly South Vietnamese, but also some Korean and Chinese captives.

Byrnes had been aware of a group of Caucasians in the prison camp and had tried to communicate with them when the guards' attention was elsewhere. Given his Asian appearance, they, like Rhodes, took him for a North Vietnamese plant. Byrnes thought the men could have been American or Australian. Shortly after he tried to make contact, they disappeared from camp. About a week later, their heads returned to the encampment on long poles. The NVA planted the poles at the gated entrance to the camp. The rotting flesh peeled from the skulls over several months: a warning to the remaining prisoners that escape attempts were futile and fatal.

If there was one redeeming value to the work battalion, it was that

Byrnes at last received enough nourishment. Starving men had no strength for the physical labor required of them. The prisoners received all the rice they could eat, plus bananas and wild fowl. A guard had been designated to hunt game animals to supplement the protein that the guards and prisoners received. The camp had its own vegetable garden with sweet potatoes, corn, cabbage, and pumpkins tended by prisoners. From a nearby river a prisoner detail caught fish daily. Byrnes had even developed a taste for nuoc mam. No longer on a starvation diet, he regained some weight and strength. Chopping down trees or sawing wood all day burned most of those calories, but also rebuilt muscle. Physically, he could have been in the best shape of his life. He and the remaining prisoners worked to turn an entire pine forest into coffins.

"How is your leg?" Tran asked.

"Until last month I would not have believed in acupuncture," Byrnes said. "That and the herbal medicine seem to have healed it completely. No more swelling. No more pain. Does that mean I will go back to using an ax on the trees?"

"Don't you like cutting boards better than felling trees?" Tran asked Byrnes.

"I miss walking through the forest," Byrnes said.

"Do you miss the danger?"

"If you mean the tigers," Byrnes said, "falling trees, tree limbs, and careless use of axes killed more men than the tigers. I only saw one. One of the guards injured two prisoners when he shot at it. And because he wounded it, they had to send a patrol after it to make certain it didn't return looking for human meals."

"True," Tran said. "And there is danger in this work, too. The saw you are sharpening or the wood you are cutting could cut or pierce your skin."

Byrnes nodded. He used a stick to measure one of the floor planks for the next coffin. There were no measuring tapes or power saws. Marks on a long stick gave him the dimensions of the typical coffin. Just as in Moscow under communist rule there was one automobile factory and one automobile design, in Vietnam there was one coffin factory and one standard design. If a dead soldier didn't fit in his coffin, the undertaker made him fit. Byrnes suspected his head would sit between his legs, if he did, indeed, take his final rest in one of the work battalion's creations.

Byrnes began to suspect Tran had something on his mind. Usually the guards wandered around camp, occasionally yelling, but mostly prodding the prisoners to work, not goof off or gossip. It was unusual for one to stay in the same spot for long. "When you finish cutting that plank, you need to report to the company clerk," Tran said.

Byrnes stopped marking the wood. He stared at Tran. Although Tran was a guard and had an AK-47 slung over his shoulder, he did not return Byrnes's gaze. Whenever a prisoner reported to the clerk, bad things could happen. "Do you know why?" Byrnes asked.

Tran turned his back to Byrnes. "Keep working," he said quietly, his eyes searching the rest of the camp. "Pretend we are not talking."

"Okay," Byrnes said. He finished marking the plank. Then he picked up his handsaw and a small file. Peering closely at the saw blade, he took the file to one tooth. The scraping noise masked their conversation. "What's going on?"

"The ceasefire has given us time to find and bury the dead. This camp will close soon," Tran said. He lit a cigarette and stared in the distance, watching as many men struggled to roll a portion of a large pine tree trunk into camp on two two-wheeled carts. The first two men tried to steer the leading cart by pulling on ropes.

Byrnes smelled the potent thuoc lao tobacco from the cigarette rolled by the guard. "What will happen to the prisoners?" Byrnes asked.

"Some will be released. Their time is up. Some have been re-educated. They will become agents for us in the south," Tran said, blowing smoke from his nose and mouth.

"Not me, though." Byrnes said. Although he had worked as hard as every other prisoner had, he had resisted re-education. The NVA had not been able to turn him against the United States.

"You and about ten others are going to join the Van Kieu, who we call Bru, when they deliver the coffins," Tran said. "The forest people have lost a lot of men. They need help making the delivery. I don't know if they are as liberal as our camp commander. He is smart enough to realize that starving, sick men cannot accomplish the goals set by generals in Hanoi."

"When will the Bru arrive?" Byrnes asked.

"Soon."

Two days later, with the heaviest of the recently constructed coffins strapped to his back, Byrnes joined a long line of shorter, darker men climbing out of the forest into the mountains along a trail leading south and west. From the air, it would appear that a long line of wooden boxes walked south on men's legs, not unlike ants carrying grains of rice. The NVA had no roads or trucks that would penetrate this forest. If it had, the communist government would not have wasted the petrol to run those vehicles in order to deliver coffins. There was a war yet to win.

Byrnes understood almost none of the Bru language. Although treated passably well for a prisoner, he found himself chained by one ankle to a tree each night. Exhausted, he realized the guards wasted their time; he scarcely moved once he lay his burden down. In addition to the sixty pounds of casket he toted seven to ten miles per day, he had to haul his own water, and the shackle and chain.

A mule lugged bags of rice and water for the delivery patrol as well as one coffin. Byrnes pitied the animal. Every man received the same size portion of rice and pork at breakfast and again at the end of the day. Most men slept in their burdens, the flat, soft pinewood being more comfortable than the rocks and tree roots along the trail.

One month later, Byrnes and the Bru trudged into Khe Ve, North Vietnam, one hundred eighty miles northwest of Hue, South Vietnam. American aircraft had bombed the once pretty village of Khe Ve heavily. Villagers lived in makeshift shelters in the woods, far from the center of the hamlet, now a ghost town of shattered buildings.

Children babbled and ran alongside the multitude of NVA, Laotians, Cambodians, Thais, and prisoners. Their hands out, the street urchins tried to sell candy or cigarettes to the men in trucks, on bicycles, in beat-up motor cars, and on foot. Most soldiers ignored the waifs. Others slapped or kicked at the pests. Old men and women worked at filling bomb craters with short shovels.

The babble of languages Byrnes heard in the NVA camp mixed together in a cacophony of unintelligible sound. He and the other prisoners helped each other and the Bru stack the coffins under a huge camouflage net. He estimated there were a thousand caskets hidden under the net awaiting their eternal occupants. *Why camouflage?* he wondered. *Were the Vietnamese afraid someone would bomb their coffins?*

After unloading the caskets, the forest people assembled into a unit and trekked north out of camp, leaving Byrnes and the other prisoners behind. NVA guards, holding their ubiquitous AK-47s, surrounded Byrnes and six other prisoners who had survived the forced march with the coffins. It was almost a relief for Byrnes to hear spoken Vietnamese again, until the corporal in charge of the guards told them their journey had barely begun. After three days to rest, they would be taking ammunition south for the *final battle.*

CHAPTER 29

Notorious for being able to sleep anywhere, through most disturbances, Wolfe never heard the intruder enter his home through the front door after breaking the side window and unlocking the deadbolt. The prowler managed to disturb Wolfe by tripping over a stool when he entered the bedroom in which Wolfe slept. Instantly fully awake, Wolfe rolled over. "Lisa? Uh, Jennifer?" he said, mixing up the names of his first and present wife. Reaching up he tapped the base of his bedside light three times, nearly blinding himself.

Chief Ralph Fulton lay sprawled on the floor next to Wolfe's bed, a pistol in his hand. Quickly rising to his hands and knees, he struggled to get to his feet.

Uncertain of Fulton's intentions, Wolfe flung himself from the bed and landed on the chief, knocking the wind out of both men. Wolfe grabbed Fulton's right wrist and hand with both of his hands. He kept the weapon pointed away from him and Fulton.

Fulton squeezed the trigger to the gun. It exploded with a loud thunderclap, making Wolfe's ears ring. The bullet slammed into the wall under the bed. Ignoring Fulton's left hand, which clawed at his head and neck, Wolfe bent Fulton's wrist back until the psychiatric patient screamed in pain and dropped the pistol. "I'm too old for this," Wolfe said and punched the retired navy chief in the stomach. "And if I'm too old, so are you."

Fulton collapsed onto the floor in a seated position, legs sprawled wide. Wolfe sat on the bed pointing the weapon at him, catching his breath. "What's going on, Chief? What the hell are you thinking? And why aren't you in Gainesville in the VA Hospital?"

Fulton shook his head, rolled to his knees, and stood in front of Wolfe. "I want you to take me to Byrnes," he said.

"Byrnes is dead," Wolfe said. "I told you that yesterday."

From his trouser pocket, Fulton pulled a switchblade. He pushed a button on the handle and the knife blade swung open. "You're hiding him," Fulton said. He pointed the knife at Wolfe. "I'll cut you if you don't take me to him."

"One step in my direction and I'll shoot you," Wolfe said. "Put the knife down. Now!"

"Dad, what's all the ruckus about," a sleepy Kayla Anne said, wiping her eyes as she entered the bedroom. "There's broken glass in –"

Fulton whirled to face Kayla Anne and raised the knife to attack this new threat. "Shit," Wolfe said, and pulled the trigger on the pistol. The bullet hit Fulton in the right shoulder blade. Fulton and Kayla screamed at the same time, but Fulton dropped the knife and fell to his knees holding his right arm. "Stay there, KayLan," Wolfe said. "Don't come any closer to this crazy man. Better yet, go back to your room; get your cell phone; go outside; find some reception; and call 911. Put some shoes on if there is broken glass in the hallway."

The ambulance arrived before the police did, but only by minutes. The paramedics refused to enter Wolfe's room until he surrendered the weapon. He refused to do that until a sheriff's deputy arrived and secured it. It took thirty minutes to evaluate Fulton, start an intravenous line, and put a bandage over the oozing bloody hole in his right shoulder. The .22 caliber bullet hadn't had the power to exit, so the medics assumed it was still in Fulton's shoulder, or possibly in his lung. His vital signs seemed stable. With the patient strapped onto the stretcher, a cardiac monitor attached to his chest, and oxygen running into the green mask on his face, the paramedics and one deputy loaded him into the ambulance. The same deputy rode in the back of the ambulance with the patient.

By the time the second deputy had finished taking a statement from both Wolfe and his daughter, Wolfe could see the glow of dawn peeking through the curtains. "Want some coffee?" Wolfe asked.

"Thank you, no," the young officer said. "I'll be on my way. Someone may call you later today to get more information if we need it. Are you sure you are okay?" The deputy directed his question to Kayla Anne, who seemed composed in spite of the excitement.

166

"I'm used to blood and guts," Kayla said to the deputy. "Dad took me to ERs and urgent cares on *Take Your Daughter to Work* days." Shifting her gaze to her father, she added, "I'm not going back to bed. Can you take me back to the dorm, Dad. I do have class today, although I doubt I'll be able to concentrate."

"Sure, honey," Wolfe said. "Officer, would you do me a favor?"

"If I can, sir."

"If you find out how Chief Fulton got out of the VA hospital, will you let me know?" Wolfe asked.

"I will. Have a good day, sir, ma'am." The deputy pushed the chair back from the dining room table and stood. He picked up his hat, and left.

"He's cute," Kayla said. "Suppose he'd fix parking tickets for me?"

"Seemed too intelligent to get involved with a woman who wanted to involve him in fraud," Wolfe said, winking at his daughter. "If you thought your mother had a hard time having a doctor for a husband, then you don't want to marry a police officer. Let me get my shoes and I'll take you to Flagler."

As the Prius left The Cascades at World Golf Village, Wolfe's phone beeped four times. It let him know that he had gotten close enough to the microwave tower that his cell phone could receive messages. He handed the phone to his daughter. "Can you check those messages for me?" he asked.

After several minutes, and just seconds before Wolfe pulled off I-95 onto State Route 16, she said, "They're all from the same guy, a Drew Jaskolski. He says he has some information for you about a Chief Fulton breaking out of the VA hospital psyche unit in Gainesville, and more information on Jimmy Byrnes. Is that the guy you knew in the navy?"

"Anything else?" asked Wolfe, grimacing at the thought of speaking with CIA Agent Jaskolski again.

"Yeah. He wants you to call as soon as you get the message. Want me to return the call?"

"No. The guy is a jerk," Wolfe said. "He can wait until I get you back to school, eat breakfast, take a shower, repair the window, take a nap...you get the picture."

"Okay." Kayla dropped the cell phone into the cup holder. Wolfe stopped on Malaga Street in front of the dorm. Kayla Anne exited the car. "See you, Dad. I love you. Drive carefully." She came to the driver's door and gave him a kiss.

Wolfe said, "Love you, too, honey." He pointed up the street a block.

"I'll be in Georgie's Diner eating a short stack of pancakes for the next thirty minutes if you need me for anything. At least I'll have phone reception there."

"Okay, Pops," Kayla said. She crossed the street carefully and disappeared into one of three identical dorms, former Florida East Coast Railway buildings.

Agent Drugi Jaskolski sat down in front of Wolfe at the precise time his order arrived: three pancakes, two over hard eggs, four sausage links and a large glass of orange juice. "Get my message?" he asked.

Not too surprised at the agent's presence, Wolfe responded. "Yeah, did you get mine?"

"You sent me a message?"

"It was sent telepathically," Wolfe said. "I hate using that language in front of my daughter."

Jaskolski laughed, a brief guttural laugh. "Funny," he said. "Is that a large enough orange juice for you? A lot of citric acid in there."

"Helps keep the kidney stones at bay," Wolfe said, taking a gigantic swig of the juice. "What do you want, Agent Jaskolski?"

"Call me Drew."

"Drop dead, Drew. And don't give me any more bull about MIAs being a national security secret," Wolfe said between swallows.

"But they are. My superiors would like to reason with you. Would you mind accompanying me to my vehicle?" The agent stood, pushed his chair under the table, and waved his arm in the direction of the front door.

"Yes, I would mind," Wolfe said. The room began to spin. Jaskolski's smile looked devious and he was out of focus.

"Yeah. I thought you'd say that," Jaskolski said. He motioned to the three men sitting in the booths on either side of Wolfe. Two men grabbed the physician under his arms and stood him up. They walked the wobbly, disoriented Wolfe to the front door. "He'll be all right," Jaskolski said to no one in particular as they left the diner, after he purposefully spilled Wolfe's orange juice and threw thirty dollars on the table.

Thirty-five minutes later, Kayla Anne Wolfe left her dorm for her class. She noticed her father's Prius still parked in front of Georgie's, but she was already late for class. She didn't stop to check on him.

CHAPTER 30

The NVA guards led Byrnes to a bicycle. To reduce its weight, the Vietnamese had removed the crank and pedals, chain, and fenders. The remainder appeared intact: two wheels, a frame, and handlebars. Hanging from the frame he found four wooden cases, two on each side. The cases held belts of machine gun ammunition. "Do not let the machine fall over," the guard said. "It will take three men to place it upright again." Blocks under the ammunition cases kept the frame vertical when at rest.

Byrnes put his left hand on an extension welded to the left side of the handlebar. His right hand he placed on another metal bar attached to the frame where the seat post had been, behind the first ammunition case. When ordered to, he rolled the bicycle forward. The guard picked up the blocks and put them in a pouch hanging from one of the cases. "Ready?" he asked.

Nodding, the American pushed the bicycle frame forward. Mud on the Ho Chi Minh Trail clung to the tires. The caravan of supplies joined a newly formed battalion of NVA soldiers marching south. The freshly trained soldiers were all in good spirits, prepared to win the final battle. Most were young men in their late teens or early twenties. Older, veteran soldiers made up their officer corps. The officers were weather-beaten, battle-hardened men, some with terrible scars, remnants of previous enthusiastic, young battalions. All had a faraway look in their eyes. Byrnes thought they seemed battle-weary, aged beyond their years. Many, he realized, had been enduring and practicing the art of war for ten to twenty years and probably represented the few lucky survivors among troops decimated by the war.

Although not supporting the total weight of the ammunition, as he had the coffin, it took Byrnes as much effort as shouldering the sixty-pound pine box to propel the bicycle forward. The convoy of reinforcements strung out over several miles. In addition there were a hundred-plus bicycles pushed by prisoners and conscripted porters from both North and South Vietnam.

Guards carried only rifles and their backpacks. They monitored the prisoners and conscripts who might desert, men at the tail end of the convoy. The effort required to march forward left little strength for talking. Conversations were few, and limited to downhill treks. "Where are we going?" Byrnes asked a guard before they started.

"There's a pass through the mountains at Mu Gia," the guard said, after seeing the jade Buddhist icon hanging around Byrnes's neck.

"How far is that?"

"About forty-five kilometers," the soldier said.

Twenty-seven miles, Byrnes thought. "How long will it take?" he asked.

"It's mostly uphill. Three or four days."

The trail at Mu Gia Pass was tortuous. Byrnes saw the rusting hulks of wrecked machines: trucks, motorcycles, artillery, and an occasional tank. Shattered rocks and trees, and the skeletal remains of dead animals – elephants, horses, buffalo, and possibly dogs – littered the sides of the trail near and in bomb craters. The NVA had presumably removed their dead comrades to the cache of caskets left behind.

Con voi is Vietnamese for elephant, Byrnes realized. He wondered at the term *convoy* in English and whether its meaning was coincidental to a long line of con voi carrying supplies. A dead elephant lay near the path, stench almost overwhelming. No one had bothered to saw off its small tusks. Visible through rotting flesh, the teeth of the elephant were massive grindstones.

"One at a time, Con co," a guard said, holding his hand out to stop Byrnes. He pulled the blocks from the pouch and propped up the bicycle. "Help the men in front of you." Byrnes joined three men pushing a bicycle loaded with sacks of rice up the steep muddy trail. Once over the crest, one man continued down the far side with the overloaded bike. The two other men helped Byrnes push his bicycle to the top of the hill. Digging his heels in, Byrnes kept the bike from running away, down the far side's slippery slope. The two men left him and joined the next cyclist.

On reaching Tchepone, Laos, after weeks of shouldering their cargo along jungle paths, through streams, across rivers, and up and down hills, the battalion commander ordered a rest. Byrnes heard grumbling among the younger NVA soldiers. The soldiers had carried their share of equipment in their backpacks: extra ammunition, RPG rounds, a spare uniform, their rifles, shovels, and bayonets, and three day's worth of food at a time. They complained bitterly, but quietly, about the political officers. Each cadre officer carried only a pistol and a small shoulder pack with cigarettes and other personal items. They didn't carry their own food. Instead they invited themselves to eat with different squads throughout the march, lessening the portions each man received. The idealism was wearing off. "Are these men going to march into battle with us?" one young man asked angrily.

"No," a combat officer said. He ordered the young man to remain silent on the subject of the political officers, his contempt for the cadre also palpable. "Keep your questions to yourself. The war is almost over. Their time will come."

During the rest stop, the battalion repaired trenches and tunnels along the side of the road. They also repaired and re-strung the camouflage netting hanging across the pathway. If American aircraft returned, the soldiers wanted to be prepared. The NVA soldiers inspected and cleaned weapons as necessary. Ambushes by the ARVN, Army of the Republic of Vietnam, remained a possibility. The way south appeared to be through dense jungle, with minimal, if any, paved roads or trails.

Three months after leaving North Vietnam, the battalion ended its march, arriving in South Vietnam by way of Laos and Cambodia. It stopped, regrouped, and then took its place alongside two entrenched NVA battalions. Officers arranged care for the injured and sick, distributed supplies and ammunition, ordered the building of new trenches and tunnels, and positioned lookouts. Not permitted to light fires to avoid detection by the enemy, the battalion had not boiled its water. Therefore it had had no tea in weeks. Bacteria that caused dysentery lived in the soldiers' water. The smell of feces was everywhere.

The other battalions had been in place for four months, awaiting orders to push north and east into Saigon. They were part of a pincer movement the NVA believed would soon crush the ARVN and capture Saigon. Already, Byrnes had heard rumors: tanks and NVA soldiers had crossed the DMZ into South Vietnam; they moved south along Highway 1 from Dong Ha toward Hue. The final battle had begun.

CHAPTER 31

Wolfe regained consciousness on a bed in a hotel or motel. A man sat next to him, pulling down the shirtsleeve of Wolfe's polo shirt. He felt a burning in his right deltoid. The man carefully recapped the needle on a syringe. "Works as advertised," the stranger said to another man. "He's awake already."

His head clearing rapidly, Wolfe sat up. He swung his legs over the left side of the double bed, where he faced another double bed, on which sat Drew Jaskolski and a third man. "Where am I?" Wolfe asked evenly, given his anger. He directed his next words at Jaskolski, "I believe kidnapping is a federal crime, asshole."

Mirth difficult to hide, Jaskolski smiled. "You weren't kidnapped, Dr. Wolfe. We arrested you. You have been detained for questioning." He pointed two fingers to the man sitting to the left of him, a tall man, darkly tanned or naturally swarthy skin color, white goatee, with a shaved head. "This is Peter Narang, my immediate supervisor. He would like to ask you some questions."

"We're not talking until I have a lawyer to represent me," Wolfe said.

"Lawyers are expensive," Narang said. "I can save you the cost of one. You are not going to be prosecuted for anything you say, unless you admit to shooting a court reporter last night. We assume Chief Fulton did that with the weapon you took from him and then used to shoot him."

"Why would he shoot the court reporter?" Wolfe asked. "And how did he get out of a locked psychiatric unit?"

Narang pursed his lips. He said, "We are investigating both of those things. As of right now, I have no answers for you."

"What do you want to ask me about?" Wolfe asked, "I may answer some questions, depending on the topic. What could you prosecute me for, anyway?"

Laughing, Narang said, "As Drew told you, we'd find something. Even if we didn't get a conviction, we could leave you destitute from legal bills. Your wife is already upset with your financial status, I believe. Imagine her chagrin if you were absolutely broke."

"Son of a –" Wolfe leaned forward on the bed and swung a fist at Narang.

Jaskolski caught the punch and spun Wolfe to the floor, twisting Wolfe's arm behind him. "Try to relax, Doc. Peter has a weird sense of humor. His point was you don't have to pay for a lawyer if you play along and answer some questions."

Over his shoulder and in considerable pain, Wolfe stared at the two men. "Okay. Let me go. But one more remark about my wife and you'll wish you hadn't made it."

Jaskolski slowly released Wolfe's arm and helped him stand and then sit again. He held both open hands out toward Wolfe. "Stay calm, Doc," he said, sitting again on the bed next to Narang.

Wolfe glared defiantly. Words came slowly, tersely, "What do you want to know?" he said, rubbing his shoulder.

"Okay then," Narang said, as if nothing had happened. "What is your interest in James T. Byrnes, III?"

"I already answered that question for Agent Jaskolski," Wolfe said. "Didn't he report my answer to you?"

"Let's pretend he didn't."

"Jimmy and I were in the navy together. We were good friends. I just found out he died," Wolfe said.

"So why go talk with his mother and sisters?" Narang asked.

"Like I told Agent Jaskolski, I went to express my condolences. And to tell them what a great guy and good friend Jimmy had been to me. Even though I was almost fifty years late."

"And why go see Colonel Rhodes? You didn't know him in the service," Narang said.

"Jimmy's sister said Rhodes was a POW with Jimmy. I wanted to hear the story myself," Wolfe said.

"Did you learn anything new?"

Wolfe stared at the men for a minute. "I think I did," he finally said.

Narang's left eyebrow elevated slightly. He frowned. "What was that?" he asked.

"Jimmy's what nowadays we call *a survivor*. Colonel Rhodes thought he died in a bombing raid. I'm not so sure. Somehow, he managed to survive a beating and being thrown overboard. It wouldn't surprise me if he lived through the airstrike, too," Wolfe said.

"I talked with Colonel Rhodes myself," Narang said. "I would be astonished if your friend survived."

"Then what am I here for? Why are you interfering with my attempts to find out what happened?"

"You applied to renew your passport recently," Narang said.

"Yeah. So what?" Wolfe said.

"Why?"

Wolfe looked at Narang carefully, trying to keep his anger under control. "My wife wanted me to go to Costa Rica with her. Bird watching."

"Why didn't you?"

"I have orthopedic problems: knees, back, shoulders. I decided I didn't want to hike around Costa Rica looking for birds," Wolfe said. "My son went in my place."

Narang held his hand out. Jaskolski pulled a passport from his inside coat pocket and laid it on Narang's hand. Narang handed the passport to Wolfe, who opened it and saw his own picture. As he shook his head at this government intrusion into his privacy and life, Wolfe heard Narang say, "Then you won't mind that we have removed SE Asia from the places you may visit using your passport. An attempt to go there will result in your arrest."

"On what charges?" Wolfe asked. "And that's breaking and entering, in addition to kidnapping."

"We'll think of something," Jaskolski said.

"Why? Is Jimmy still alive? In Vietnam? Or Laos? Or Cambodia? What the fuck is going on, if I should be so forward as to ask in polite French?"

Narang let out a slow sigh. His smile returned. He said, "I don't imagine your friend is still among the living, Dr. Wolfe. Most MIAs died instantaneously, their bodies blown into so many fragments that they couldn't be found. We know some were captured, tortured, and killed, or died of wounds or disease in captivity. It's been forty-six years since anyone saw Byrnes alive. Actuarially, he'd be an outlier, seventy years-old in a hostile, if not deadly, environment. Don't you agree?"

Wolfe bowed his head. He understood the logic. He didn't like it, but he appreciated it. "Maybe you're right," he said. "What's the harm in finding out? He's not the only MIA. I think Jaskolski told me there are still 1600, or more, from Vietnam alone."

Relaxing, Narang allowed his shoulders to droop. He intertwined his fingers around his knee. "You've heard of Bowe Bergdahl?"

Wolfe nodded. "The confused kid who left his post in Afghanistan, believing he could somehow reach a peace settlement with the Taliban?"

"Right," Narang said. "There were a number of servicemen in Vietnam who deserted, for whatever reason. A few may have thought they could affect the course of the war. Some may have been psychotic or drugged — there were a lot of illicit drugs used among the army's enlisted. Some may have thought they fought on the wrong side. We had reports of Americans siding with the NVA."

"Jimmy wouldn't do that," Wolfe said.

"You understand the Stockholm Syndrome, Doctor?"

"A hostage learning to like his captors? Yeah, I get that," Wolfe said. "It's one of the reasons I am trying to figure out exactly what kind of guy Jimmy was before he joined the navy. So far, I don't see him capitulating like that."

"Well, Washington doesn't want the MIAs found. If found, they don't want them repatriated. In addition, we have new wars going on now. There are missing soldiers all over the world, Doctor. The war on terrorism is world wide. It's World War III, in case you didn't notice. And it hasn't been without casualties or MIAs. If a few are alive and brought home, they might prove to be a huge embarrassment to the government. Like Bergdahl. Or they might be double agents. As for the Vietnam-era MIAs, what should we do with a traitor who comes home fifty years after the war has ended, Doctor? Hang him?"

"We didn't even hang all the convicted Japanese war criminals after World War II," Wolfe said. "Why would we hang our own people?"

"I can't say," Narang said. "If you want to continue investigating James T. Byrnes, III, I can't stop you. If you publicize what you find, I promise you, you'll end up in jail. If you attempt to visit SE Asia, the same is true. Understand?"

"Are we finished?" Wolfe asked.

"No," Jaskolski said. "We're not one hundred percent certain that Chief Fulton was responsible for the wounding of the court reporter. We're examining his contention that someone killed all his friends who participated in throwing Byrnes off the *Oriskany*. If you pursue your investigation, you may be putting your life at risk. We aren't going to protect you. You're on your own. Understand?"

Wolfe stood. He thought about throwing another punch at Narang or Jaskolski, but the pain in his shoulder precluded that. "Now, are we finished?" he said.

"Yes, sir." Narang said. He stood and offered his right hand to Wolfe. The doctor stared at it for several seconds, and then turned away without shaking it. "Jaskolski, do me a favor and drive the good doctor to his car."

Bill Yancey

CHAPTER 32

Byrnes and three other prisoner-porters sweated in the humid, hot dense jungle near the Mekong River delta. They had followed a North Vietnamese Army soldier along a barely visible trail to the position held by five battalions of NVA. Although he knew hundreds, if not thousands, of men surrounded him, Byrnes had great difficulty spotting them. Camouflaged, from foxholes, from trenches, and from tunnels men called to one another. "First company ready. Third squad ready. Pass the ammunition boxes."

A hand gripped Byrnes's ankle, almost pulling his foot out of his sandal made from the tread of a used tire. Startled, Byrnes looked down. The hand elongated into an arm. An NVA soldier stood in the shadows of a cave carved into the side of a deep trench. "Pass the ammunition boxes," he said again.

Byrnes knelt and lowered his box to the soldier. The other porters handed their boxes to Byrnes, who passed them on to the soldier, who passed them to invisible men, hidden deeper inside the dark cave. "Is that all of it?" the soldier asked.

Byrnes looked behind him. The three prisoners nodded. "That's all there is," Byrnes said.

"Okay. Go back north and get some more, in case this battle lasts longer than we think it will." The man laughed at his own joke and then spoke to the prisoners' guard. "We will be attacking the enemy's position shortly. I suggest you get as far away from here as possible, or drop into that shallow trench behind you until the assault is finished.

The enemy has mortars and artillery. We know they are running short of ammunition, but you don't want to be in the open if they use them."

Silently, the private in charge of the porter detail motioned them with his AK-47. Holding the rifle horizontally he herded the men into the smaller slit trench. When standing, the top of the trench came to the porters' waists. The men sat with backs to the muddy wall, heads below ground level. The NVA private sat on a log a short distance from the trench. He pulled a cigarette from his shirt pocket. Lighting the cigarette, he inhaled. The scream of a mortar shell falling to earth interrupted his smoke break. "Phao kich! *Incoming!*" many men yelled at the same time. Followed by, "Enemy soldiers!"

A whistling sound grew louder, seemingly sucking in air. The guard stood, intent on jumping into the trench. The whistling ended with a loud crack, as if lightning had struck nearby. The first mortar shell exploded at the guard's feet. The man disappeared. A twisted rifle barrel fell into the trench, followed by a whiff of tobacco smoke and a spray of blood. "Into the cave," Byrnes told the three others, although he was not entirely certain they understood Vietnamese. Hoping the law of averages and the overhead jungle canopy would keep another mortar round from landing in the same spot, Byrnes scrambled out of the shallow trench. He slid on his abdomen across the slimy trail, and fell into the deep trench where the soldier who had taken the ammunition had been. The three other porters followed him.

After a minute, Byrnes's pupils adjusted to the darkness. The cave was a portal to an underground network of tunnels. As far as Byrnes could see in the darkness, the first tunnel was empty. He heard voices ahead and slowly crept forward until he came to a lashed bamboo ladder. Above him a gun crew manned a heavy machine gun. Unaware of his presence, they talked to one another. The hammering of the machine gun drowned most of their conversation. "Here they come." "Hundreds of them." "Thousands." "On the left." "Grenade!" Then, *Whomp!* Smoke wafted into the tunnel. Byrnes smelled cordite. The concussion of an exploding grenade digging into the mud and spraying shrapnel into the gun crew knocked Byrnes to the mud floor. He heard the men above him: "I'm hit!" "Can't reload." "My leg!"

After a short while Byrnes heard only silence from the machine gun position. He crept forward again. Hearing nothing, he slowly climbed the ladder and found himself within a fortified gun position. The NVA had surrounded the gun pit with logs and mud packed between tree stumps. One gunner had lost a leg and apparently bled to death. A second had shrapnel wounds in his chest and head. He no longer breathed either.

The third gunner struggled to load the machine gun with only his left arm, the other ended at the elbow. Obviously weak from blood loss, he kept trying to pull the bolt handle and re-feed the metal belt of bullets into the weapon. Byrnes could tell the barrel of the weapon no longer functioned. He grabbed the soldier by his belt and dragged him to the ladder. Slinging the man's right arm stump over his shoulders, Byrnes carried him into the tunnel.

Once underground, the porters hauled the gunner deeper into the tunnel, away from the gun pit. Byrnes ripped off the soldier's shirt, tore it in long pieces, and used strips of the cloth to tourniquet the shattered arm. The tourniquet covered a tattoo on the soldier's inner arm. Byrnes had seen the same sentiment written on many of the younger NVA soldiers. It was one of the few Vietnamese phrases he could read: *Born in the North to Die in the South.* "We can't quit now," the soldier said. "The enemy is…is overrunning our position. Go! Fire the machine gun. Go quickly."

"The gun is broken," Byrnes said. "It can't be fixed."

"Then get our rifles. In the back. In our quarters," the soldier said, pointing to the dark tunnel. "Hurry." None of the prisoners moved. "I have let my men down," the soldier spoke softly, voice fading with his strength. "I have shamed my ancestors and my village. So close to victory. After seven years of combat. So close. You see my uncle? He's standing there."

The men all turned their heads and looked where the soldier pointed. There may have been someone in the tunnel. It was too dark to tell. Byrnes assumed the man hallucinated. "It's all right," he said, placing his hand on the man's forehead. "We'll get you some medical attention. Hang on." At the same time, the soldier's eyes stopped moving. His vision seemed to focus on the ceiling, pupils dilating. He sighed once and stopped breathing.

"Dau hang! *Surrender!*" a voice shouted at the cave entrance. "Dau hang!" another voice screamed from the gun pit.

"Don't shoot!" one of the prisoners yelled in Vietnamese. "We are hostages of the North Vietnamese, forced to deliver ammunition. We are not armed."

"Come out slowly. Hands where I can see them," the voice said. "How many of you are there?"

The prisoner continued the conversation. "Three dead NVA gunners.

Four prisoners." Slowly, the men made their way toward the voices with their hands elevated, palms outward in front of them. As soon as they entered the trench, a squad of ARVN troops pulled them to the ground level one at a time.

"Anyone alive in there?" a sergeant with an M-16 in his right hand and an AK-47 in his left asked the prisoners. The camouflaged cloth name strip on his fatigue read Doan.

"We were only as far into the tunnels as the gun position," the first prisoner said. "The tunnels go on after that but I don't know how far. They may connect with other positions."

"Corporal Ha," the sergeant said, "take some C-4 and collapse that tunnel as far back as you are comfortable going." The corporal pulled off his backpack and extracted a handful of C-4, along with what Byrnes assumed were a timer and wires to connect the two together. He disappeared into the tunnel. "And who are you four?"

Using excellent Vietnamese, the Korean spoke first. "Lieutenant Roh So-dong, South Korea, 9th Division, 29th Regiment. Captured during Operation Hong Kil Dong near Tuy Hoa. Home Base Ninh Hoa."

"Welcome back, Lieutenant," the sergeant said. He tossed the Korean the AK-47 he held in his left hand. "You may need this. You'll find ammunition on some of the bodies we left behind."

"Thank you," the lieutenant said.

"And who are you men?" the sergeant asked.

"Hai Quang," the second man said. "Textile merchant from Saigon. I was kidnapped – "

"Can you use a rifle or an assault weapon?" the sergeant interrupted.

"No." Hai said.

"Next?"

The third porter said, "Thao Linh. Air force mechanic. Corporal. Kidnapped while on leave. I have used an M-16 in the past."

The sergeant tossed his M-16 at Thao. He said, "Don't lose it. I want it back when we return to Saigon."

"Yes, Sergeant."

"And you?" the sergeant pointed to Byrnes, as the corporal backed from the cave and climbed out of the deep trench.

"Four minutes," Corporal Ha said.

"Never mind," the sergeant told Byrnes. "I'll give you a chance to answer when we get back to our lines. Corporal, lead these men to our trenches. Pick up weapons you need and ammunition you see on the way. I'll find Captain Vinh. I expect the NVA will be making a counterattack shortly. Don't waste time."

CHAPTER 33

Wolfe sat at a desk in the showroom of Aikens Ford, surrounded by dividers, half wood, half glass, that separated him from other cubicles and ten or twelve beautiful new Ford automobiles. Through large plate glass windows in the front of the building he could see acres of similar vehicles, some new, some used. Colorful banners flapped in the warm Orlando breeze. A salesman walked by with a young couple, "The new Mustangs are outrageously beautiful," he said. Wolfe watched as the trio opened the driver's door to a red convertible version of the pony car.

"Dr. Wolfe?" a voice said.

Wolfe turned in the chair and found a muscular man about his age with gray hair and matching mustache. The man extended his right hand toward Wolfe. Rising, Wolfe shook it. "Mr. Aikens?"

"You can call me Pete. Peter Cottontail was my childhood nickname," Aikens said. "Come on back to my office. Care for some coffee?"

"No thanks. Barely finished this cup. Had one of your donuts, too. Can you make money giving away food?"

Aikens chuckled. "Have to match or beat our competition," he said. "It's part of the cost of doing business, like advertising." Limping slightly, he led Wolfe down a long hallway to a plush office. After they entered he pointed at a leather chair for Wolfe. Aikens circled his desk and fell into a taller leather seat, spinning it so he faced Wolfe.

"Nice office," Wolfe said, scanning the plush carpet, solid wood paneling, and autographed pictures of celebrities in front of their automobiles.

"It's incredible being close enough to Daytona that I can meet a lot of personalities at the race track," Aikens said. He pointed an index finger directly over his head to an autographed picture of him shaking hands with Donald Trump, in front of a yellow Mustang wearing asymmetrical wide black racing stripes. "Sold him that Shelby for his daughter."

"Beautiful car," Wolfe said.

"Yeah, but you didn't come here to talk about cars," Aikens said. "I know you drove at least two hours to get here, and in a Prius, too. Sure I can't sell you a more comfortable vehicle while you are in Orlando?" Aikens laughed good-naturedly.

"Can't afford it," Wolfe said. "The M.D. after my name does not stand for *mucho dinero*, if you know what I mean."

"Okay. That's settled. I have some time before we have a sales meeting. What can I tell you about J.T. Byrnes?"

"Well," Wolfe began, "as I told you on the telephone, his sister gave me your telephone number. She thought the two of you were good friends. Apparently you and other classmates spent time at his house in the summer between plebe and youngster years."

Aikens nodded. He leaned back in his chair and put both hands behind his head. He crossed his ankles on the corner of his desk and stared in Wolfe's direction. He tried to recall his relationship with Byrnes from fifty years before. "We were more rivals than good friends, I guess," he started, playing a video in his mind of the two young men interacting.

"Rivals concerning what?" Wolfe asked.

"It started with 150 pound football. Do you know about that?"

"An Ivy League light weight football conference." Wolfe said. "Yeah, his sister, Tammy, lent me Jimmy's Annapolis yearbook."

"Jimmy? Oh, yeah, James T. We always called him J.T. at Annapolis, when we didn't call him something less socially acceptable, like Cato. That was the name of the Pink Panther's Asian sidekick. We also called him other names when we were mad at him: Gook, Slope, Charlie."

"Why would you have been mad at him?" Wolfe asked, having also been on the wrong end of Byrnes's intellectual barbs at times.

"The guy was too perfect. He made good grades. Hell, academically I think he was first in our class when he dropped out. I know he was in the top ten. But mainly it was football for me. He played my position, cornerback. So, I ended up playing third string," Aikens said. "And there was Emily, too."

"Emily Rose? His girlfriend from high school?"

"Yeah. She damn near got me killed," Aikens said.

"How's that?" Wolfe asked.

"We met at J.T.'s house. Several of us stopped in Alexandria on our way from Annapolis to Norfolk to catch a ride to our summer cruise ship. The navy had a plane going to Puget Sound from Norfolk Naval Air Station. We had just finished plebe year. After being locked up in Mother B for a year, that's Bancroft Hall by the way, all women looked good to us. Especially Emily. And she was a flirt. Anyway, after he quit school, they broke up. I had been unable to get her out of my mind for six months, so I called her. To console her, I said. You know how that goes."

"You started dating?" Wolfe asked.

"Yeah. Hadn't been for her search for *a real man*, I wouldn't have signed on with the marines," Aikens said. Almost forgetting Wolfe's presence, he continued, gaze fixed on the wall above Wolfe's head. "One year after graduation, I had finished all the combat infantry training at Quantico and found myself in Vietnam as a platoon leader in Da Nang. Daily, we went on patrol outside the perimeter. Charlie knew we were coming. Headquarters hadn't gotten smart enough to let us decide when and where or how to vary the patrols, yet. They wanted the same areas cleared every day, so the gooks couldn't get close enough to rocket the base or to interfere with flight operations. Consequently, the VC knew where we were going and frequently set traps for us. We got damn good at spotting the ambushes before we fell into them, but they cost us some lives. And we didn't find them all.

"About a month before I was to be rotated to Saigon – at the time, we did six months in the field and six months at a desk – I led a patrol into Indian Country. The guy in front of me stepped on a land mine. Cost him two legs, and me one." Aikens made a fist and rapped his knuckles on his left leg at the thigh. The hollow sound echoed in the room. "Our government was pretty good at making promises: to the Vietnamese, to our troops, to our countrymen, and to others. But they stuck us out in the field of battle with so many restrictions on how to fight back, it seemed like they abandoned us."

"I'm sorry," Wolfe said.

Aikens dropped his feet to the floor and again sat facing Wolfe. "Not your fault. If I hadn't broken up with Emily my second-class year and thought that my being a marine might get her back, it wouldn't have happened. Worse things have happened to guys over women." He chuckled. "She ended up marrying a guy she knew from high school, a peacenik demonstrator, no less. Bet that killed her dad."

"Can you tell me more about the 150 pound football?" Wolfe asked.

"A little, I guess," Aikens said, looking at his Rolex. "I've got some time. Most of the guys who played one-fifty were offensive or defensive backs in high school. So, it's a fast game. Problem is everyone wants to continue being a back when they get to Annapolis. Someone has to play the line. And there was only one cornerback position, because Annapolis used a rover cornerback who switched sides of the field. You know what a 4-3-4 defense is?"

"Yeah," Wolfe said. "I played rover in high school."

Aikens nodded. "As plebes, we couldn't play with the varsity against other schools. Back then the NCAA didn't allow lowly freshman to play any varsity sports at any college. There were no frosh 150 pound teams to play against, either. So we ended up being the blocking dummies for the varsity. We played the roll of the upcoming opponents each week. Didn't take the coaches long to figure out who was really good, who could make weight every week, and who was smart."

Wolfe nodded knowingly. "Jimmy."

"Yeah. I was his back-up as a plebe. Played some middle guard. Ballooned to 175 pounds on the youngster cruise, too. Had a hell of a time making weight youngster year. That year J.T. started. I played third string behind a firstie, first class midshipman, who liked J.T. even less for taking his position."

"I told you over the phone that Jimmy was a POW in South Vietnam, right?" Wolfe said.

"Yeah. That's a shame. The gooks committed all sorts of atrocities. We found guys with their private parts stuffed in their mouths, beheaded, skinned, burned alive, buried in ant piles, and worse. It wasn't pretty. Some of those people were true war criminals," Aikens said, and paused. "Had some of our own war criminals, too, I guess. Lt. William Calley at My Lai comes to mind."

"Jimmy seems to have survived at least three years, according to Colonel Rhodes," Wolfe said.

"If there were a guy who could exist under those conditions, J.T. would be the one. He was a resourceful guy. I'll give you an example. We rented a car in Charleston, S.C. to return to Annapolis after the summer cruise. The air force landed us in Charleston. Anyway, on the way north, we got stuck in traffic behind two ladies whose fan belt had broken. They were on a bridge on I-95, blocking half a lane with an overheated engine. When we pulled past them, J.T. pulled over to see if we could help them.

"He talked one of the women into pulling off her nylon pantyhose. He cut one of the pant legs off. Using it in place of the fan belt, he tied the nylon around the flywheel, generator, and water pump. It worked. We followed them to the nearest gas station, where they got a real fan belt."

"How did he know to try that?" Wolfe asked.

"I asked him the same thing," Aikens said. "He told me his dad always had a subscription to *Mechanix Illustrated*, but seldom read it. Apparently, Captain Byrnes was out of town a lot. J.T. used to read the magazine religiously, cover to cover, and he rarely forgot the tips he picked up."

Wolfe smiled and said, "Jimmy made a light bulb puller for the hangar deck. It was a thirty-foot pole with a set of wires and springs on one end that could squeeze a light bulb on the ceiling of the hangar deck. It saved us from having to move aircraft and drive a forklift around to change the burnt out bulbs. Now I know where he got the idea."

Aikens continued, "He was solid. Hit like a mountain. He was stoic. He was smart. If I were a POW, I'd want him there to help me, too." Again Aikens looked at his watch. He said, "I've got to go. If you can wait an hour or so, it would be my pleasure to take you to dinner after this sales meeting. You can tell me about J.T. as a petty officer. Bet that was a trip."

CHAPTER 34

Lt. Roh So-dong of the South Korean army gave his fellow ex-POW, Byrnes, a short course in using the AK-47. They had picked up four of the weapons while running to the ARVN lines, along with arms full of magazines for the assault rifles. "This is about the same difficulty to use as an M-16," Lt. Roh said. "It's not as accurate, but it packs a more substantial punch. And it doesn't jam, even filled with dirt or water. It's a peasant's weapon."

"I'd be happier with my old M-1," Byrnes said. Seeing the NVA approaching, he added, "Here they come." He had read in military history at Annapolis about the swarms of Chinese soldiers that had engulfed the American troops in Korea. Now he knew how his ex-girlfriend's father and his Marines at Chosin Reservoir had felt. He could see wave after wave of NVA spilling from the jungle into the firing lanes the ARVN had cleared.

"Aim low," Lt. Roh said. "Keep it on single shot. Automatic wastes ammunition." .50 caliber machine guns behind Byrnes cut loose on the enemy. Mortars shells landed among them. Then artillery shells rained down from the heavens. Still, they pressed on, almost closing with the ARVN troops before being beaten back, or dying in their tracks.

"That was close," Byrnes said, surveying the destruction. Hundreds of dead littered the field in front of him. As a high school student, he had taken a field trip to Gettysburg and had been told about the Confederate soldiers attacking the Federal troops in wave after wave, knowing they would likely die in the charges. *How strong had their beliefs been? In their country? In their God? In an afterlife?* he wondered. *Not to fear charging up those hills. And these men. For communism?*

Puff the Magic Dragon, A South Vietnamese C-119 gunship circled the field of battle when the second attack started. Byrnes heard a loud ripping sound, similar to the tearing of a stiff canvas. Dirt flew in front of him, a round from the mini-gun on the aircraft slammed into every square yard of the contested field. A wave of dying North Vietnamese fell.

"Why do they do this?" Byrnes asked Lt. Roh during a short pause. "Don't they know they're going to die? Is their country worth this massacre?"

"They aren't doing it for their country," Roh said. "They are doing it for their comrades and ancestors, and to prove they aren't afraid. The same as us. Are you afraid?"

"Afraid they might make me a POW again," Byrnes said. "I think I'd rather die."

"There's your answer," Roh said. "Sergeant Doan, they're massing for a third attack. Looks like we're outnumbered about ten to one."

Sgt. Doan laughed. "Then we have them right where we want them, Lieutenant," he said. "Don't waste your ammo, though. The artillery unit backing us up is running out of shells. We're already out of mortar rounds. I expect we will need all the ammunition we have left to get back to Saigon. All right, ladies. One NVA per bullet."

The third wave faltered fifty yards from the defensive position of the ARVN. "Cease fire," Corporal Ha yelled, as soon as the charge had broken. "Save your ammunition." The artillery had fallen silent before the NVA charge had stalled.

"Okay," Sgt. Doan said. "Capt. Vinh says Can Tho has fallen to the communists. Our next line of defense will be the outskirts of Saigon. Let's get to the Landing Zone and evacuate. Everyone saddle up. Bring the wounded. Leave the dead."

No helicopters showed up at the LZ. They were visible in the air overhead. Byrnes saw dozens of Chinooks and Hueys flying below the gathering rain clouds. They all seemed headed east. *What could be going on east of us?* he wondered. The thirty-mile retreat to Saigon from Long An took the remnants of the ARVN battalion all night, a ten-hour march. Most of the severely wounded died during the withdrawal. The living laid them on the side of the trail, covered the bodies with their dark green ponchos, and kept moving. The NVA followed the ARVN at a discreet distance, in no hurry to close on the South Vietnamese soldiers. The NVA bided their time, having had their noses bloodied by the stiff resistance put up by what remained of the battalion.

Expecting government troops to challenge them on entering central Saigon, they found instead complete chaos. No one paid attention to them. No police or reservist troops manned the checkpoint on the bridge where Highway 10 crossed a tributary to the Saigon River. Dark smoke billowed into the sky from small fires in the suburbs. People milled about the streets, evidently in shock.

As the last officer alive in the battalion, Capt. Vinh called to Corporal Ha, who had taken over the field radio from a wounded radioman. About 10:30 a.m. he said, "What do you hear on the radio?"

Ha stood in the street, tears streaming from his eyes. Byrnes watched as the corporal handed the radio to the captain. "It's over," he said. "The government has capitulated. Acting President Duong Van Minh has agreed to an unconditional surrender. He has ordered all ARVN combatants to lay down their weapons. He says he has surrendered to prevent a massacre of civilians and the wholesale destruction of Saigon. NVA tanks have already entered northern Saigon. The enemy controls Tan Son Nhut airbase. One tank is sitting in the US Embassy compound. The Americans have all gone, flown to a massive fleet east of Saigon."

"Not quite all of us," Byrnes said quietly, realizing then where the choppers had been headed. As he watched, the word of the defeat spread quickly and quietly through the ranks of hundreds of men surrounding him in the street. Without a sound the soldiers began to disperse, leaving behind weapons, uniforms, even their boots. Within an hour, Byrnes stood alone with Lt. Roh on the deserted bridge. Civilians walking around in a daze ignored the weapons and uniforms. They apparently understood that to be caught with some of the soldiers' possessions by the North Vietnamese would be tantamount to treason and probably earn a death sentence.

A jeep-like machine drove past Byrnes and Roh. Seated in the back of the vehicle, a woman in the uniform of an NVA soldier held a tattered flag. On the faded, tattered flag were two horizontal bars, the upper one pink, and the other a light blue. A large gold star filled the middle of the flag: the NVA battle flag.

"Now what?" Byrnes asked Roh.

"I don't know about you," Roh said, "but I could use a beer. I've been too long a captive of the NVA. I need some good food and a drink. With luck it will take them days to weeks to organize the capture of Saigon. Maybe by then we will be gone."

The idea of a good meal and a Coke appealed to Byrnes. "I can't drink alcohol," he said. "Do you know some good restaurants?"

"I was stationed in Saigon prior to being assigned to Ninh Hoa," Roh said. "My apartment wasn't far from the US Embassy. With luck, there will be some empty apartments. We can take showers. If the occupants left in a hurry, we might find some real clothing. There is a restaurant, the Viet-My, *Vietnamese-American*, not far from the apartment. May I treat you to a meal if the café is still open for business?"

"I'd like that," Byrnes said. He unloaded and checked the chamber of his AK-47, heaved the magazine into the water below them, and dropped the assault rifle on the bridge pavement. Roh did the same with his M-16.

CHAPTER 35

Wolfe's cell phone rang while he drove along I-4 headed north toward St. Augustine from Aikens's dealership after spending the night in Orlando. Brain-washed to believe that even-numbered interstates ran east and west, he always marveled how he ended up north of Orlando on I-4. Checking the cars around him, he pulled off the interstate at the next exit and coasted to a stop at the side of the road. Pulling out the cell phone, he noted the low battery charge. Then he checked his messages and found that Jimmy Byrnes's sister, Tamiko Kimura, had left a brief message asking him to call as soon as he received the voice mail.

Pushing a button to return the call automatically, Wolfe looked in his rearview mirror and watched as a black sedan pulled off the exit and onto the dirt shoulder about a hundred yards behind him. *Weird*, he thought. *What are the odds two drivers would do this at the same time?*

"Tammy? It's Addy. You called?" he said when Kimura answered. Before she could reply, he added, "Sorry I didn't answer right away. I was driving. I pulled off the road. Don't like to drive and talk at the same time. What's up?"

"I apologize for interrupting your trip," she said.

"No problem. I was visiting with one of the men you pointed me to, Pete Aikens. Nice guy. Owns a Ford dealership in Orlando. But that's not why you called. Tell me what you need."

Kimura exhaled audibly, and then said, "I have some bad news. My mother died early Monday morning. I thought you should know since you were so kind to her."

"I'm so sorry for your loss, Tammy," Wolfe said. "Another stroke?"

"We don't know. The hospital had transferred her to a rehab facility about a week ago. She was doing well. Yaz spent most of the day with her Sunday. When the nurses went to check on her after breakfast, she was gone." Wolfe heard Kimura sniff, catching a tear.

"I am truly sorry, Tammy," Wolfe said. "You have my condolences. I'll pack and catch the next flight to Washington. When will the services take place?"

"You don't have to catch the next flight, Addy," Kimura said. "She's going to be buried with my father in Arlington. There's a seven or eight week backlog there. When I know the exact date, I'll let you know. Has Mr. Roh contacted you?"

"Who?"

"A Mr. Roh. He's Korean. Works at the Korean Embassy. He called this morning after seeing my mother's obituary in the Washington Post. It mentioned that Jim and my father had predeceased her. He called to see if J.T. III was the same man he had known in Vietnam. He was in the Korean infantry during Vietnam and also a POW. I gave him your name and telephone number."

"Oh, okay. No, I haven't heard from him. Is there anything I can do for you or Yasuko?" Wolfe asked.

"I don't believe so. If I think of something, I'll let you know," Kimura said. "Thank you for the offer. Good-bye."

"Bye," Wolfe said. He turned off the cell phone. Again noting the very low battery level on the phone, he plugged it into the car to recharge it. Taking the tri-folded piece of paper and pen he always kept in his shirt pocket, he wrote a reminder to buy a sympathy card for the sisters. Looking at his rearview mirror, he saw that the black sedan had not moved.

Wolfe started his engine and finished driving off the exit to an intersecting two-lane street. The ramp back onto I-4 north beckoned directly across the road. He ignored it. The sedan had begun moving almost as soon as Wolfe's vehicle had. He turned to his left and looked for a fast food outlet, intermittently checking his mirrors. The sedan followed him, about a hundred yards behind.

Not yet convinced he was being tailed, Wolfe turned left into a Burger King, drove around the building, and waited for the sedan to pass the structure. When the sedan pulled into the parking lot, Wolfe pulled out, turned right, and headed back toward I-4. Passing by the onramp again Wolfe continued east on the two-lane road. The sedan followed. Doing math, trying to remember what the probabilities would be that the car would stop behind him, make the same left turn, and then the same right turn, Wolfe decided the chances were less than one in eight. He pulled into an Arby's and parked. Taking his cell phone with him, he went inside and ordered a sandwich.

Unable to park next to Wolfe's vehicle, the sedan pulled into a slot directly in front of the building, rear bumper toward the fast food outlet. Wolfe could see the car as he slowly ate his curly fries and roast beef sandwich. He could not see through the darkened windows. The license plate didn't appear to be a government plate. In Florida, rental cars no longer had distinctive plates, to cut down on tourist ambushes, so he couldn't tell who tailed him. The chances of outrunning the sedan in a Prius seemed slim.

Wolfe walked to the counter and asked to speak with the manager. When she appeared, he told her his name and that he would like to speak with her in private. She led him to her office. "And what can I do for you, Dr. Wolfe?" she asked, after she had closed the office door.

"May I use your telephone?" he asked. "I may be in some danger. I suspect someone is following me. A man broke into my house three days ago and tried to stab my daughter. I'd like to call the police."

"Sure thing," she said. "I'll step outside so you can talk in private."

"If that black sedan parked under your sign leaves, please let me know," Wolfe said. He picked up the telephone and dialed 911.

A Seminole County Sheriff's Deputy had been eating lunch at the Burger King down the road. He arrived quickly, and after hearing Wolfe's tale, walked out to the black car. Wolfe watched as the deputy stood by the open driver's door. The driver handed papers to the deputy. The deputy spoke to dispatch through the radio microphone attached to his right epaulet. After several minutes, the deputy handed the papers back to the driver, who never left the vehicle. The deputy backed away from the sedan and the driver closed the door. The brake lights came on. The car started, the back-up lights shone, and it backed out of the parking space. Slowly it exited the parking lot, drove back onto the two-lane road and disappeared going east.

The deputy returned to the Arby's. He smiled at Wolfe. "Japanese tourist," he said. "Lost. And hungry. He thought you might have known something about the Burger King, so he followed you here. Said he didn't want to upset you, so he was waiting for you to leave before he came in to order."

"Really?" Wolfe said.

"That's his story. I called in his identification, passport, driver's license, and license plate. He's clean. The car is a rental. Came from the Orlando airport about two hours ago. I suppose we have to believe him, Mr. Wolfe. Is there anything else I can do for you?"

"No. Thank you, deputy," Wolfe said, not entirely convinced. "I guess I'm still anxious after the break-in. Sorry to put you to all that trouble. May I buy you a sandwich and a drink? Oh, do you remember the man's name?"

"Shima Ichiro. He said it means *first born island*, or something like that. My lunch is waiting for me in the cruiser. Thank you, anyway, sir. Have a good day."

Wolfe pulled his piece of paper from his pocket and wrote down the tourist's name. He didn't see that particular black sedan on the remainder of the drive to St. Augustine.

CHAPTER 36

Lieutenant Roh emerged from the bathroom in the second floor apartment with a bath towel around his waist. He dried his hair with a second towel. "My first shower in many years," he said to Byrnes. "With lots of hot water. Your turn. Find any clothing or money, Con co?"

Roh had found his old apartment virtually unchanged, with the exception of a new recliner and a newer television in the living room. The key he had kept hidden under a statue of Buddha in an outside decorative rock garden remained where he had left it. At the front door had been three days worth of two newspapers, the *Chin Luan*, a Vietnamese paper, and the *Saigon Post*, an English language newspaper. Roh had shared the apartment with another South Korean officer, who worked in intelligence. His tour would have ended long before. They uncovered no sign of the newer occupants, evidently he or they had departed three to four days earlier. The absence of most of the occupants of the apartment building reminded Byrnes of an post-apocalyptic movie.

Naked to the waist, wearing only the faded, worn, khaki pants given him by the NVA, Byrnes nodded. "In the apartment directly above us, I found clothing that will fit you. The occupants must also have left quickly. I saw family pictures on a bureau. May have been an employee of the Americans. No looters have hit this apartment building, yet. Seem to be some original residents here. Across the hall is a nice lady. She said there was a man about my size who left a week ago. She used to clean his apartment for him. Gave me the key. I found a few pair of trousers, shoes, socks, even three dress shirts," he said, pointing to two piles of clothing he had dropped on the couch in front of a small television set. "But no money."

"Some underwear? I've missed my underwear." Roh scanned the room, eyes falling on the broadcast displayed by the black and white television. Tanks rolled past the US Embassy. Crowds waved hands and NVA battle flags.

"Didn't know if you wanted to wear someone else's underwear," Byrnes said, "but I brought three pair for you. Seven pair of tighty-whities for me." He held one pair up for Roh's inspection.

"Nice. I prefer boxers, though."

Byrnes showered. He spent thirty minutes under the running water. He stood under the stream until the hot water began to cool. *No mud, no animals, clean warm water, soap, heaven*, he thought.

Roh rapped on the door. "Are you done?" he asked. "According to the reporter on television, the communists have declared a curfew. Anyone on the streets after 9:00 p.m. will be detained. Or shot. Or both. Looters are subject to arrest and execution without a trial. All former ARVN troops are to surrender their arms at the Presidential Palace."

"Great," Byrnes said. "You might want to leave that watch you found in the apartment. Don't know about you, but I'm starving. Where is that restaurant you bragged about?"

"The watch will help us keep track of time and the curfew. Restaurant's near the American Embassy off Hong Thap Tu. We can walk it in thirty minutes, provided we aren't detained by the NVA," Roh said.

"Yeah, and you said it would only be an hour's walk to this apartment building, too," Byrnes said, skeptical of Roh's time estimate.

"How was I to know the streets would be impassible?" Roh asked. "If you don't want to go out, there is food in the kitchen and probably more in some of the other abandoned apartments."

"May as well see Saigon before the communists destroy it," Byrnes said. He slipped on a pair of thin nylon socks and tried to put his feet into a pair of short engineer boots he found in the upstairs apartment. "Crap."

"What's wrong?"

"Shoes are too small," Byrnes said. He pulled off the boots and then stuffed the socks in them. He had also rescued a pair of worn leather sandals from the other dwelling. "These feel good," he said after slipping them on.

"Boots and socks fit me," Roh said, after sitting on the couch and slipping them on. "Thanks. Oh, I found a wad of bills in a hollow book on the shelf. Looks like 100-200,000 piasters."

"Is that a lot?" Byrnes asked.

"Depends on how bad the inflation has been over the last six to eight years. A US dollar was worth about 200 piasters when I was captured in 1967. I guess we'll find out at the restaurant." He stuffed the entire wad of bills into his pocket.

Byrnes had no idea where they were, or how to find anything in Saigon. He walked with Roh, speaking quietly in Vietnamese, even though Roh spoke perfect English. Both men had shaved off sparse mustaches and beards after their showers. Byrnes told Roh about the pack of razor blades he had bought prior to leaving the States on the WestPac cruise. He expected a single blade to last him the entire cruise. Roh laughed. The only change in his appearance had been slightly shorter and squared off sideburns and the loss of a small patch of chin hair. "Europeans show their ice age heritage," he said. "They needed hair to keep warm."

The walk northwest along Pasteur, led them within a block of the South Vietnamese Presidential Palace. They saw hundreds of NVA processing thousands of ARVN troops. The South Vietnamese presented in various stages of dress. Some were fully clothed in combat fatigues or dress uniforms. Others sat or stood in their white boxer shorts and bare feet. Byrnes saw every combination of clothing between those extremes.

At Han Theuyen, the men turned right and walked past the Notre Dame Cathedral. "That's probably one of the reasons they surrendered," Roh said.

"To save the cathedral from destruction?"

Roh nodded. "Saigon has a long history. Cathedrals, pagodas, museums, palaces. Ho Chi Minh would have wanted it preserved, too."

More vehicles piled with revelers yelling and waving flags drove past the men as they walked northwest again on Duy Tan. "There certainly are a lot of people celebrating for a country that was at war two days ago," Byrnes said. "Do you suppose they were all communist sympathizers?"

"They're being pragmatic. You may not realize this, but many South Vietnamese fought with the Viet Minh against the French, and then came south to escape the communists. Their loyalty has been divided for years: pro-independence, anti-communist. If pushed they can display either. Most have recently switched sides in order to prolong their lives, I suppose," Roh said. "I had many a southerner tell me he admired Ho Chi Minh for his resistance to the Japanese and his ability to throw out the French. Everyone, even the South Vietnamese, called him Uncle Ho. The original southerners, and those who left North Vietnam after the Geneva Accords divided the country in 1954, had no desire to be communists. Especially the Catholics. Entire Catholic hamlets packed up and followed their priests south, marching in the night to avoid soldiers, or taking boats down rivers to the South China Sea and following the coast south. Many died trying to escape. The North Vietnamese communists detained many more. Still, they all admired Ho."

Byrnes could smell smoke. Behind a ten or twelve foot tall cement wall along Hai Ba Trung a plume of black smoke drifted into the air over the trees that lined the road. "What do you suppose is burning over there?" he asked.

Roh sniffed the air, smelled the acrid odor. "Probably secret documents. Behind that wall is the US Embassy. See that tall building with the flat roof? That's a helicopter pad. One way to hide is in plain sight. We will walk down Hong Thap Tu, past the embassy. I doubt the NVA would expect fugitives to do that. Keep your eyes open, though."

Furniture, papers, typewriters, adding machines, wastebaskets, even staplers and paperclips littered the road near the embassy. "Jesus, what a mess," Byrnes said. "Looters?"

"You wouldn't think so. If the communists find American equipment in someone's possession, he'd have a lot of explaining to do," Roh said, then laughed.

"What's so funny?"

"I figured it out. Some people did ransack the embassy, probably angry that the Americans left without them. And when they got to the street and heard the NVA tanks, they thought better of the idea, dropped their booty, and ran."

"Makes sense," Byrnes said.

In the courtyard, behind a huge metal gate that evidently had been damaged by an armored vehicle, sat two Russian or Chinese T-34 tanks. Their crews, men who looked like fourteen- and fifteen-year-old boys, but in reality were older teenaged combat veterans, lounged on the decks of the tanks or in the grass nearby. Roh waved. Some soldiers smiled and waved back. Byrnes copied Roh's gesture to the NVA soldiers.

Several blocks off the main thoroughfare, they found a small brick establishment. Huge posters covered the windows and walls in front, advertising for the nearby Pink nightclub. They depicted guitar-toting stars: Elvis Phuong and Anh Tu.

The proprietor of the Viet-My restaurant, a toothless old man with sparse white hair, recognized Lieutenant Roh. "Good evening, Lieutenant," he said. "I haven't seen you in years. In fact, I don't believe I have seen a Korean national since the South Korean Army left in 1973. Are you a correspondent now?"

Initially surprised that all South Korean troops had departed Vietnam, Roh recovered quickly. "Yes. Yes. I'm a foreign correspondent covering the war. I guess now I'm covering the peace," he said. He pointed to the taller Byrnes. "My friend, Con co, and I thought we'd get one last local meal before seeing about leaving Saigon." When the waiter, an older man with a bad limp and a withered left arm, appeared, Roh ordered an American meal of steak, vegetables, and baked potato, along with a beer for himself and a Coca-Cola for Byrnes.

While the waiter delivered their order to the cook, Roh pointed to the menu and prices, written in colored chalk on the large blackboard behind the bar. "Inflation has been brutal," he said. "An apple used to cost about half an American dollar in this restaurant, about 100 piasters. They were cheaper in grocery stores, of course. Now an apple is worth 1250 piasters here, according to that menu." As they watched, the owner of the restaurant erased the prices with a dish rag and added 1000 piasters to each as he rewrote them. "Paper money is worthless in a time of crisis, Con co. Probably one of the reasons the most recent occupant of my apartment left it behind. It would be of absolutely no value wherever he went outside Vietnam."

When the waiter returned with their food, Roh pulled the wad of bills from his pocket. "I think I'll pay you now and give you your tip while I can still afford it," he said. He thumbed through the bills, then shook his head and handed all but 1000 piasters to the waiter. "Easy come, easy go," he said in English.

CHAPTER 37

A surprise awaited Wolfe when he drove in the front gate at The Cascades, part of World Golf Village. Teddy, the guard, had called him minutes before. Wolfe had dutifully pulled off the highway and answered the call. A man waited at the guard shack for Wolfe. Ted said the man wanted to talk to him about a mutual friend.

Parking his Prius along the side of the road, Wolfe walked over to the gate, where the man waited in his vehicle, a late model BMW sports car. The convertible top lay open. Within the shade of the guard shack, the man sat inside his vehicle smoking a cigar. He wore an Hawaiian shirt and cargo shorts similar to Wolfe's favorite shorts. Wolfe couldn't see the man's feet, but he assumed he wore sandals, if he wore anything at all.

Wolfe stood next to the driver's side of the car. "I'm Addison Wolfe," he said to the heavy-set stranger with a full head of gray hair. "You want to talk with me?"

"Dr. Wolfe," the man said. He pushed the driver's door open and stood. Grabbing Wolfe's right hand, he shook it with a firm grasp. "Is there a place where we can talk?"

"You don't look like an assassin," Wolfe said. "Who are you and what do you want to talk about?"

"Pardon me? Oh, I'm George Crouch," the stranger said. "My friends call me Zorro, although now I look a lot more like Sgt. Garcia." He patted his midsection. "That was my call sign in the Navy. I flew F-8s and F-4s in the navy." He chuckled. "Can we chat about J.T.? I talked with his sister yesterday after I heard about his mom. We keep in touch. J.T. and I were roommates during Plebe Summer at Annapolis. You were kidding about being an assassin, right?"

"I wish," Wolfe said. "Follow me to the club house. That's a fairly public place. On warm summer days there are usually a number of people around the pool. And we can get drinks if you want."

"Okay."

Wolfe told Teddy to let the BMW through the gate. Crouch followed Wolfe to the clubhouse and, after parking, joined him at one of the tables around the pool. Wolfe had picked a spot between the indoor and outdoor pools, relatively isolated from the crowd around the grill and bar. "Want a beer?" he asked Crouch.

"Pepsi's fine, Doc," Crouch said. "I'm flying later today."

Wolfe retrieved two Pepsis from the concession stand. He set one in front of Crouch and sat with his back toward the pool. "You mentioned flying later," he said. "What do you do, Mr. Crouch?"

Crouch took a sip of his Pepsi. He said, "Call me George, Doc. I work at the Cecil Commerce Center, what used to be Cecil Field until the navy closed it. A friend of mine buys F-5s and T-38s from countries all over the world. They are being retired from most air forces. Then he rebuilds them and sells them to rich civilians who want to fly supersonic jets. I'm his test pilot for the refurbished aircraft. They only cost one to two million once he rebuilds them. Want one?"

"Can't afford one. I always wanted to fly," Wolfe said, smiling. "My uncle was a military pilot. Flew F-86s in Korea. When I graduated from medical school, I applied for astronaut training. Didn't work out."

"I'll call you next time we test a T-38. Those are the two-seaters. Be happy to take you up with me," Crouch said.

"Don't know if I'd go," Wolfe said. "I've gotten used to being Earth-bound. They let you do that at your age?"

"At my age, I'm expendable. And I have a lot of experience that comes in handy occasionally. If you change your mind, let me know," Crouch said. "Tammy said you were on a mission to learn more about J.T. She said you and he were buddies on the carrier. *Oriskany*, right? Never flew off her. Oldest one I was on was *Midway*. Anyway, since I live close by in Ponte Vedra I thought I'd stop by. Why are you worried about assassins? Tammy didn't mention that."

Wolfe told him about having to shoot Chief Fulton, and the black sedan earlier in the day. He laughed, "Some poor lost Japanese tourist, afraid to eat the local food. My paranoia, I guess."

Crouch sipped his Pepsi and then said, "So Fulton said these guys threw J.T. overboard? That's disturbing, even more disturbing than the navy believing he had committed suicide. And Colonel Rhodes shared captivity with him for about two years? Crap. What a way to go. Bombed by your own countrymen."

"He seems to have survived in places most of us would have died," Wolfe said. "Any inkling of that ability as a plebe?"

"I don't know about the rest of plebe year, because we were no longer roommates or in the same company. He showed real resilience first and second sets during Plebe Summer. He had *Reef Points* memorized before the rest of us. All the famous quotes by presidents, naval heroes, and others. So much trivia. He knew the phonetic alphabet and Morse code before we did, too. Being a military brat may have given him a head start on some of it. Either way, he was a smart guy. Resourceful. You wanted him as friend. There wasn't anything he wouldn't do for you then. You didn't want him as an enemy, either."

"Why?" Wolfe asked.

Shifting his weight in the chair, Crouch said, "I saw him steal food from meals and take it to friends who were being harassed by upper classmen in the mess hall and had no time to eat. I also suspect him as being the guy who sabotaged some upperclassmen, got them demerits for being late to formation, rooms out of order, etc. He could break into any room. He set traps for them, too. Water balloons. Burning bags of dog crap. All sorts of stuff. And never got caught."

"Anything else?"

Crouch laughed and said, "He could pass for a Filipino mess boy, and frequently did. I know of two occasions when he left the academy and went downtown Annapolis dressed as a civilian. I guess that's where he found the balloons."

"Pete Aikens said they called him Cato, after Peter Sellers's sidekick in the movie *Pink Panther*."

"You only did that once," Crouch said. "He never forgot an insult. He never showed his feelings, either. Sometimes you didn't know you had slighted him until he paid you back. And although you couldn't prove it, you knew it when he retaliated." Briefly, Crouch admired the granddaughter of one of the Cascades residents as she walked past their table. He continued, "A friend of mine, also a high school classmate from Columbia, South Carolina, was a bigot. Couldn't stand blacks or foreigners. They were in the same company during the academic year. One day he insulted J.T. Starting the next day, none of his computer programs ever ran correctly on the IBM 360 on which they taught us Fortran. That was back when we used punch cards. Every time this guy ran a program, the computer would go into an infinite loop and spit out his punch cards. Even the professors couldn't figure it out. They finally had to give him a pseudo ID. I know J.T. did that."

"He admitted to it?"

"Never," Crouch said.

"Sounds like he thrived during Plebe Summer," Wolfe said.

"He made some mistakes, and paid for them, too." Crouch said. "One of the upperclassmen happened to pop into a plebe's room late one night. J.T. was in the room without authorization, helping the guy polish his shoes. He heard the firstie open the door and slipped into the closet. The upperclassman started to harass the other plebe about failing inspection that morning because he hadn't folded his underwear correctly. He flung open the closet door to see if the plebe had remedied the deficiency and found J.T. standing there." Crouch grinned. "I can still see the smirk on the upperclassman's face when he told us about it later. They fried him, of course. Gave him a shitload of demerits. He marched them off with his M-1. J.T. had looked at the firstie innocently and said, 'Going down, sir?'"

"That's funny," Wolfe said.

"Yeah, it was," Crouch said. "You know the academy is a perverse place. A common saying is IHTFP, *I Hate This Fucking Place*. And most of us stayed because we were afraid to quit and face our family or our peers. Some of us feel J.T. had more balls than we did, because he went home to face his dad, a Captain in the navy at the time. I certainly would not have."

"Don't know that I see your point, but I'll take your word for it," Wolfe said.

"I guess it's similar to combat," Crouch said. "Sometimes you do things more because you worry about what other people think than you worry about the consequences. Maybe marriage is like that, too." He chuckled. "So what's next, Doc?"

Thinking about his own marriage, Wolfe laughed. He told Crouch about the CIA and their prohibition on his travel to Vietnam. "Their attitude makes me even more tempted to find my way to Southeast Asia. I know the odds are long that he could have survived, or that I'll find him if he did. Just the same, I feel obligated to try. I have led a comfortable life since I left the navy. Maybe not as luxurious as some would assume since I was a doctor, but very pleasant compared to his existence. I wouldn't want to miss the chance to help him if I can. Do you suppose there was a chance Jimmy could have become a traitor? It's one of the possibilities the CIA mentioned."

"One of the more famous quotes we memorized plebe year at Annapolis was: *non sibi, sed patriae.* The class of 1869 inscribed that on the chapel doors. J.T. personified those words."

"What does it mean?" Wolfe asked.

"Not self, country," Crouch said.

"Yeah, I don't believe he'd turn his back on his country, either."

Crouch stood. "I've got to go, Doc. Have to preflight an F-5 and test fly it. You let me know if you need transportation or a retired navy fighter pilot for some reason, even sneaking into Vietnamese airspace. I know my way around the sky in what used to be North and South Vietnam, also Cambodia and Laos."

"I will," Wolfe said.

CHAPTER 38

About two hundred yards from the apartment they had appropriated, Roh put his hand in front of Byrnes, stopping him on the sidewalk near a parking lot full of bicycles and mopeds. A single 1940s vintage, black, Citroen taxicab sat in the lot, without a driver. Standing next to his three-wheeled pedal cab parked at the curb, a cyclo driver leaned on his vehicle and smoked a cigarette. The street and sidewalks glistened with puddles of water, the monsoon season having started days before. It had poured while they ate dinner. Stars shone in a clear sky. "Did you leave the lights on in the apartment?" Roh asked.

"No. I turned them all off," Byrnes said, looking at the three-story brick building a half block in front of them. He saw lights in the second floor windows. "Are you sure that's ours? Both those buildings look alike."

"I'm certain. I used to live in the second one, the one with the giant antenna on the roof." Roh turned to the pedal cab driver who had taken his seat on the cyclo. "How far will 1000 piasters take us, father?" he asked the older man.

The old man with sinewy arms and legs grinned, revealing only six to eight teeth. "Half as far as it would have yesterday, about six blocks. The new curfew takes effect in twenty minutes. Where do you want to go?"

"Four blocks straight up this street," Roh said. He and Byrnes slipped into the seats of the pedal cab in front of the driver. An awning hung over their heads, protection from bright sunshine or rain, when needed.

The old man stood on the pedals and pushed downward. He pulled up on the handlebars, straining every muscle in his body. His thick thigh muscles labored to move the cab forward. Taking a quick look to make certain no motorized traffic moved in his direction, he steered the cab to the middle of the brick paved street. With no suspension, the sturdy frame of the cyclo transmitted every crack and bump in the ancient cobblestones into Byrnes and Roh's bodies. "Rough ride, uncle," Byrnes said.

"Life is rough," the driver said.

As the cab glided past the twin apartment buildings, Roh and Byrnes saw the woman from the apartment across the hall standing in front of the building. She spoke with two bo dois, NVA foot soldiers, in dark green uniforms. They wore pith helmets and carried AK-47s, in addition to leather holsters and pistols on their belts. Inside the lighted room of the apartment, another soldier walked past the window.

"She turned us in," Byrnes said, in English. Both men turned their heads away from the woman and the soldiers as the cyclo glided past the building.

"She's ingratiating herself with the new political regime. I remember her. She's part of the landlord's extended family. Three generations of them live in two or three of the apartments," Roh said. Switching back to Vietnamese, Roh spoke to the driver. "Take us as close to Doan Thi Diem Street as you can on the money I gave you. Give yourself a tip out of it. Oh, and be home before curfew."

Three blocks later, the cyclo coasted to a stop in front of the Notre Dame Basilica. "It's not a long ways to Doan Thi Diem Street from here," the old man said, "about two blocks."

"I know the way," Roh said. He handed the bills to the driver. "I would appreciate it if you forgot you gave us a ride."

The man's eyes twinkled. "That watch might lock my lips," he said pointing at the watch Roh had found in the apartment.

Roh slid the watch from his wrist and handed it to the old man. "Thank you, father. Have a good night. Get indoors quickly."

"Where are we going?" Byrnes asked after the cyclo disappeared around the corner.

"Not Doan Thi Diem," Roh said. They walked past the intersection of Doan Thi Diem and Hong Thap Tu, to Le Van Duyet and took a right. The street led them northwest. No traffic and few pedestrians crossed their path. Of the persons they saw, there was an inordinate number of individuals with amputations, ex-soldiers missing one or more limbs. The injured men hurried on, looking away from Byrnes and Roh, not knowing if they were communist sympathizers. Sirens began to wail in the city. "Curfew," Roh said. He strode off the road and closer to the structures on the side of the boulevard, sticking to the shadows of the buildings. The farther they walked the sparser the dwellings appeared. Villas with large lawns and walled yards replaced smaller apartments, businesses, and restaurants.

After entering the residential district in western Saigon, the two men passed a grisly scene as they stayed close to the homes along the street. In one house the lights were on and the front door lay open. A man in the uniform of an ARVN general lay sprawled across the entranceway, the left half of his head blown away. An American .45 automatic lay on the concrete step, inches from the dead officer's hand. Behind him in the well-lit hallway lay an adult female and two small children, all dead of gunshot wounds. "Some people won't want to be taken prisoner," Roh said quietly.

Byrnes followed Roh. "That includes me," he said.

The Korean took a left and stopped six blocks farther down the road, across the street from a corner mansion. "Still standing," he said.

"What's this?" Byrnes whispered.

"My girlfriend's house," Roh said. "She works for the Saigon City public works. Her father runs an import company, really a smuggling operation, I assume. They were never too clear about the family business, but they are fabulously wealthy. They were probably among the first people to leave Saigon on a jet for the Philippines or the United States."

"Will it be safe for us to stay there?"

"For a day or two," Roh said. "The communists will eventually search all these villas for their capitalist owners. They will punish or execute them, depending on their crimes against humanity, in other words: earning a living and having employees. *Exploiting the masses*, as the communists call it."

"We should probably get off the street," Byrnes said.

"I'll go first," Roh said. He ran across the street and leaped onto the cement wall to the right of a large iron gate. Pulling himself to the top of the wall, he lay along the top and waved at Byrnes.

Byrnes jumped up and grasped the Korean's hand. Roh pulled him to the top of the wall. They both slid off the wall to the interior of the lot. "Don't think I could do that twice," Byrnes said, bent at the waist and blowing out a huge breath. "I'm not as fast or as strong as I used to be."

Roh laughed. He whispered, "We'll get you a YMCA membership

when we get out of Vietnam."

Roh led Byrnes to the rear of the residence. He tried the French doors one after the other. Stealthily, he turned the handles. One opened and he entered. Byrnes followed, directly behind him. Byrnes pulled the door closed silently and turned to face Roh. A voice in the darkness said. "You might die, looter." In the gloom of a large kitchen, Byrnes saw a man with a weapon that looked like an Israeli Uzi pointed at him and Roh.

He and Roh put their hands in the air. "We are not looters," Roh said.

"Well, you are not the postman, either," the man with the Uzi said. "Who are you and what is your business if you are not thieves?"

"I am looking for Dang Tu," Roh said. "Does she still live here with her family?"

"And who are you?" the other man asked.

"Roh So-dong, an acquaintance."

"Lt. Roh So-dong is dead or a prisoner of war," the man said. He pointed the weapon at Byrnes. "Who are you?"

Byrnes saw no benefit in hiding his identity. He said, "An American. James Byrnes. Until two days ago a prisoner of the North Vietnamese. Lt. Roh and I have recently escaped from the NVA."

A flashlight suddenly shone from behind the man. A circle of light lit the floor at Byrnes's feet and then slowly climbed his body. "He doesn't look American," a woman's voice said, when the light shone on his face.

"Tu." Roh said. "Is that you? Tu?"

The flashlight swung to Roh's face. It suddenly fell to the floor, the light winking out as it hit the tile and the filament in the bulb broke. "So! So-dong," the woman screamed. "It really is you." From behind the man with the Uzi, an obviously pregnant Vietnamese woman rushed to Roh and threw her arms around him. "Father, it is So-dong." She laid her head on his chest and began to cry.

The man dropped the barrel of the weapon toward the floor. "Come," he said. "Tu, take these men to the basement, where no light can be seen. Send your brother up here to guard this door. Tomorrow we will have to figure out how to secure it better."

"Yes, father," the woman said. She led Roh by the hand through the interior of the darkened home to the basement door. Byrnes followed quietly. A pale light escaped from the basement as she opened the door. The three walked down the steps. In the basement proper thirty-some Vietnamese adults and a score of children ranging from infant to pre-teen in age greeted them.

"My father has arranged for us and our extended family to leave Saigon tomorrow," Tu said to Roh. Blushing, she held her hand out to a man who stood in the crowd wearing black trousers, black shoes, and a traditional, embroidered, white cotton shirt that hung over his belt. "This is my husband, Truong Truc." She began to weep again. "I thought you were dead."

Byrnes admired Roh's stoicism, the Korean holding his emotions in check, obviously happy for Tu and sad for himself. Byrnes watched the young woman weep with her head on her husband's shoulder and holding his hand. Roh quickly turned his back to Byrnes and the couple, hiding his expression from Tu.

CHAPTER 39

Transporting fifty-some people to a boat without attracting the attention of the communist vanquishers of Saigon proved difficult, but not impossible. The communists had yet to consolidate their hold on the city. The sudden collapse of the South Vietnamese government had been as much a surprise to them as it had to the population. In the midst of hurrying administrators south from Hanoi, the army had to take the reins of government temporarily. In order to do that, they had to rely on city officials already in place, and on those citizens willing to swear loyalty, for whatever reason, to the new regime. That left huge gaps in security. It proved impossible to prevent an exodus of local officials and South Vietnamese who had worked for the Americans. Most had assumed correctly that their actions warranted the death penalty if captured by the North Vietnamese.

"Where are we going?" Byrnes asked Roh. The two men accompanied a woman with three small children, meandering slowly north and west. They took random turns at street corners, occasionally doubling back. Roh watched for NVA soldiers or civilians who might be following them, or showing undue interest in their tortuous stroll.

"Can't tell you," Roh said. "If the NVA question us, I don't want you or Mrs. Hung to know, yet."

The small group approached a bridge across a small man-made channel of water. Roh stopped the group. He leaned over the bridge railing, looking at the brown water and pointing to various landmarks. The children listened intently as he explained part of the escape plan to

Byrnes and their mother. "This canal eventually leads to the Saigon River, south of where it meets the Dong Hai River. From there the combined rivers flow southward to the Binh Dong, the East Sea. Or, as the Americans call it, the South China Sea."

"That's a long swim," Byrnes said. "We have water wings, I hope."

Roh laughed. "Better than that," he said. "Mrs. Hung and I will stay here, Con co. You go to the far side of the bridge and cross over to the other side. Wait until no one is around. There is a path down to the river. The vegetation and bridge will hide you from sight. You will find a boat there. I will send the others down one by one. Get them onto the boat."

"Will you be down last?" Byrnes asked.

"No," Roh said. "I have more trips to make. We should have everyone together by nightfall. The password is, 'Father Chinh?' Once you say that, someone on the boat will say, 'He has gone to Mui Ne.' Any other response means the northerners have found us out."

Byrnes nodded. He walked as nonchalantly as possible to the far end of the bridge and crossed the street. A captured ARVN armored personnel carrier, sporting the NVA battle flag, traversed the bridge going the opposite direction. The lieutenant sitting in the command seat ignored Byrnes. No one manned the seat behind the .50 caliber machine gun. Other than two pedal cabs in the distance, Byrnes saw no other traffic. He waited until the APC disappeared from sight, checked the area for other pedestrians, and then dropped onto the dirt trail next to the bridge.

Directly underneath the bridge, hidden by land and water vegetation, Byrnes found a large sampan, not dissimilar to the one that had saved his life in the Gulf of Tonkin. Slapping his hand on the side of the boat, he called, "Father Chinh?"

From the stern of the covered section of the sampan a short man with bad acne and dragon tattoos on a bare chest pulled back a curtain. "He has gone to Mui Ne," he said. "Are you alone?"

"No. there will be three children and Mrs. Hung shortly."

"Fine. No names. Be quick. Tell the children to be quiet."

Byrnes had climbed almost to street level when the youngest of the children, a girl approximately six-years-old, met him on the path. He held her hand and walked her to the boat. As the boat rocked gently in the wake of another sampan passing by, Byrnes handed the child to the sailor.

Next he brought the youngest son, followed by Mrs. Hung. The oldest boy arrived last, accompanied by Lt. Roh. "I thought you weren't coming." Byrnes said.

"I'm not. Just checking on conditions. You need to stay in the boat, out of sight," Roh said.

"Mr. Dang really believes he can sneak fifty people out of Saigon on a sampan?"

"This is no ordinary sampan, Con co," Roh said and smiled. "It has a large, powerful inboard engine. In addition, it has a compass and a radio. It is capable of sea-going operation. To a smuggler, it's worth its weight in gold. Mr. Dang used it to meet with larger ships offshore. I'll be back in about two hours. Get some rest. We'll set sail after dark."

Byrnes climbed onto the fifty-foot boat. The sailor who had greeted him sat near the tiller, smoking a cigarette, reading an old edition of the *Nhan Dan*, a North Vietnamese newspaper. He nodded to Byrnes, pointing to the hatchway that led to the covered portion of the boat. Byrnes pulled back the plasticized drape and stepped inside.

In a fairly roomy interior Byrnes found a score of men, women, and children. He estimated the humidity on the river hovered at nearly 90%, and the temperature had climbed to the mid eighties by the early afternoon. The children lay on the deck naked. Adults sweated. They read or slept in silence. In the hold below the compartment Byrnes saw sacks of rice and tins of water. Children lay on the rice bags. One baby nursed at its mother's breast. Byrnes sat near the entrance. People whose names he could not remember from the night before nodded to him and smiled wearily. Body odor, the smell of raw vegetables, fish, sewage in the canal, and fear hung in the air.

Throughout the day and evening others arrived singly and in pairs. Monsoon rains poured on either side of the bridge intermittently. Byrnes counted fifty-three occupants before Mr. Dang, his wife, Tu and her husband arrived with Roh. Fifty-eight fugitives on the small sampan. All the refugees squeezed into the lower hold. The two crewmen of the sampan covered the hold with boards and laid fishing equipment on top of the boards. In the claustrophobic darkness, parents whispered to their children, trying to comfort them.

As the sun set, Roh and Byrnes joined the men on deck to augment the crew. Jumping into the canal, they helped push the sampan from the reeds under the bridge. The sailors had given them simple cotton pants and sandals to replace their civilian clothing. To the unsophisticated eye, they passed as crew. Using a small outboard motor, the tattooed sailor navigated the channel north and east, toward the Saigon River. The big inboard motor ran at idle, in reserve if needed.

Saigon buildings were dark. Few street lights shone in the city. Bridges were deserted of pedestrians. Byrnes saw no vehicular traffic anywhere. The curfew of the second night of occupation kept people in their homes, either planning for escapes or accepting their fate, he guessed.

A police boat pulled alongside the sampan about an hour after they cast off. The small powerboat flew the NVA battle flag as banners from its bow and stern. An infantry sergeant in dark green khakis stood on the bow of the boat. Two armed soldiers positioned themselves behind him. A third man steered the boat. He wore a white T-shirt and dirty white pants. The nose of the police boat nudged the sampan, which was about twice its size. "Where are you going?" the sergeant asked.

"The East Sea," the sailor with acne replied. "Tide goes out early this morning. We will be trapped inland unless we leave now."

"We have orders to inspect all boats," the sergeant said.

The sailor with the dragon tattoo threw the sergeant a line. "Fine. Come aboard." After lashing the two boats together, the sergeant stepped across the gap to the sampan. He followed the sailor into the compartment. Obviously not a sailor, the sergeant wobbled while moving about the boat. He saw the fishing equipment covering the deck, but did not ask to see the hold. He had been unaware the sailor had kept his hand on the hilt of the long knife in a leather scabbard on his belt, prepared to end the soldier's life if necessary.

"Okay," the sergeant said. "You may continue. Bring us some fresh fish when you return. I have written your boat's number down, 513. Don't forget, or there will be trouble." He jumped across the gap between the boats and, after loosening the line, tossed it into the water. The sailor pulled the rope into the sampan and coiled it on the deck.

"Yes, sir," the sailor replied. He returned to the tiller and cranked up the outboard. Slowly the boats parted. The police boat made a U-turn and continued west.

Two hours later the sampan puttered into a larger body of water. "Saigon River," Roh said quietly to Byrnes. "The Dong Hai is north of us. The East Sea is south of us. There are not many channels between here and the ocean. Mr. Dang's crew knows them all. We have to hope the NVA are not yet aware of them."

When the sampan cleared the south edge of Saigon, the sailors pushed the fishing gear to one side and opened the hatch to the hold.

They allowed the sweating, confined passengers to come up on deck four or five at a time for brief respites of fresh air and to relieve themselves over the side of the boat. The gunnels sat barely two feet over the brown water.

"I'm surprised the police didn't open the hold," Mr. Dang said to Roh when he took his turn on deck.

The tattooed sailor laughed. "Boss," he said. "That was no water policeman. The NVA probably detained all the real river police. He was a land-lubber for sure. A real sailor would have noted how low in the water we sit. He would have known there is a hold filled with something below the compartment."

"I guess we should be thankful that they replaced the water patrol with their own people," Dang said. "How much longer until we reach the East Sea?"

"We are taking our time," the sailor said. "We will reach the Nha Be River shortly. I hope to have us at the East Sea by dawn. Then we can use the big engine. We have more than enough fuel to reach Malaysia. Do you still want to go southeast?"

Dang shook his head. He said, "My informants say the Americans are escorting a vast number of large and small Vietnamese boats to the Philippines. We should go east. With luck we will be picked up by a larger ship."

"Aye, aye, sir."

The muscular throb of the powerful inboard motor woke Byrnes as he dozed on the deck. He rolled over and looked into a fat, red, rising sun, surrounded by pink billowing clouds on the horizon over the open sea. Then he heard the gunfire from behind the sampan. Dang had returned to the deck, wearing only his underclothes. "Faster!" he yelled. The inboard growled louder.

Tracer rounds hit the water near the bow of the ship. Byrnes turned his head and saw another patrol boat to the south, closing quickly. "Better surrender," he said.

"Never!" Dang said. The man pulled an M-16 from inside the compartment and began to return fire.

A third patrol boat north of them opened fire on the sampan with a machine gun. Bullets stitched the water, climbing into the boat, feet from Byrnes. He heard screams from the passengers below. Dang tumbled into the water, covered with blood. The tattooed sailor, the second crewman, Roh, and Byrnes stood on deck, hands in the air. The machine gun fell silent.

CHAPTER 40

"So, Mr. Wolfe, you are not familiar with Mr. Fulton?" the court appointed psychiatrist asked Wolfe.

"I'm sorry, Dr. Nichols," Wolfe said, looking across the desk at the pretty, slight, black woman. A whiff of perfume wafted across the desk and dissipated quickly. "I knew Chief Fulton a long time ago when he was a third-class petty officer in the navy. He worked in disbursing on one of the ships on which I served. The only time I saw him was when payday rolled around and we were headed into port. Otherwise I left my pay in the bank."

"He's convinced you want him dead. I'm trying to determine if he is delusional, paranoid, or some other type of mentally ill," Nichols said. "You understand?"

"Of course," Wolfe said. "I did shoot him, but only to keep him from stabbing my daughter. He broke into my house and threatened to shoot me. I'm a retired physician, by the way."

"Sorry. I knew that. Would you prefer I call you Dr. Wolfe?"

Wolfe smiled. He wondered if Dr. Nichols were psychoanalyzing him. "Addison, Addy, or even Doc – that's what the kids at the elementary school call me – is good. Doctor, rather than Mister, if you want to be extra professional, though."

Nichols grinned. "Touché, Doc," she said.

"How seriously did I wound him?" Wolfe asked.

Nichols leafed through Fulton's medical chart, stopping on a yellow page. She said, "He got a chest tube for about a week. Surgeon took the slug out of his right lung. He has healed. No physical complications are expected."

"Did Fulton shoot the court reporter? Was she seriously injured?" Wolfe asked.

"They took the bullet out of her thigh. She's walking with crutches. They did ballistics on the bullet. We're not positive who shot her, yet. Fulton denies it. The same weapon you used to shoot Fulton was used to wound the reporter, though. I don't understand why he would have shot the court reporter, if he did. Or who did it, if it wasn't Fulton. The reporter didn't see who fired through her sliding glass kitchen door."

"Have you done a physical work-up on the Chief? Any lab or scans to check him for the other things that might make him hallucinate, like thyroid abnormalities, drug use, brain tumor, or whatever else is pertinent?"

"All negative," Nichols said, nodding. "His story about the fight and throwing a man overboard is consistent, however. Do you know how true that is?"

"Maurice Noble was a second-class petty officer at the time who is also a retired chief now. He was on the same ship with Fulton and me. He told me Jimmy Byrnes did disappear from the ship during its last deployment. I wasn't on the ship then. The navy wrote the incident off as a suicide. I met with Jimmy's sister recently, and an ex-POW. They say Jimmy survived the push or fall from the ship and ended up in South Vietnam as a POW."

"So there's a chance he wasn't thrown overboard, but jumped or fell." Nichols said.

"At this point I don't think all the evidence is in," Wolfe said. "Losing sailors over the side of a ship is a constant worry. That's why they conduct *man overboard* drills. As a psychiatrist, you know there is a subset of people who are depressed and attempt suicide. And what better way to remove a witness to a crime or an enemy than to toss him overboard when no one is looking?"

"Man overboard drill?"

"It's even more common on carriers than other ships. Pilots and planes sometimes go into the ocean," Wolfe said, nodding.

"Mr. Fulton mentioned trying to yell, 'Man overboard,'" Nichols said. She stood and pulled off the jacket to her gray pantsuit, revealing a frilly pink blouse. She rounded the desk. Hanging the jacket on a hook on the back of her office door, she walked to a filing cabinet and opened the top drawer. After fingering through the filed psychiatric dictations, she pulled one out and took it to the desk. Sitting, she turned the pages of the chart over the top of the manila folder until she found the passage for which she searched. "We record our sessions," she said. "This is a typed transcript. Saves me from having to remember every detail. Fulton said, 'I yelled man overboard. The ship is a noisy place, especially the hangar and flight decks. No one heard me. Then Deke, that's Deke Jameson, grabbed me by the face. He threatened to throw me overboard, too, unless I shut up. He would have, too. He was a huge man. And angry. Byrnes had made him really furious, by getting him tossed into the brig and costing him his stripes.' Does that sound possible, Dr. Wolfe? Could Byrnes truly have been beat up and thrown off the ship?"

"I knew Deke Jameson. Obliquely," Wolfe said. "We weren't friends. He was a bully, an arrogant SOB. And large. If Fulton is correct about there being a smuggling ring within the Supply Division, and Byrnes had cost them a lot of money by testifying against Deke when he stole some laundry, then yeah. That's not only possible; I'd say it's likely. It would not have been easy, though. Jimmy knew some martial arts. I've seen him deck guys with a single punch, but only someone who had attacked him first. He was no bully. I expect it would have taken several guys to incapacitate him."

"That, too, is consistent with Chief Fulton's account," Nichols said. "Byrnes survived the fall and was later a POW?"

"Yes," Wolfe said.

"Can we get him to verify this chain of events? It would go a long way toward having Fulton declared mentally incompetent. I think his break with reality might have been the result of years of dealing with the guilt of not being able to save Byrnes. He's certain Byrnes died."

Wolfe shook his head. He said, "Jimmy didn't die from the fall from the ship, or drown. But he can't testify. The air force pilot who spent time with him as a POW says he was killed in a USAF bombing raid."

The psychiatrist wrote herself a brief note and placed it in Chief Fulton's chart. After a minute of staring at the note, while Wolfe wondered if the interview were over, she said, "Do you know anything about the men Fulton claims Byrnes killed? Obviously that's not possible if the man died in Vietnam, right?"

"You mean the members of Jameson's gang, the guys who were stealing from Supply?" Wolfe asked.

"Yes. The men in Fulton's scrapbook. Why would he feel they were murdered?"

Wolfe thought for a minute. He said, "I think you could probably explain that better than Chief Fulton or I can, Dr. Nichols. I suppose the responsibility the Chief felt for Byrnes's assumed death might make him wish they had died at Byrnes's hand. That would mean Byrnes wasn't really dead. Or, maybe Fulton killed them himself, or arranged their deaths?"

Nichols pulled her upper lip under her lower lip, contemplating as she jotted notes. She said, "You know, at one point he claimed you were trying to kill him. And you may have killed those other men."

"I did shoot him," Wolfe said. "Until three weeks ago, I had no idea that Jimmy was dead or that they had tried to kill him. Otherwise, I might have done precisely that."

"Okay," Nichols said. She lay the dictation on her desk. "I believe that's all I have for you now. Would you mind coming back if I need more information?"

"Not at all, if I'm available," Wolfe said. "Sometime this summer I will be attending Mrs. Byrnes's funeral. The date isn't set yet, and that can take a while at Arlington National Cemetery."

"Okay, thanks, Doc," Nichols said. "Looks like I'll send a deputy to Chief Fulton's home, to see if there are any receipts for plane trips on the dates of these men's deaths." She stood and shook Wolfe's hand. "Thanks for coming in."

"My pleasure, Dr. Nichols."

CHAPTER 41

Wolfe sat in a folding chair in the large living room of the brick colonial house in Alexandria. All the furniture that had been in the room on his last visit had been removed and replaced with Mrs. Byrnes's casket, several stands of flowers, and an altar draped in white paper. Tammy Kimura told Wolfe the altar was a Shinto shrine and the paper was meant to ward off evil spirits.

After all the visitors had viewed Mrs. Byrnes's body, a Buddhist priest conducted the wake ceremony. Kimura and her sister had dressed the dead woman in a white kimono, her wooden geta sandals, and white socks with the gap between the first and second toes. They had placed six coins, pictures of family members including Jimmy and his father, and a package of her favorite chocolate candy in the coffin.

The casket sat obliquely in the corner with Mrs. Byrnes's head pointed toward the back window and feet toward the side window. "She was specific about having her head point north for the wake," Kimura said to Wolfe. "The coins are for her to pay to cross the Sanzu River, the Buddhist equivalent to the Greek mythological River Styx."

Wolfe sat through the Buddhist ceremony, understanding none of what the priest said in Japanese. The smell of incense and flowers drove him outside after the ceremony. Many of the guests stood on the broad lawn. Almost all the men, except Wolfe, wore black suits with white shirts and black ties. Wolfe's only suit was a dark navy blue.

"I'm so glad you could come to the wake on short notice, Addison," Kimura said as she approached him with a shorter Asian man in tow.

"Buddhists prefer the wake to be held on the 3rd, 7th, 49th, or 100th day after death. Not knowing when the funeral will be scheduled, we chose the seventh day."

"Still no date from Arlington National Cemetery?" Wolfe asked. He glanced at the white-haired gentleman. Someone had tucked the right sleeve of the man's coat into his right armpit after folding it. Two large safety pins kept it neatly pressed to his side.

"They say in late August. Yasuko calls every day. She suspects the calendar varies with the number of boys coming back from Syria through Dover, Delaware. They promised a firm date by the end of next week." Kimura turned to the man standing next to her. "I want you to meet Mr. Roh So-dong. I told you about him earlier over the phone. He works in the Korean embassy."

The man with one arm bowed slightly toward Wolfe. He held his left hand out. Wolfe shook it with his left hand. "Mr. So-dong," Wolfe said. "A pleasure to meet you. Oh, I'm sorry, that's your first name isn't it? I forgot that the Koreans, like the Vietnamese, place their surname first. Mr. Roh, correct?."

Roh shook Wolfe's hand. "Correct. James told me much about you, Dr. Wolfe. Tammy has praised you, also," Roh said, surprising Wolfe.

"Mr. Roh was in Vietnam with Jim," Kimura said. "He told us about their time together. After reading about my mother's death in the *Washington Post* obituaries, he contacted us. He spent a long time on the telephone with Colonel Rhodes, too. The colonel couldn't make it today."

"You knew Jimmy in Vietnam?" Wolfe asked, surprised. "As a POW? With Rhodes?"

"Not with Colonel Rhodes," Roh said.

Kimura interrupted. "You two have a lot to talk about," she said. "I have to see to the guests. Please excuse me. Talk with me before you go, please." She patted both men's shoulders and left them together. Wolfe saw tears in her eyes.

In the spacious front yard, Roh and Wolfe wandered in silence between guests until they arrived at a sparsely populated, small Japanese rock garden to the left of the house, between the front entrance and the basement garages. Once out of earshot of the others, Wolfe said, "You work in the South Korean embassy?"

Roh nodded. "I'm the ROK, that is Republic of Korea, Civilian Intelligence Attaché."

"And you read obituaries as part of your job?"

"I read every word of the Washington Post, the New York Times, and the Wall Street Journal, every day they are published," Roh said, laughing. "You'd be surprised what you can learn about the military in this country by reading obituaries. Admiral J.T. Byrnes, Jr., was a hero in the war against Japan. An ace, in fact. When I saw the name of Mrs. Byrnes's predeceased, I knew I had found James's family."

Wolfe nodded. He asked, "How did you meet Jimmy?"

Roh told Wolfe about the NVA capturing him, forcing him to be a conscripted porter, the ARVN freeing them, the shock of the surrender of Saigon, and their attempted escape from the city two days later. "Obviously he survived the B-52 strike," Wolfe said.

"And a lot more," Roh said. "The patrol boats towed our sampan to land. Including Mr. Dang, the machine gun fire from the patrol craft killed three people. The NVA separated the men from the women and children. We never saw the women again, but it's safe to say they lost all their possessions. The NVA probably sent them to a New Economic Zone for punishment. Hundreds of thousands of South Vietnamese died in the NEZs and re-education camps, starved or beaten to death, or executed. I guess they could have ended up in the new collective farms in the south, but the collectives were a failure. Even the northerners admitted to that eventually."

"And you and Jimmy? How did you lose your arm?" Wolfe asked.

"The NVA considered young, healthy men without papers to have been in the military, ARVN. They treated all ex-military to re-education – hard labor, starvation, and communist propaganda. They initially thought James and I were Vietnamese. After they learned our real identities – it took a long time for them to believe us – they also sent us to a re-education camp in the north. Older men, obviously wealthy exploiters of the masses, suffered worse fates.

"Immediately after we reached shore and in front of their families and us, the NVA executed some men from the boat. They thought we were lowly crewman, or, at worst, smugglers. Since we were healthy, they tied us together and packed us onto captured American army trucks or Russian Molotova army trucks and shipped us north. We held on to the sides of the trucks and each other to keep from being bounced out of the vehicles. NVA tanks had destroyed the roads as they moved south for the invasion of South Vietnam. Tied together at the wrists, fifty men stood in the back of a truck, exposed to the elements, unfed, for three days until we reached the first re-education camp."

"First camp?"

Roh nodded. He said, "Do you mind if I smoke? Nicotine calms my nerves. It's not easy re-living these memories. They moved us frequently, to discourage escapes."

"Of course," Wolfe said. He watched as the one-armed Korean pulled a pack of cigarettes from his coat pocket with his left hand, shook the pack until a cigarette popped up, stuck it in his mouth, replaced the pack, and lit the cigarette with a Zippo lighter.

Roh showed the lighter to Wolfe. On one side, Wolfe saw the insignia of a Korean infantry battalion; on the other the map of South Vietnam. "A gift from my battalion when I returned to Korea in 1979."

"That's a long time to have been in Vietnam," Wolfe said. Smoke from Roh's cigarette wafted upward in the warm summer afternoon breeze.

"I was lucky to leave alive. For four years they alternately starved us or forced us to do hard labor. I suppose we were in six or seven labor camps. They moved us around to keep us confused about our location. All that time we received communist indoctrination as well. They released some prisoners after six months. Many more died of malnutrition, or beatings and executions. Some, I'm sure, are still held captive. We harvested rice from paddies, planted potatoes, constructed buildings, paved roads, chopped wood, whatever, until the Vietnamese invaded Cambodia to throw out the Khmer Rouge."

"Did they make you carry ammunition for that war, too?"

"Worse. The Chinese communists thought the Vietnamese acted under the direction of the Soviets and were trying to expand their influence in Southeast Asia. The Chinese invaded northern Vietnam and occupied part of it for several months. When the Chinese declared victory, they pulled out in March, 1979, leaving behind large mine fields."

Wolfe had already figured out how Roh lost his arm. "You guys had to disarm the mines?"

Roh nodded. "I made a mistake with one. James was nearby. He put a tourniquet on the stump. The Vietnamese thought I was going to die. They had minimal medical facilities. Rather than waste time and medicine on me, they contacted the Korean Embassy and turned me over to them. The embassy doctor had to amputate what remained of my arm in order to remove an infection and save my life. I survived. Obviously."

"What about Jimmy?"

"The last I saw him, he was headed back to the minefield to disarm more mines. I think about him every day. I tried for years to get my government to ask the Soviet government to coerce the Vietnamese to release him. To no avail. Even your government seemed less than interested."

"Yeah," Wolfe said. "I believe I know why. I had an unintentional meeting with the CIA. They are in no hurry to rescue MIAs. Did you tell his sisters about Jimmy?"

"They were delighted to hear he had not been killed by the B-52s, but devastated to think he could still be a prisoner," Roh said.

"Do you think he could still be alive? That's a pretty harsh environment. He was born in late 1946. He'll be seventy years old later this year if he is still with us," Wolfe said.

Roh shook his head. He said, "James didn't have many friends among the Vietnamese. Of all the prisoners, he had the most to gain by pretending to believe the Marxist-Leninist nonsense they spouted in the re-education courses. He never did. I saw no signs that he ever would give them the satisfaction of even thinking that he had changed his allegiance. I have to believe he is dead by now."

CHAPTER 42

"This man!" the Vietnamese officer in the starched, neatly pressed, green uniform yelled. He pointed at Byrnes, asleep on the straw mat laid over a wooden pallet.

Two beefy guards dragged Byrnes to his feet before he had awakened completely. One slapped the back of his head. "Stand upright. Look the major in the eyes," he said. A dog barked in the distance.

Byrnes opened his eyes wider, trying to see the officer in the dim light of the prison barracks, a hot, corrugated metal building with only dim, dirty skylights for light and ventilation. Scores of other prisoners lay scattered on pallets and the dirt floor around him. Most feigned sleep, not wanting to participate in the harassment of their comrade.

"He claims to be an American, yet he speaks fluent Vietnamese with a northerner's accent," the officer said. "Is that correct?"

"Yes, Major Binh," the second guard said, pulling Byrnes more upright by his shirt. "What should we do with him? He has spent months in isolation and years in indoctrination. Still he defies us."

"Put him in my car. I want him interrogated in Hanoi," Vong Binh said. He paused, sniffed the air and made a disagreeable face. "No. Wait. I don't want to ride with this smelly scoundrel in my car. Find him some clean clothes. Make him take a shower before putting them on. Do you have soap and shampoo?"

"Yes, Major," a guard said. He pushed Byrnes from behind toward the cinderblock outbuilding that housed the latrines and a single shower that served 250 prisoners. "Move it, Con co." The barking increased when the men stepped between the buildings into the dirt prison yard surrounded by concertina wire, machine gun towers, and guard patrols.

"Have him ready to go in thirty minutes," Vong said. "I will be in the camp commander's office collecting his papers."

"Yes, sir."

About forty-five minutes later, Byrnes found himself in a large, black Russian made Zil automobile. The guards had handcuffed his hands in front of him. A chain connected the handcuffs to a pair of leg irons around his ankles. He sat in the spacious rear seat of the vehicle with Major Binh. Two more people could have fit comfortably between them in the large car. The major appeared familiar in some way, but Byrnes could not place where or when they may have met. *Certainly, I would have remembered the scar that runs from the man's chin to his right ear*, he thought.

Vong remained silent for the entire four-hour drive to Hanoi from Lang Son and the re-education camp near the Vietnam-China border. Near the end of the trip, the Zil crossed a bridge over a large river. Within the city, Byrnes became aware of hundreds of scooters, small motorcycles, and bicycles on the streets. There were few automobiles visible. "That was the Red River," Vong said, speaking for the first time, "the ancestral home of our people, if you remember your history from school. You saw the sign, I'm sure."

"I don't read Vietnamese very well," Byrnes said.

Vong ignored Byrnes's response. He said, "And you may remember seeing pictures of the presidential palace." Vong pointed to a yellow building that Byrnes thought would have looked more at home in Paris, or at least in Europe. "A French architect designed it. I believe it's called Italian Renaissance architecture."

There were few multi-story buildings in the city, the majority being single-level with orange tile roofs. The few tall buildings stood out, giants among the pygmies. The Zil stopped in front of one, a soaring, gray stone, severe-looking, functional building. "This is the Ministry of Defense, and is where I work, Prisoner Byrnes. Your hands, please."

Byrnes held his hands in front of him. The major unlocked the chain that ran to the ankle cuffs, and then unlocked them. The chain and leg irons fell to the backseat floor of the vehicle. He left the wrist cuffs on Byrnes. "You are in the middle of Hanoi, Prisoner Byrnes. There is a small chance you could run away from me, but you would have difficulty escaping from the city, especially with the handcuffs on. Do you understand?"

Byrnes said, "I'm enjoying my day away from the minefield, Major. I am in no hurry to return. It's nice to rest for a while, too. Why am I here?"

"Insolent prisoner!" Vong said. He slapped Byrnes's face. The door behind Byrnes opened, held open by the driver, who reached in and pulled Byrnes out of the vehicle by his collar. The man made a fist and reared back to punch Byrnes.

"No!" Vong said. "I suspect he understands he should remain compliant now. True, Prisoner Byrnes?" Byrnes nodded. "Good. Driver, you are dismissed. Someone else will return this prisoner to Lang Son this afternoon or tomorrow."

"Yes, Major," the driver said, closing the back door. He walked around the black car and opened the front door. He spoke before climbing into the vehicle, "Major?"

"Yes, Corporal?"

"I doubt we will meet again, sir. Enjoy your retirement. It's been a pleasure being your driver for the last five years."

"Thank you, Corporal Bui. You have been a most helpful assistant. Have a long and happy career, soldier," Vong said.

"Thank you, sir."

Vong and Byrnes stood outside the building. They watched the Zil recede in the distance, returning to the military motor pool. "Moron," Vong said.

"Insults, now," Byrnes said. "May I know why I am here, Major?"

Vong laughed. "I meant the driver, not you, Con co. Corporal Nguyen Bui is an idiot. The slap to your face was for his benefit. I apologize," he said. "You don't recognize me, Con co? After all we meant to one another? You got me beat up in the south for letting a prisoner carry my AK-47, while I carried Thien Vu. The man who lost his leg."

Byrnes stared in disbelief. Uncertain, he said, "Binh. "Vong Binh, my friend." Byrnes's disbelief became incredulity when Vong unlocked Byrnes's handcuffs, removed them, and slipped them into his uniform coat pocket. He then shook Byrnes's hand.

"Why did you do that?" Byrnes asked.

"We are no longer at war, regardless of what my country thinks. I want you to come to my office," Vong said. "Your new papers are there. We wouldn't let prisoners walk around the Ministry of Defense, would we?"

"I don't understand," Byrnes said.

"You will. From now on, if anyone asks your name, it is Vong Sang. You are my brother. One year younger than I. You have been a guard in the re-education camps since the end of the war, and you, too, are now retiring," Vong said. "Understand?"

"You have a brother?" Byrnes asked.

"Missing and presumed dead by my family since the battle for Quang Tri Province in 1972, ten years ago. Your military called it the Easter Offensive. It was the first province liberated in the south," Vong said.

"What if your brother returns?"

"He won't. Ten years is a long time. We lost a half million soldiers in the war against the United States. More than half of them are buried in unmarked graves, or are missing in action. Unfortunately for us, fortunately for you, the records kept by my government are far from complete," Vong said. He opened the heavy metal door that led into the building.

"Won't they miss me in camp?"

In a low, flat tone, Vong said, "I have already sent word to your camp commander that you will be executed for crimes against the state."

Stunned, Byrnes followed Vong into the building and up four flights of stairs. They passed two young women in bright green uniform pantsuits, who chatted among themselves after acknowledging the major. Vong nodded silently toward them and kept walking. "No elevator," Vong said. "We won't have them until the power grid is restored. No one likes being trapped in an elevator when the power goes out." He chuckled. They encountered no one else in the hallways or on the stairs.

In his office, Vong handed Byrnes a set of clothing, including new underwear and new sandals. "We'll see about a haircut and shave when we get home," he said, as Byrnes changed. No sooner had Byrnes buttoned his white shirt and Vong had placed his prisoner's garb in a bag than there was a knock at Vong's door.

"Enter," Vong said. He stood upright and saluted when he saw Colonel Vu enter. "Good afternoon, Colonel."

"At ease, Major," Colonel Vu said. "Or should I say Mister Binh?" Seeing Byrnes, he added. "I'm sorry, Binh, I didn't realize you had a guest. I just wanted to wish you well in your retirement. You have been a fine asset to our operations group."

Vong held his left hand out toward Byrnes. "Colonel Vu, this is my younger brother, Sang, one of the heroes of Quang Tri. He came from our village to accompany me home. He is also retiring. Until a month ago he was a guard at one of the re-education camps."

Byrnes made a slight bow toward Colonel Thuy Vu. The colonel took a step toward Byrnes. He made a slight bow and held his hand out to Byrnes. Byrnes made a quick glance at Vong, who nodded his head. Apprehensively, Byrnes shook the officer's hand. "The State, the People's Army, and the Party thank you for your sacrifices, Sang," Thuy said. He then shook Vong Binh's hand. "Your ancestors must be particularly proud of your family, Binh. Have a safe journey home. Think of this old soldier occasionally."

"Yes, sir," Vong said. Thuy left the room, closing the door quietly behind him.

After he had been gone several minutes, Vong said, "Not bad, brother Sang. On the way home, we'll have time on the train and bus to teach you some greetings customs."

Byrnes smiled, "You mean other than the one where you are slapped or punched in the face on meeting?"

Vong laughed. "No longer, little brother. No longer."

CHAPTER 43

Standing on the manicured front lawn of the Byrnes's home, among a hundred people he didn't know, Wolfe thought about slipping out of the post-wake social party. He decided to say good-bye to Tammy Kimura first. In search of her, he found her sister, Yasuko Barnes, instead. "I'm going to leave, Mrs. Barnes," he said. "First, I'd like to say good-bye to Tammy. Do you know where I can find her?"

Reading her dislike for him on Barnes's face proved easy for Wolfe. The words out of her mouth surprised him, however. "Oh, Dr. Wolfe," she said, frown pinned to her face. "I'd like you to meet Datu Ocampo. He's a diplomat at the Philippine Embassy in D.C. He was Jim's roommate at Annapolis during plebe and youngster years."

The short, dark-skinned, plump, white-haired man put his right hand out toward Wolfe. "A pleasure to meet you, Doctor."

"Did she say, *Daytoo* Ocampo, sir?" Wolfe asked, shaking the man's hand. "Oh, and call me Addy or Addison."

The older Filipino smiled. He said, "She did, but my kids have been calling me Data, ever since *Star Trek the Next Generation* came out. Friends my age call me Dat."

"I'll leave you two to talk," Barnes said, almost pleasantly. "Tammy went to see about more refreshments, Dr. Wolfe. She should be back within a half hour."

"Thanks, Mrs. Barnes," Wolfe said.

Barnes answered clipping her words with loathing. "You are welcome, Doctor Wolfe."

Wolfe shook his head. He spoke to Ocampo after Barnes left. "I'm afraid she doesn't like me very much," he said.

"I've known Yaz for over fifty years," Ocampo said. "She doesn't like anyone very much. She lives in her own little world. If anyone intrudes without an invitation, they are an interloper and not to be trusted. Don't worry about it. It took her twenty years to warm up to me. She said you knew J.T. in Vietnam?"

Wolfe nodded. He took a sip of sweet ice tea. "Not exactly Vietnam. Jimmy and I were shipmates on the USS *Oriskany*. It's an aircraft carrier. Or was. It's an artificial reef off the coast of Pensacola, Florida, now. We spent time in the Gulf of Tonkin launching aircraft against the North Vietnamese, actually moving aircraft around the hangar deck. We also visited Japan, the Philippines, and Hong Kong. It was like a working, sight-seeing cruise at times."

Ocampo laughed. He said, "After I graduated from Annapolis, I returned to the Philippines and became an officer in the Philippine Navy. I also spent some time in the Gulf of Tonkin, on a destroyer the Americans lent my navy, BRP *Datu Kalantiaw, PS-76*. It and I shared a first name. It was renamed after one of the first Filipinos to make a pact with the Spanish in 1565."

"I didn't realize foreign students attended the US Naval Academy."

"Up to sixty each year," Ocampo said. "That's how J.T. and I became roommates after Plebe Summer ended and the academic year began. Some upperclassman decided J.T. looked too Asian. He was a good guy. It broke my heart to see him resign. He would have been a good officer. He had a great sense of honor and duty. I suppose he got some of that from both his mother and father."

"You got along well, I take it," Wolfe said.

"Not at first," Ocampo said. "You have to remember the Philippines was raped by the Japanese during World War II. Many of my family died in concentration camps. My grandfather and father served in the US Navy as messmen. They happened to be home on liberty when the war started, on December 8, 1941 in the Philippines. The day after Pearl Harbor. Both were stationed on the USS *Houston*, but couldn't get back to Panay Island before the *Houston* sailed. Eventually, they joined the Filipino resistance. The Japanese captured and executed them. I had vowed never to trust a Jap."

"The same *Houston* that was the first American ship to go down in battle after Pearl Harbor?"

"The same," Ocampo said. "Their fate would probably have been the same had they gotten back to the ship before it sailed. In any event, it took me three months to learn to like J.T."

"What changed your mind?" Wolfe asked.

"The first day in the swimming pool. In order to avoid mandatory swimming lessons we were required to swim across an Olympic-sized pool and back. We plebes stood in lines along the side of the pool. We were supposed to jump in, swim across, swim back, and climb out unassisted. He told me later that he had looked at the other end of the pool when some plebes jumped in and disappeared under water. He assumed that was the deep end of the pool. He expected to hit the bottom when he jumped in because he thought he stood at the shallow end. Consequently, he didn't bother to take a deep breath when he jumped. It was twelve feet deep. There was no shallow end. He came to the surface sputtering. I thought we might have to pull him out, but he managed to swim across and back. Barely. When he told me the story, I realized he was human, not inhumane. It broke the ice."

Wolfe smiled. Byrnes had told him that the navy thought Byrnes should hold his breath, sink to the bottom, and walk, if the ship ever sank. They didn't think much of his swimming ability. Now Wolfe knew why. "I saw him swim at the enlisted men's pool in Subic," Wolfe said. "He did tolerably well. Apparently you liked him well enough to room together the second year."

"Yeah. We had filed down all the sharp edges by the end of plebe year, before the youngster cruise. We caught the USS *Robison*, a destroyer, in Puget Sound, went to Hawaii, where J.T. swam in the Pacific and almost learned to surf. At some point, he realized he had to paddle out about a mile to catch a wave. We didn't have surfboard leashes connecting our ankles to the boards back then. He thought if he lost his board it might be a long swim to shore."

"Where else did you go on the cruise?" Wolfe asked.

"I got to show him around my home town, Manila. He made friends with everyone in my family, even the veterans from World War II. Then we went to Japan. I met his extended family in Tokyo when the ship docked in Yokosuka Naval Shipyard." Ocampo's eyes watered. He wiped away some tears. "They treated me like family. I've been back many times as a diplomat. Each time I stop in and see his family. We are close friends, now."

Wolfe waited until Ocampo had regained his composure, then asked, "What happened the second year?"

Grinning, Ocampo recounted their return to the Naval Academy.

"When we got back, it was like vacation from vacation. No more bracing, no chopping in the middle of the passageways or square corners, as much food at meals as we wanted, no more recitals of minutiae about formations or meals for the upperclassmen. We *were* upperclassmen. Academics required attention, of course, but without the plebe harassment, we easily got through our studies. I played soccer; he played 150 pound football. We had it made."

"Until the knee injury?"

"Yeah," Ocampo said. "When they twisted his knee after the interception in the Army-Navy 150 pound game, he said he heard a pop. His leg collapsed when he tried to run to the sideline after he was tackled. The docs at the academy weren't especially helpful. They told him he'd never fly; he wouldn't pass the physical. That ate at him and ate at him. He threw books around the room. 'Why study when they won't let me fly?' he said many times. Finally, he gave up and quit. There was nothing I could do to stop him. Captain Byrnes tried to reason with him, too. He told him there were more careers in the navy than flying. So did his girlfriend, although she wanted him to be a ground-pounding jarhead anyway."

CHAPTER 44

Byrnes had never ridden on a train before, except for the trip from Annapolis to Philadelphia for the Army-Navy football game. The conductor curried favor with Vong, still dressed in his green NVA major's uniform. The national railway employee practically fell over himself leading Vong and Byrnes to a relatively comfortable bench seat in the front of the passenger car. He placed Vong's small, weathered duffle bag in the storage area in front of the seat. "No one will bother it, I assure you, Comrade Major," the conductor said. "You and your brother have a pleasant trip. Be certain to let me know if you need anything."

After the man had moved toward the rear of the car, Vong said quietly to Byrnes, "Everyone is scared of the uniform. The only thing they fear more are the cadre, enforcers of the peoples' will." He had slipped Byrnes a second set of identity papers before they boarded the train to Sa Pa. "Everyone in my village will know you are not my brother, Con co. You are ten centimeters taller than he was. You are now Thien Sang, almost like Thien Vu's younger brother. And I'm going to return to calling you Con co, okay?"

"Vu? The man who lost a leg to the B-52s?" Byrnes asked.

"The same," Vong said. "He is now an administrator in Ho Chi Minh City. With luck, you will get to meet him again some day. He says he owes you his life. We both know that's true."

"Where did you get these papers?" Byrnes asked.

"I dealt with forgers and thieves for years as part of my job in national security," Vong said. "The black market is our only real economy. The only criminals we sent to jail or executed were the opium dealers and anyone in open revolt against the state. Corruption is rampant. If we put all the lawbreakers in detention camps, there would be no one to run the country." Vong laughed. "Anyway, I have, or I had, access to the best forgers in the country. Many of whom owed me favors. Your identification papers are better quality than those made by the government. In fact a man who makes documents for the government produced them. He steals their ink and papers and substitutes inferior quality materials."

"And my picture? How did you get that?" Byrnes asked, scanning his papers.

"That's a complicated story. My job in the Ministry of Defense put me in contact with most of the prisons, jails, and detention and re-education camps. After all, that's where we sent the criminals we caught," Vong said, quietly, even though the racket made by the ancient locomotive drowned his words before they reached anyone else in the car. "I thought you might have survived the war. I knew you never made it to Hanoi, once I saw the records of POWs repatriated to your country. Yours wasn't included. Eventually, I discovered where you were – I found out after the Korean blew himself up in the mine field. After that, it was easy to obtain your picture."

With a sudden lurch the train moved forward. It took fifteen minutes of halting acceleration, with black coal smoke drifting into the compartment through open windows, before the engine attained a decent speed. "Our infrastructure suffered terribly from the American bombing," Vong said. "This is supposed to be a nine-hour trip. It will take much longer than that."

The car reminded Byrnes of black-and-white movies he had seen. He imagined Bogart and Bacall as spies on a train through pre-World War II Europe, or maybe he remembered such a motion picture. All the wooden church pew-like seats faced forward. Two persons sat in each seat. Packed to the limit, several unfortunate villagers stood in the aisle. Byrnes suppressed the urge to stand in order to give an old woman his seat, an act that he supposed Vong would have difficulty explaining.

Every thirty minutes to an hour, the train pulled into a small station, sometimes pitching left and right on uneven tracks, always with a loud screeching of the brakes and a sudden, stuttering stop. After the passengers in the aisle regained their footing, they usually filed out, replaced by a new set of local residents. Byrnes saw trussed pigs, chickens, and ducks carried by farm boys and young women.

"Buses take even longer," Vong said, wrinkling his nose to an unfamiliar odor. "And the roads will be the last to be repaired, after the canal system, the railroads, and the electrical grid. We have much work to do. Some still curse Ho Chi Minh for not surrendering to the Americans, although they praise him for his tenacity against the Japanese and French. Ten years after you defeated the Japanese, you made them a world-class economic power. Imagine where we would be."

Byrnes fell asleep listening to the clack-clack of the train wheels. He woke in absolute darkness, the train motionless. Unsure of where he was, having started the day in a prison camp, he waited for his senses to take in his surroundings. "You missed the announcement," Vong said. "Engineers are checking the bridge ahead. There has been a lot of rain recently. They want to make certain it is structurally sound."

Shortly after that, the lights came on in the cabin. "Everyone will have to disembark," the conductor said. "The train will go across the bridge first. Then we will walk across the overpass." A chorus of moans greeted the announcement. "Or you can take your chances in the train. If the bridge doesn't hold its weight, you will die." The moaning stopped.

"In the dark?" Vong asked the conductor.

"No, Major," the conductor said. "I apologize for the inconvenience, sir. We will wait until dawn. Try to get some rest."

There were no more incidents after the passengers re-boarded the train on the far side of the trestle. On reaching Sa Pa, Vong had good news for Byrnes. "We won't have to wait in a hotel room overnight for the bus, since we spent the night on the train. Our bus leaves in thirty minutes."

Unfortunately, there wasn't a conductor to curry favor with Major Vong on the bus. He and Byrnes squeezed in along with the overload of passengers. The driver tied crates of birds and pigs to the roof and the back of the bus. Seated near the front, Byrnes thought he could make out French instructions written on the dash. The ancient diesel billowed clouds of oily black exhaust as it worked its way up and down the mountains. Slowly up, and too quickly down.

What should have been a two-hour trip, 72 kilometers to Lai Chau, took four hours in the Renault passenger bus built with a truck-like front end. There were places along the mountainous road when the collective passengers held their breath looking down into a ravine along the side of the dirt highway. Byrnes almost liked his chances with the landmines better. In Lai Chau, the passengers disembarked.

"So this is your hometown," Byrnes said to Vong.

Vong laughed. "This is the big city compared to our village," he said. "Be thankful you don't have a heavy bag to carry."

"Why?" Byrnes asked.

The nine-mile walk on the dirt road to Phong Tho took the two men four hours, up and down the switchback road through the mountains. A man on a bicycle and a woman on a Honda motorbike passed them, going in the opposite direction. Both waved. On the way, they passed a deserted village, overgrown by the forest. Byrnes saw thatched roofs no longer in place, trees growing through foundations, fences crumbling, and weeds poking through the cobblestones. The surrounding fields, once meadows of tall grass, gradually had been invaded by trees. "What's that place?" Byrnes asked as they sat by the road resting.

"Tam Duong," Vong said. "After the French defeat at Dien Binh Phu, the villagers abandoned it. They left the north for the south."

"The whole village?" Byrnes asked.

"A million and a half northerners went south after the Geneva Accords," Vong explained. "Mostly Catholics. Confucians converted to Catholicism by the French. The Buddhists in the south didn't like them any more than the Confucians or communists in the north, but they couldn't live under communist rule. In the middle of the night, whole villages left everything behind and marched south with their priests. They slept during the day, to avoid the Viet Minh patrols."

"So why haven't new villagers moved in?" Byrnes asked.

"Most young people gravitate to the bigger towns and cities these days, our workers' paradise. It seems no one wants to be a farmer any longer. They all want to work limited hours in factories or go to university. Besides, we don't have the population to replace those who went south. One and a half million left in 1954; another million northerners died in the war."

"What happened to the northerners who left their villages?"

"Most made it to the coast, caught boats to the south. Some crossed the DMZ on foot. President Boa Dai granted them abandoned French property in the Mekong delta. Your older brother, Administrator Thien Vu, has been trying for six years to collectivize their farms. He says it's not going to work. The southerners are too independent minded. As fast as he punishes them by sending them to the New Economic Zones, they bribe officials and return to their property."

Byrnes laughed. "The southerners might turn you northerners into capitalists, yet."

Turning serious, Vong said. "Don't laugh. We need Vu to succeed and remain an administrator in Ho Chi Minh City. He is trying to find you a way out of Vietnam. It may take a while. You need to be patient."

"So far, I have been here fifteen years, Binh. That's a long time."

"Perhaps. Remember, the war for Vietnamese independence dragged on for some forty years. On your feet, Con co," Vong said, lifting his body off the ground and picking up his duffel bag. "Use those long legs to finish the climb up the mountain."

CHAPTER 45

His search for Tammy Kimura led Wolfe back, into the house. Guests gradually diminished in number as they expressed their condolences, said last prayers in front of the casket, and bade their farewells to the sisters. Wolfe heard Kimura's voice upstairs, along with other guests. As he climbed the stairs he caught a glimpse of a black trouser leg entering the hallway bathroom and the door closing behind the gentleman who wore it. He found Kimura in her brother's bedroom talking with a gray-haired woman.

"Mom cut them all out, except this one," Kimura said, pointing to a photograph in the book, "probably because it wasn't labeled with your name."

The white haired woman chuckled. She said, "I never thought your mother liked me very much."

Wolfe waited patiently for a pause in the conversation. When Kimura finished talking, he said, "Tammy, sorry to interrupt. I have to go."

"Oh, Addy," Kimura said. "We were just going to look for you. I want you to meet Emily Rose. It used to be Emily Rose, then Emily Thornton. She's gone back to Rose, says she'll keep that from now on, no matter what husbands three, four, and five have for their last names."

"Tammy!" the diminutive woman said, blushing.

Kimura continued, "She was my brother's girlfriend his senior year in high school. Emily, this is Dr. Addison Wolfe. He was on the aircraft carrier in Vietnam with Jim."

Rose turned to face Wolfe. She was short, less than an inch over five feet tall. Her blond hair had morphed into a beautiful silver gray. Her genes had been kind. She didn't look more than fifty-five years old, although Wolfe knew she was in her late sixties. "A pleasure. Call me Addy," Wolfe said, holding his hand out to the woman.

She took his hand with both of hers. "It's nice to meet a close friend of Jim's," she said.

"Is that you?" Wolfe asked, pointing to the half-page picture in the open high school yearbook. It depicted a well-built blonde high school student with a pixie haircut, standing next to an exceptionally tall, handsome young man. The boy was easily a foot and a half taller than the girl. The caption read, *Mutt and Jeff: Editor of the* Salvo *interviews basketball star.*

"Yes," Rose said.

Kimura explained, "The *Salvo* was the school newspaper. My mother didn't cut that picture out. They didn't use Emily's name in the caption. Guess Mom missed it."

"Who's the tall guy?"

"That's my first husband, Max Thornton," Rose said. "We got married after college. The marriage didn't last long."

"Sorry," Wolfe said. He heard the toilet in the hallway flush and water run in the sink. No one exited the bathroom, however. Wolfe had a sudden inspiration. He turned to Kimura. "Would you mind if I borrowed that yearbook again, Tammy. I'd like to do some more research."

Kimura looked at Rose. Rose shrugged and nodded. Kimura said, "Sure, Addy. Could you bring it back when you come for the funeral, or mail it back if you can't make it?"

"No problem," Wolfe said. "Are you finished with it for now?" Both women nodded. Wolfe pulled out the tri-folded piece of paper he kept in his shirt pocket and placed it between the pages and then closed the book. The plastic book cover stuck to his hands when he picked it up, so he held it by one edge in his left hand.

Wolfe put his right arm around Kimura's shoulders and squeezed her to him. "I'll be here for the funeral," he said. "Your mom was a nice lady. Too bad I didn't get to know her better. I'm sure you and Yasuko will miss her."

"Thanks, Addy."

To Rose, Wolfe held out his hand. He said, "It was a pleasure meeting you, Emily. Maybe we'll meet again some day."

"That would be nice," Rose said, shaking his hand. "We could talk about Jim."

"That would be great," Wolfe said.

As Wolfe reached the first floor, he heard the bathroom door open. "Ready to go?" A man's voice asked.

***

"I don't know, Dr. Wolfe. What would this request have to do with Ralph Fulton, and whether or not he is fit for trial?" Psychiatrist Yolanda Nichols asked as she shook her head. She held Fulton's chart on the desk in front of her. "I don't see the connection."

"Chief Fulton says Byrnes told him to inject the bolus of potassium into Clemons, right?"

"Yeah, but what's that got to do with fingerprints in a fifty-year-old yearbook?"

"What if I could prove that James T. Byrnes is alive and living in the United States?" Wolfe asked. "Wouldn't that change things? Admittedly, Fulton's mental health is fragile. Seeing a ghost could certainly push him over the edge."

Nichols's face showed her surprise at the statement. She said, "What are the chances? You said it looked like he died in a friendly-fire accident in Vietnam."

"I heard recently that he survived the airstrike. He lived long enough for the North Vietnamese to send him to a detention camp near the Chinese border. I met a fellow inmate, a Korean soldier who disarmed landmines with him. That man was repatriated by the Vietnamese after more than ten years as a prisoner."

"Was Byrnes repatriated?" Nichols asked.

"I don't know. Right now, I can't prove he was. But if I find his recent fingerprints on that book, that will be a different story. I do know that the CIA threatened me with jail if I pursued my investigation. They don't want MIAs found, they said. Or, maybe, they want to exploit MIAs in some fashion and they don't want that exposed."

"You realize that you are beginning to sound a bit paranoid, don't you?" Nichols asked, shaking her head. "Okay, Addy, I'll see what I can do. The district attorney isn't going to be happy with the expense, though. This isn't a murder case. The alleged victim was already dead. It may be an attempted murder case, or a theft of hospital property with unauthorized use of medication case, a competency case, or a purely question of insanity case. The DA has more important legal matters he'd like to send to trial, or close."

***

"Dad! Watch out!" Kayla Anne yelled.

While driving, Wolfe had looked down and reached for his cell phone when it rang. He was digging in his pocket for the phone when the Prius rolled up on a man walking toward him in the middle of his lane, on North Legacy Trail in the Cascades. Looking up, he slammed on the brakes, stopping ten feet short of the tall, gray-haired man. The man continued his jaunt, walking around the driver's side of the Prius.

Wolfe rolled down the window. "Hey, old man," he said. "Get out of the middle of the street."

Never slowing, the man said, "I don't like the sidewalks here. They're uneven. I tripped once and skinned my knees. Nearly broke my wrist." He continued to walk, skirting the Prius and continuing down the middle of the lane.

Irritated, Wolfe yelled, "We'll put that on your tombstone, moron!"

"Dad!"

Blushing, Wolfe shrugged. "Well, it would look good there," he said. *"Rather be a hood ornament than have skinned knees.* Yeah, that fits." He shook his head. "We have some neighbors with early dementia. I guess that's why your mother chooses to spend a lot of time away from home."

"She and Junior will be back next week," Kayla Anne said.

"Good timing," Wolfe said. "I'll be out of town at Mrs. Byrnes's funeral."

When they pulled into the driveway and stopped, Wolfe finished fishing out his cell phone. "Go ahead in, KayLan," he said. "I have to return this call. Reception's better here in front of the house." He pushed the button on the garage door remote. The door slowly retracted into the garage.

Kayla Anne exited the car. "Make sure you close the door, Dad. We don't want the cookie zombies returning."

Wolfe smiled and nodded. He listened to the message on his phone and returned the call to the fingerprint expert.

CHAPTER 46

"Con co!" Vong called to Byrnes as the American returned from the terraces one evening.

Exhausted from a day of harvesting rice and clearing irrigation ditches along the terraces, Byrnes smiled and waved. He needed no excuse to halt his steep climb uphill to the hamlet. "Binh," he said, sitting on a log at the edge of the forest. He placed his long wooden shovel between his legs. "What brings you to the workers' paradise? I thought you village administrators couldn't stand physical labor."

Vong surveyed the dry mud caked on Byrnes's arms, chest, and feet. Bare-chested, he wore only cotton pants, also covered in mud. He said, "I have been looking for you. Have you been working the fields again?"

"Widow Mai Kim-Ly's share of the collective rice field needs harvesting. I do what I can for her," Byrnes said. "It helps me fit in. Also, I learn many customs from her."

Glancing around to make certain no one else could hear their conversation, Vong noted the path through the woods was empty as was the trail down the edge of the terrace. "Have you told her you are an American?"

"No," Byrnes said, "I told her only what you wanted me to tell people. Like everyone else, she believes that my mother was a French nun raped by the Japanese during the war. That I grew up in an Hanoi orphanage until I escaped and lived as a street urchin with no schooling. Needing cannon fodder, the NVA drafted many of us into the service. All that explains my lack of manners, lack of education, and my inability to read Vietnamese."

"You seem awful close to widow Kim-Ly," Vong said. "Not that it's a bad thing. A woman needs a man, especially those women whose husbands died in the war."

"Another good reason not to tell her I'm American," Byrnes said, nodding. "She cares for certain of my needs, and I do the same for her. And she's teaching me Vietnamese history and to read."

"Is she your first woman?" Vong asked.

"No!" Byrnes blurted, then reconsidered, "Well, yes, but don't tell anyone. I'm sure many of your comrades were still virgins when conscripted by the army."

"Many remained virgins until their deaths," Vong said, shaking his head. "Many wives became widows. Also, some wives could not wait for their husbands to return. Fortunately, my wife remained faithful." Changing the subject, Vong said, "I have good and bad news, Con co."

"I am sitting. Tell me the bad news first," Byrnes said.

"There is an ongoing investigation into your disappearance. My ex-driver apparently asked about you to someone in the Ministry of Defense."

Stunned, Byrnes said, "It's been nearly three years, Binh."

"The Party is slow, but it has the memory of an elephant. Three men are on their way here to interview me, to see if I know why you did not return to your re-education camp. There is no record of your execution," Vong said. He sat on the log next to Byrnes. "We have to go south. I sent a letter to Thien Vu. He should have it in a week or so."

"How much time do we have?" Byrnes asked.

"Transportation has not improved much since our journey here. And the Party is slow, as I said. I assume we have a week to leave the village. Depending on how rapidly security personnel respond to my family, you, and me being gone, we have about that long to depart the country after we make it to the south. We must hope Thien Vu has made sufficient arrangements."

"Are you willing to leave the country because of me?" Byrnes asked.

"Me and my family. Rescuing you always carried a risk. Thien and I both knew that. He will have to come with us, too. All our lives are forfeit otherwise," Vong said.

"Your family is all right with leaving?" Byrnes asked. He thought of Vong's three children, two girls and a boy in their early teens. "What's the good news?"

"In his last letter, Vu said he thought he had solved *our problem*. He knows how to get you out of Vietnam," Vong said, smiling. Trying to lighten Byrnes's mood, he added, "It will be a great adventure.

"Vu and his family have been preparing to leave for years. Except his wife. She died of tuberculosis. The government medical services couldn't treat her, even though Vu is a Party member in good standing. The government has no money for medications. The harshness of the Party's oversight and the corruption in the government have discouraged him. Fortunately, he knows all about fraud and bribery, dealing with it on a daily basis. He has helped others escape. Getting his children, their families, and us out should be easy for him. Besides, the government is actively encouraging some people to leave. The Party chased the Chinese out of northern Vietnam and Saigon. They ignore misfits bribing officials to leave. The Party even encourages successful escapees to send money to their families that remain in Vietnam. Without that money the economy might collapse."

***

Vong let everyone in the village know the Communist Party had summoned him and his family to Hanoi in order to receive a medal from the premier himself, Pham Van Dong. He said he supposed the award was for his work against corruption and the black market. When leaving the village, he wore his faded green major's uniform. Medals hung on his shirt pulling the pocket almost to his waist. His family followed him down the dirt road to Lai Chau. Twenty or thirty residents lined the pathway near the hamlet to wish him well on his journey. Even the geese seemed to celebrate his departure by honking louder than usual.

Byrnes left the village two days later. He took the widow Mai Kim-Ly's Honda motorbike, the widow Kim-Ly, and a small cloth suitcase with all her possessions. They told no one that they would not be returning. He wore everything he owned. In Lai Chau, they sold the motorbike, taking payment in paper Dong and some aluminum coins. With that money, they paid for their seats on the same old bus Byrnes and Vong had ridden to Lai Chau three years before. Early the next morning they arrived in Sa Pa and met Vong in front of the railway station.

"What's this, Con co?" Vong asked on seeing Mai Kim-Ly. "Did she come to say good-bye?"

"There's a small complication," Byrnes said, pulling Vong to the side in order to speak privately. "She's pregnant."

"You're the father?" Vong asked.

"Do you know anyone else who has slept with her since her husband was killed?" Byrnes asked.

"No," Vong said. "Have you told her you are an American?"

"Not yet," Byrnes said. "Give me some time. As you know, you arranged this trip suddenly. She'll know before we reach another country. I promise."

"All right," Vong said. "I'll procure another ticket. If it is running on time, the train will be here in an hour." He left to enter the building and to buy another ticket.

He had not been gone long when the train arrived, an hour early. Byrnes could tell a new engine pulled the passenger cars, although those cars appeared more dingy and worn than they had three years before. Looking as if they had slept in their clothes, three men in wrinkled green uniforms of officers in the Peoples Army disembarked. Each carried a small suitcase and identical briefcases. Byrnes thought one officer was a major. He didn't recognize the rank of the other two, although the major seemed to defer to them. The three men marched down the street in the direction of the bus station.

"That's yesterday's train," Vong said when he returned. "The coal burner blew up on the tracks fifty kilometers north of Hanoi. The railroad authority sent this new diesel to finish the trip. The stationmaster gave me a choice: take this train south, or wait for the next one in about two hours."

"What did you tell him?" Byrnes asked.

"The sooner we leave the better," Vong said. "I told him we'd leave now."

"Good. I think the officers on your investigation board arrived on that train. A major and two other officers got off while you were inside. They walked toward the bus station."

"Yen," Vong said to his wife, "I'll take the children. I can't do this in my uniform without attracting their attention. You follow those officers. See what ranks they have. Don't get close enough for them to see you. One of the officers may recognize you from Hanoi. Hanh Ca, bring your sister. Giang Hai, gather the luggage."

Byrnes helped Mai Kim-Ly into the passenger car. She wore only a peasant's black pajama-like pants, black shirt, and a woven bamboo hat. Byrnes stuffed her small bag under their seat. He refrained from holding her hand in public. They sat opposite Major Binh and his family. Vong Yen returned. When the train got underway, she whispered into her husband's ear. Vong Binh listened to his wife and then nodded in Byrnes's direction. No obsequious steward or conductor smoothed Major Binh's way to Hanoi on this trip. The trip took only ten hours with the new diesel pulling the cars mainly downhill from the mountains. Three days later they were in Ho Chi Minh City.

CHAPTER 47

Arlington National Cemetery scheduled Mrs. Byrnes's funeral for a Saturday morning. Wolfe decided to drive to Washington in the Prius two days ahead of time. He left Kayla Anne with her mother's Subaru. She also had access to the van conversion in an emergency. "Pick your mom and Junior up at the airport," Wolfe told his daughter as she lay in Junior's bedroom, hands over her eyes to block the light. 6:00 a.m. was much too early for a college senior who had finished her summer classes. "And don't let them leave until I get home. Got it?"

"Like she'd listen to me," Kayla Anne said. "When will you be back?"

"Probably Monday or Tuesday. Love you."

"Love you, too, Pops. Drive carefully," Kayla Anne said. "Don't use the cell phone while you are driving."

"What? Am I the kid now?" Wolfe asked, laughing. Twelve hours later, he returned to the same hotel he had stayed in before in Crystal City. Using his laptop and the internet, he had no difficulty finding Emily Rose's address and telephone number in Fairfax City.

The next morning, Friday, he called her to make certain she was at home. "Sure," Rose said, "I'd love to talk with you about Jim. My husband won't be home until later, so the neighbors will gossip." She giggled. "I like being the source of their entertainment."

Wolfe found the older, small brick rambler, near George Mason University, without difficulty. A newer VW sedan sat in the driveway. There was no garage. Parking the Prius behind the Bug, Wolfe exited the car. He opened the screen door and knocked on the wooden door, using a brass knocker shaped like a lion with a ring in its mouth.

In seconds, the inner door swung open. The tiny Emily Rose beckoned him into the living room. She held her hand out to Wolfe and then engulfed him in a hug. "So good to see you, Dr. Wolfe," she said.

He returned the hug tentatively and released her. He said, "Addy, please. May I call you Emily?"

"Of course," she said. "May I offer you some sweet tea? Some chips? Have a seat on the couch." She pointed to a leather couch under the front living room window.

"Tea would be great," Wolfe said, sitting. "I really am thirsty."

She retrieved the tea and chips from the kitchen, and then sat across from Wolfe in a matching loveseat. For about an hour, Wolfe and Rose reminisced, telling each other their favorite James T. Byrnes stories. She told him about the senior class trip to Great Falls. He shared stories about R&R in Hong Kong.

A motorcycle rumbled into the driveway. "Would that be your husband?" Wolfe asked.

Rose nodded. She said, "He teaches at George Mason. Actually, he's a history fellow there."

"Teaches about the Vietnam War," Wolfe said.

Rose's eyes grew larger. "How did you know that, Addy? I don't believe I told you about him."

"You didn't," Wolfe said, "but I learned quite a bit about him from the internet. His last name is Thien, first name Vu. A widower, he escaped from Vietnam in a sampan in 1985, along with his children. And grandchildren. Went to Thailand, then Canada, and immigrated to the US, after marrying you."

Stunned, Rose sat with her mouth open. She did not stand when the front door opened and Thien Vu stood in the doorway. Only slightly disappointed that Thien wasn't six inches taller, Wolfe rose from his chair and walked to the door, right hand extended. "Good afternoon, Mr. Thien, I'm Dr. Wolfe, a friend of Jimmy Byrnes. I met your wife at his mother's wake. Your wife and I were entertaining each other with some stories about him. I have reason to believe you knew him as well."

Thien looked at his wife, eyebrows raised. She shook her head. "I didn't tell him anything. He figured it out by himself," she said. "I guess it wouldn't hurt to tell him what happened to Jim when you left Vietnam."

Wolfe scanned both their faces, hoping to tell if they would be honest. He had never been able to interpret peoples' body language or facial expressions, except for gross displays of anger or mirth. "Would you mind?" he asked Thien.

"Please, have a seat," Thien said. "I'll be right back." Thien left the room and returned with a large glass of what could have been sweet iced tea, but looked a little more like bourbon on the rocks. Limping slightly, he walked to his wife's side and sat with her on the small loveseat, holding her hand.

"Before you begin," Wolfe said, "tell me how you two met."

Thien grinned. He squeezed his wife's hand hard enough for her to make a face. "Con co gave me her name and address before we left on our journey."

"Con co?"

"A nickname we gave him in Vietnam when he was a POW. It means stork. He was much taller than the rest of us," Thien said.

"You were a POW, too?"

"No. I was in the North Vietnamese Army," Thien said. He briefly outlined Byrnes's capture, escape, and recapture, and how he and Binh vowed to rescue him. "He saved my life," Thien explained, tapping on his prosthetic leg. "He could have taken Binh's AK-47 and killed us both. Instead, he helped Binh find medical help for me. For that act of kindness to an enemy soldier he remained a prisoner for many years.

"I was an administrator in Ho Chi Minh City. You know it as Saigon. After the storms and floods of 1979 almost destroyed our economy – made worse by attempts at collectivization – I made plans to leave Vietnam if the opportunity presented itself. You never knew who the communists would use as scapegoats for their failures. I also knew that helping Binh and Stork might be a death sentence.

"The day before he, Kim-Ly, and Binh's family arrived in Ho Chi Minh City, I had received the letter Binh had written about the investigation into Stork's disappearance. I was expecting them, though, because the Party had put out an order for their arrests. I had a safe house I used in the city, so I put them up there.

"I had gotten people out of Vietnam before. Some went across the Mekong River to Cambodia after our armed forces defeated the Khmer Rouge. Many were caught and turned back by Vietnamese patrols there, though. I heard that many Chinese, like the Hoa in the north, took junks and sailed to Hong Kong...but China eventually closed its other ports. If the junks didn't make it all the way to Hong Kong, the Chinese turned them back to Vietnam. Many perished.

"The only way out for us, in 1985, was to sail on the East Sea;

Americans call it the South China Sea. We could sail to the Philippines, Indonesia, Malaysia, or Thailand. At that point, only about fifty percent of escapees actually left the country. My government caught many and placed them in re-education camps or the New Economic Zones, which proved death sentences for some. The courts executed a number of people who attempted to escape. Many returned home to find all they owned confiscated by the communists. The officials waited for these resourceful individuals to rebuild their wealth. Then those same dishonest officials received more gold and silver in bribes the next time the people tried to escape. Corruption was rampant.

"Only about half of those people who actually made it to the East Sea survived. The lucky ones were picked up by larger ships. Many shipping companies ordered their sea-going vessels to ignore the refugees. Many expatriates died of starvation or thirst. Sailing south to Thailand exposed the escapees to the pirates in the Gulf of Thailand, who raped, killed, and kidnapped many women. They also brutally slaughtered children, and men. They stole food, water, and treasure from the escapees. They rammed and sank their boats. I have seen statistics that suggest there were two million Vietnamese refugees between 1975 and 1992. We think one-half to three-quarters of a million of them died trying to escape the communists."

"A national tragedy," Wolfe said.

"No. A world tragedy," Thien said, shaking his head. "We were abandoned to die, either at the hands of our own government, at the hands of pirates, by starvation and thirst, from storms at sea, or from cruel twists of fate. It was not like Vietnam had not suffered enough already."

"Obviously, you made it out okay," Wolfe said. "Are those just stories Vietnamese immigrants tell for sympathy?"

"No!" Emily Rose said. "Tell him Vu. Tell him how Jim died."

Wolfe took in a deep breath through his nose, forcing himself to remain calm. He admired how Thien kept his emotions under control. "Please, go on," Wolfe said.

"My office received reports on the search for Vong Binh, his family, and Stork, so I knew how close the investigators were getting," Thien said. "On the day they had narrowed their search to central Ho Chi Minh City, I left work early and went to the safe house. Altogether, we had a crowd of twenty or more, with my children and grandchildren and Binh's family. I gave everyone instructions on how to take different routes to the Ham Tu wharf in Saigon. We split up into five or six groups and made our way to a taxi boat, arriving in a staggered fashion. The taxi made three trips in the canals to the village of Luong Hoa, southwest of Ho Chi Minh City. There is a boat yard in Long An Province, close to the village.

"I had provisioned a boat over the previous month, in preparation for leaving Vietnam in case I had come under suspicion. It was a large sampan, previously owned by a smuggler. The marine patrol had confiscated it. As administrator, I took charge of it and used it for operations against black marketers. The crew was loyal to me. All were previous South Vietnamese sailors whom I had pardoned from re-education or NEZs.

"My crew had loaded the boat with coconuts, fish, beans, rice, sausage, dried squid, cookies, water, and fuel, but no weapons. If the authorities caught us I didn't want to face execution for treason. We took two days to meander through the canals and small tributaries to the Mekong River, traveling mainly at night to avoid detection. A coastal patrol boat stopped us in one of the smaller rivers. They fired a machine gun over our heads. We all assumed they would arrest us and send us to prison. Instead, the captain sent a man over to our boat. He held out his hat and said, 'Give me your gold, and we will let you go.'

"I collected some jewelry from the passengers, and threw in about one-fourth of my silver. We handed that to the sailor. He returned to his boat, but came back. 'The captain says that's not enough,' he said.

"We made another collection. I handed them half of my gold. The sailor returned to his boat. He waved at us from the patrol craft. 'Have a nice voyage,' he said, and snorted an evil laugh. Shortly after that we were alone on the river. Evidently, the additional jewelry and gold made the bribe acceptable.

"The second night we hit a sandbar. It took us two hours to rock the boat off the shoal. Stork and the crew spent those two hours in the water. Fortunately the tide was coming in and we were close to the East Sea. It was enough to lift us off the shelf.

"Patrol boats went past us in the dark many times during those two hours, but did not see us since we were close to shore and in the dark. Once the crew had us into the ocean, the East Sea, we turned south toward Malaysia. The shortest distance to safety was also the most dangerous. We knew the pirates might find us. They did.

"At one point we sailed through a cluster of drowned bodies, maybe thirty or forty children and men. Pirates had evidently kidnapped the women for the sex trade, and probably sunk the boat on which they traveled. We did not see their boat, only their bloated bodies. They were tied together at the wrists.

"I woke up on the third or fourth morning to find a Thai pirate boat bearing down on us. They moved so much faster than our loaded sampan could. Thai pirates painted their fishing boats with dragon designs on their sides. I'll never forget that evil-looking dragon. Once the fishing boat drew near us, a pirate climbed onto the bow and fired a pistol in the air. Our crew shut down our engine. The pirates drew along side and tied our boats together. Five or six pirates jumped onto our boat. Most had machetes. The one we thought was the captain had a pistol. Another man stood guard on the pirate boat with an AK-47 in his hands.

"They lined everyone up on our boat, all twenty-six of us. Holding the pistol to cover us, the captain had his men search each of us for gold and jewels. They took great pleasure in checking the women, hands in intimate places. Then they explored the cabin and hold. When finished, they separated the men and children from the women, and began taking the women to their boat.

"My son objected to seeing his wife stripped and mounted by one of the pirates. He ran toward the pirate boat screaming at the bandits. A pirate slashed at him with his machete, cutting his arm off, and then his head." Thien took in a deep breath. He bowed his head, and then looked at Wolfe. Tears welled in his eyes. "My boy fell dead in the ocean."

"I am so sorry," Wolfe said, unable to express his deep feelings of outrage adequately.

"I need a minute to recover," Thien said. He stood and walked into the kitchen with his empty glass.

CHAPTER 48

When Thien returned, he had refilled his glass, without ice cubes. He sat closer to Rose. She put an arm around his neck and kissed him lightly on the cheek, tears visible in her eyes. "You don't have to continue, dear. I can tell him the rest."

Thien shook his head. He said, "No. My life. My story. I will tell him."

"Please," Wolfe said softly.

Thien nodded and continued. "Seeing the pirates' brutality, Binh's wife, Yen, screamed from the pirate boat at Binh, 'Do something!' A man hit her in the face with his fist, knocked her to the deck, and started to remove her clothing. Binh raised his fists at the pirates. Two men with machetes stepped toward him. The man with the pistol laughed. He put his arm out to stop his men, and then lowered the pistol to the deck. Pulling the trigger three times, he put holes in our water cans and the bottom of our sampan. He waved the pirates back to their boat, intent on leaving the men and children on the sinking vessel.

"As he turned to jump to his boat, Stork stomped on his foot, breaking bones. I heard them snap. At the same time he grabbed the man's pistol with both hands, pulling it downward and hitting the man in the face with the top of his head. Blood went everywhere and the two fell overboard. I hurried to the side of the boat to see what would happen. Stork pushed the pistol under the man's chin and pulled the trigger. The bandit's head exploded, blossoming like a red flower underwater. Then Stork disappeared under our boat.

"The man with the AK-47 began shooting at the water, trying to hit

Stork. More bullets hit our sampan, putting additional holes in it. The rest of us scattered. Women and children screamed. The water deflected the bullets from Stork. Swimming under the pirate boat, he surfaced on the far side. He shot the man with the AK-47 in the back as the pirate leaned over the side of the boat looking for him. When a second man with a machete tried to retrieve the AK-47, he shot him, too. After pulling himself onto the fishing boat, Stork picked up the AK-47. Before the remaining pirates could react, he had killed them all."

"So you were saved." Wolfe said.

"Almost," Thien said. "Our sampan was sinking, and it was tied to the pirate boat. It could have pulled the Thai's fishing boat under, too. Leaving the pirates' bodies and the raped women where they lay, Stork grabbed a machete. He called to us to bring the children and jump to the pirate ship. To prevent the pirate boat from sinking with our boat, he hacked at the ropes holding the boats together, freeing the sampan.

"When we climbed into the pirate boat, he jumped back onto our sampan. As it continued to sink, he threw water cans, and food to us. We stood on the side of the pirate ship, women crying and screaming, the men calling for him to jump clear of the sampan. After passing us the compass, Stork was waist deep in water on the deck. The boats drifted apart. Soon only the top of the cabin was visible. Suddenly, the boat rolled over, taking Stork under water. He never surfaced. We watched for an hour as the sampan drifted away. It took us three hours to start the engine on the fishing boat. By then our boat was gone."

"It sank?" Wolfe asked.

"I assume so," Thien said. "Either that or it drifted so far away that we couldn't find it when we searched for it after the outboard engine started."

Wolfe felt nauseated by the descriptions of the rapes, murders, and fighting, but he needed to finish his inquisition of Thien. "Then you went to Malaysia?"

"Malaysia turned us away. Two of my grandchildren died of thirst. In the Gulf of Thailand, a Thai destroyer gave us water and food. Then it turned us away also. Among the packages of food, I found a note with directions, 'Go 250 degrees. Songkhla.' One of the sailors must have put the instructions in the package. We steered 250 degrees on the compass. Two days later we arrived, nearly dead, on Songkhla Resort Island in Thailand. There was also a refugee camp there. Eighteen months later, I arrived in Canada. Once in Canada, I contacted Emily through the American Red Cross, as Stork had requested."

Wolfe turned his attention to Rose. "And a marriage of convenience followed?"

"No," she said. "I listened to his story and arranged for Mai Kim-Ly to come to the United States. My congressman sponsored a bill for her, since she was the wife of a dead American POW. Vu eventually followed me home, got a job here, and started studying at George Mason."

"Wow," Wolfe said. "I'm exhausted just listening to your tale, Vu. May I call you Vu?" Thien nodded. "Good. Call me Addy. I'm certain it was difficult to relive your journey and the death of your son."

"Yes," Thien said. He seemed devastated and drained by the recounting of the ordeal. "It is difficult, even after thirty years. One never recovers from the death of one's child."

Wolfe stood. "Well, I have to go," he said. "I'm afraid I need a good, stiff drink." He stepped closer to Rose and Thien. Holding his right hand out first to Rose and then to Thien, he shook their hands. He then turned and walked to the front door. He paused in front of the screen door and turned his head toward the two.

"Good-bye," Thien said, too emotionally drained to stand.

"Will we see you at the funeral tomorrow?" Rose asked, also remaining seated, arm around Thien.

"Definitely," Wolfe said. "And by the way, I'm not buying it. Oh, I believe most of that yarn is true, Vu. But, I've heard too many times how Jimmy Byrnes has died, only to hear later of a miraculous escape and a later death. You can tell the CIA that I have proof he's alive. Both his and a guy named Thien Sang's fingerprints are on that high school yearbook Tammy lent me. In fact they are identical matches. They are the same person. One set is in the navy archives, the other is in Canada as an immigrant registered by the United Nations High Commissioner of Refugees. And we found the prints on the page with the picture of you and your first husband, Emily. Unless the CIA can give me a believable explanation, I will tell the *Washington Post* to print the story I gave them last night. Good day." He opened the door, stepped into the bright sunlight, and strode to his car.

Bill Yancey

CHAPTER 49

The Welcome Center at Arlington National Cemetery throbbed with hundreds of visitors. Wolfe could see why there were plans to raze all of Fort Myer, which bordered the cemetery. Arlington needed space for more graves. Dying for one's country was a booming business. Among the multiple groups waiting for funerals, he found Tammy Kimura and her sister talking quietly with friends and relatives. Wolfe edged closer to the group, but stayed at the periphery. He didn't like funerals, or the coat and tie he wore – his last suit and last tie. Both were reserved for funerals, including his own, despite what his wife said. He rather liked the fact that his wife called him a beach bum. It fit his personal image of himself.

Within the gathering, Wolfe spotted several people he had met over the previous weeks. In addition to the Byrnes sisters, he glimpsed Colonel Richard Rhodes, Thien Vu and Emily Rose, Pete Aikens the Ford dealer from Florida, and George Crouch the pilot. All had known Emiko Byrnes and had helped sustain her after her son's reported suicide.

The crowd of mourners almost filled the gray navy bus that took them to the gravesite. George Crouch fell into the long back seat next to Wolfe, when the bus lurched forward. He slapped Wolfe's knee. "Glad you made the party, Doc," he said. "She was a grand old girl. It's a shame J.T. can't be laid to rest with his parents. Unless you do go back to 'Nam and find him or his body."

"Yeah," Wolfe said, wondering if everyone in the bus was in on the conspiracy, or if they were all clueless. He remembered what Mrs.

Byrnes had told him after her first stroke, 'My Jimmy like you very much. You go see him. Okay?' Had she known?

"You seem a little distracted, Doc," Crouch said. "Still worried about the CIA?"

"No," Wolfe said. "I don't think they are going to be a problem in the future."

"Did you get permission to go to Southeast Asia?"

"No," Wolfe said, not looking at Crouch. "I suspect my quest is over."

"Well, if you think you need my help, you let me know," Crouch said. Wolfe smelled alcohol on the pilot's breath. Crouch turned and started a conversation with a younger woman to his right. "You're too young and pretty to go to funerals," he said. Deep in his own thoughts, Wolfe didn't hear her reply.

The bus stopped. Wolfe knew they weren't far from JFK's burial site because he saw the tourist crowds wandering along in the distance.

Wolfe stood apart from the family and behind the crowd as the pallbearers bore the casket, following the chaplain to the gravesite. Mrs. Byrnes's body had not arrived on the horse drawn caisson, but in a navy gray hearse. An NCO oversaw the placement of the American flag, over the coffin and secured against the brisk wind. With the flag in place, the chaplain faced the family members, Kimura, Barnes, and their children, and invited them to sit in chairs in the shade under the green cemetery tent.

Wolfe scanned the crowd. Slightly edgy and distracted, more than curious about how the day would end, he missed some of the ceremony. The same Buddhist priest Wolfe had seen at the Byrnes's home followed the navy chaplain's service with one of his own in Japanese. When the priest finished, the chaplain asked the family to rise. The rifle volley stirred him from him thoughts. He looked up, at the immaculately dressed navy seamen. Behind them, some fifty yards in the distance, he saw a white-haired Asian man facing the grave, intently watching the ceremony. He was in the shadow of a large tree, and partially hidden by smaller trees. Wolfe could not identify him.

When the bugler sounded *Taps*, the man in the distance bowed his head. After the bugler's last note floated away to join the ending ceremonies nearby, the chaplain asked the family to be seated again. The navy NCO folded the flag and presented it to Byrnes's daughters. Friends and relatives milled about the grave and expressed their condolences to the family. Wolfe watched as an elderly Asian woman and three young men separated from the crowd and began walking toward the man near the tree.

Weaving his way through the larger group as they returned to the navy bus, Wolfe circled the grave. With failing hearing, intent on catching the man and his family, who started toward JFK's memorial, Wolfe didn't hear the black sedan roll up behind him.

"Dr. Wolfe," a voice called. Wolfe didn't look back. He raised his hand to wave good-bye and kept his attention on the small group, which ignored him and walked swiftly away.

The sound of shoes hitting the pavement rapidly behind him drew Wolfe's attention. He looked back to find three men in dark suits jogging in his direction. *Crap*, he thought. He hadn't run in over a year, having had to stop for orthopedic reasons, but he hadn't forgotten how. With a thirty-yard head start, he thought he might catch his quarry before the men caught him. He ran, as fast as a sixty-eight year-old with arthritic knees and a bad back can run.

"Sir!" the man said as he grabbed Wolfe's elbow. "Stop!" A second man grabbed his other arm. The two men held on tightly. Wolfe was unable to wriggle free.

They pulled him to a halt, but not before he had gotten within ten yards of his goal. "Jimmy! Jimmy Byrnes!" Wolfe yelled. The couple, followed by three younger men, did not look back. They continued their walk toward the eternal flame on JFK's grave.

"Dr. Wolfe," the man who held his left arm said, "Mr. Narang would like to speak with you, sir." The men pivoted Wolfe around and walked him back to the street. There a chauffeured black limousine pulled to the curb to meet them. A third man opened the back door.

Thrust into the back seat of the vehicle, Wolfe found himself sitting down and facing agents Peter Narang and Drew Jaskolski of the CIA. One man sat to Wolfe's right. Another climbed into the vehicle on his left, pinning him in the middle of the large bench seat. The third man joined the driver in the front of the limo. "Gentlemen," Wolfe said, only mildly surprised. "Fancy meeting you here. Was that really Jimmy Byrnes I saw?"

"I thought we had an agreement, Dr. Wolfe," Narang said. He handed a legal-sized manila envelope to Wolfe. "And I guess you broke it. I believe you left this with a *Washington Post* correspondent the day before yesterday."

Wolfe opened the envelope and pulled out the typewritten exposition that detailed his attempt to find Jimmy Byrnes. He nodded. "How did you get it?" he asked Narang.

"We've had contacts at the Post since Watergate," Narang said. "Besides, Jeff Bezos is still feeling his way around the newspaper business. He occasionally asks us for our take on international, national, and other sensitive news. He thought this fairy-tale might involve national security."

Slipping his narrative back into the envelope, Wolfe said, "So now what?"

"I'm afraid you have put us in an untenable position, Doctor," Narang said. "We'll have to have a conference at Langley."

Resigned to his fate, Wolfe slumped in the seat and watched glumly as the limousine turned onto the George Washington Memorial Parkway and headed north toward CIA headquarters in Langley, Virginia.

CHAPTER 50

The limousine stopped at the front gate to CIA Headquarters. A man with a semi-automatic weapon checked the driver's identification and those of the passengers. He then watched on three monitors as the vehicle was scanned for electronic and explosive devices. Wolfe saw multiple close-up views of the undercarriage on one monitor, evidently from cameras built into the road below the car. He heard the guard say, "You're good. Cleared to Building 104."

The chauffeur drove past the huge parking lot filled with vehicles of employees to a six-story building behind the main building. A circular ramp sank into an underground garage. Narang and Jaskolski silently led the way to an elevator at the far end of the garage. Wolfe followed. The three other men trailed him. Despite the seven or eight buttons on the elevator panel, the stainless steel box stopped at B1, one floor above the garage. The doors opened and Wolfe found himself in a large room with what looked like a Transportation Security Administration airport checkpoint on steroids. Five men with assault rifles stood spread out in the windowless room with bare concrete walls. A woman sat in front of a screening booth. Two flat screen monitors faced her and her keyboard.

"Should I take off my shoes?" Wolfe asked, only partially in jest.

"No," the woman said. "Hold your arms over your head and walk through slowly." To Narang, she read from one of the monitors, "Belt buckle, pen in shirt pocket, car keys, cell phone has been disabled. Reading glasses in pocket with pen. No explosives. No weapons."

"Thanks, Jackie," Narang said. He and the four other men duplicated Wolfe's dance through the booth.

The screener did not call out their metal objects. She said, "Matches ID for – " and gave the agent's name.

Still following Narang, Wolfe walked into a waiting elevator on the far side of the room. Jaskolski pushed the button for the sixth floor. When the door opened Jaskolski and the three other men went to the left. "Follow me," Narang said to Wolfe. He turned to the right. "Don't get any ideas. They aren't that far away."

"My arm still hurts from the visit with you in the hotel," Wolfe said. "Ideas are for younger men, I suspect."

Narang stopped in front of an unmarked office door. "I will not accompany you into this room," he said. "I can tell you that we are authorized to use deadly force, should that become necessary. Do you understand?"

Wolfe tried to swallow, but his tongue stuck to the roof of his dry mouth. He nodded. "Noted," he said, barely able to speak.

At the far end of the large room, a white-haired, dark-skinned man sat at a small desk. Wolfe did not recognize him. Face directed downward, the man moved a pen across a stack of papers. Two walls near the desk displayed large maps of SE Asia, with the depiction of Vietnam reaching from the ceiling to the floor directly behind the desk. Two 8 X 10 blow-ups from reconnaissance aircraft or spy satellites depicted changes in foliage and were taped over the map. One appeared to say *1973 TH* in missing flora, the other *USA K*. Maps of the Middle East, Europe, the Philippines, and Indonesia covered the third wall.

Eyes glancing upward at Wolfe, the man grimaced, raised his head, and said, "You've been an aggravation for me over the last month, Addy." He stood and walked around the desk, right arm thrust in Wolfe's direction. "I'm afraid we're going to have to eliminate you."

Wolfe froze. He recognized the man immediately upon seeing his face. The jade Mother of Quan pendant on a short necklace looked familiar, too. "Eliminate," he said. "Why?"

"You know too much. Our recovery program is in danger. Never mind, I'm pulling your leg, Addy," he chuckled. "You are one persistent s.o.b. How have you been, my friend? How long has it been?"

"Jimmy Byrnes, you bastard!" Wolfe said. He wrapped his arms around his friend. "What the hell is going on, man? I've heard that you died in so many ways, and here you are...." His eyes filled with tears. He put a hand on each shoulder and held Byrnes at a distance staring. "It's great to see you, Jimmy."

"Actually, my legal name is Thien Sang," Byrnes said. "That's the name I had when I left Vietnam. Look, have a seat," he said, pointing to two stuffed chairs near a large window.

Wolfe sat in one of the chairs, back to the view of the CIA complex. "How? What? Why the secrecy? Son of a—" he said, unable to verbalize his thoughts.

"Brother Vu said you know most of the story. The final chapters are pretty simple, really. Our boats drifted apart. Mine didn't sink completely, but by the time I escaped from the flooded hold and got back to the upper deck, we were too far apart to swim. You know what a great swimmer I was. They couldn't find me after they got their engine going. I drifted south to Indonesia over the next two weeks. Had plenty of food onboard. It rained enough that I had fresh water. I just had to bail all day, every day, so I wouldn't sink when I fell asleep. I couldn't patch the bullet holes in the sampan.

"It took the UNHCR (United Nations High Commissioner of Refugees) folks about ten months to find Kim-Ly and Vu. I got to Canada in time to meet my son before she came to the US as the widow of a POW. The Company found me shortly thereafter. Only a few people know I returned."

Stunned, although he had suspected, and then knew, Byrnes was somewhere in the United States, and probably local since his family lived in Alexandria, Wolfe remained speechless for a moment. Eventually words migrated from his brain to his tongue. "You work for the CIA?"

"It's a special unit. I've been its director for the last ten years. We specialize in following up on rumors of MIAs. Initially, we concentrated on the war in Vietnam, and in Laos and Cambodia, of course," Byrnes explained.

He pointed to a map on the wall. "We've had some success. Before I joined, the CIA had dreadfully little luck. They were too unwieldy, too noticeable. A small army. They couldn't surprise anyone. Whenever they went on a mission they invariably found the enemy had executed the POW or deserter before they tracked him down. Ultimately, they decided to announce the cancellation of the MIA recovery efforts and make the Recovery Unit top secret. If the Vietnamese thought we had given up looking, there was a better chance we would find the MIAs alive, so the theory went. They insisted I keep my name and remain an

MIA. Very few people know I survived being a POW for eighteen years. Unless you have a need to know, you don't. You're the first person I know of who has tracked me down."

"Don't people recognize you?" Wolfe asked.

"Oh, sure, some think they do. When I show them my driver's license with my new name and speak broken English, they shake their heads and apologize. Many of my high school and academy classmates are dead, of course. We're at that stage of life. More, including me, don't look anything like we did when we were younger. And besides, to a lot of white folks all Asians look alike." Byrnes said. He smiled.

"Do you have a family?" Wolfe asked, remembering Thien Vu's mention of a widow to whom Byrnes had been close. "Was that Kim-Ly I saw?"

"Kim-Ly and I have three sons. You saw them from a distance earlier today at my mother's funeral. The oldest is almost thirty-two. Youngest is twenty-five."

"Have you been back to Vietnam?" Wolfe asked.

"Who better to search Vietnam for POW-MIAs than me? I'm fluent in the language and can pass for a national," Byrnes said. "We've had some accomplishments. Granted, most MIAs were killed in action or died in captivity, but we have managed to recover some alive and returned some remains. Who and how many is also secret. You won't read about the live ones in the papers, or hear about them on the news. Only their immediate families are aware. Most have no problem with the secrecy, or of being a part of the WWPP, *war witness protection program* as they like to call it. Anything to help rescue others."

Wolfe sat quietly, trying to digest and understand all that he heard. "You're really going to let me walk out of here with all that knowledge? You're not worried about what I may have told the *Washington Post*?"

"Addy, I run the Recovery Unit now. If I didn't trust you, you wouldn't be here now. Besides, my involvement in the program ends at midnight tonight. The papers on my desk are my retirement papers. I'm an old man, sixty-nine. Soon seventy years-old. I'm going to travel for fun in the future. Kim-Ly wants to visit her home again. So do I. It's beautiful in the mountains when the rice is full-grown. It's like golden wheat on the terraces."

Another loose thread intruded on Wolfe's thoughts. "What about Chief Fulton? Did you really tell him to kill Clemons? And those other guys who threw you overboard? Did you or the CIA have anything to do with their deaths? As a matter of national security?"

Byrnes's face became stern. The corners of his mouth turned down, but he couldn't hide the gleam in his eyes. "If I told you, I'd have to kill you," he said, then laughed. "Just kidding. We did not assassinate any of those men. You have to admit that criminals and servicemen live uncertain lives. I did see Fulton. I had stopped in to see Clemons in the hospital. It was my last chance to tell him I had forgiven him. When I left the room, he was still alive. As I left the hospital, Fulton met me in the lobby outside the ER. He didn't look well. I had seen him three or four times in the past. I thought I had explained that I didn't hold a grudge against him or the other guys, including Jameson. Trying to soothe him, I reiterated that he shouldn't feel remorse for being too afraid of Deke to yell *man overboard*. The guilt ate at him anyway.

"Nevertheless, he asked if I had killed Clemons. I told him no, that it would have been easy to do. All I would have needed was some medication off a crash cart in the ER, if I really wanted him dead. I also told Fulton that I thought Clemons would pass shortly in any event. In his abnormal state of mind, I imagine he must have interpreted that as an order to kill Clemons. The written note was entirely his idea. Certainly stirred things up here at CIA headquarters. Put a burr under your saddle, too."

"Is he going to go to prison for attempted murder?" Wolfe asked.

"No. We, the CIA, had a brief conversation with the St. Johns County DA's office. They will transfer Fulton here to the VA Hospital until his delusions are under control. Then he'll go home. We compensated the court reporter, too. We'll probably never know what he was thinking when he attacked her. His mind is full of conspiracies. We're so lucky that he didn't hurt her seriously. Same with you and Kayla Anne."

Emotionally drained, Wolfe put his hand on his friend's knee. "I'm sorry about your mother. And father, of course. And not knowing about you, too, I guess," he said.

"They both knew I was back. We'd get together, far from Washington, occasionally. The hardest part for them was not letting anyone else know. Tammy and Yaz did well leading you away from me, but you were too persistent."

"So this is your last day on the job," Wolfe said. Out of questions, he stood. "I guess I'll be on my way. Do I need an escort out? I suppose I'll stop by your sister's house and say good-bye."

Byrnes stood. He shook Wolfe's hand, and then pulled his friend close in a hug. "Narang's outside the door. He'll see you out. In fact, he'll drive you to the cemetery to get your car. Thanks, Addy. You are a real friend. I'll be at my sister's this evening with my family. By the way, so will your family. The CIA put Jennifer, Junior, and Kayla Anne on a chartered aircraft from Jacksonville about two hours ago. They will arrive about 4:00 p.m. at Reagan National. You may as well plan on spending the weekend here with us. We have a lot more catching up to do."

The End

Epilogue

In my humble opinion, the Vietnam War was as unnecessary as it was inevitable, given: European colonial competition, World War One, Bolshevik Revolution, Treaty of Versailles, League of Nations, and Ho Chi Minh's failed attempt to extract his people from French colonial rule in the 1920s. Both the United States and Vietnam had fought against the Japanese, and were and are wary of the Chinese. At times we have been allies. Had President Roosevelt or President Truman persuaded the French and other European countries to give up their colonies peacefully after WWII, the series of wars in Indochina might never have taken place.

Millions of people died in the Indochinese wars to end colonial rule. Many were combatants. Many more were innocent civilians caught in a struggle between ideals.

The American-Vietnam War could have ended sooner, could have ended with better results for both the Americans and the Vietnamese people. North Vietnam might have benefited from losing the war. Ask Japan and Germany about that. Their quick recoveries only happened because the USSR existed and the USA feared it more than it feared its WWII enemies. Nation building is not usually an American specialty. See Iraq and Afghanistan for examples.

The North Vietnamese won. They struggled from 1940 until 1975 to become an independent country, ruled by Vietnamese only. They fought successfully against Vichy France, Japan, the Republic of France, and the United States. By all accounts, their success seems to have been a disaster. Communist rule over the south has cost at least one million more lives.

We Americans let the South Vietnamese down, a combination of the result of President Richard Nixon's impeachment (he probably would have sent the B-52s back to Hanoi and Haiphong in 1975 when the NVA invaded South Vietnam) and war weariness in the US. We had no will to fight a war that should never have started. Brave soldiers died on both sides, many for an ideology they didn't believe in, didn't care about, and for which they would not have fought given a choice.

My hope is that present day politicians and diplomats are not setting up the world for more unnecessary wars in the future. I also expect that Vietnam and the USA will normalize relations eventually. Communism is a bankrupt ideology. Although, the path to democracy and capitalism can be daunting, too. See how China struggles walking the tightrope.

With luck we'll heal this gigantic wound and learn to get along. Maybe then we'll find out what happened to American MIAs, Vietnamese MIAs, and millions of civilians.

About The Author

Bill Yancey had the privilege of being the son of an air force officer and the grandson of an army officer. As a result, he lived all over the world, but never really grew up. He attended four high schools, a prep school, and five colleges. After bouncing out of an engineering curriculum, and spending time in Vietnam as a result, he finally obtained an undergraduate degree in general science from Virginia Tech in 1971. The Medical College of Virginia still regrets giving him an M.D. degree in 1976. He writes for his own entertainment, and hopes you see the humor in it, too.

Author's Statement

I have not asked my family or friends to read this book and/or put inflated reviews on the internet. I would appreciate it if you would put an honest review (good or bad) on the internet when you finish reading it. Even something as simple and short as, *I hated it*, *I loved it*, or *It was OK*, would be appreciated.

Also, you may contact me at: https://www. Goodreads .com/ You can direct comments or criticisms to me on my author page at that address. Thank you for spending your money and taking the time to read this novel. I hope you got your money's worth.

Sincerely,
Bill Yancey